Fragrance of Lilacs

A Love Story

Alene Roberts

Published and Distributed by:

Granite Publishing and Distribution, L.L.C.
868 North 1430 West • Orem, UT 84057
(801) 229-9023 • Toll Free (800) 574-5779
FAX (801) 229-1924

First Printing: March 1999
Second Printing: May 1999
Third Printing: September 1999
Four Printing: February 2000

Cover Artwork by: Jennett Chandler
Cover Design by: Tamara Ingram
Page Layout by: Brian Carter / SunRise Publishing, Orem, Utah

Library of Congress Catalog Card Number: 99-94316
ISBN: 1-890558-53-2

Acknowledgments

I would like to thank Lael W. Hill for graciously giving me permission to use her beautiful poem: "FIRST LOVE."

I feel great satisfaction to thank publicly the following: First: My son Whitney and his wife, Lisa, who were enthusiastic readers and valuable critics; Whitney, as the first to read any of the manuscript, prophesied with gusto: "Mom, this is going to be published, I know it!"

I also appreciate the rest of my children who cheered from the bleachers, giving me support and encouragement: Emily and Mark Lauritzen, Christie and Doug Atkinson, Dwain and Caroline Roberts, and Cynthia and Jeff Shaw. I might add that I always take serious note of Emily's 'feelings.' Though not having read the manuscript, she also stated with conviction: "I know you will be published, Mom."

Second: I appreciate and thank Granite Publishing and Distribution for taking a chance on me. When I met all the publishers at a Utah League of Writer's Round-up, Jeff Lambson, President of Granite, stood head and shoulders above the others; of course...he's six feet four inches tall. In actuality, I took my manuscript to Granite because I was impressed with Jeff. And a very special thanks to Jeff's wife, Darla, for her satisfying reaction to this book.

Dedication

To my husband, Elliott, who is the better writer, but who is happy for my success. Who has been my toughest critic and my greatest help. Who has spent many hours reading over my revisions and suggesting more. Who even suggested I write more about a certain thing in the book, and when I said I couldn't face writing about that part and asked him: "Would you write it for me in my style?" he did...three-fourths of a page! Who, when I had moments of self doubt, said just the right thing, even giving me a gentle reprimand when needed. Who would come home and find me still at the computer at 6:00 P.M., and, with a twinkle in his eye, ask: "Are we going to have dinner tonight?"

Who I can't live without.

Chapter One

Torry's brisk walk up the two lane asphalt road turned into a run as she felt another wave of anger swelling inside her. Ten minutes later, gasping for breath, she slowed to a walk. The grim set of her mouth softened as she breathed in the scent of the honeysuckle blossoms hugging the scraggly barbed wire fences on each side of the road. The warm afternoon sun flickered through the branches of the tall Elm trees that lined both sides of this street leading to the vegetable farms...lifting her spirits. At last the anger ebbed away.

Now able to be more objective about the call from her father, she asked herself why she'd become so angry? Long ago, she quit caring what her father said to her, never allowing herself to become emotional over it. So why now?

It was just about a year and-a-half ago that her forty-four-year-old husband, Jack, a seemingly healthy ex-football player, died suddenly of a heart attack. Sitting on the couch, cheering loudly over a televised football game, he grasped his chest in pain. Three days later, he died in Denver General. She could still feel the shock of it, and wondered if it would ever diminish. But as devastating as the death itself, was the legacy of unanswered questions Jack left behind.

Her big, fun loving, lovable husband had gradually changed into a dark, morose, unhappy man—and she didn't know why. When Torry first became aware that something was not right, she talked to Jack about it, but his immediate reaction was denial that anything was wrong. His denial became an insurmountable obstacle to her. As time went on, finding out the cause of Jack's unhappiness became an all consuming focus for Torry, especially that last year when his life took a frightening downward turn. She almost gave up hope. But hope became her enduring companion, hope that she would eventually find the answer, hope that faded, then rekindled through fervent daily prayer, hope that never died...until Jack died. Suddenly bereft of hope, she felt lost, cut off as though stranded in mid-sentence. She had failed in her marriage and didn't know how or why—and for Torry Anderson, whose life-bread was understanding, this was almost more than she could cope with.

After struggling with grief and confusion for almost a year, she decided to move from Denver and all the things that evoked memories of Jack. She felt this was the only way she would be able to survive and once more become a productive human being.

Torry waited until the end of the year for her son, Scott, to return from his mission. She needed to discuss the decision with him and his older brother, Jim. To her surprise they were more than supportive, they were happy about her desire to move, even though Denver had been their home since childhood.

With this decision firm, Torry called her parents in Salt Lake. Their response was eager and immediate, urging a move to be near them.

"I will seriously consider Salt Lake," she told them, "but I don't know if it's where I should be right now."

"Of course it is, Torry," her father said in adamant tones. "You're alone. Since your boys are both at BYU now, you could see them more often, and your mother and I can look after you."

"Dad," she said wearily, "I'm forty-three years old."

"Well then," her mother chimed in, "you can look after us."

Torry managed a small laugh. "I promise I'll think about it seriously." And, she did. How safe it felt, the idea of living near her mother. And how wonderful it would be to live closer to her sons so she could see them more often. But her prayers about moving to Salt Lake brought only a stupor of thought. Frustrated, she fasted and prayed about where to move and as she did so, memories of Grandmother Thomas filled her thoughts.

Six weeks out of every summer, from childhood to junior high when Grandmother died, was spent with her and Grandfather in Green Valley, Utah. These were special memories.

Suddenly, somehow, the idea of living in Green Valley came to her mind. She rejected it, telling herself it was just a wish to escape her present pain by retreating to happier times of the past. Her attempts to consider many other places, including Salt Lake, proved useless. It was strange—but Green Valley was the only place that felt right. In desperation, she made the decision to move to the small town. Kneeling, she earnestly prayed for a confirmation, and as she did so a powerful peace came over her, relaxing and soothing every taut nerve in her body. There was no doubt where she was supposed to go. Her mother would understand. However, it would be impossible to explain this to her father, so she and the boys kept it a secret. Only when the house was sold and she was ready to move, did she call and tell her mother, explaining that her son Jim wanted to tell his grandfather a little later, hoping he could soften the shock.

When at last she moved, and when she was somewhat settled, she called Jim at school and gave him the go ahead to call his grandfather. Her father's response to the call from his grandson, was the call to her this afternoon. It began with a tirade.

"I can't believe you didn't call your mother and me to inform us you were moving. We learn of it from Jim after it's already done. I can't believe you could be so thoughtless, Torry."

"I didn't want to hurt you by doing it this way, Dad, but I had to. You would have been upset at my decision to move here and would have told me it was a stupid idea and..."

"It is a stupid idea. There's nothing in that hick town for you."

"How do you know, Dad?" she asked quietly.

Her father passed over the question. "I could kick myself for letting you go down there every summer to spend weeks with that woman. All she did was put harebrained ideas into your head."

"Please don't call Grandmother Thomas 'that woman'."

"You're just wanting to escape into the past, Torry. You don't want to face the reality of your situation."

"May I speak to Mother, Dad?"

"She isn't here."

"I thought so. You wouldn't talk to me like this if she were."

"Are you going to live on Jack's life insurance?" he demanded, ignoring her remark.

"I am for a while, but I'm going to start a business and..."

A harsh blast of laughter came through the phone. "A business? You've never worked in your life, Torry. And how could a business in that hick town produce enough income to live on?"

The edginess growing inside her suddenly erupted into anger. How dare he talk to me like this? "I've got to go Dad." She hung up abruptly, leaving him hanging on the other end. She paced the kitchen floor, but the anger continued to broil within her. Soon, as she always did in times of extreme stress, she ran out the front door to walk it away.

Walking slower now, she began to sort out the reasons why her agitation had turned into anger, causing her to hang up on her father.

From the day the moving truck deposited her belongings into the plain, stale smelling, dusty little house on Farm Road 6, a kind of numbness set in. Her father's outrage this afternoon broke through this protective shell, and left her feeling even more alone. But it was more than that, somehow. His final insult seemed to strip something away. What was it? She began to feel anxious. Maybe Dad's right, maybe I can't make a go of the business. She'd never felt this way before. Ever since she could remember, she felt she could do anything she set her mind to do...until now. Her father had stripped away her confidence! No—she corrected herself, he didn't do it, he merely knocked off my blinders. "No wonder I lost my cool," she said aloud. Feeling a lack of confidence was more than uncomfortable, it was totally alien. How did this happen? She knew immediately. Since she'd failed as a wife, deep down she felt she might fail at anything she tried to do.

In spite of the discomfort, a sense of relief pervaded her whole being. At least she understood. If she could understand something, then dealing with it one way or another was possible. Still, she was stunned by this new insight. For Torry, a sense of fear in her own abilities was a new experience.

A faint smile played upon her lips as she remembered one of the many times she and Grandmother Thomas sat on the lawn together shucking corn, freshly picked from the cornfield. Grandmother held up an ear of corn, pale-yellow and succulent. Turning it slowly around as though examining it, her grandmother then leaned forward and looked intently at her granddaughter.

"Torry, many people are born like a shucked ear of corn, all the tender kernels bare and easily torn." She picked up an unshucked ear. "But you, my dear, came into this world clothed in the protecting layers of the green husks of self-confidence."

A cool late afternoon breeze brushed against Torry's face and arms, bringing her back to the present. A truck, heading toward town, roared past, reminding her that it was time to turn around and head for home. She took a deep breath, squared her shoulders and now with greater resolve, changed direction.

A pickup drove slowly by, and a young man yelled, "Hey beautiful, wanna ride?"

Torry smiled. "No thanks." Wouldn't he be chagrined to know I'm old enough to be his mother? she thought. Another truck drove by with a load of scruffy, dirty farm hands in the back, all whistling and hooting at her.

"I guess forty-three isn't so old after all," she whispered to herself. Somehow, this released a little of the tension over what she had to face tomorrow morning—the first step toward pioneering a new business, the first step toward trying to support herself financially. Never wanting to work outside the home, she now found it a welcome necessity—hoping it would help her focus on something outside herself, outside the heavy baggage of heartache and failure.

Chapter Two

Henry, the neighbor's rooster, crowed loudly, flamboyantly at 4:30 A.M., waking Torry from a fitful sleep. Glancing at the clock, she groaned.

"Darn rooster!" She knew it was useless to try to go back to sleep; her mind already racing. Sitting up, she turned on the lamp, shivering in the early morning chill of mid-April. Pulling a blanket around her shoulders, she opened the scriptures and read until 5:15, then slid off the bed for her morning prayers. She got up feeling calmer and more rested. Morning is my time, she thought, as it was her grandmother's. While dressing, she remembered her brother's grumbling over Grandmother's early hours. Always on the first night of their visit, Grandmother would give her usual lecture.

"Now Billy, I don't hold with anyone who sleeps past 5:00 A.M. Your spirit wants to get up at that hour and if you let your body languish in bed past that, your body and spirit are out of harmony for the rest of the day." Because of this, Billy's visits lasted only a few days each summer. Torry didn't mind. She loved having Grandmother to herself.

Grabbing a sweater, she went out for her usual thirty minute walk, grateful she was settled enough to be back into this morning routine which gave order to her life. It had always been her way of coping with the daily pressures, worries and anxieties that came unbidden through the years.

Her chosen route, 5th Street, ran perpendicular to, and dead-ended at Farm Road 6, directly in front of her property. Trying to ease the tension in her shoulders, she walked rapidly up the side-walk past the orchard, homes and park on her left, reaching Main Street, where she turned around and headed back. Arriving again at the park, her route veered into and through it, following the smooth walking path that was still lit by lamp light. The serpentine-like path deposited her back on the 5th Street sidewalk, where she turned right, quickly arriving back home.

Breathing heavily, she walked up the steps of the small front porch and entered the house. She looked at her watch and sighed.

6

"Still three-and-a-half hours until the bank opens."

She stood there in the small foyer staring into the front room of this two-bedroom frame house she'd rented. Restlessness compelled her to walk into it, stepping carefully over and around the unopened boxes resting on the ugly two-toned brown carpet. She had unpacked only the necessities so she could paint the dingy brown walls throughout the house. She was pleased that the off-white paint had brightened it, making it seem more spacious, enhancing the unusually large cheery windows in each room.

Her eyes rested longingly upon the two dear and familiar pieces of furniture that had belonged to her grandmother: the charming round bentwood lamp table placed in front of the first window, and the elegant old double-doored china cabinet on the opposite wall. Both looked out of place among the boxes...in this plain little house.

She was glad she'd sold all of her furniture before moving from Denver, all except her drawing table and five pieces that had belonged to Grandmother.

She entered the bedroom. Grandmother's large cherrywood armoire and the two matching lamp tables looked more at home because of the large colorful patchwork quilt that Grandmother had pieced and quilted herself. The quilt didn't fit their king-size bed in Denver, but made a nice bedspread for this new queen-size bed which she purchased from Johnson's Furniture store immediately upon arriving here in Green Valley.

Even with the few pieces of warm familiar furniture, this little house still felt strange and lonely. Not like home. But then...where was home?

She glanced in at the small second bedroom which would double as her work room. There was only room enough for the pull-out couch she had just purchased for the boys, her drawing table, easel and paint supplies.

Frowning, she remembered selling the nice furniture that belonged to her sons. They each had a bedroom set that they themselves helped choose when they were small. In later years, they had talked of giving it to their own sons one day, but as moving time came closer, they requested she sell their sets. She refused, explaining that she could rent a storage unit. Both Jim and Scott were equally adamant that they needed the money. She had argued, telling them she would give them the money **they needed**, but they wouldn't budge. At the time, she wasn't strong **enough** emotionally to match their fierce determination—but now **something** nagged at the back of her mind. She hadn't divulged the financial situation their father left her in, so why were they so insistent?

"I need to talk to them again about this some time," she mumbled. She walked into the kitchen and sat down at the small dinette set, also purchased from the local furniture store. The table, white formica trimmed in natural wood and four wooden chairs covered in white leather, added much to brighten the small kitchen, she felt.

Feeling more nervous than hungry, she got up and fixed some toast and hot chocolate. Trying to quell a fluttering stomach, she reminded herself of her careful research and preparation previous to the move from Denver. Before putting her house up for sale, she had flown to St. George, rented a car and driven to Green Valley to find a place to live. When she discovered that this little house and ten acres were for sale or lease, the idea for the business came into her mind. For the first time since Jack died, she felt a stirring of interest in doing something new. Putting a deposit down for a temporary lease, she returned to Denver. She located several similar enterprises in the outlying areas of a couple of other cities and gleaned from them the cost, profits and risks of the business. The library was used for further research. The more she found out, the more convinced she was it could be done successfully.

She flew to Salt Lake on the pretext of visiting her parents and sons, and only Jim and Scott knew the real purpose of the trip. It was to visit some of the better restaurants, to explain the uniqueness of her product and solicit their business. All of them were very interested.

The next decision she had to make was how to finance the venture. She and Jack had been paying off their home mortgage for eighteen years, and the value of the house had gone up. She decided that the profit from the house could be used for the business, but when she pulled the mortgage papers from the files, she was confused. Then shocked. Jack had remortgaged the house and had forged her name! She sat there in a stupor—wondering why, what for? The shock of his death seemed to reverberate like the tremors of an earthquake resulting in one shock after the other. This was the third. The second had come a week after Jack's death when she finally had presence of mind to call Hank Taylor, one of the vice presidents of the sports equipment company and Jack's boss, to tell him of Jack's death. After Hank had expressed his shock and sympathy, he thanked her for calling him.

She numbly blurted out the obvious, "I didn't want you to wonder why he didn't return to work next week."

"To work?" Hank asked, surprised.

"Yes."

"Uh...didn't Jack tell you? He hasn't worked here for a year now."

Stunned, she tried to comprehend the words. "He...hasn't?"

"No."

She felt stupid. "I uh...don't understand. Why?"

Hank Taylor hesitated, then told her. "We fired Jack."

Torry was dumb with shock. "You...you fired him?"

"I'm sorry to add to your grief, Mrs. Anderson, but Jack's performance had been going down to the point of almost no performance. He changed. He just wasn't the same cheerful personality guy who became our top regional sales manager."

"Do you have any idea why he changed?" she managed to ask, hardly daring to hope. Wanting, needing to know, yet dreading the possible answer.

"No. Jack and I had more than a few discussions about it but he was very vague and always had some excuse or other."

"Do you know where he went to work after you fired him?"

"I have no idea. I couldn't even give him a letter of recommendation. But..." Hank Taylor hesitated, then continued, "I heard through the grapevine, that he wasn't working."

"Do you remember who you heard this from?"

Hank thought a minute. "You know, it's been so long, I don't. I'm sorry."

"Do you know of anyone in the company who could tell me anything...someone who might have an idea what was wrong with Jack or where he went? You see, he still went away for two weeks out of the month, just as if he were still going to work."

"He did?" There was a long pause before Hank spoke, "I'm

sorry, Mrs. Anderson, but the men he worked with in the field and the employees here at the corporate offices all asked me at one time or another what was wrong with Jack."

Another dead end, she thought. "Thank you, Mr. Taylor. If you hear anything at all that could shed some light on this, I would appreciate it." She then gave him her phone number and her parent's phone number.

Jack had lied to her! She realized now that he was using the mortgage money for them to live on. He had told her the company wasn't doing well and that the corporate heads cut everyone's salary. However, he quickly assured her that business would pick up soon.

But where did he go those two weeks, where did he live? She again wondered if there was another woman in his life. She had asked him this more than once. Each time, he angrily denied it.

One thing she felt sure of, the money from the second mortgage was gone. He certainly hadn't put it in their savings or checking account. Even though Jack always paid the bills she should have been more aware of their financial situation!

Torry was grateful that her father, who recently retired from a highly successful insurance business, had talked Jack into buying life insurance because of his constant traveling. She would be able to live on that and the dividends from the company stock for another two years...if she were frugal. At least Jack hadn't touched those. In her heart, she knew eventually he would have.

The profit from the sale of the house was small. It turned out to be only enough to pay for the move to Green Valley. After a lot of thought and prayer, she decided she didn't want to sell any of the stock. It was the only security she had. Her parents could easily loan her the money, but her father's attitude made it impossible for her to ask. The only other alternative she could think of was a bank loan.

She glanced at her watch and sighed. Time was dragging; she still had two hours to kill.

Feeling scattered and unfocused, she walked into her work room. Sitting down at her drawing table, she idly began to sketch, trying to make the connection between hand and eye that produced the many portraits she'd drawn and painted. A relaxing pastime usually, but this morning it wasn't. Her hand shook slightly. With a sigh, she gave it up. Knowing she needed physical labor that would also occupy her mind, she decided to unpack the books.

The sandstone fireplace, almost overpowered by the ugly brown paint of bookcases on either side, was now, with their new paint job, an attractive centerpoint of the room.

She opened the boxes and worked quickly. As the last box was unpacked, she looked at her watch and saw that it was time to get ready. She stood back to admire the fireplace and the newly painted bookcases full of books—but instead, found herself wishing it felt as 'homey' as it looked.

While brushing her short, closely cropped, charcoal-brown, naturally curly hair, she stared in the mirror at her attire: faded jeans and a red and white cotton shirt, held in by a worn red leather belt.

"Dad would really have a fit if he saw me dressed like this to go to the bank for a loan," she said out loud, feeling more than a little nervous. She had spent much time several days ago going through her wardrobe contemplating what to wear. Deciding that a dress and heels would not be as convincing or credible for her type of business, she chose the blue jeans. Not feeling as sure as she had a couple of days ago, she wavered, then reassured herself that it was best to wear 'work clothes.' Hoping fervently that she was using good judgement, she left the house.

Since it was only six-and-a-half blocks to Main street and it was a beautiful spring morning, she decided to walk. She crossed the street to the corner, took a few steps and stopped. A sudden inclination to turn back immobilized her. Taking a few deep breaths, trying to gain control, she wondered—is something trying to keep me from going to the bank? This thought fired her determination. She moved on.

After passing the small orchard on the corner and the first block of houses, she came to the town park where she had exercised this morning. This park was where Grandmother's home used to be, the big red barn and the chicken coop. This was where she spent many happy hours climbing trees in the orchard, eating apricots, cherries, and apples. Years ago, after Grandmother died, her mother had sold the property.

Looking at her watch, she realized there was time to relax on one of the park benches and relive for a moment the happy times. She found a bench close by and sat down.

She looked around and realized that her favorite apricot tree had probably been close to this very spot. She remembered checking the green apricots every day until the first blush of orange appeared. Unable to wait more than a few days longer, she ate them, feeling certain they couldn't possibly taste any better fully ripe.

Torry sighed. This failed to bring the comfort she sought. In fact, to her distress, she could feel nothing.

Children were playing on the playground the other side of the park. An elderly gentleman snoozed on a bench near them. Further off to the right, stood a charming white gazebo with a set of white bleachers about ten feet in front of it. Torry vaguely wondered what kind of performances were held there. Petunias of all colors were blooming in the well-tended beds and she could hear the bees humming as they moved from one flower to the next. All this, usually so delightful to Torry, did nothing for her. She could almost hear her mother's voice on one of her visits to Denver eleven months after Jack died.

"Torry, you're suffering from depression."

"Depression?" Torry questioned in astonishment. "I'm grieving! I've lost my husband of twenty-three years. I'm grieving, Mother."

"But there is a fine line between healthy, healing grief and depression, my dear."

Torry, always a little impatient with people who allowed depression to take hold, found this idea abhorrent. "You've never lost a husband, Mother, how do you know that?"

"I've had quite a few friends, Torry, who have lost their husbands." Her voice was gentle. "And I began to notice how differently people grieve, so I watched and studied them through the years. I found that depression took hold when a person had depended too much on their mate for emotional security instead of dealing with it in the right way. I found that depression sometimes took hold when the person felt there were serious unresolved issues in their relationship with the lost mate."

The latter struck a nerve and tears fell. "You know which one fits me don't you, Mother?"

"Yes. Your independence and cheerful front even fooled me for a while, Torry, but then I discovered something. My daughter, whose zest for life infected everyone around her, could no longer enjoy one of the things she was most noted for, joy in the simple things of life."

She thanked her mother, realizing she was right. Judgmental over this weakness in others, she now found the mote in her own eye. Once again she was compelled to humble herself. She went about trying to overcome the depression, which she soon recognized was even more than that. It was a black feeling inspired by the adversary. Through much prayer and after several blessings from her home teachers and the bishop, the blackness left. But despondency remained. Nothing looked good; nothing felt good. Try as she had, she couldn't enjoy anyone or anything.

It was at this time she decided to move. She managed to put on a cheerful front until her sons returned to school. Desperately fighting the despondency, she focused outward, continually looking at the sky, clouds, the trees and people. She prepared the house to sell, working long hard hours until she was so exhausted she fell into bed at night.

Now, here in Green Valley, she focused on the new business, on painting the little house, but the bleakness still remained. The chirp of a bird in a nearby tree startled her. Looking up she saw a Robin. She studied it wistfully.

"Sorry little bird, if the Meadowlarks can't cheer me, I'm afraid you can't." The Robin retorted with another chirp.

Getting up, Torry walked on toward her unscheduled appointment. Today she only glanced at the neat, brick in-town homes with their green lawns, landscaped with spring flowers, blossoming lilac bushes and varieties of shade and fruit trees. Passing the last home, she stopped at a lilac bush that edged the sidewalk and drank in the smell. Without even thinking she broke one off and walked on.

Arriving at Bell's Bakery, she turned left on Main Street and walked past the barbershop and Allen's Cleaners to the Green Valley Drugstore—where she found herself slowing down. She walked over and looked into its windows as memories of long ago surfaced. This dear old drugstore, repaired and restored, so much like it used to be when Grandfather owned it, today only cried out his absence. Tears stung her eyes. What is the matter with me? She stared unseeing at the display of gifts in the window.

Facing it once again, she knew, as she did last night on her walk, she was scared. How she longed to run to Grandmother right now and explain that some of the green husks of self confidence were torn. Could she fix them—as she had fixed her Sunday dress, torn while climbing the cherry tree?

Suddenly, the memory of her mother's face full of frustration as she had seen it so often, flashed into her mind.

"That is too big a project to take on, Torry. You have school work, seminary, chores here at home, the school newspaper, and the choir. You can't stoke ten fires at once and keep them all blazing well."

But in Torry's mind she could. Always forgetting the disasters that invariably followed, flunking a test, catching a cold from no sleep, Mother and sometimes her brother, Bill, having to come to her rescue to finish the projects.

"But a Broadway musical would be so much fun and so good for the ward. All the kids and adults who have always wanted to be in something can be in it. And I'll take over the scenery. I've got the greatest ideas for the set."

"I'm sure you do, Torry Ann," sighed her mother. "But what do Sister Clark and Brother Jensen say about this undertaking?"

"Oh, they're shaking in their boots," she said in a tone of disgust. "I just don't understand why people get so scared about doing things like this."

"Someday maybe you'll understand, Torry."

"You're right, Mother," Torry whispered in the present. I think I'm beginning to understand...now...finally. But, oh how I need that fearlessness right now! I'm sorry for self-righteously judging others...but at the same time I'm grateful to have been born with the trait that helped me get to this point.

"But Heavenly Father, please, I need a repair job..." she whispered, blinking back tears. Lifting her head high and squaring her shoulders, she waited. It came. The old natural self-confidence that she had always taken for granted, the feeling that she could do anything she put her mind to, pulled her up out of the mire of fear, rescuing her.

"Thank you, Heavenly Father," she whispered. Taking a deep breath, she walked next door to the Green Valley National Bank. Her white rubber-soled walking shoes made no sound on the shiny stone floor that led to a graceful mahogany desk planted firmly in the middle of an elegant green and rose rug. The motherly gray-haired woman behind it smiled at Torry.

"Hello, I'm Mrs. Ames, may I help you Miss..."

"Mrs. Anderson, Torry Anderson. I would like to speak with a loan officer if I may please."

"Oh yes, Mrs. Anderson. I believe you opened an account with us several weeks ago."

"Yes, I'm leasing the Harris house and property on Farm Road 6."

"That's right and if I remember correctly, you moved here from Colorado."

"Yes, Denver."

After more friendly questions and conversation, Mrs. Ames said, "I believe Mr. Baker is free now, let me introduce you."

Mrs. Ames led her to a private, sunny office. As they entered, the tall barrel-chested man immediately stood up. His suit coat thrown over a chair, his white shirt sleeves rolled up, suggested to Torry a comforting informality. Sunlight from the window behind, haloed his blonde hair. His blue eyes were warm and welcoming.

"Mr. Baker, this is Mrs. Torry Anderson who just moved here to our community from Denver."

"I'm happy to meet you, Mrs. Anderson," he said smiling as he leaned over the desk and shook her hand. "Please have a seat."

Torry sat down feeling at ease with this kind-faced man.

"Now, Mrs. Anderson, how may I help you?"

Unconsciously, she lifted the lilac and smelled it.

Tom Baker smiled. "You like lilacs too?".

"Oh," Torry smiled, chagrined, "I forgot I had this in my hand. I'm afraid I snitched it from a bush as I was walking to the bank."

Tom Baker was disarmed. People wore many different faces when they came into his office to discuss getting a bank loan, but he'd never seen the face that Torry Anderson wore. In one sentence, she revealed a charming, unabashed honesty and naturalness.

Thirty minutes later, a flustered Tom Baker stood in David

Mayer's office, running his hand through his hair, revealing his feeling of frustration. David looked up in surprise.

"Dave, would you see this woman, Mrs. Torry Anderson? She won't take no for an answer...or to be more accurate, I can't tell her no."

David had never seen Tom like this. He was the smoothest, most diplomatic, albeit the toughest loan officer he'd ever known and could handle anyone Mrs. Ames brought to him. David stared at him. "You...can't tell her no?"

"No," he said lamely, shaking his head.

"All right, give me a couple of minutes to collect myself, then send her in."

Even though it was only a little after 10:00 A.M., David Mayer felt bone tired. Last week had been an unusually trying and difficult week and yesterday had not turned out to be any better. He felt irritated at this woman. He would make short work of her he decided. Straightening himself in the chair, he pushed aside the papers he'd been working on and waited. Allowing his weary mind to imagine what kind of woman Tom Baker couldn't say no to, he visualized a tall, tight-lipped woman with the piercing eyes of a strict school marm. Maybe she was a large, formidable looking woman with bushy eyebrows. He braced himself.

"Mr. Mayer?" she asked. He noted that her voice had a melodic quality that belied her appearance. A petite young woman stood there, wearing a checkered shirt and faded jeans, revealing a small waist and nicely curved hips. Her oval, but somewhat angular face, framed by a short crop of dark-brown curls, wore a puzzled look or was it irritation, he couldn't decide. Taken back by her appearance, David Mayer just stared. He didn't know what he had expected, but this was certainly not it! The silence stretched out.

Torry Anderson refused to be intimidated by the silence. Her look of irritation was plain now.

"I'm Mrs. Anderson. Mr. Baker sent me in to talk to you."

"You...are...Mrs. Anderson," he said slowly.

Torry was puzzled. This was not a question. It was as if who she was would not sink in.

"Yes, I'm Mrs. Anderson. I've been trying to explain to Mr. Baker my proposal and need for a loan...but he seems somewhat uh...nonplussed."

An involuntary smile came across David Mayer's face. He was beginning to understand what Tom Baker was up against.

Torry frowned. She intended to be taken seriously. Walking over to a chair in front of the desk, she pulled it around the desk, sat down, facing Mr. Mayer directly, her knees only inches from his. David gasped inwardly. She had just taken from him the subtle protection that this formidable piece of furniture always gave him.

"Mr. Mayer, the title on your desk says that you are the president of this bank so I certainly hope you will be a little better at understanding my proposal and need for a loan than Mr. Baker."

David's unease heightened. Somehow he just knew he was not going to handle this young woman any better than Tom.

Irritated by the strange expression on the man's face, Torry tartly assured him that there wouldn't be a risk to the bank so would he please allow her to explain it to him? She waited for his response. More silence. Was everyone in this bank crazy? To quell her growing uneasiness, she lifted the lilac and breathed deeply of its calming scent.

"What's that?" David Mayer blurted out.

"Oh I uh...you see lilacs are my favorite flower and as I was walking to the bank, I passed a lilac bush and I'm afraid I couldn't resist taking one. I...uh...." She realized things were not going as she had planned and in an effort to gain control, she spoke abruptly. "Now may we get on with business, Mr. Mayer?"

He was beginning to understand why Tom was flustered. She hadn't even begun her story and somehow he felt—off balance.

"Mr. Mayer, I have never been in a bank to ask for a loan before," she said in frigid tones, "but you and Mr. Baker hardly seem to handle business in a businesslike manner."

He stared at her, and for a horrified instant, he felt as though he might start laughing. He swallowed, cleared his throat, biding time in hopes that the feeling would pass. It didn't. Unwanted laughter came out in choking, gasping sounds. Quickly swiveling his chair around...away from Torry Anderson, his hand shielding his face, he unwillingly gave into it, his shoulders shaking.

Torry jumped up, shocked and concerned. "Mr. Mayer....are you...are you crying?"

David Mayer's laughter stopped, momentarily shocked at the

question. Swiveling his chair back around, he looked at her, tears threatening at the corners of his eyes...then losing all control, he threw back his head and laughed out loud.

Torry's fierce determination dissolved into confusion. She stood there immobilized. He had been laughing!

The president of Green Valley National Bank finally got himself somewhat under control, at least enough to gasp a few words to his potential customer.

"Forgive me, Mrs. Anderson, but I...uh needed that. It's been a hard week and I..."

By now, Torry's confusion had turned to indignation. "You certainly are not forgiven, Mr. Mayer," she stated, her hazel eyes glinting with fire. "I do not appreciate being your comic relief of the day. May I ask you what you found so amusing?"

He tried to answer something intelligible but began laughing again.

"That does it!" Torry said, slamming her lilac down on the desk. "I'm going to take my business elsewhere." She turned to leave but David, suddenly sobering, grabbed hold of her wrist and stared at the lilac that lay limply on the desk—then up at her.

"Please don't go Mrs. Anderson, I'm sorry. My actions are inexcusable. Please sit down and give me another chance."

She glared at him for a moment, then at the hand that was holding her wrist. He let go immediately.

"Then may I ask you again what you found so amusing?"

He thought a moment then shook his head and stood up. "You know I don't think I can put it into words."

"Please try," she said, her voice a quiet ultimatum.

"I assure you, Mrs. Anderson, it wasn't you...it was...uh the situation, Baker, me..."

"And that's an explanation?"

"No it isn't, but I'm afraid I can't do much better than that."

"All right then, thank you for your time, Mr. Mayer," she said, walking to the door.

"Mrs. Anderson," he said following her, "let me give it one more shot, and if I can't do any better, you may leave." Taking her silence as approval he began, "let me put it this way," then pausing, he ran his hand through his hair, "have you ever been in a situation where people didn't act in their usual manner, people were not what you expected and things didn't turn out as you expected?"

"Yes, that describes my visit to your bank perfectly."

He stared at her a moment and then laughed. "Touche, Mrs. Anderson, touche."

She couldn't resist smiling, and David, taking advantage of it, offered her the one remaining chair in front of the desk. Hesitating a moment, she stepped over to it and sat down. David Mayer returned to his own seat. Feeling much more in control now that the desk was between them, he proceeded.

"Mrs. Anderson, tell me...you need a loan for what?"

She took a deep breath and blurted out, "A chicken farm."

"A...chicken farm? Well, that is a surprise. That's the last thing I expected to hear...but then I should have expected the unexpected, right?" They both laughed, releasing the tension between them. "A chicken farm is...uh...an interesting venture. Will your husband be helping you run this farm or is he employed elsewhere?"

"My husband died a year and a half ago." She straightened up, trying to make herself look taller, more capable. "I'll be running it myself. I will be starting small so that I'll be able to handle it. When I'm financially able to expand, I'll hire some help, maybe one of my sons."

David could visualize this over-eager and over-confident young mother letting her young son feed the chickens and gather the eggs, breaking more than he gathered. He heaved a sigh over what seemed to be an utterly unrealistic and impractical plan.

"Uh...Mrs. Anderson, why did you choose this particular business? You seem like an educated person, surely..."

"Yes, I could renew my elementary education certificate and teach."

"Now that sounds much easier and less risky to me."

"It is, but you see, I don't want to be tied up all day at work. I want to be free to enjoy my grandchildren when they visit and a chicken farm will give them a special kind of education as well as give them a lot of good memories."

"Your grandchildren?" David was visibly shocked. "You certainly are planning far into the future, Mrs. Anderson."

"My sons are twenty-one and twenty-two, and both in college, so it won't be long before they're married and have children. At least I hope not," she added with a smile.

David Mayer gaped at her. "You have sons twenty-one and twenty-two years old? I thought you were no more than thirty!"

"Thank you, Mr. Mayer, but I'm forty-three."

David, trying to rethink it all with this startling new information, was silent.

"Mr. Mayer, your silence and strange expression...are we going to have a repeat of..."

"No no," he smiled. "I assure you there will not be a repeat of my bad behavior...it's just that I was thinking one way, assuming you were a young mother with young boys, and now I...Mrs. Anderson, may we start all over?"

Chapter Three

David Mayer stood up and stretched, grateful that it was five o'clock. Even though busy with one appointment after another, the day seemed to drag after Torry Anderson left. He noticed the wilted lilac lying on the corner of his desk and smiled. He picked it up, studied it, then smelled of its still strong aroma, a heavenly fragrance he'd never experienced before. Turning to the book case behind him, he pulled out a heavy book on banking and carefully placed the lilac in it, piled several more on top, then walked to the door.

As he turned off the light and stepped out, he glanced over at Tom Baker's office and was relieved to see that he'd gone home. David was grateful for the reprieve tonight. Tomorrow Tom would want a report on how he had handled Torry Anderson and he would have to confess what a fiasco it turned out to be. Knowing Tom's indefatigable sense of humor, he would thoroughly enjoy every minute of it and never let him live it down!

As he drove home, he smiled, remembering how difficult it was convincing Torry Anderson to go out to dinner with him tonight in order to discuss a loan for the proposed chicken farm.

"Mr. Mayer, surely this isn't the usual procedure you have for discussing loans is it?" a look of irritation again on her face.

No it isn't, but my eleven o'clock appointment is here and you have just begun telling me about your business. We would have to get together again anyway, it might as well be over dinner."

"Thank you, Mr. Mayer, but no. May I come in this afternoon or tomorrow?"

"No, I'm all booked up."

"The next day?"

"I'm afraid not."

"Mr. Mayer, really!" she said in exasperation. "I was married for twenty-three years, it would be awkward for me to...uh..."

"This isn't a date," he'd quickly assured her, "it's only business. I've been married also, but I've been single a long time and I'm tired of eating alone. It's as simple as that."

He was keenly aware of the struggle she was having with herself while weighing the options, and he knew her final acceptance was only because she was desperate for the loan.

~~~~~~~~~~~~~~~

At six o'clock sharp, David Mayer was standing on Torry Anderson's small front porch with an armful of lilacs. Torry opened the door and gasped in delight as she saw the huge bouquet, but just as quickly the delight turned to dismay.

"Mr. Mayer, this doesn't look like...business to me."

"This is just an apology for my rudeness and unbusinesslike behavior this morning."

"Well...all right," she said hesitantly. "Thank you, come into the kitchen with me, and I'll find a vase."

David stepped inside and followed her through the small foyer and into the kitchen.

She stopped, turned around and looked up at him. "Oh dear, I forgot, my vases are still packed. I know," she said, turning to a cupboard and stretching to reach the top shelf, "I'll use a glass pitcher."

"I wonder where I've been all my life, Mrs. Anderson," he said as he watched her fill the pitcher with water, "I've never seen a lilac before coming to Green Valley, and until now I've never smelled one."

"I'm glad you've been introduced to them," she said, smiling as she took them from his arms. Putting them in the pitcher she arranged the bouquet and placed it in the middle of the kitchen table. "Mmmm they smell wonderful. I would like to have a bouquet of lilacs in every room during the season—which is far too short."

"Did you have lilacs in...I haven't even found out where you are from yet. We didn't get that far did we?"

"I moved from Denver. No, my husband Jack didn't like them because the bushes grow very large and full. He thought they would take up too much space." She broke off a single lilac to take with her.

"I'm ready, Mr. Mayer. Where are we going?"

He noticed that the faded jeans had been replaced by a simple navy blue linen suit and pearls.

"I hear that Hilltop House draws tourists from all over, and I've always wanted to find out why."

"How long have you lived in Green Valley, Mr. Mayer?" she asked as they walked to the car.

"Only a year." He opened the door for her and she got in.

"Do you mind if we roll down the windows?" she asked as he placed himself behind the wheel. "The Meadowlarks are singing, and the air smells good."

"Not at all," he said pushing the window button. "I've never heard a Meadowlark."

"They aren't nocturnal birds, so they're singing their last songs of the day. Listen and you'll hear them."

"Beautiful. I have heard them this spring, but I didn't know what kind of birds they were."

"Can you hear what they're saying?" she asked, a teasing smile on her face.

"No, what are they saying?"

"Green Valley's a pretty little place." He looked askance at her. She explained. "If you say it fast with the lilt of the Meadowlark's song, it sounds like it." She repeated it with the lilt in her voice. "Now listen to their song again."

He listened carefully, then chuckled. "You're right! When did you discover this?" he asked, starting the car and backing out onto the street.

"My grandmother Thomas told me about it...and..." her voice trailed off as she stared out the window.

"And what?"

"Oh, also she often said, 'You always need to listen carefully to the birds, Torry, because they sing about the joy of life.'"

David Mayer was silent for a moment, then he smiled. "Thank you for sharing that with me. I don't remember when I've just listened to the birds, in fact I don't think I did much of it as a boy, that I can recall anyway."

Torry looked at him and her heart tugged for some reason, but she quickly checked herself. Emotionally she felt depleted. She had even gone to the bishop of her ward in Green Valley and requested that he give her some time to work things out before calling her to a position. She didn't even want to get to know anyone at church yet, though she attended weekly. She needed to be alone for a while, even though the loneliness was distressing. This morning, before going to the bank, was one of the loneliest times she had ever experienced. But—as she thought about it now, it suddenly came to her attention that after returning from the bank, the feeling of loneliness was gone. She decided it was probably because several things took its place: hope, uncertainty, amazement at the strange experience she had with Mr. Mayer, and amusement at the comedy of errors it seemed to be. All this intermingled with trepidation over going to dinner with him.

Glancing at her, David saw that she was smelling the lilac.

Torry realized he was watching her and remembered her own unbusinesslike behavior—carrying a lilac into the bank and at a very inappropriate moment, taking a whiff of it.

"Lilacs make me think of my grandmother Thomas," she confessed.

"Oh?"

"The city park is where my grandmother's house stood. Lilac bushes lined both sides of her front lawn."

"Too bad it's not there anymore, I would have liked to see it."

As they traveled, each engrossed in their own thoughts, they strangely felt comfortable with the silence. After heading out of town a short distance, they came to a sign announcing 'Hilltop House, Restaurant and Inn.' Turning off, they wound higher and higher, the trees becoming thicker and greener, with a smattering of pine trees mixed in. Torry shivered as the evening air, tinged with the scent of pine, blew in brisk and chilly. Arriving at the restaurant, Torry uttered an exclamation of delight.

"What a picturesque old Victorian home!"

"I was told that it was built in 1900."

A young man, dressed in a Victorian costume, offered to park the car. The hostess, also in costume, greeted them as they entered and led them up to the second floor, seating them in front of a large window which overlooked the beautiful country surrounding the inn. The decor was elegantly authentic. Rich colors of deep wine and several shades of blue were predominate in the furniture, the flowered wallpaper and the tasseled drapes. Small tiffany lamps graced each table.

"I can't believe that the town of Green Valley has a restaurant and inn like this," marveled Torry.

"Tom Baker said that this belonged to a wealthy eccentric from the east who married a Mormon girl."

"What was the name?"

"Randolph, I believe."

"Oh yes, I remember my grandmother mentioning the Randolph mansion on the hill."

"Tom said that the inn is crowded all spring, summer and fall. The people who stay at the inn drive into town to hear The Barbershop Quartet sing at the Old Mill where they serve home-made root beer and sandwiches on homemade bread."

"Really? Barbershop is one of my favorite types of singing. The name of the barber shop in town is called The Barbershop Quartet, could that be them?"

"It is. And it also is a tourist attraction. When they're through cutting a person's hair, if he or she is satisfied with the hair cut, they all four sing a short harmony, in celebration they say. A very clever idea and a way to advertise their group while getting some practicing in."

"I can hardly wait to get a hair cut, I need one."

"You need a hair cut?" David asked as he scrutinized her short curls.

"Yes," she said, running her hand impatiently through her hair. "It's too long."

"It's too long?" he repeated, dubious.

"I don't like spending time on it and if I keep it short, the natural curls are easier to manage...but why am I telling you this?" she said, annoyed with herself.

"Amazing."

"What's amazing?" asked Torry.

"That you don't want to spend time on your hair."

"Most women don't, that's why they go to beauty salons."

"How often do you go to the salon?"

"About every two months."

"As I said—amazing."

"It seems we are going around in circles, Mr. Mayer," she said, exasperation in her voice.

David just smiled and shook his head. "Speaking of circles, in my circle of acquaintances, from my youth on, women spent hours in the salons, two or three times a week, including my mother."

Torry, noticing the sparkle in his eyes diminish momentarily when he mentioned his mother, said more gently, "Mr. Mayer, may we look at the menu and order? We need to get on with the business we came here to discuss. It's difficult in this nice atmosphere, but I need to. Hard work is going to be my therapy."

He studied her a moment. "You must have loved your husband very much."

Torry winced. "It's much more complicated than that, Mr. Mayer."

An hour-and-a-half later, they were finishing a dessert of vanilla custard after a delicious dinner of fresh salmon, scalloped potatoes, asparagus sprinkled with shaved almonds, hot rolls and a fresh fruit salad. They were also finishing up the details of Torry's research on chicken farming.

"Mrs. Anderson, I'm doubtful that you can begin to compete with the big chicken producers and their prices."

"I don't intend to try to compete with them. This chicken will be produced for the more elite restaurants, not fast food places. My grandmother taught me some secrets of raising chickens and never have I tasted chicken like hers. Because of the way chickens are mass produced today, and the way they're fed, the meat doesn't taste the same. I've already talked to several four star restaurants in the Salt Lake Valley who seem enthused about trying my chicken. I have also arranged with a middle man, Chelsey Farms, just south of Salt lake, to process the chicken and deliver to these restaurants. They have two divisions, the processing plant and a hatchery. I will also be purchasing the chicks from them."

"For now I want to buy about 150 quality day-old chicks and feed them to be broilers, fryers in other words, which will take eight to nine weeks approximately. Then I'll get another batch of chicks and start over. By that time I should be able to find out how the restaurants like the chicken and I, of course, will keep several back to try myself. I think it will be better tasting meat but I suspect it won't taste like grandmother's until I raise several generations of layers and hatch the eggs myself. I will never want to go into the processing part of the business."

"Is ten acres large enough?"

"No. The ten acres will be used only for test and research farming. Large chicken farms, I'm afraid are rather odiferous, so I plan to buy acreage outside of town when I expand."

"I see, and you say you want to borrow sixty-five thousand dollars?"

"Yes. That is what the owners of the property and I have agreed upon. I have enough money from the life insurance to pay for it in cash. I will give the bank the deed to the property as collateral."

"When do you think you can start making a profit?"

"Hopefully in two years. The profit will be small but as I expand, it can be very profitable."

"Do you have an income until the business can support you?"

"Only the rest of my husband's insurance and a small monthly dividend from stocks. It should carry me for at least two and a half years."

"Sixty-five thousand isn't very much. You might be under-financing, depending on how elaborate you intend to make your building and how much and what kind of equipment you intend to use. So many businesses fail because of this very reason."

Torry frowned. "I'm concerned about borrowing more...I..."

"No matter, Mrs. Anderson, I'm afraid the board of directors will not even consider approving this loan."

"Why? If the business isn't successful, the bank can take over the property and sell it for the same amount I've borrowed."

"That makes sense, Mrs. Anderson, but the fact is, that particular piece of property has been up for sale for about ten years and you are the first potential buyer. It's not large enough to make a farm out of it and there isn't much demand for residential property, especially in that location, so I'm afraid it would be a risk for the bank."

"I see, I didn't know it had been on the market that long." she said slowly, raw disappointment on her face.

David quickly added, "Maybe I can come up with a solution for you. I'm impressed with your preparation and research. Let me give it some more thought and get back to you in the next couple of days or so."

Torry's face brightened. "I would appreciate it very much if you would. Thank you." She glanced at her watch. "I don't want to take any more of your time, Mr. Mayer. The dinner was delicious and this place is wonderful, thank you."

"And thank you, Mrs. Anderson." His eyes smiling, intimate, caused Torry to squirm uncomfortably. "I appreciate you accepting my invitation so that I didn't have to dine alone."

For the first time, she noticed the color of his eyes. They were bluish gray, mostly gray—then she became conscious of something she'd noticed this morning. The moment she saw him, she was keenly aware of the magnetism in his eyes. It was ever present, smiling or unsmiling. It seemed to come from a light deep within that surfaced as a sparkle of familiarity, humor, warmth, drawing people to him. Realizing she'd been staring at him for several seconds, she stood up, smiling. The smile remained on her face as they walked to the car. She felt sure that if David Mayer dined alone, it was definitely by his own choice.

Torry shivered as they began their descent down the small mountain. "It has turned cold up here."

David rolled up the windows, now concentrating on the narrow road as light from up-coming cars came one by one, almost blinding him. "I can't believe that there are so many late night diners on a Tuesday night. And April seems a little early for tourists."

Back on the highway, David Mayer's thoughts returned to Torry's business. He already had a solution in mind for her, but decided to give her another option, proposing both at once, letting her choose. But would she accept either proposal? Torry Anderson was like no other woman he'd ever known. He smiled, remembering when he first saw her this morning, standing in the doorway of his office.

Frowning, Torry wondered how David Mayer could possibly find a way to finance her venture if it was too risky for a bank. She felt hopeful anyway. Impatience made her want to ask when she could expect to hear back from him on this. Instead, she focused her thoughts on trying to think up other alternatives herself.

Both were surprised to find the trip back very short.

Reluctantly, David turned into Torry's driveway. She waited, pleased when she saw he wasn't going to open the car door and walk her to the porch. That and the fact that he had stuck strictly to business all evening was proof she'd been foolish to feel nervous about going to dinner with him.

"Here's my card, Mrs. Anderson," he said as she opened the door to get out, "it has my office and home phone on it if you need to contact me before I get back to you."

With her thanks she said good night, leaving a wilted lilac on the seat. Picking it up, David smelled of its fragrance as he watched her walk to the door.

Chapter Four

Wednesday afternoon, Torry looked at her watch for the hundreth time. It was 4:55 and David Mayer had not called. Her impatient nature was a curse at a time like this. Yesterday was the day marked on her calendar to start the wheels in motion, but David Mayer's verdict, last night, effectively derailed all her careful planning. The time-frame she had set, in order to achieve the goals toward starting her business, could not be realized.

All day, she fought the urge to call him, and ask if he had any intimation when he could come up with a viable solution for her. Would it be two or three days, a week, two weeks? Knowing herself, she knew it would be almost impossible to wait more than a week.

Because of her anxiousness, it turned out to be a most unproductive day. Standing up in the midst of the half unpacked boxes and piles of things here and there, she sighed. In her distracted state of mind, she seemed to have created more chaos than order. The phone rang. Her heart lurched...hoping. Stepping quickly out and over the clutter, she ran into the kitchen.

"Hello?"

"Mrs. Anderson, this is David Mayer."

"Oh hello, Mr. Mayer. It's nice to hear from you," she said, trying not to betray her eagerness.

"This is late notice, I know, but I just heard about it a few minutes ago. In an hour, at six o'clock, The Barbershop Quartet is giving a short thirty minute concert at the park. If you can make it, why don't we meet there and listen to it. Afterward we can go somewhere and discuss several solutions I've come up with concerning the financing of your business."

Torry felt a mixture of relief and disappointment. "Mr. Mayer, why is it we must socialize before we discuss business?"

David was silent. He thought he was being subtle by suggesting they meet at the park rather than picking her up.

"Mr. Mayer?"

"As Jack Benny would say: 'I'm thinking, I'm thinking.'" He heard a giggle.

"Mr. Mayer, why don't we meet at the drugstore at 7:00 and I'll buy you a soda while we discuss business?"

"Fine. I'll see you then."

Torry hung up the phone. Her anxiousness gone, at least for the present, she smiled. Even though she had declined David Mayer's invitation to meet him for the performance, she definitely intended to go to it on her own.

Throwing a sandwich together, she munched on it while rummaging through the closet looking for something to wear. A long dark blue slightly gathered denim skirt looked appropriate enough. To go with it she chose a peach boat-necked shell and small peach earrings. It had been a long time since she noticed her wardrobe needed refurbishing and for some reason...she noticed tonight. Her light mood evaporated remembering the last time she inspected her wardrobe.

About two years before Jack died, she went on a shopping spree for one purpose only and that was to get his attention. She came home with a new dress, a couple of blouses and pants, hoping that Jack would notice. He didn't. Hurt and frustrated, she finally gave up trying to dress for him. She had never dressed for herself, always for Jack. During the first years of their marriage, his enthusiastic appreciation of her was very satisfying.

Wrenching her thoughts away from Jack, she went into the bathroom and began brushing her hair with fierce intensity. She checked the time, then quickly applied the usual thin layer of base, a touch of blush, eye shadow and lipstick. Torry was grateful for short, natural curls and full, dark lashes. Both saved her time. She didn't have to bother with perms, mascara and eyelash curlers. She studied herself in the mirror, dismayed that she couldn't tell how she looked. A sob escaped and tears blinded her view. Why is it, she thought, that a woman needs a man to validate her appearance? The sob left as quickly as it came. Drying her eyes, she walked to the front door and down the steps at 5:35, hoping to get a seat on those white bleachers. She walked quickly. Half a block from the park, she heard a voice some distance behind her.

"Hey Torry, wait up!"

Turning around, she saw Zelda Blackburn. She and her husband, Zak owned Henry the rooster and the farm next to her property on Farm Road 6.

She could tell Zelda's walk two blocks away. The cowboy boots she always wore, made her walk seem a little masculine. Raising and training thoroughbred Paint horses was a hobby of hers, so her everyday attire, except for church on Sundays, was blue jeans and cowboy boots. Though no taller than five-feet-four-inches, her broad hipped, sturdy figure was very trim. Her plain face, framed by a delightful disarray of curly, shoulder-length light-brown hair, pulled, pinned or tied exotically here or there with a flower, scarf or stretch band to match the colors of her blouse, invariably took on a glamorous appearance.

Zelda was the only neighbor she knew, the only one who welcomed her to the town. She and her two teen-age sons, Ivan and Gilford had come to Torry's door carrying a pot of soup, homemade bread and a small apple pie. They also offered their help. She thanked them for the food, but declined the help. Zelda had come over several times since to visit and to offer help.

Torry smiled as Zelda walked up with that ever present, contagious smile. "Hello Zelda, it's good to see you."

"Good to see you too." Her face became serious as she studied Torry. "What's happened? Anything I should know about?"

"Why do you ask that?"

"You look...uh...different somehow."

"I do?" Torry asked, surprised.

"Yes, I can't quite put a finger on it but..."

"Are you going to the performance in the park?"

"You bet, I wouldn't miss it."

"Good. Let's get a seat on the bleachers. Where are Zak and the boys?" Torry asked as they walked briskly toward the park.

"Oh, I couldn't get any of them to come and get a little culture. Are you unpacked and settled yet, Torry?"

"Not yet, but it's coming. I've finished all the painting."

They found the bleachers just beginning to fill and a few families were spreading blankets on the grass. They settled on seats midway up.

Shortly after sitting down, David Mayer walked up to the

bleachers, his suit and tie exchanged for casual pants and shirt. Seeing Torry, he waved, climbed to the top and sat down.

"Do you know him?" asked an obviously impressed Zelda.

"Yes, he's my banker."

"Lucky you! Isn't he handsome?"

"Handsome? I've never thought about it."

"You're joshing me. He has all the single women in town looking like sick calves. I have one friend who remarked that his rugged features remind her of the way they describe the hero in the paperback romances."

Torry raised an eyebrow as she studied Zelda's expressive face, noticing the mischievous twinkle in her eyes. "You aren't serious, Zelda."

"You bet your cowboy boots, I am."

"I read a few of those romances when I was young and I remember, the heroes had 'steely eyes and a jutting jaw'."

Zelda laughed. "My friends would probably say you weren't well-read at all and then tell you that David Mayer's eyes are far from steely, that they make them feel all liquid inside."

"Come on, Zelda," Torry said smiling and shaking her head.

"It's true! One friend told me she thinks that his hawk-bridged nose fits perfectly with his strong jaw...not 'jutting,' Torry, strong. And his smile, she said, makes her heart set off on a cross-country run."

"You know, Zelda...I am not interested in what your friends say."

Zelda continued as if she hadn't heard. "I think he's about two inches under six feet, because one of my taller girl friends can almost look him in the eye. But, she said she didn't care because his fascinating looks, and masculine hands make up for his lack of height."

Torry rolled her eyes in exasperation. "You certainly have a lot of single friends, Zelda."

"I do, and I would like to find them each a husband. Several have never been married, a couple are divorced. They all find any excuse they can to go into the bank. He's probably being mobbed right now—if you dare look."

"I really don't care about Mr. Mayer's looks...or his personal life, Zelda."

"You mean his personal problems don't you?" Zelda said as she turned and looked up at the top row of bleachers. "There is a woman on each side of him vying for his attention. Oh oh, there are a couple of my friends sitting just in front of him—and turning around chattering at him."

"Please don't gawk, Zelda, you're making me uncomfortable."

"Not as uncomfortable as David Mayer I'll bet. He looks as miserable as a stallion caught in a swarm of horse flies."

Torry giggled. She couldn't resist; turning, she looked up and indeed found David Mayer in the situation Zelda had described, but...glaring ominously in her direction. Shocked, Torry turned around quickly.

"Well, can you beat that, he gave you a dirty look, Torry. Now why would he do that?" Zelda asked, eyeing her with suspicion.

"How would I know? I'm not his keeper."

Zelda chuckled. Fuming, Torry stared at her, which only succeeded in making Zelda giggle. Finally succumbing to the humor of the situation, Torry joined Zelda, their giggles reaching the point of embarrassment. She couldn't stop, Zelda didn't want to, each infecting the other with laughter like a couple of teenagers. A voice over the loud speaker announcing the program sobered them. It had been a long time since she had laughed like that. It felt good.

Torry couldn't remember hearing a better barbershop quartet. They sang several humorous songs with actions to match, thoroughly entertaining the appreciative audience. It was over far too quickly.

"Thanks for your company, Zelda—I think." They both laughed as they climbed to the ground.

"Come over sometime, Torry," she said as she was walking away, "and I'll give you a gallon of the best Jersey milk you ever tasted."

"Thanks, Zelda, I'll see you soon."

A hand gripped her arm. "Mrs. Anderson, how are you?"

She looked up into the desperate face of her banker. Noticing the menagerie of women around him, she smiled sweetly, "Mr. Mayer, you're right on time for our appointment."

Feeling relief that she quickly sized up the situation and helped him out, David recovered his manners. "May I introduce you all to one of my customers, Mrs. Torry Anderson?" He muddled through the introductions, and they each begrudgingly acknowledged Torry's acquaintance.

After managing to disengage himself from the group, David walked with Torry through the park. Torry was having trouble holding back more giggles.

"If you'd been with me, I wouldn't have been ambushed," he growled.

Torry stopped walking and stared up at him in disbelief. "You mean, my job is to be your protector?"

Looking a bit sheepish, he shook his head. "Well...no, but you and your friend needn't have enjoyed my predicament so immensely."

Torry couldn't hold in her amusement any longer. Grabbing the first park bench, she sat down weak with laughter. David stood above her, glowering.

Finally gaining control, she said mockingly, "Thank you, Mr. Mayer, I needed that...it's been a hard week and..."

"I don't appreciate being your comic relief of the day, Mrs. Anderson." he replied on cue, his eyes twinkling as he sat down beside her.

"Now we're even." Torry stated.

"You mean I'm not held accountable anymore for my bad behavior yesterday?"

"I didn't say that, I just said we're even." She studied him closely, noting that Zelda had forgotten to mention his nice, dark, slightly curly hair.

"Uh, why are you looking at me like that?"

"Oh...uh nothing."

"Is something wrong?"

"No, nothing is wrong. I was looking at you because my neighbor, Zelda, the one who owns Henry said you were handsome." Embarrassed, now that she had said the words, the color rose quickly in her cheeks.

"Who is Henry?"

Relieved that David Mayer focused on Henry instead of the other, she replied, "He's the loudest mouth in the neighborhood. When I first got here, he woke me up at 4:30 every morning but now I'm used to him so I can usually sleep until 5:00."

"What does he do, holler?"

"No, he crows."

"Oh. Henry's a rooster." He laughed.

"I can't believe this." Torry said shaking her head, suddenly serious.

"What?"

"I can't believe our business relationship has deteriorated into this casual banter. Trying to stay businesslike with you, Mr. Mayer, is like trying to drink milk with your mouth closed."

David smiled, his eyes twinkled with mischief. "Why fight it, Mrs. Anderson, we were meant for far greater things."

"Mr. Mayer, please."

"Well then, at least, let's give up the encumbrance of Mr. and Mrs."

Torry sighed in resignation. "We might at well, they seem out of place now."

"Good. Is Torry short for Torrance?"

"Yes, my grandmother's name was Torrance Ann. My father was determined that I wasn't going to be named after her, but Mother was equally determined, so they compromised and named me Torry Ann."

"What part of this park was your grandmother's?"

"All of it." Torry told him where the house had been, the orchard, the barn, the chicken coop and the swing.

"Where were the lilac bushes?"

David Mayer's sincere interest triggered an attack of nostalgia. She told him briefly of her six-week visit each summer: the activities, the association with her grandparents; all inexplicably dear to her.

"I would like to hear more details," he said, a hint of longing in his voice.

Torry studied him, wondering. "Did you know any of your grandparents?"

"No, but what was that about buying me a soda?"

"Are you trying to change the subject, Mr. Mayer?"

"David."

"David," she repeated.

He stood up and held out his hand for her. "I'm just thirsty for a soda, how about it?"

Ignoring his hand, she stood up and they walked in silence to the drugstore. Entering, they found themselves in the midst of teenagers and the din of talking, laughter and music. They found one booth left and sat down smiling at each other.

"Sorry," Torry said, "I didn't know this was a teenage hangout."

"It looks like the same bunch that was over at the park," David said, looking around.

"How do you like the music?" Torry asked.

"It sounds great—goes with the surroundings. Every time I come in I feel I'm back in the 1930's.

"I heard they play music from the 30's, 40's and 50's. The decor is certainly authentic. It looks like it did when Grandfather owned it, but improved."

"Your grandfather owned this? You didn't mention that when you took me down memory lane."

A small sigh attached itself to her smile. "I spent many happy hours in here, as a child and as a teenager, eating sundaes, malts and floats and so on."

A young harried waitress came to take their order. Both decided on root beer floats. She jotted it down and disappeared into the crowd.

"Tell me about your grandfather."

"He was kind of the town character, but a little on the periphery of my life because he was always so preoccupied, in a world of his own." Torry smiled. "Sometimes people would mistake this as being absent minded or unaware and would try to take advantage of him. But they soon found themselves the recipient of a salty reprimand or his unwanted counsel, whichever he felt they needed at the time. I think he rankled nearly every one in town at one time or another."

They sat in silence for awhile, letting the music flow around them as they watched the youth laugh and talk with each other.

The root beer floats arrived. They sipped them for a moment, then David asked, "How did your grandfather rankle people?"

"There was one instance I remember well. Grandfather was a good pharmacist and one of my favorite places when I was a child was on a small stool behind the counter in the pharmacy area. I liked listening to him interact with the customers."

"There was a town whiner called Bertha who seemed to have every ailment in the book at one time or another and was always coming in with a prescription for the newest complaint. One day when ol' Doc Haslem called in a prescription for Bertha, Grandfather's irritation had reached its peak and he chewed him out for giving in to her and prescribing useless medications. When Bertha came in to get it, Grandfather handed her the prescription in a sack." Torry chuckled. "Well, she got the surprise of her life when she got home and opened the sack. She found a brown bottle with a label on it that said: 'Prescription to Take Your Mind off Yourself.'" David laughed.

"Inside the bottle, she found three slips of paper rolled up with a typed message on each. A tearful, whining Bertha came back and handed Grandfather the sack with the bottle in it, complaining how unfeeling and hardhearted he was for not understanding the illnesses that always plagued her."

"What did your grandfather do?"

"He just handed her a sack with the real prescription in it, totally unperturbed and said, 'Thought you'd be back, Bertha.'"

David chuckled. "But I want to know what he typed on those rolled up pieces of paper."

"So did I, or rather I wanted to know what was in that sack. I was on my little stool that day and having more curiosity than was good for me, I grabbed the sack off Grandfather's work counter and pulled out the bottle. When I read the label, I giggled. Grandfather turned around and looked at me as if it was the first time he realized I was there, then shooed me with his hands; 'Off with you, Torry Ann!' I grabbed the sack and bottle and ran out the back door, anxious to look at the contents with Grandmother."

"She and I had a hilarious good time over it. One message was, 'Visit Widow Nielson weekly.' Another one was, 'Take a meal into old Granny Turner once a month.' And the third, 'Don't talk about yourself, ask after the welfare of others.'"

"Wonderful!" David exclaimed. "Did it help Bertha?"

"It so happened that was one of Grandfather's successes. Bertha actually took his advice, to the relief of her poor husband, as well as the whole town, now spared their daily recitation of her ailments. She rarely had to go to the pharmacy for medicine. But, when she did, she smiled and even managed to talk without a whine in her voice."

"An astounding story. And...an astute little girl who grabbed the sack and ran." He smiled, his eyes holding hers as he visualized the little girl of long ago.

Feeling uneasy under his gaze, Torry blurted out with more abruptness than she intended, "Mr. Mayer, I mean David, I wanted you to know a little of the history of this old drugstore, but I think we need to get on with the business we came here to discuss."

"All right, but you must tell me more stories about your grandfather sometime. Now to get down to business. I have a solution to the financial backing of your farm. Actually it's one solution with two choices." He paused a moment, noticing her hopeful expression. "I would like to put up the money personally."

"Why?" she asked abruptly.

He smiled.

Torry frowned. "Why are you amused?"

"Because you reacted like I thought you would," he said still smiling. "Hear me out. The first choice is a partnership with me." He waited for her reaction.

"A partnership? Why...why would you want a partnership with...me?" she asked guardedly.

"Because it sounds like an interesting and promising business, and I may even be able to actually give some physical help at times. The second choice is that I personally loan you the money, and I'll earn interest until you are able to pay off the loan."

Rubbing an imaginary spot on the table, Torry tried to sort out her thoughts and feelings. Seconds stretched out. Conscious of David's scrutiny, she finally looked up. "I don't know why I'm surprised at this since we've...uh...become acquainted so quickly. I...I've never felt so comfortable with anyone in such a short time as I have with you. It's rather unsettling."

David, pleasantly taken back at Torry's candidness, smiled; it made it easy to express his own feelings. "I feel just as comfortable, Torry, but I must admit, it feels great to me."

She frowned at his admission, but went on. "I don't know about the second choice, but I can't envision a partnership at all. I came here needing to be alone, to work alone, and now I find myself with the possibility of a 'hands on' partner."

"Hands on?" Mmm, sounds nice to me."

She looked at him in alarm. "That remark makes me suspicious of your motives, David Mayer," she said, quickly scooting out of the booth and standing up.

"Whoa there, Torry, just teasing."

"Are you really interested in my business?" she asked, her voice thick with skepticism.

"Yes," he answered honestly.

The expression on her face indicated she was not convinced. "Thank you for the offers. I'll think about them and let you know." She fished around in her purse. "Here's the money for the floats." She tossed a five dollar bill onto the table then wheeled around and briskly walked to the door and out.

David heaved a sigh, thoroughly annoyed with himself. "Damn! I've managed to louse up again," he whispered to himself.

He got up, slowly walked to the cashier and paid the bill, pocketing Torry's change, an excuse to see her again he thought, his spirits rising.

Out on the sidewalk, he stopped, noting that she was already out of sight. With slow deliberate steps he headed in the same direction to retrieve his car. Turning the corner, a distant lamp light illuminated a small figure, briskly moving toward home.

"Why wouldn't Torry be suspicious of my motives, I made them plain enough," he said aloud. "But why?" He could be as careful and subtle as he chose to be. He had learned that in the business world, so why did he allow himself to be so transparent tonight? The answer came immediately. Habit. There was never a need for subtlety with any of the women he'd known. Most of them aggressively let him know their desire to become better acquainted, turning him off completely. And the few who didn't pursue, annoyed him with their eagerness.

At forty-three years of age, David had no patience with the dating games. However, as he thought about it, he decided that discretion and caution were definitely called for when dealing with this spunky, unpredictable woman.

It had only been two days since he met Torry Anderson and his life had done a complete about-face.

It had been a year-and-a-half ago in Dallas that his friend Gabe, recognizing the signs of physical and mental burnout, finally, after many discussions, convinced him that he needed a respite in a small community away from the stresses of big business and big city life.

It had taken David six months to arrange his business affairs and, with Gabe's help, find a suitable town. He had to designate some one to take over the day-to-day management of his holding company. Meetings were held with executives in New York, Chicago, Boston and other parts of the country to inform them of the pending changes, and to whom they would now report. He explained that he would be checking in with them periodically.

The next challenge was to find the place. For David's change of pace, Gabe, being of the Mormon faith, had suggested a small Mormon community, explaining that their way of life would afford him a more relaxing atmosphere and lifestyle.

David's life, as far back as his youth, had been all work and still needing to continue work at something while taking this sabbatical, he researched and investigated more than a few small towns and businesses. It finally came to his attention that a major stockholder of three small banks in the West wanted to sell out. Since one of them was located in the small town of Green Valley Utah, he became interested. After some investigation, he purchased the controlling stock. According to Gabe, this town was made to order for David.

The first ten months of the year spent here in Green Valley were as good for him as Gabe had predicted. The slower pace of living and the small town were welcome changes from the frenetic lifestyle in the cities.

The people in this Mormon community with their friendly, kind ways, reflected, he felt, their religious beliefs. He knew nothing of Mormonism, but he had never known such a large number of basically good people. He could even see the influence of the Church in the mannerisms and way of speaking of those who didn't practice their religion.

It had been a boost to his morale to associate with Tom Baker who, he knew, lived what he believed. Tom had invited him to his home to meet his wife, Jenny, and their seven happy, rambunctious children who instantly made him a part of their lives, from sixteen-year-old Josh down to four-year-old Missy. Jenny had invited him to dinner many times. He accepted only about half the invitations, not wanting to take advantage. Instead, he chose to take them all out to eat now and then, to the delight of their enthusiastically grateful children. Watching a real family, a loving family in action was soul satisfying to David, and he became more attached to them than he wanted to be.

There were others who adopted him. Jesse Jones and Dan Higley, a couple of crusty old farmers whose colorful vernacular would starch the petticoats of a too proper English teacher, as they would say, but who awakened in David a renewed vitality in life. The duo, who had neighboring farms, were fast friends. Both, overdue in their retirement, continued to work long hard hours. Yearly, they borrowed money from the bank and when the crops were in and sold, they paid off the loan.

Weekly, they made trips into town for a sandwich and a malt at the drugstore, to relax, talk politics or see who could tell the funniest or wildest yarns. They, for some reason, took to him and insisted that he join them. It wasn't long before he looked forward to the weekly get-together. Some days he returned from the meeting, his sides aching from the belly laughs that their stories evoked. Other times, he entered the bank meditative after listening to the inspirational stories and experiences they were able to share without forcing their beliefs upon him.

The unpretentious, down-to-earth people in this town made him feel comfortable and at ease in every situation except one, and that was when they were in larger groups such as a town council meeting. They seemed to have such a common bond with each other, he felt like an outsider looking in. It occurred to him one day this might be the cause of the bleakness that had begun creeping over him about two months ago.

Loneliness had been his companion as long as he could remember, but the bleak emptiness that eventually took hold of him was worse than anything he had ever experienced. Unable to find relief, he decided, with much regret, that his time in Green Valley was up.

He was about to make plans to move on, when Torry Anderson walked into his office. Because of the comical episode that followed, he failed to recognize, at first, that the depressive emptiness had vanished. For two months, day and night he had suffered this devastating emotion and now, in one moment, it was gone!

When Tom asked him to talk to Torry Anderson, he had waited for her, feeling the total exhaustion and restlessness that the despondency seemed to bring. The minute he saw Torry, it was all forgotten—then it was gone. Though a pragmatic man, and a cynic of 'love at first sight,' he was significantly humbled at the powerful phenomenon...Torry Anderson had filled the painful void.

The immediacy of it perplexed him, leaving unanswered questions in his always questioning mind. Mulling it over constantly for two days and nights, his need for a logical explanation and understanding gave way to a greater need—happiness.

Now what in the deuce was he going to do about the unprecedented and most difficult challenge of his life—Torry?

~~~~~~~~~~~

Out of breath from walking so rapidly, Torry sat down on the front steps of her little home. The disappointment and frustration were gone but doubt remained—doubt whether she should have walked out on David Mayer like she had.

Why was she feeling this? The intimate way he talked to her was out of line, she was certain of that, so why was she questioning her actions? Why did he feel he could say that? She hadn't encouraged him in any way. Or had she? Something nagged at her, prompting her to review the whole evening, starting from the program in the park. She found herself smiling at the incident on the bleachers and as she did so a thought struck her.

"It's Zelda!" she exclaimed out loud. With Zelda added to the equation, it made more sense. It was Zelda who made her aware of David's problem with the women. It was Zelda whose remarks made them both giggle like a couple of school girls. It was Zelda who insisted on relating how enamored her friends were over David's physical appearance. And it was Zelda's own remark that had influenced her to blurt out those embarrassing words to David about his looks! She felt her face flush as she thought of this...this intimacy she herself had indulged in. What was it that made it feel so easy and natural to joke with and relate personal memories to David Mayer? After all, he was a new acquaintance, and her banker no less.

Rising suddenly, she paced up and down the walk, rubbing the evening chill off her arms while trying to put a name to it. Unsuccessful at both, she sat down again, and hugged her knees. It was something indefinable, something she couldn't pinpoint. One thing she was certain of, it was amazingly comfortable to be with him. Yet, having been married so long, feeling comfortable with a single man was, at the same time, uncomfortable! What a bundle of contradictions she was.

Examining every detail of the evening, again brought Zelda into focus, not Zelda herself Torry realized, but something she said, "You look different somehow." It was a simple enough statement, but now it jolted Torry. As the rising sun dispels the lingering shadows of night, Torry felt a sudden glow of understanding—the depression was gone! Not quite believing it, she sat there in awe, feeling, examining. It was true!

Heartache over her failed marriage was still there, but the despondency that came with it a year-and-a-half ago and had remained with her until...she didn't know when, was now gone! Stunned, she sat up straight, savoring the relief.

"Heavenly Father, when did this happen?" she asked aloud. Then bowing her head, she thanked Him for releasing her from the smothering grayness that had hovered over her day and night, like a cloud eclipsing the sun. Tears fell onto the denim skirt. She reached into her pocket for a tissue and wiped her eyes.

When did the depression leave? She stood up and began pacing more slowly this time, trying to think back over every detail of the past two days.

Walking to the bank yesterday morning, she felt oppressed, weighed down by a sense of depression and fear. How did she feel in the bank? After the bank? How could one tell after that absurd encounter with David Mayer? And his insistence on discussing business over dinner that night, had left her feeling unsettled for the rest of the day.

The bouquet of lilacs! When she took them from David, the joy in their beauty and fragrance had filled her soul. She was now certain by that time the depression was gone. Whether or not it left at that moment, she didn't know, but she marvelled over the suddenness of its passing. And while walking to the car with David, the pleasant smells of early spring and the songs of the Meadowlarks had assailed her senses. This kind of awareness had eluded her since her arrival in Green Valley. She rejoiced in this revelation.

Drawn inward by despondency, the enjoyment of people had diminished to an unbearable level, but at the park she had truly appreciated Zelda and her colorful personality for the first time. And thanks to David Mayer's willing ear, the remembrance of times spent with Grandmother and Grandfather Thomas brought even greater joy.

How we take for granted the ability to feel, she thought. How strange she hadn't noticed the change in herself until tonight! How did it happen? Why did it happen this way? She decided that at the moment, the hows and whys didn't matter. All that mattered was that she could once again, as her mother said, enjoy the simple things of life.

She sat down on the steps smiling, contemplating it all. However, the smile slowly disappeared, replaced by a puzzled frown. The same nagging question remained. Why did she feel so comfortable with David Mayer? She had only known him two days?

"Maybe," she sighed pondering aloud, "it's as simple as an indication that I should accept a loan from him."

A familiar old dinged-up blue pickup turned into the driveway, screeching to a halt, spewing gravel in all directions. Zelda jumped out carrying a gallon of milk.

"We have too much milk, Torry, so thought I'd drop this by and save you a trip over for it."

Torry smiled, glad for the company. "Thank you, Zelda, I'm anxious to taste the milk. My grandmother had a Jersey cow, and as a child I thought it was the best milk in the world."

Zelda looked pleased as she set the milk on the porch and sat down beside Torry. "I saw you and your banker walk off together. What's going on with you two?"

"Why Zelda," laughed Torry, knowing that this was the real reason for bringing the milk, tonight. "You are a curious soul."

"You mean nosy don't you?" Zelda chuckled.

Torry smiled. "You said it, I didn't."

"Well?"

"Zelda! I had an appointment with him to discuss the financing of my business."

Zelda's eyebrows arched. "Discussing business in the park?"

"Believe me, there is nothing going on between us personally...and there can't be."

"Why?"

"Be...because," she spluttered in annoyance. "I don't...uh think he is a member of the Church and..."

"He isn't. And..." Zelda was eager to add. "he's Jewish, did you know?"

"No I didn't, so that means he probably doesn't believe in Christ. But, even if these weren't the issues, I can't get emotionally involved with any one."

"Why?"

"Zelda! You are nosey."

"I know, why?"

"Because," Torry said in exasperation. "I have some things to work out."

"Maybe it will help," Zelda said, knowingly, "for you to know that David Mayer is a multi-millionaire. Not only is he handsome, but he's rich."

Torry stared at her. "How do you know this? I knew that he must be well-off but..."

"I have my sources," Zelda said with smug assurance.

"I need to know if they're reliable sources. Please, Zelda, this is important."

"They are reliable, I promise you."

Unsettled by this information, Torry turned indignant. "Why that low-down, sneaky...uh"

"Jew," added Zelda grinning. "But"...her eyes suddenly widened with astonishment, "why does that make you angry?"

"Excuse me, Zelda," she said, standing up and stepping up onto the porch, "I need to call Mr. David Mayer right this minute."

"All right, I'll be off, but you've got me as curious as a cat on a kitchen counter. I'll check with you later, you can count on that."

"Thanks again for the milk," Torry said, grabbing the handle of the plastic container and almost slamming the screen door in Zelda's face.

~~~~~~~~~~~~~~~

Driving to Torry's house, David Mayer's pulse quickened as his emotions seesawed between excitement and concern. Torry's call, demanding in a brusque, business-like tone that they meet again tonight, came an hour after he had returned to his apartment. He was sitting down thinking about the evening when the call came. He rushed out immediately. Parking in front of Torry's house, he stared at it wondering why he responded so quickly to her demands. With any other woman he would have let her cool off, and only if and when he was ready, would he comply. He knew the answer. He got out of the car and walked slowly to the front porch and knocked on the screen door. Torry appeared immediately, opening the door. "Please come in, Mr. Mayer."

"Back to formalities, Torry?"

Ignoring the question, she led him into the kitchen. "Please sit down."

He sat down and leaned over to smell the lilacs. "Mmmm, they still look fresh."

Torry abruptly shoved the bouquet aside, and sat down, facing David squarely.

"Thank you for the offers you made tonight, but I can't accept either."

"I'm sorry about my teasing, Torry. It was in bad taste, but surely you're not turning me down over that?"

"No."

"Then what is this all about? What has happened since I saw you earlier?"

"Someone informed me tonight that you are a multi-millionaire. Is this correct?"

He looked shocked, then puzzled. "What in the deuce does that have to do with anything?"

"Is is true?"

"Am I supposed to feel guilty about it?"

"Is it true?" she snapped.

"Guilty as charged!" he replied angrily. They stared at each other in smoldering silence.

"Why in the hell does that make a difference to you?"

"Don't swear at me!"

"I didn't swear at you."

"You did, you said 'h-e-l-l'."

David gazed at her, a smile tugging at the corner of his mouth. "I'm sorry. I'll try not to swear again. But will you tell me why it makes a difference that I'm rich?" He paused, the smile becoming broader. "Most people would not find this to be a problem."

The smile on David's face only validated Torry's feelings. "You aren't interested in my little chicken farm, you are just toying with me."

"What do you mean by that?"

"If you are a multi-millionaire, you have many businesses and investments that are much more interesting and challenging, and which, I'm sure, make you much more money than my little chicken farm ever could."

His eyes narrowed. "What do you mean by toying with you?"

"That I'm just a diversion in your life of big business, a possible momentary amusement, relieving the quiet uneventful life of a small town."

He scrutinized her a moment, then got up, walked to the back door and stared out its window, seeing only his own reflection in the darkness. How could he rebut the logical, but totally false conclusion she had just thrown in his face? Unwilling to confront Torry until he found a way to clear up her misconceptions, he remained standing, his back to her. Moments passed, the silence thick with tension.

A flash of insight brought an answer for himself as well as Torry.

Turning around, he said, "First of all, how do you know that your 'little chicken farm' as you put it, won't make as much money as my other businesses? How do you think I became a multi-millionaire? I know how to make a business grow. I know how to make money."

"I'm sure you do but..."

"I'm not finished." He walked to the chair he'd been sitting in and stood behind it, his hands gripping the back. "And how can you judge my motives? What do you know of my life? Do you know why I came here to this small community to work in a bank when I have a conglomerate to look after?"

Torry was silent, her eyes wary.

"Well, do you?"

"You know I don't," she said quietly.

"Of course you don't. But I'm going to tell you." David stopped, his brows furrowed, aware of the edge of bitterness in his words. "I have a friend, a good friend, in Dallas who was concerned about me. He could see that I was exhausted, burned out, needing a change. He finally convinced me I needed the slower pace that a small town would give me. I decided to take his advice, did some research and chose Green Valley. Being here has been good for me as my friend predicted. But the last two months have...well, when you and your 'little chicken farm' presented me the possible opportunity of being as actively and physically involved as I chose or had time for, in a low stress outdoor business, it didn't take long for me to make up my mind." He walked back to the window again, his back to her, grateful he realized, in time, this other need: to be physically involved in Torry's business. He was sure that he sounded much more convincing than he would have otherwise. It also disguised the main reason he wanted the partnership, his desire to be with her, to get to know her better.

He walked back to the chair. "This is business, Torry, and the offer of the loan or partnership still stands. I prefer the partnership but if you don't choose to do either, that's fine too." Studying her as she listened, he noticed that the tight line of her mouth had softened, returning her lips to their enticing fullness. "I'll be going now, I think we both need to sleep on it—good night." He turned abruptly and left the kitchen. He stopped, turned around and walked back in.

"I forgot to thank you for the root beer float. Here is your change." Depositing the money on the table, he smiled, his eyes communicating warmth. Torry opened her mouth to say something, but he was already out of the kitchen heading for the front door. Halting again before going out, he returned, stopped at the kitchen door and peered in.

"Oh by the way, Torry Anderson, I have the money to buy or start any business I want to. If you don't accept the partnership or the loan, I think I'll start a goat farm...maybe next door to your chicken farm. Good night, Torry, call me when you make up your mind."

As soon as she heard the screen door slam, Torry wearily put her head down on her arms. Soon her shoulders were shaking with laughter.

Chapter Five

R evealing his state of mind, David Mayer drove into the bank parking lot too fast, Thursday morning, making it necessary to swerve abruptly in order to park in the usual place.

A lock of his dark hair fell forward as he got out of the car, suggesting only a cursory comb before leaving home. His jaw rippled as he walked with brusque, purposeful steps to the back door of the bank. He unlocked it, slammed it shut and relocked it.

Tom Baker, having arrived earlier, was sitting at his desk getting caught up on paper work when he heard the door slam louder than usual. He looked up just as David appeared at the door of his office. He smiled.

"Good morning, Dave."

"It's not going to be a good morning for someone in this bank!"

"Have a seat," Tom said, surprised at David's anger.

David remained standing. "Did you know that I'm a wealthy man...a multi-millionaire?"

Tom Baker, astonished by the question, was silent.

"Well, did you?" demanded David.

"You're serious."

"Very!"

"Since you're serious, you must be a multi-millionaire."

"That's not what I asked."

"No, I didn't know," Tom answered slowly, his deep voice patient. "I know that you are the major stock holder of this chain of banks, so naturally, I assumed that you were quite well off...but it had not occurred to me that you were a multi-millionaire. I hadn't given it any thought."

"I'm sorry, Tom," he said, finally accepting the invitation to sit down. "I didn't mean to accuse you, but someone in this bank has gone to a great deal of trouble to find out my financial status."

Tom leaned forward in concern. "How do you know this?"

David explained briefly, emphasizing the effect the knowledge had on Torry Anderson.

Tom smiled. "Most women would have been delighted to hear you were wealthy."

"Exactly! But Torry Anderson is not like any woman I've ever known, Tom."

Tom grinned. "I figured that. But Dave," he continued, his face becoming serious. "I can't think of one employee in the bank who would know how to find out that kind of information. It would be difficult even for me."

They sat in silence, thinking.

"Several women come in the bank often, Dave, and it's apparent to everyone why they come in."

"I know. Several sat by me on the bleachers in the park last night."

"Have you ever noticed any of these women talking to a particular employee of the bank?"

"Only the teller for a few minutes to cash a check or make a deposit. Have you Tom?"

"No."

"Wait a minute, I may have an idea," David said. "Do you know Silvia Barber, the new attorney in town?"

"You mean that sleek, blonde that has taken you to lunch several times on the pretext of getting your business?"

"That's the one."

"Silvia Barber...I wonder if she's Mildred Barber's daughter."

"Her mother's name is Mildred."

"Has Silvia asked you pointed questions about your businesses?"

"Yes, but I didn't think I divulged anything of importance. But...you know, Tom, as I think about it, being an attorney, she would know how to find out quite a bit from what I told her, if she chose to. But how would that have gotten back to Torry Anderson?"

"Well, there may be one way. Mildred is what I would call the town socialite, so to speak. As much of a socialite as one can be in any small town populated mainly by Mormons. And, she is somewhat of a talker. She likes to talk about her connections, hinting at affluence, name dropping and that kind of thing."

"If Silvia went to the trouble of finding out your financial status, then told her mother, Mildred may have bragged about Silvia's association with you and hinted broadly about your wealth. Just a guess, Dave."

"It's very probable. I've met her mother. If she's the source, there is nothing I can do about it, so I'm going to forget it." David stood up and stepped to the door, then turned around, "I'm just glad it wasn't you, Tom."

Tom smiled. The affection in his eyes for his employer and friend was apparent. "Me too, Dave, me too."

Chapter Six

It was only 5:00 A.M. Thursday morning when the phone rang. Torry had just begun her morning scripture reading, when she heard it. An expression of concern crossed her face as she ran to the kitchen.

"Hello?"

"Torry, how are you dear?" came the welcome sound of her mother's voice.

"Is everything all right, Mother?"

"Yes. While your dad was still asleep, I wanted to see if you were all right. Did he upset you, Torry?"

"Yes, but it's all okay. He actually did me a favor. I'll explain when I see you. I'm sorry I upset Dad but..."

"I understand, Torry."

"I was going to call you today, Mother, to tell you some good news."

"I could use some, I've been so concerned about you."

"My depression is gone!"

"Oh...Torry, that is good news. When did this happen?"

"I don't know for sure. One minute it was there and then it wasn't. But the strange thing is, it had been gone for almost two days before I realized it wasn't there anymore."

Her mother was silent.

"Mother? Are you all right?"

"More than all right." she said, choking back tears. "Can your father and I come down and see you?"

"Of course. You don't have to ask that, I want you to. I don't have a nice room for you as I did in Denver, but I have a pull-out couch."

"That's good enough, Torry. I don't know when we'll be down, but we're coming, I want to see where you're living and hear all about this business of yours."

~~~~~~~~~~

The call from her mother had lifted Torry's spirits. On her walk, energy surged through her body; her stride was rapid. How good life seemed. The songs of a variety of birds cheered her on while cheering her up. Sounds from other early risers of the community harmonized with them. The cows were mooing to be milked; rooster's crowed from several backyards; dogs barked. Farm trucks were heading out Farm Road 6. All were country sounds she missed in suburbia Denver. How good it was to hear, to feel, to enjoy!

Her mind returned to her dilemma. Only a little over two days ago, she had two choices for financing the business: use her own funds or borrow from the bank. Soon after finding out that a bank loan was not possible, she found herself with three options. She could accept one of David Mayer's offers or use her own funds.

Why did it have to be so complicated? Why was everything concerning David Mayer complicated? His arguments, the night before, had confounded her, leaving her uncertain about him or his offers. She had no more success this morning at coming to a decision than she had last night, in spite of her prayers for guidance. Her impatience was probably impeding her progress. Stepping back from it for awhile might be helpful, she decided.

Arriving home from the walk, she stopped in the foyer, feeling edgy as she looked at the full and partially unpacked boxes covering the floor of the front room.

"How can I make a decision when this house is in so much disorder?" she asked aloud. She determined right then and there that unpacking was her first priority, and as she did so, a calmness settled over her.

After breakfast, she began unpacking. She worked feverishly, feeling happier and more hopeful for the future. Whether she accepted one of David Mayer's offers or borrowed on her stocks, it didn't seem to matter at the moment. For some reason, his proposals had strengthened her confidence that she could be successful in the poultry business.

Late afternoon, three days later, Torry walked through each room of the house, pleased with the order she had achieved. A gentle breeze blew in through the open windows and through the open back and front screen doors, filling the house with fresh air. As she walked into the front room, the sweet smell of freshly mown lawn attached itself to the breeze.

She looked out the first window at the lawn, newly mowed by Gil Blackburn, Zelda's oldest son. This morning, feeling the need to hurry, she had backed the van out of the one-car, detached garage and driven over to Zelda's house to hire Gilford.

As expected, Zelda besieged her with questions.

"Torry, am I glad to see you. My curiosity has almost been driving me to drink warm milk. What happened that night after you called David Mayer?"

Already prepared, Torry answered in generalities. "As you know, I called him, he came over and everything is fine. I just haven't made up my mind about the financing of my business."

"And that is an answer?"

Torry smiled. "Yes."

"Did you tell him off?"

"I have to get home and finish up a few things, Zelda. I came over to see if Gilford would like to earn some money by mowing my dandelion-filled lawn."

"I'm sure he would, that seventeen-year-old kid is into driving and dating so he's always in need of money. I'll call him in as soon as you answer my question."

"I don't want to answer your question."

"Why?"

"Because, I'm a private person."

"And, I'm a perennial Nosey Josey who finds out the answers one way or another. You see, it's my hobby. Some people knit, some people crochet doilies or paint, but I get into other people's business, especially those I like."

Torry laughed. "I'm glad you like me, Zelda. All right, I'll answer your question. Yes, I told him off, in a way."

"And?"

"You said question, not questions, Zelda."

"Oh, I lie a little too. But—I want you to know that even though

I'm nosey, I'm not a gossip, I keep secrets. When someone tells me something that they don't want anyone else to know, my mouth is as tight as our mulish old mare, Nellie, when she doesn't want a bridle on."

Torry smiled at the simile, but it was a tight smile. She didn't know quite how to handle this kind of persistence.

"Torry...I'm your visiting teacher."

"You are?" Torry asked, surprised.

"Yep. The day after I took the meal into you, I called the Relief Society president and asked if she could put you on my route."

"You did? You are a Relief Society president's dream, Zelda."

"Oh no, they had been threatening to add another Sister to my route so I just beat them to the trough."

"Who is your companion?"

"For the present, Bishop Price only wants me to visit you."

"The bishop?"

"When I asked for you, the Relief Society president said that I would have to see the bishop. He had told her that she wasn't to assign anyone to visit teach you until she talked with him. When I asked him if I could be your visiting teacher, you should have seen his face. He's been worried about you and didn't know who to assign to you. When I asked, he looked mighty relieved and thanked me, saying that I was the perfect one. So what does that tell you, Torry?"

Torry was touched beyond words, then she smiled. "Visiting teachers are not supposed to be nosey, Zelda."

But Bishop Price knows how nosey I am, and he said I was the perfect one." She grinned. "So...as I said, what does that tell you?"

"That I had better give up and answer your questions. You are incorrigible, Zelda."

It was difficult for Torry to reveal personal details about her life to anyone but family and even then she was a careful communicator, not wanting to burden unnecessarily. A listener most of the time, she was uncomfortable confiding. She grappled with the wall of pride that had grown up around her for months as she denied a need for help from another human being, other than an occasional priesthood blessing.

She decided to confide selected parts of her life here in Green Valley. She started with the day she first went into the bank to ask for a loan, knowing Zelda would enjoy it immensely. Zelda's giggles punctuated the incidents, her colorful remarks added more humor to her already comical interaction with David Mayer. Neither of them, however, could figure out why David was so amused.

Zelda shook her head, puzzled. "It must be a male thing."

Torry also enlightened Zelda about what happened after she brought over the milk, and explained the struggle she was having making a decision and why. She found in Zelda an interested and caring listener, sensing, to Torry's surprise, when not to ask probing questions.

Torry returned home, her mind clearer, her heart freer, feeling humbled. Thinking back to her visit with the bishop, she remembered how she had told him she needed to work things out alone for a while. Tears of gratitude filled her eyes, realizing that once again, as throughout her life, the Lord knew better—and had provided a friend.

Turning away from the window, she studied the bare front room, trying to analyze what kind of furniture would fit best, but all she could see was the depressing two-toned brown carpet.

"This carpet has to go."

A rap on the screen door caused her to jump.

"I'm sorry if I startled you," came the low mellow voice of David Mayer.

"You did startle me, especially since you caught me talking to myself," she said, smiling sheepishly as she opened the door. "Come in."

"Thank you, and what were you saying to yourself?"

"That this brown carpet has got to go."

David studied it. "I agree, it doesn't look like you."

"Thank you for that!"

"But you know," he began thoughtfully, "there is something familiar about this room since you've cleared it out and put your books in the bookcase."

Her eyes widened in surprise. "Really?"

"I can't figure out why."

"Does it remind you of your own home as a child?"

My home?" his laugh was bitter. "Quite the opposite, I lived in a mansion growing up."

Torry was puzzled. "Then why could this..."

"I don't know." He turned silent, his mind searching.

After a while, Torry felt prompted to ask, "did you ever as a child, visit a humble home like this?"

"A humble home? Why yes, I had a childhood friend named Paul who lived in a home very much like this, only a little larger as they had a big family. Yes! Paul's house looked like this one. It had a fireplace with books on both sides and large windows. You know...I spent many happy hours in that home with my friend. It has been years since I've thought of Paul and his family." He glanced away. A faraway expression of longing filled his expressive eyes. Pulling himself away from these memories, he noticed Torry watching him intently.

He took a deep breath. "Well, now that we have that figured out, let's get on with business. I came to tell you that I'm leaving town for a week, and I didn't want you to call or come to the bank and think I'd skipped town or reneged on my offers," he said, the smile in his eyes more compelling than the smile on his lips.

"Thank you for coming by to tell me. I haven't made up my mind yet, but I'm certain I will have by the time you return."

"Good! I'll see you when I get back. I'm anxious to find out whether I'm going to have a goat farm or a chicken farm." He grinned, then pivoted quickly and walked to the door and was out before she could answer. Her laughter followed him as he walked away, lifting his spirits, which had been low. Perhaps, after all, the three days of silence since they had last talked didn't mean she was going to turn down his offer.

Torry stood staring at the screen door, feeling somewhat unsettled that David left so abruptly. She sat down thinking, wondering about him and his friend Paul whose home felt more like home than his own.

Chapter Seven

Torry sat at the kitchen table after David left and wondered what she was going to do for a week. She looked around the plain little kitchen.

"First thing, I'm going to put up some cheery wall paper in here," she said out loud. "In fact, I am going to get rid of that brown carpet." She smiled, nodding her head, "and—while I'm at it, get some new front room furniture." With typical feminine logic, she felt these changes would make it easier to deal with David and the decision she had to make.

Tomorrow is Sunday, she reminded herself. She needed Sundays. Sacrament meeting was her lifeline. After the block of meetings, I'll call the boys and find out when they can come down. She felt a stirring of happiness. Maybe I can get on with my life after all without trying to solve the unsolvable. The moment this thought entered her mind, she knew it wasn't so. Knowing herself, she knew she had to find the answers about Jack—but how? A cloud eclipsed the brightness of her new found happiness.

The phone rang, startling her. After picking it up and saying hello, she heard two voices,

"Hi, Mom!"

"Hi, Mom!"

"Jim, Scott! I can't believe you called right now, I was just thinking about calling you to find out when you could come down."

"You were?" questioned Jim. "Scott and I were discussing the same thing."

"Of course," Torry smiled. "This isn't the first time something like this has happened to us, right?"

"Right," chimed in Scott, her youngest. "Boy, you sound good, Mom."

"You do," corroborated Jim. "Things must be going well for you. Tell us about everything."

"Well, I finished all the painting, totally unpacked and am ready now to buy some furniture and maybe some new carpet. Wish you boys could see the before and after."

"We could have seen the before if you hadn't insisted you didn't want our help."

"It wasn't that I didn't want your help, Jim, I didn't want you to miss school to do it. You know that." This wasn't altogether the whole truth, she acknowledged to herself. She had needed some time and space to overcome her feelings of despondency.

"Tell us about the business, any progress on that?" he asked.

"Some." She told them briefly about her banker and his offers, without the extraneous details that were woven into the fabric of her relationship with David Mayer.

"Mom, are you sure this man is trustworthy?"

"I think so, Jim, but before I sign anything, I'll do some checking."

"Also, be sure to read the fine print, I don't want anyone taking advantage of you," insisted her practical and protective first born.

"I agree with Jim," added Scott, "but it sounds like this might be a good opportunity for you, Mom. You sound happier than I've heard you in a long time." She smiled. Her youngest son had always been the intuitive one, able to hone in on her moods and needs.

"When can you boys come down?"

"We both have such different class and work schedules, it will take some doing to work it out—but we'll be down. We're anxious to see you and check out that little house you live in. Scott or I will call a few days before we come."

"Good. I've bought a pull-out couch for you to sleep on. I'm sorry you don't have your nice bedrooms to come home to, or at least to your bedroom furniture."

"That's all right." Jim replied quickly, a little too quickly Torry thought.

"I could have stored it for you," she reminded him.

"Mom, it was just too big a hassle to find a storage unit for it...and we needed the money."

"But Jim, you each chose the furniture with your dad when you were little boys."

"I know. We didn't want the furniture!" he blurted out emphatically.

"Does not wanting the furniture have something to do with your dad?" Neither boy answered. Torry's heart sank. Why did she think they wouldn't be aware of the years of neglect? She had tried to make up for Jack's failures, tried to cover them up so they wouldn't notice too much. Scott had asked her about his dad's behavior before he left for his mission and Jim had remarked on it after he returned from his, but she didn't realize it ran so deep.

"I...I'm sorry boys," tears choked off the last word.

"Mom, please don't be upset, we're all right," pleaded Scott.

"Mom, why didn't you want the furniture that Dad helped you pick out?" interrogated Jim.

It was Torry's turn to be silent. Reaching for a tissue in her pocket, she blew her nose. "I see the three of us need to have a talk one of these days soon, right?"

Silence.

"Right?" she insisted.

"Mom, I need to go," hedged Jim. "I have a test Monday and I need to study."

"We love you, Mom, everything's okay," reassured Scott.

"Yeah, we love you, see ya, goodbye." Jim's phone clicked.

"Goodbye, Mom, we'll call." Scott hung up.

She stared at the phone in her hand, the dial tone screaming at her. Slowly she hung it up. Tears fell, culminating in sobs of grief for her sons.

Chapter Eight

The week turned out to be a flurry of activity for Torry. Since Green Valley serviced several small surrounding communities, Johnson's furniture store also carried a fair selection of carpet, enabling Torry to get everything she needed except kitchen wall paper.

Veering from her usual colors, of blue and rose, she selected a taupe carpet that the store already had in stock. She was delighted to find two light green love seats which she could place in front of the fireplace across from each other. A small magazine table caught her eye. It was the shade of wood that matched Grandmother's furniture and a perfect size to put between the love seats.

After a year-and-a-half of emotional dreariness, she wanted cheerful bright colors to match her mood. Luck was with her. She found two small, high backed, upholstered chairs in floral prints with some of the same light-green color as the two love seats, but with major florals of sunshine yellow and gold.

At home, she found a box of silk flowers she brought with her from Denver. Pulling out the colors she needed, flowers of sunshine yellow, peach, gold, with a touch of lavender and some greenery, she put together a bouquet for the magazine table.

Even with all the excitement of decorating, however, the pending decision would pop into her mind. As it did, she would go over the three options, weighing the pros and cons, each time feeling unnerved by indecision.

Nevertheless, she found herself singing as she chose pictures, vases and other decorative items, from her collection, to accent the new furniture and carpet. This little frame house, so unlike her lovely home in Denver, would be her home for some time to come, and she felt happiness while making it hers.

In five days the carpet was in and the furniture delivered. She stood in the foyer looking at it, pleased...but feeling slightly uneasy now, thinking again what a hole it had made in the insurance money. The uneasiness soon passed, however, because she knew that at this time of her life, cheerful surroundings were important for her emotional well being.

She sat down in one of the upholstered chairs which she had placed on both sides of the bentwood table in front of the first window. Across from them was Grandmother's china cabinet. Both pieces now gave the room a special feeling of warmth as well as a look of distinction. She smiled. She knew her mother would approve, but what would her father think? As she began to look at it through her father's eyes, she felt anxious.

What if he and Mother came down in the next couple of days before the contract to this property could be signed, whichever way her decision went? She knew she had been precipitous in spending money on carpet for a house she hoped to own but as yet did not. And, she knew what her father would say. She jumped as she heard a car drive into the driveway. She got up and stepped quickly to the screen door, half expecting to see her parent's white Mercedes. Instead, she saw a well-used blue pickup. Stepping out onto the front porch, she waved at Zelda.

"Zelda! What a relief to see you!"

"A relief?" she asked, walking toward Torry. "Most people are relieved when I leave."

"Well, actually, Zelda, it was your pickup I was happy to see."

"My pickup? I wish Gilford was happy to see it. All he can see is our new pickup. He doesn't want his girlfriend to even get a peek at this old truck, let alone ride in it. So who is relegated to drive and ride in the bumpy old relic, his father, me and his disgruntled fifteen-year-old brother, Ivan."

Torry chuckled. "I know, I've been there. Come on in."

Zelda stepped into the foyer and stared, her eyes wide with shock. "Are we in the right house?"

"Torry smiled. "We are. Do you like it?"

"Like it? I'm wild about it! How did you do it so quickly?"

"I happened to like what Johnson's had on the floor. Now all I have to do is hang pictures and wallpaper the kitchen."

"I'm here, let's hang pictures. I can't help with the wallpaper; I need to learn how to hang my own."

"If you'll help me hang pictures, I'll help you put up your wallpaper."

"You know how to hang wall paper?"

"I do."

"It's a deal, Torry."

"Come on in and sit down on one of my loveseats. It's nice to have a place for guests to sit besides at the kitchen table."

"Hey, these are comfortable, Torry," Zelda exclaimed as she settled on one of the small couches. "And pretty too. A rare combination. Now," she said as she crossed her legs, her jeans riding up, revealing a classy cowboy boot, "why the attachment to my old pickup?"

Torry laughed. "I was very happy that your old pickup drove into my driveway instead of my parent's white Mercedes." Zelda's eyebrows arched questioningly. "My father is not pleased that I moved to Green Valley instead of Salt Lake. And he doesn't think I can be successful in starting a business here. They're coming down soon, and if they come down within the next few days he will wonder, rather vocally, why I put new carpet in before the contract on the property is signed, sealed and delivered."

"Mmm, good point."

"I'm afraid my long suit is not patience. I've been known to be optimistically impulsive at times, getting myself into hot water...minor things but..." she frowned, "this isn't so minor."

"Nope."

"Zelda, you certainly aren't making me feel any better."

"Sorry, my nice soft saddle blankets always come with a cocklebur or two under them."

Torry smiled. "I'm beginning to find that out."

"So where are you with the big decision?"

"Nowhere."

"Why?"

"Because I don't want to borrow on my stock, I don't want to borrow from David Mayer and feel beholden to him, and I don't want to go into business with anyone, especially David Mayer."

"So?"

"So I keep putting off the decision."

"What if your folks drive up in their white Mercedes?"

"Ouch, that cocklebur is prickly."

"You bet."

"Thanks, Zelda. Just the same I'm going to take a chance and put the decision off a little longer while I finish the decorating."

"In that case, why don't we run down in my beloved pickup and peruse the wallpaper at Nelson's Hardware. They have a good selection and a sale on some they already have in stock."

"Sounds good, Zelda." sighed Torry.

Chapter Nine

Sunday evening, the sun, hanging low on the horizon, cast a golden hue upon the scraggly hollyhocks that someone had, once upon a time, planted next to the house. Its golden rays also spread out over the weed-filled acreage behind the house, making it look meadow-like—inviting.

Torry, staring at the metamorphosis, opened the screen door, stepped out onto the back porch and filled her lungs with the sweet spring air. It was almost the first of May and the evening crispness was giving way to the soft mellow promise of early summer.

She walked down the steps and wandered over to the barbed wire fence that separated the house and yard from the rest of the property. On impulse, she pushed open the wooden gate that hung limply on one hinge and stepped into the enclosed area, startling several large grasshoppers who jumped adroitly out of her way. Gingerly taking another step, tiny ones jumped to safety. Intrigued by their pastel colors, she hunkered down and grabbed a small yellow one by its hind legs, studied it and smiled, then let it go.

Winding her way through the milkweed and thistles, stepping where the grass grew, she found herself in the middle of the ten acre field. The Meadowlarks were singing their last songs of the day and a calf bleated for its mother in the Blackburn's green pasture next to her weed-filled one. She saw Zelda's prize thoroughbred Paints nibbling on the grass in the upper pasture. A dog from the farm on the left barked, another one, from somewhere, answered it.

All the pleasant sights and sounds only penetrated the surface of Torry's consciousness. She stood alone in the sunlit meadow, feeling alone as she wrestled with the turmoil of indecision. She turned and started back, noticing that the back view of the house, a homely box-like structure without any trees, looked as dismal and lonely as she felt. Why would someone build a house and not plant trees? she wondered.

Back in the house, she found herself meandering through it aimlessly, putting off the inevitable. She scrutinized the pictures that Zelda helped her hang and felt satisfied. She had gone through her collection of paintings and decided to hang the large watercolor by the Utah artist, Norma Forsberg, above the mantle of the fireplace. Zelda went wild over it, exclaiming over the colors and shades of the partly cut, ripe wheat field with its background of blue hills. The painting, the silk flowers and several throw pillows for the couches, matching the florals in the two chairs, tying it all together, pleased her aesthetic sense.

Friday night and most of Saturday, she had helped hang wallpaper in Zelda's kitchen. They had such a good time while they were at it, that Zak and the boys grinned and shook their heads.

Staying up late Saturday night, she hung wallpaper in her own kitchen and was pleased with the improvement.

Now—she had no more diversions to hide behind. David Mayer had been gone eight days and tomorrow, Monday, he was sure to be back in the office.

Painfully aware that the moment of decision was here, she curled up in one of the chairs by the open window and gazed out at the salmon hues of early sunset. Still feeling terribly alone, she knew this decision was one only she could make. The gentle breeze refreshed her mind as she once more went over the different sides to each option. She finally allowed herself to face the real cause of the struggle—fear! Fear of doing the business alone, fear of failure, fear of a partnership with David Mayer, fear of turning it down. The deterioration of her marriage was still causing ripples, disturbing everything she tried to do. Fear—the Devil's tool. Sliding off the chair to her knees, she pleaded with the Lord to take away the fear—but it remained, along with the confusion.

Staying on her knees, she pondered. The thought came, "God is not the author of confusion." She concluded finally, the only way out of the confusion was to make a decision. But, she realized, the only decision she could make at the moment was to choose the least fearful but the least desirable option, the partnership with David Mayer. Contemplating this for some time, and then with this choice in mind, she prayed fervently for guidance. She waited, listened. No help came. Of course not, she chastised herself. God was a strong task master when the heart wavered. Persuading herself to settle firmly on this choice, she at last became resolute in the decision to accept the partnership. She prayed for a confirmation. It came. The fear left and peace suffused her whole being—not as powerful as the first time when she prayed about coming to Green Valley—but it was an unmistakable confirmation, an answer to prayer. She shed tears of gratitude to her Father in Heaven. And she cried because she wasn't sure this was the answer she really wanted.

~~~~~~~~~~

Morning brought no qualms. Still feeling at peace, Torry called David Mayer's office at 9:00 A.M., an hour before the bank opened, hoping he had returned.

"David Mayer speaking."

"Hello, David, this is Torry Anderson."

"I recognize your voice. How are you, Torry?"

"I'm fine, thank you. It's good to have you back in town."

"Thank you. Actually, I've been back for a couple of days, but had so much to catch up on, I didn't call to inform you I was back."

Torry was so taken back, she couldn't reply. Silently she scolded herself. How quickly she had begun to take David Mayer's charming eagerness for granted. David waited out the silence.

"Is your offer of a partnership still open or have you changed your mind?"

"Why should I change my mind?"

"Well...you seem a little different. I don't want you to feel obligated...maybe starting a goat farm sounds more profitable?"

David chuckled. "I don't feel obligated, this is business. And I tend to think that a chicken farm may be more profitable."

"Good. When shall we get together to draw up the partnership?"

"Let me look at my calendar...today is filled, how about tomorrow morning at 9:00 here at my office?"

"Fine," she answered, feeling disappointed that it wasn't today. "My calendar certainly isn't full."

"Good, I'll see you then."

Torry hung up the phone and stood there thinking, wondering. This was the second time David Mayer left her feeling unsettled.

Sitting down at the table she stared at the three lovely lilacs standing in a small vase. The bouquet that David brought her was long gone and the lilac season was fast drawing to a close.

Late Saturday afternoon on the way home from a quick trip to the grocery store, she had pulled her van over and stopped before a lilac bush, still with a few blooms left. These three lilacs were hanging over the sidewalk like three unwanted children, so she broke them off and brought them home.

On impulse, she picked up the vase, took it to her work room, got out the watercolors and began reproducing lilacs that would not wilt.

"Damn!" exclaimed David under his breath as he hung up the phone from Torry. He wanted to see her today. He wanted to see her two days ago. He could hardly keep his mind on business while out of town for thinking about her—and now, purposely, he put off their meeting until tomorrow, all because he knew it was important to give Torry lots of room.

The momentary frustration soon gave way to the excitement over Torry's acceptance of the partnership. Barely able to contain his happiness, he got up and walked out of the bank and next door to the drugstore for a cup of coffee. He sat in the booth, thinking of the little girl of long ago who spent time here eating ice cream confections or sitting on a stool behind the pharmacy counter, listening to her grandfather.

Chapter Ten

Tom Baker walked to the front door of the bank Tuesday morning at 8:55. One minute later, Torry Anderson appeared. Tom unlocked the door, swinging it open, smiling broadly.

"Good morning, Mrs. Anderson, it's good to see you."

"Good morning, Mr. Baker."

"Dave asked me to watch for you and let you in, he's tying up a couple of loose ends on the contract. Congratulations. You're going into business with a great guy."

"Really? My sons asked me to get references on him and I told them I would, but I forgot."

Tom smiled. "Good for them. Well, I'm a good reference. Tell them that David Mayer is as honest as Abe Lincoln."

Torry smiled at this warm friendly man. "That's quite a vote of confidence." They began walking slowly toward David's office.

"Another reference even better than mine is Missy, our four-year-old. She said, and I quote: 'I'm going to marry David when he grows up.' Torry laughed. "But Dave is sure that he can't grow up fast enough to catch up with her. He thinks she's four going on fourteen."

"Thank you. That takes care of the references," she said still smiling at Missy's remark. This was certainly another side of David, she thought.

Arriving at David's office, Tom said, "Go on in, I'm sure he's ready now."

David looked up from his desk to see Torry standing at the door, a different Torry than the one who presented herself thirteen days ago. Gone were the faded jeans. Instead, she was wearing a teal green silk blouse with gold accessories, an ivory colored knee length skirt, and matching heels, revealing shapely legs. In her hand was a brown leather briefcase.

"And your name, Miss?"

"Torry Anderson."

"You are Torry Anderson? I think there must be some mistake."

"Oh, I assure you, Mr. Mayer, I am. You know, the one who has that wonderful business opportunity for you—a chicken farm?"

"A chicken farm? I'm sorry but you don't look like you could run a chicken farm, dressed so elegantly. There was, however, a young lady here thirteen days ago, wearing faded jeans, who I think maybe could..."

"Did they help?" Torry asked, smiling and helping herself to a chair in front of the desk.

"What?"

"The jeans."

"Help what?"

"Help me seem more credible as a chicken farmer?"

He gazed at her, not knowing how to answer.

"I spent three days going over my wardrobe trying to decide what would be most appropriate to wear. I'm curious. May I ask you again, did they make me seem more credible as a person who could run a chicken farm?"

Her face was serious, demanding a serious answer and once again David, as he had on their first encounter, fought a desire to laugh. Ducking his head and feigning a coughing spell, he gained control.

"The jeans helped all right, Torry, they helped you look...uh I wouldn't use the word credible exactly...." His eyes betrayed him and the laugh lines, at the corners, crinkled.

Torry stared at him, her mouth open slightly not believing her eyes. "Don't you dare laugh, David Mayer."

He cleared his throat. "As I was saying, the jeans...uh let me put it this way, they added much to the whole charming package."

"Charming package? That isn't what I intended." She jumped up and walked to the window and back. "I didn't want to be a charming package."

David laughed. "I'm sorry, Torry, I had nothing to do with it."

"I was talking more to myself than to you," she said feeling embarrassed by her childish outburst.

"Torry, you are delightful."

"I don't want to be delightful. I mean...I want to inspire confidence that I can run a business."

"You don't have a worry there, Torry. I strongly suspect that you've been successful in everything you have ever tried to do."

"You really mean that?" she asked, a little uncertain, sitting down again.

"You bet I do." His warm and serious eyes validated the confidence he expressed. "However, I am curious about one thing. What made you finally decide to accept the partnership?"

Torry was surprised at her sudden desire to tell him of her prayers and confirmation. Immediately, she squelched it. "Because," she began cautiously, "it took me a long time to make this decision, and," she finished with frankness, "it was the least fearful of all the options."

He grinned. "That's good to hear. I'm glad I'm the least fearful thing in your life right now. Since you've decided to accept my proposal, I would like you to go over the contract carefully. I want you to be totally satisfied with it before we sign anything."

Torry looked through the contract, reading a little here and there. When she was through, she handed it back.

The partnership was drawn up with Torry as the working partner, David the investing partner. Tom Baker was called in to witness the signatures as a Notary. Then Mr. and Mrs. Harris, who had been asked to be there at 10:00, were called in to consummate the sale of the property. David in a burst of optimism, had previously taken care of all the legal work: a survey, the title search and so forth. By 10:30, everything was taken care of and Torry sat staring at David, her head swimming.

"Is it really all taken care of? I can't believe it all happened so quickly."

"I've had to learn how to cut out a lot of red tape, Torry. Sometimes the secret to success in the business world is the ability to move fast."

"I'm all for that. Patience is not one of my virtues."

"Do you have any questions?"

"I feel like I should have. My sons wanted me to check on you before I signed anything."

"Good for them." He smiled. "Did you check up on me?"

"Yes. I got several good references."

"Oh?" he asked, surprised. "Who in the world might that be? I didn't think you knew anyone I've had dealings with."

Torry smiled. "Well, I don't know one of them at all, and I know the other one only slightly."

"They don't sound like very reliable references to me."

"Oh they are reliable, I can assure you."

Puzzled, David leaned forward. "Are you going to tell me who they are?"

"I...don't know," she said, deliberately pausing. "It might be breaking a confidence." A tiny smile played at the corners of her mouth.

"Torry!" David exclaimed, standing up and walking around the desk. He towered over her, a menacing expression on his face. "I must warn you that when my curiosity isn't satisfied, I'm liable to do anything."

"Oh?"

"Torry," he laughed, shaking his head, "you are the most exasperating woman." He sat down opposite her and growled, "Now spill it."

"All right, if I must. "Tom Baker is one. He said you were as honest as Abe Lincoln and his four-year-old Missy, the other reliable one, said she's going marry you when you grow up."

David's chin dropped, then he threw his head back and laughed. "You're right, they are reliable references. Especially Missy's. You'll have to meet her sometime. She's really something."

The buzzer on the desk alerted David to the time. He looked at his watch, stood up and reached for the button. "Yes, Mrs. Ames."

"Your 10:45 appointment is here."

"Thank you, Mrs. Ames, give me five minutes." Turning back to Torry, he smiled. "I hate to end this charming conversation about Missy, but I'll have to. May I study your research on the business?"

"Yes, it's all in this briefcase," she said, handing it to him as she stood up.

"We'll need to get together to decide our next step. When can you meet and where?"

"Would tonight about seven be convenient with you?"

"Yes. Do you have a preference where?"

"Why don't you come over to my house...I mean 'our' house, I now have places to..." She stopped, "Oops."

"What?"

"Oh dear," she whispered, her hand over her mouth, her eyes wide and troubled.

"What is it?" David asked.

"I've really pulled a blunder, David."

"You have?" he asked, alarmed at the concern on her face.

"Yes." She stood up, turned her back to him. "How could I have done this," she mumbled.

"Torry, don't keep me hanging, tell me." He stood up, fighting the desire to turn her around and shake the answer out of her.

The buzzer on his desk rang again. "Just a minute, Mrs. Ames, I'm not ready."

Torry turned to face him. "I've got to go...your buzzer...your appointment..."

"To hell with the...I'm sorry. The appointment can go to blazes! Spit it out, Torry, don't leave me wondering."

"David I uh....I hope you won't be too upset," she said, stepping to the door.

"Torry wait!" he blurted out, stumbling over a chair trying to stop her.

"You'll find out tonight, David," she muttered as she hurried out, leaving her new partner dumbfounded, worried and thoroughly frustrated.

"How could I?" she whispered, running out of the bank. Out in the parking lot, tears blinded her as she tried to locate her van. "How could I be so stupid? How could I?!"

~~~~~~~~~~~~~

As David pulled into the driveway at five minutes to seven, he saw Torry sitting on the front porch, hugging her knees, the folds of a light blue cotton bib dress covering her legs. He got out of the car, Torry's briefcase in his hand.

"Hi partner," he said, grinning. "What's up?"

She gave him a feeble smile. "You probably won't want me for a partner when you know what I've done."

He sat down beside her. "Whatever it is, it can't be too serious, listen to the birds. Remember your grandmother Thomas said they sing about the joy of life."

A tear rolled down her cheek. "Oh, why did you say that." She wished with all her heart that she could be a little girl again and sit on Grandmother's lap.

The urge to take her in his arms and comfort her was overwhelming, but instead David just watched and waited. The breeze gently blew her short curls, the late evening sun creating a dancing tangle of highlights and shadows, almost hypnotizing him.

She wiped away the tear with her fingers and blinked. "I feel foolish, David, for what I've done...and for boo-hooing about it here in front of you."

He was helplessly charmed. "Whatever it is, your foolishness can't begin to match mine. Remember me laughing like a hyena when you first visited my office?"

She smiled. "Thank you for that."

"Are you ever going to tell me?"

"No. I'm going to show you. Come into the house."

He followed her, but stopped in the small foyer and gaped. "Wow!" he blinked in amazement. "I can't believe it, Torry. Just a week ago it was a plain little room and now it's...it's lovely, inviting, and superbly decorated. How did you ever do it in only a week?"

"Zelda helped me hang the pictures," she said in a small voice.

"Zelda?"

"You know, the one that owns..."

"Henry the rooster, of course. I like Zelda," he mused. "I want to meet her."

Torry looked askance at him. "Only because she thinks you're handsome."

He grinned. "Of course. And also because she helped you hang the pictures."

"David,"...she began hesitantly, "the carpet is all through the house."

He looked at her blankly. "Oh? Well, good. That's good."

"But it's one thing to paint and another thing to put carpet all the way through."

He stared at her puzzled. "You've lost me, Torry, what are you trying to say?"

"But it's your house, David."

"It's half yours."

"Yes, and it's half yours."

"Right...so?"

"So...I had no right to choose carpet and put it in without your approval."

"But Torry, we just signed the papers this morning."

"I know, David, that's the point! A week ago, I knew that it was a possibility that I would choose the partnership...so why didn't I wait like a businesslike individual and ask your approval before decorating?"

"Oh." Relief flooded through him. "You mean this is what all that...I mean, this is what you were upset about when you left the bank this morning?"

"Yes."

A smile teasing his lips, he replied, "I don't know, why didn't you wait like a businesslike individual and ask my approval?"

"Because I'm so impatient and impulsive. That's why! I didn't want to live with that brown carpet another minute." She walked toward the fireplace and stood there, her back to him. He noticed the buttons down the back of the bib dress, the way it hugged her waist, enhancing it by the fullness of the skirt. The blue and white pinstripe blouse added the final enchanting touch.

"I kinda liked the brown carpet."

Torry whirled around, "David, I'm serious!"

"But" he said trying to appear as serious as possible. "What if I wanted to keep the brown carpet?"

"What do you mean?"

"I mean, what if you waited and asked my opinion, and I told you I liked the brown carpet?"

Stumped for a moment, she paused. "Well, then I would have paid for the carpet out of my own funds. Would that have been all right with you?"

"I thinks so, you're the one who has to live here."

"David, I want to assure you that the carpet is all paid for. You won't have to help foot the bill for it—or the paint."

David was certain that this girl had just dropped right out of heaven. His face must have betrayed his thought, because Torry walked over and looked up at him, studying his face.

Torry couldn't read the peculiar expression on David's face. "I'm sorry I started our partnership off on the wrong foot. I hope this doesn't diminish your confidence in me as a business partner."

"It doesn't Torry. I hope my stupid attacks of laughter haven't diminished your confidence in me as a business partner."

She smiled. "No, they haven't."

The anxiety gone, Torry came to her senses. "I should invite you to sit down—in fact, I'm excited to have a place for you to sit besides at the kitchen table. Come and sit down on one of my loveseats."

"Love...seats? Hmmn."

"No more teasing like that, David."

"Sorry, no more teasing like that." He sat down across from her.

"David!" she exclaimed, her mouth open.

"What now?" he asked, alarmed.

"You're wearing jeans."

"Oh, is that all." He blew out a big gust of air. "That's a relief. I can never tell with you what will happen next, Torry Anderson." Then he grinned. "Well...I'm glad that you finally noticed my jeans." He stood up, straightened his shoulders and strutted to the middle of the room. "How do I look?"

His shirt, with the wide stripes of light and navy blue, enhanced his dark hair and brought out the blue of his blue-gray eyes, making her uncomfortably aware of his whole appearance, his broad shoulders, muscular thighs...and the silly grin he had plastered on his face.

She giggled. "You look...uh...stunning."

His face fell. "I don't want to look stunning. I want to look credible, like I could help run a chicken farm."

Torry giggled again, resisting the urge to throw a pillow at him.

David walked back to the couch and sat down, smiling at her.

Torry sighed. "I feel better now that everything is out in the open."

"That makes two of us. I hope I don't have to go through another day like this one."

"I hope so too," she said apologetically.

"Now, let's get down to business, Torry. I have something for you." He pulled out a check book from his shirt pocket, opened it, tore out a check and handed it to her.

Puzzled, she took the check, looked at it and gasped, "David, this is five thousand dollars!"

"I know."

"What is it for?"

"Your salary for this month."

"My salary?" What salary?"

"It was in the contract."

"It was in the contract," she echoed.

"Don't repeat me, Torry," he said in a warning tone.

"But I can't accept this."

"Why?"

"Because we didn't even discuss it."

"Torry, I thought I gave you enough time to read the contract."

"Well, you didn't...at least not enough time to read it thoroughly."

"How was I to know? I asked you if you had any questions. You said no—and you signed it."

"I'm not used to reading contracts as quickly as you, David. You took advantage of that."

"I what?" he asked, shocked.

"You took advantage."

"I can't believe this." He stood up and paced to the center of the room, running his hand through his hair—then wheeled around. "Explain to me how in the deuce that is taking advantage?"

"You took advantage of my inexperience."

"Inexperience?"

"Yes."

"Go on"—his eyes were smoldering, daring her to make sense of such nonsense.

"I'm not your favorite charity."

"Charity?"

"Yes, charity. Do you pay this kind of a salary when a business is just starting out?"

"It depends on the business," he said, now wary of the direction the conversation was taking.

"Let's talk about this business."

David ducked his head, ran his hand through his hair again and smiled. "Okay, let's talk about this business."

"You are an astute businessman, how much should the starting salary be for this small business?"

"Torry," he said sitting down, "you are an astute 'businessman' yourself."

"You didn't answer my question."

"Well," he admitted ruefully, "maybe five thousand is a little high."

"May I see the contract again, David."

"You may. I have your copy of it right here in your briefcase." He opened it, pulled it out and handed it to her.

She glanced through it and found the section concerning salary. "David, this only says a salary will be paid monthly and that the amount will be decided by both of us, so why didn't you discuss it with me?"

"How do you do it, Torry?"

"Do what?"

"Make me feel guilty for being rich?"

"Why did you hand me that check without discussing it with me?" she persisted.

"You are a widow, Torry and..."

"I knew it!" she exclaimed, jumping to her feet and distancing herself behind the couch. "Don't you see how foolish that makes me feel? I want you to treat me like you would any other business partner."

"I see that I've been traveling in the wrong circles."

"What do you mean?"

"Never in my career, has anyone ever objected when I chose to pay a..."

"You have now. How can this business partnership work if...if you treat me differently because I'm a widow?"

"I'm sorry, Torry. I'll try not to treat you differently."

"You'll try?"

"All right, I won't."

"I know we have to go over the plans, David, but we had better call it a night. We both need to think about this partnership and what it will take to make it work."

"You know what, Torry?" he said, standing up and smiling a little wanly.

"What?"

"I'm not going to object to calling it a night—to tell the truth, I'm exhausted."

Chapter Eleven

The plans for the chicken house Torry had put together while still in Denver, and the list of equipment were spread out on Torry's kitchen table at 7:45 Wednesday morning, ready for David's perusal. He had called at 7:00 and suggested they finish their business before the bank opened.

David arrived at their appointed hour, 8:00 A.M. Torry opened the door and smiled.

"Come in, David, you're looking rested."

"I feel great, Torry. Slept like a log."

"Me too," she said leading him into the kitchen. "Sit down. Can I get you something to drink, juice, a cup of cocoa?"

"I could use another cup of coffee."

"I'm sorry, I don't have coffee in the house."

"Oh, that's right, Mormons don't drink coffee. Never mind, I wouldn't care for anything. Uh...Torry, before we get started, can I take care of some business I didn't get to last night?"

"Of course."

"I'm afraid I'm going to stick my finger in the light socket again, but here goes. Remember, I told you I wouldn't treat you with special consideration because you are a widow? Well, I assure you I'm not. First, here is a check for your salary this month. If it doesn't meet with your approval, I'll tear it up and write another one that will meet with your approval."

Torry took the check and saw that it was for two thousand. She frowned, thinking.

"Is it enough?"

She gazed into David's inviting and inquisitive eyes. "Since I'm not paying rent anymore, I think fifteen hundred would be the right amount," she said, handing the check back.

As agreed, David took the check, tore it up and wrote out one for the stipulated amount. He handed it to her.

She smiled at him. "Thank you, David."

He smiled back. "Good. And this," he said, handing her another check, "is to pay for all the time and money you spent on the business: researching and traveling, that I'm now going to benefit from. It's only fair that you are remunerated."

"David, this is five thousand dollars!"

"Hold on, Torry. Stop and think a minute. Calculate your expenses and you'll see that five thousand may not even quite cover your time, car expense, air fares and so on." He waited while she did some mental calculations. After a few moments, David continued, "If you were financing yourself, Torry, would you consider your preparations as business expense?"

"Yes," she said, still doubtful about accepting the check. "I wish Grandfather were alive, and I'd ask his advice about all this. People all over the county came to him for advice. On second thought..." She smiled. "I'm afraid I would be the recipient of a salty reprimand over purchasing the new carpet before I owned...I mean before we owned the house."

"And," David added, smiling, "he might even suggest that the brown carpet still had plenty of wear in it."

"How did you know? That is exactly what he would say." Torry laughed.

"Did people come to the drugstore to seek his counsel?"

"No, he never allowed that. They came to the house with no warning whatsoever, but Grandfather, always the hospitable host, invited them in. A few went away unhappy with the advice, but most of them were respectful and appreciative."

"How do you know? Were you sitting on your little stool eavesdropping again?" His eyes softened as he pictured the Torry Ann of long ago.

Torry looked down, away from those eyes that were so unsettling, intimate. Why did he have to look at her that way? But wasn't it her fault? Hadn't she told him personal stories? Taking a deep breath, she tried to analyze the situation with a kinder view of herself. She had eventually come to that during the years when her marriage was falling apart. Her self accusatory introspection had at last given way to a clearer view. Though she had failed somehow, she realized she had done all she could and a sense of self-acceptance replaced her sense of guilt. David Mayer was just interested in people. It was as simple as that.

David watched her, curious, as different emotions expressed themselves on her face, emotions he couldn't read.

"You don't have to answer that, Torry, if you don't want to, I didn't realize..."

"Oh, I uh..." Torry stammered, feeling foolish at not answering such an innocent question. "It isn't that, I...my mind wandered a bit. Yes, I did eavesdrop. Sometimes I would follow Grandfather and his visitor into the parlor, totally unnoticed, and sit behind Grandfather's chair. I didn't understand the conversations very well, but I liked to peek at the guest and watch him, feeling proud at how smart Grandfather was. However, it wasn't long before I got bored and tried to sneak out. When I was almost safely out the door, Grandfather would call me back. 'Come here, Torry Ann, I want you to meet this fine gentleman.' Then he'd proceed to tell him that I was Ruth's daughter. The gentleman would always ask about her, then Grandfather would brag on her, on me, and my brother, Bill, until I got so wiggly that he'd tell me to run along—to my great relief."

Torry noticed David smiling. She was both amazed and annoyed at herself over her eagerness to share these memories with him.

David chuckled. "I can picture it all."

"Did you know your grandparents, David?"

The smile disappeared and his face closed. "No I didn't." Glancing at his watch, he said, "I guess we'd better get on with business," He focused on the plans.

Curiosity over David's continued refusal to discuss his family caused her to stare unseeing at the plans.

"How big do you want to start, Torry?"

"What? Oh, as you can see from the plans, I'd like to build a brooder about 300 square feet because I only want to start out with a flock of 150 quality day-old chicks. And it needs to be wired for electrical heat."

"What kind of flooring?"

"Cement, which will be covered with litter, which is straw. I also want an outdoor chicken-run four times that size."

"Are you sure you don't want to start larger, Torry?"

"As I said, this is going to be the experimenting station until we're sure that we have the quality and taste just right. We may or may not be able to expand after just a couple of broods, but of course if we do, it will have to be outside of town because of the odor."

David scrutinized the plans while Torry explained about the incubators, the feeders, heat and ventilation, the automatic watering troughs and lighting. She pointed out that the small attached storage room would hold supplies of mash, grains, litter, etc.

David figured that the greatest expense would be the plumbing and equipment. He decided it wouldn't take long to build once the plumbing and electric wiring were finished. Finding skilled men to install the equipment might prove a problem in this small town, but David knew he was good at solving any problem—except a problem like Torry. Here, he felt like a complete novice.

They agreed that David would hire a plumber, electrician and builder and Torry would oversee the work, with input from David whenever he had time. Their meeting ended at ten thirty.

Torry picked up the five thousand dollar check, still indecisive about whether she should keep it. David studied her, then enfolded her hand that held the check in both of his and looked into her eyes.

"You can trust me, Torry, your grandfather would tell you that it is good business." Holding her hand a little longer than necessary, he gave it a squeeze, smiled and let go.

He stood up. "See you soon, partner." He turned to go.

"Wait, David." She tore the check in half. "I'll take three thousand." She stood up, handed him the torn pieces and said, "Thank you." She smiled up at him, appreciation in her eyes. "It's a very secure feeling to be in partnership with someone who is a good businessman, and who can afford to practice good business and...is generous enough to do so."

Chapter Twelve

Tom Baker had just handed David a list of people in town who were builders, plumbers and electricians, when his phone rang.

"Excuse me a minute, Dave. Hello."

"Are you busy, Tom?" his wife Jenny asked.

"Oh, hi sweetheart. Yes, I am a little, I'm talking to Dave."

"Oh. Do you think David would have time to talk to me?"

Tom put his hand over the receiver. "Jen wants to talk to you, do you have a minute?"

"You bet!" he reached for the phone. "I always have time to talk to you, Jenny."

"That isn't the way it looks, David. You've turned down all of our invitations lately."

"I know," he said apologetically, "It's just that I haven't been very good company lately, but I'm feeling great now."

"That's what Tom tells me. When can you come to dinner?"

"Oh Jen, you see I have this new business partner, Torry Anderson and..."

"Invite her to come too," she added eagerly.

"I was hoping you would say that. I want her to meet all of you, especially Missy, since she is one of Torry's references."

"What?" she could hear her husband and David laughing. "Explain that David."

"I'll let Tom explain, Jenny. Thanks for the invitation but I can't invite Torry to come to dinner...yet. Our business relationship is uh...a bit tenuous, to say nothing of our personal relationship."

"Well, the invitation stands. Let me know when, okay?"

"I will, and thanks Jenny. Tell the children hello for me." He handed the phone to Tom who told her he'd call back in five minutes. They both returned to their study of the plans.

"Dave, this is the most complicated chicken coop I've ever seen."

"It's a rather unique business she has in mind. That's one of the reasons I chose to go in with her."

"Oh?" Tom questioned, raising a knowing eyebrow.

"I said one of the reasons, Tom, there are others."

Tom grinned. "That's what I figured. Let me know if I can help with anything else," he said, handing him the plans.

"Thanks, I will." David turned and walked out of Tom's office toward his own.

Tom's face turned pensive. A couple of months ago he and Jenny watched despondency take hold of David, and there was nothing they could do. He turned down every invitation and didn't offer any of his own.

Since he and his family had become acquainted with David, they and the children prayed daily for an opportunity to introduce this man of Jewish blood, to the gospel of Jesus Christ.

From the day Torry Anderson walked into the bank, David was a different man. When he told Jenny about this, her romantic nature overrode her usual practical one, and she began watching for an opportunity to help things along. He, on the other hand, was not feeling totally comfortable about Torry Anderson.

~~~~~~~~~~~~

David had just finished making some calls and setting up interviews with potential builders, when Jesse Jones and Dan Higley, hats in hand, ambled into his office. They were wearing their usual attire. Dan's hip waist jeans hung loose on his thin frame and Jesse's overalls looked comfortable over his slightly rotund belly.

"Hey there, David, we've been waiting in the drugstore. What's keeping you?" asked Dan, his grin deepening the lines on his lean weather beaten face.

David looked up in surprise. "Oh, oh, I forgot, it's Wednesday isn't it?"

"You bet your shiny, city slicker shoes it is," Jesse added, the grin on his round face creasing the sun tanned laugh-lines around his eyes.

"I'm coming, I'm coming, if you two ol' reprobates can wait a second or two."

Soon, the odd threesome walked out of the bank together to the drugstore next door. Settling themselves into a booth, Dan asked

David, "How come you forgot it was Wednesday? Don't tell me that running that puny bank would make you forget a lunch appointment with two of your best customers?"

"It's not running the bank that made me forget, it's my new business." David grinned.

"New business?" they asked almost simultaneously.

"Yes. I'm going to be a chicken farmer." David watched in glee as they both stared at him, stunned. Then, as he expected, they both hooted with laughter.

"I'm serious, fellas and I'll be working it as I have time."

This brought on louder hoots. "What does a city slicker like you, David, know about chicken farming?" asked Jesse.

"I don't, but I have a partner who does."

"Oh? Anyone we know?" asked Dan.

"Nope—she just moved here."

"A 'she'?" they asked at the same time. David nodded.

"Well, I'll be an overgrown turnip! What's her name?" queried Jesse.

"Mrs. Torry Anderson. She lives in the Harris house on Farm Road 6. That's where the chicken farm will start on a small scale."

"You're serious," stated Dan, "Where's her husband?"

"She's a widow."

"Oh ho!" exclaimed Jesse, looking at Dan. Their eyebrows raised knowingly. "We want to meet her."

"Oh no, not you two characters. You'd upset the hay wagon, it's already riding on only two wheels."

"That can't mean the business then, David, you're too shrewd a business man. That means personal, right?" asked Dan.

David laughed. "You two are the sharpest, cunningest pair I know. Would you like to help me run my banks?"

"Oh, no!" they exclaimed.

"I wouldn't trade my grief for yours, David, for all the money in the world," Jesse said.

"Me either. In fact, Jessie and I have been plotting a way to get you out of that rat race because you haven't acted yourself the last couple of months."

"But," interjected Jesse, "it seems that you're back to your old self today."

"Even better than your old self, David," added Dan. "We'd like to meet this Mrs. Torry Anderson."

Chapter Thirteen

It had only been ten days since she and David signed the contract and already the plumbing was in and the framing up. Torry was impressed. David certainly knew how to get things done. Early in the week, he had ordered metal hoods and portable walls for the incubators from the addresses she had given him, also feeding troughs and an automatic watering system. The only thing she had done toward the project was go to Dale's feed store, three blocks south, and order the grain and special meal needed for the chicks.

Looking out the kitchen window, she saw that David was already out there, in his jeans...and it was only 4:45 P.M. She learned that his usual hours at the bank were long, beginning early and lasting until 6:00 or 7:00 P.M. Since starting work on the chicken house, he had cut back on his hours. He had also begun to take most of his lunch hour to check on things and confer with her. Torry wondered when he was eating. Maybe he, too, had been living on snacks and sandwiches like she had.

Vaguely it had occurred to her that perhaps she should prepare a meal for him, but as quickly as the thought came, she dismissed it. She consoled herself that by doing so it might be construed by David or others as a change in their relationship.

Though not that involved with the building, she found it unbearable to stay in the house. She kept herself busy pulling weeds and preparing soil for flowers while keeping an eye on the workers and conferring with them as needed.

She'd come inside for only one reason—to take care of a task she'd been dreading. Taking the phone from its cradle on the wall, she sat down at the table and dialed her parents. She needed to tell them about the partnership, or rather prepare her father so he could digest it a while before he met David.

"Hello," came the welcome sound of her mother's voice.

"Mother, I'm glad you answered."

"Torry!" her mother exclaimed. "Is everything all right? You sound worried."

"Everything is more than all right, Mother. I'm sorry for sounding worried. I just don't want to talk to Dad, but of course I have to. Get him on the phone will you? I have some good news."

A few minutes later, she heard her Dad's cool voice, "Did you call to apologize for hanging up on me, Torry?"

"I called to tell you some good news."

"Do you think you can tell it without hanging up on us?" the sarcasm still evident.

"George, do you want to hear the news or would you like Torry to tell us why she hung up on you?"

The patience and gentleness in her mother's voice when addressing her father, always amazed Torry. This question silenced him. She was sure he didn't want her mother to know how he'd talked to her.

Her mother spoke into the silence. "Go on and tell us the news, Torry, we both want to hear."

Torry explained as briefly as she could about starting a chicken farm and the partnership with her banker.

Always allowing her father to speak first, her mother was silent. Torry waited uneasily for his response, and when it came it was as she expected, negative.

"I have only two things to say, Torry. First you know nothing about chicken farming. Secondly, you don't know this man very well, do you?"

"Of course not. I just moved here. But he's well liked and I have two very good references by two reliable people." In spite of the tension, Torry almost laughed as she said this. "If you'll come down, I'll explain it all to you and mother, and you can meet David Mayer, my partner."

"We'd love to Torry," her mother said, "when would be a good time?"

"We're building the chicken house now. If you want to wait and see it when it's finished, it may be completed in about three weeks—I hope."

There was silence as Ruth Conway waited for her husband to make the decision. When she could see it wasn't forthcoming, she said, "All right, Torry, we'll be down in about three weeks. Good luck, dear."

"Thank you, mother. See you soon. Goodbye, Dad."

The next call was a pleasant one. She called her sons. Scott's voice answered.

"Hello, Scott."

"Mom! How great to hear from you. What's up?"

"Is Jim there to get on the phone, too?"

"No, he's at the library."

"I could use some help from you and Jim this weekend if you can possibly come down. The fence around the chicken run needs to be put up."

"It's about time you let us help."

"Now if you have dates, pressing studies or tests to study for, don't come. Do you hear, Scott?"

"I hear, Mom. Neither of us have dates this weekend. I can swing it but let me talk to Jim, and we'll call back as soon as we know."

"Thanks, Scott. I love you."

"I love you too, Mom."

A knock on the front door sent Torry running. She saw through the screen, two older men standing on the porch. She opened the screen door.

"Yes?"

"Are you Mrs. Torry Anderson?" asked the one in overalls.

"Yes I am."

"You look like you might be," said the thinner one, eyeing her appreciatively.

"I'm Jesse Jones," said the one in overalls, "and this is Dan Higley. We're friends of David's. We've brought you a little something to congratulate you both on your new business."

"I'm glad to meet you. Let me call David, he's..."

"No, don't do that," said the one called Dan, "we'll go around back later and say hello."

"We've brought you some sucker shoots from our lilac bushes," said Jesse.

"You have?" Her eyes were wide with astonishment.

"We asked David what we could contribute," said Dan, "and he told us that you both like lilac bushes and could we bring over a couple of lilac saplings since the yard was so bare. Would you like to tell us where to put them?"

Shaking her head in amazement, Torry stepped out onto the porch and walked down the steps with the two men.

"We've actually got more than a couple, We have fifty," explained Jesse.

"Fifty!" exclaimed Torry. "Uh...did you buy some too?"

"No, didn't cost a penny," said Dan. "We each have a lot of lilac bushes and we got the sucker shoots and saplings from under our own bushes."

"This is wonderful—thank you!"

"Now where do you want us to plant them?" Jesse asked.

"Well let me see...over there along that fence and...oh wait a minute, I made a mistake by making a unilateral decision about this house once, I'm not going to do it again. I'll get David."

She ran around the house and called David. He looked up, then came running over to her.

"What's up?" he asked.

"Follow me, and you'll find out."

As they turned the corner of the house, David's face lit up. "Dan! Jesse! It's great to have you come by." He shook their hands affectionately. "You brought the lilac saplings?"

"They brought fifty!" exclaimed Torry.

"Fifty!" David laughed. "You ol' rascals."

"Well, a lot are going to die because most of them are only sucker shoots, and we wanted to make sure they'd be enough left," explained Dan. "If you don't want that many, that's okay, we needed to pull them up and clean out under our bushes anyway."

"We want all fifty," stated Torry. "I mean...is it all right with you, David? You see, Mr. Jones and Mr. Higley, this is half his property and..."

David laughed. "You bet. I see you've already met these men, Torry."

"Yes, we've introduced ourselves," Dan said.

"These two farmers" David explained to Torry, "corralled me about a year ago and insisted that I join their weekly lunch at Green Valley Drug Store, so I could be an audience for their wild yarns."

"We had to initiate this city boy, somehow," Jesse said, grinning as he addressed Torry, who was smiling over their affectionate by-play.

"You almost look human in those blue jeans, David."

"Thank you, Dan."

"Mr. Higley and Mr. Jones," Torry began...

"We're Dan and Jesse, Mrs. Anderson," corrected Dan.

"Thank you. I'll call you that if you'll call me Torry."

"It's a deal," Jesse said. "So what were you going to say, Torry?"

"I was going to ask you if either of you knew my grandfather, Joseph Thomas who owned the drugstore?"

"I'll say we knew him," Jesse said.

"You're his granddaughter? Ruth's daughter?" asked Dan incredulous.

"Yes."

"I can't believe it! exclaimed Jesse. I always wished that beautiful mother of yours were ten years older."

"No wonder this young woman is a beauty, David, you should see her mother," said Dan.

Torry ignored the reference to herself and smiled, "Yes," she agreed, "my mother is beautiful."

"Old Joe Thomas, your grandfather, did a lot for people around here," Jesse said.

"And your grandmother, Torrance took care of a lot of sick people through the years, a grand family, grand," Dan said.

"Thank you. I spent six weeks out of every summer here for years."

"Wait a minute. Could you be that scrawny, little girl with the fly-away hair, hiding behind her grandfather's chair the night I went by to get some financial advice from him?" asked Dan.

Torry laughed. "I'm the only scrawny little girl that eavesdropped on grandfather's advising sessions, so I must be."

"Well I'll be darned."

David grinned from ear to ear as he listened to the exchange. "It is certainly a small world in this small town." They all laughed.

"I reckon we better get these here sucker shoots planted and watered before sundown," Jesse said.

"You're going to plant them for us, too?" asked David.

"You bet. Part of the gift," Dan said.

"But we got an extra shovel in the truck if any city dweller thinks he has the muscles to keep up with us," Jesse said, grinning.

"I don't think I can, but I'd sure like to try," David said.

As Dan and Jesse went over to their truck to get the plants and shovels, another visitor drove up. Zelda parked her pickup out front since her place in the driveway had been usurped.

Torry turned to David and smiled. "We have another visitor."

They watched Zelda wave at Dan and Jesse, and then get out. She went around to the passenger side, opened the door and picked up a covered glass baking dish with hot pads and walked toward them.

"Zelda! What have you got there?"

"Oh, just some chicken and seasoned rice. I've got a salad and an apple pie still in the truck."

"Boy that sounds good!" exclaimed David impulsively.

"It so happens that it's for you too," Zelda said grinning. "It's a congratulation meal for yours and Torry's new partnership."

"David, this is Zelda Blackburn."

"The one who owns Henry," he stated.

"Yep," replied Zelda.

"And the one who thinks I'm handsome."

"Right on, cowboy."

David laughed. "Thanks for the compliment and the meal. Let me take this into the house for you."

Torry chuckled to herself as she walked to the car with Zelda to get the rest of the food.

"I would have been over sooner," explained Zelda, "but one of Zak's horses was sick. I could see all the activity going on over here and couldn't get over. It about killed me."

"How's the horse?"

"We thought we were going to lose her, but I think she's going to make it."

David came out and took the rest of the food from them and carried it into the house.

"I like him, Torry."

"Apparently a lot of people do. He certainly seems to relate well with everyone."

As David returned, Zelda said, "Hey David, how about you and Torry giving me a tour of the chicken coop?"

"By all means," he said, grinning. "It's our pride and joy."

Torry and David sat in the kitchen enjoying Zelda's delicious meal, each in deep thought.

To David, this had been an amazing week. He felt like a new man. The fresh air and sunshine were a welcome change from the fluorescent lights and air conditioning of the bank. But more importantly, seeing Torry twice a day and talking with her had brought such happiness he could hardly internalize it—the miracle of it.

Torry shook her head and sighed. "I can't believe this day."

"It has been an interesting day," David said, his smiling eyes pulling her in.

Torry looked down quickly. "Uh...I want to do something special for Zelda. She's been such a good friend to me since I moved here." She looked up and smiled, "I like your friends, Dan and Jesse."

"And I like your friend, Zelda."

"Of course you do," she smiled knowingly. "By the way, we are going to have extra help this weekend—maybe."

"Oh, who?"

"My sons, Jim and Scott, if they can work it out."

"Great! I'm anxious to meet them."

"They'll be good help, David. They know how to do about anything, and they're hard workers."

He smiled. "I'm not surprised."

"My parents are coming down in about three weeks. I hope everything is done and the chicks are here."

"That's cutting it close, Torry."

"I know...but I was hoping because...never mind, it doesn't matter." She stood up and walked to the kitchen counter, frowning as she cut the pie. Why did she care if everything was in place and going before her father came down? she wondered.

Placing a piece of pie in front of David and one for herself, she sat down and smiled. "You like apple pie?"

"Do I!" Taking a bite he exclaimed, "especially this one."

Chapter Fourteen

It was almost 8:30 Friday night and the boys had not arrived. Though they were supposed to be there around eight, Torry talked herself out of worrying, deciding they probably got away later than they expected. Where was David? He was supposed to drop by and meet the boys. Just as she asked herself this, he knocked on the screen door.

"Hi, David. At least you're here. Come in."

"Since I only saw your van in the driveway I gathered the boys weren't here yet."

"I left my van in front of the garage so they would know that this was the place. They should be arriving shortly." She noticed that David was still in his suit, which meant that he'd come straight from the bank. He must have had a busy day today, she thought, because he hadn't been over to check on the building.

A car door slammed, and they heard running feet. Two young men dashed through the screen door, each hugging their mother in turn and exclaiming how great she looked.

"Boys, I want you to meet David Mayer, my banker, who is also my partner in the chicken farm business."

"Glad to meet you, Mr. Mayer, I'm Jim," the taller boy said, shaking David's hand firmly.

"I'm Scott," the other said, shaking David's hand just as firmly as his brother. "We appreciate you helping our mother."

"Thank you, Scott, but I think it's mutual."

"Mom," exclaimed Jim, "this is a neat looking little house."

"From what you told us, this is a complete transformation," added Scott.

Jim, walking over to the fireplace, rubbed his hand over it. "I like this sandstone fireplace."

"You were able to get all your books in the bookcase," Scott said studying them. "It looks nice."

They both exclaimed over the new furniture, then Jim said, "Now let's see the rest of the house."

"Okay, follow me." She started for the hall and stopped. "Oh,

David, do come with us, I don't believe you've seen all of your house have you?"

"No," he said smiling. "But I'm a little tired. I think I'll wait out here in one of these comfortable chairs by the window."

The truth was, David didn't want to infringe on their reunion, so he just listened to the happy voices, the interaction of this close family. A family who didn't seem to need any one else in their lives at the moment.

A flash of memory came unbidden... He was a little boy alone, in his bedroom, hearing his mother and father talk and laugh in theirs. Entering their room was forbidden, so he just listened, longing, wanting to run to them, join their fun and closeness. But he couldn't. The old dreaded gut-twisting pain grabbed at his insides and beads of perspiration appeared on his forehead. A gentle voice from far off called his name.

"David?" Torry repeated, "Are you all right?"

Slowly coming back to the present, he could still hear the voices off somewhere—and saw some one kneeling in front of him. It was Torry.

"David, what is it? You looked as if you were in pain."

He noticed the concern on her beautiful face. Why did this happen here? he questioned himself. Now?...Damn! Thoroughly embarrassed, he stood up. She stood up, too, looking up into his face, anxious for the answer.

"Torry, I'm fine. I was just...uh...a million miles away."

"But you looked like you were in pain."

"I did?" he asked, trying to sound surprised. "If I was, I'm not now." He managed a smile.

"Mom, why did you leave the tour?" queried Scott, entering the room. "We almost got lost."

She put on a smile. She couldn't explain to them that her action was prompted by a sudden overwhelming feeling that David needed her. "You boys hungry?" she asked, changing the subject.

"Always!" exclaimed Jim, grinning.

"David, you and the boys come into the kitchen and sit down at the table, and I'll put the food on."

"I can't stay, Torry. I just remembered something urgent that I didn't do today. You three have a good visit, and I'll see you boys early tomorrow morning."

"I'm looking forward to working with you, Mr. Mayer."

"Me too," Jim said.

Concerned, Torry followed David out onto the porch. "Are you all right, David?"

"I'm fine, Torry, really." He forced himself to smile. "I just have to take care of something very important."

David's thoughts raced as he drove home. Anguish filled his heart. Why did he have another episode? He thought they were over! It had been a long time since he had one—so why now—why at Torry's of all places? It shouldn't have happened! The urgent thing that needed doing was something he hadn't done for a week, and that was—reading the Bible.

When David was a young boy, Hildi, his mother's housekeeper had given him a Bible. One day, many years later, during an emotionally desperate time, he had picked it up and began reading from it. He found great solace and from then on things went better in his life, especially if he read it every morning. But this last week, he was so caught up in the excitement of the building over at Torry's he had neglected his reading.

When he entered his apartment, he wrenched off his tie, threw his coat over a chair and sat down by the lamp. Leaning over, he placed his elbows on his knees, and resting his head in his hands he prayed aloud.

"Dear God, why? Why? Please help me, help me..." then turning on the lamp, he picked up the Bible, held it a moment—then turned to the New Testament.

~~~~~~~~~~~~~

For David, morning always brought hope for a better day. He was hopeful that last night's attack was just an aberration and wouldn't happen again. After all, he hadn't had one for several years.

He looked forward to working with Torry's sons this morning. He thought of them as he fixed himself breakfast. He decided that Jim, tall, blonde and broad shouldered must look like his father. Scott, on the other hand, not quite as tall as Jim, was of a more slender build and had naturally curly dark brown hair like Torry.

They were both clean cut, nice looking boys—somewhat like the sons he always dreamed of having. This thought dampened his spirits. Since becoming an adult, he had always been successful in anything to do with the world of big business, but it had taken most of his adult life to overcome his so-called upbringing. Now it was too late to have children. Immediately, he shook the thought away. Of course he could have children. All he had to do is marry a younger woman....but then...there was only one Torry.

David arrived at Torry's house at 7:00 A.M. and found the boys already outside working, carrying a roll of chicken wire to a more convenient place.

"I'm impressed," David said, grinning as he walked up to the boys. "I didn't think college boys got up so early."

"Good morning, Mr. Mayer," Jim said returning the greeting.

"Please, both of you call me David. Mr. Mayer sounds too formal since we're going to dig post holes together."

"Thank you, David," Scott said, "Mom thinks we can do anything, but Jim and I need some guidance here on how to put up this fence around the chicken run. We've never put up a fence made of chicken wire before."

"My friends, Dan and Jesse, told me how to do it last night, or I wouldn't know either."

They worked hard and fast for an hour-and-a-half, digging the holes with post-hole diggers borrowed from Dan and Jesse, then Torry stepped out on to the back porch and yelled,

"Breakfast is on!"

"Great! More home cookin'," exclaimed Jim.

"Come on in, David, Mom is expecting you for breakfast too," Scott said.

"Thanks, but I've had breakfast." He saw a look of disappointment on their faces which gratified him immensely. "Besides, I have an errand to run. See you in about thirty-to-forty minutes."

"Where's David?" their mother questioned, as the two boys sat down at the table.

"He's had breakfast," replied Jim.

Torry frowned.

"Mom, I think you had better invite him ahead of time after this," Scott counseled.

"I guess...maybe...but I really don't want to. I would like to keep our relationship as businesslike as possible." The boys glanced at each other.

When David returned, they were just finishing up. He knocked on the back door and then stuck his head in, "Hi," he greeted. "I would like to invite the three of you out to the Old Mill for dinner tonight, as kind of a celebration for our new business."

The boys looked at their mother. "Don't look at me, you two. Do you want to?"

"Do we!" said Jim exuberantly. "Even at school we've heard about that quartet and that home-made root beer."

"Thank you, David," said Scott, grinning widely. "We accept the offer."

Chapter Fifteen

Inspecting the lilac shoots that Dan, Jesse and David had planted only ten days ago, Torry saw small green sprouts starting on some. Excited, she got the hose and watered each one as she had every day since they were planted. She was finishing up the last three, when David's car drove up.

It had been seventeen days since they had begun the chicken house and today, Friday, they had completely finished it. They were now waiting for the arrival of the equipment.

"David come here and look," Torry yelled.

Laying down a roll of white paper on the front porch, he walked over to where Torry had been watering.

"Look at these, David, there are new green sprouts on these!"

"Well, I'll be darned. Our lilac bushes are growing."

"Isn't it wonderful?" She stood up, beaming.

"It is," he said, glowing inside at her enjoyment of such a small thing.

They both walked back to the water faucet next to the front porch, and Torry turned it off. A small whirling gust of wind encircled them, blowing the roll of paper off. David darted after it. Rolling it back up while walking back to Torry, he grinned.

"Whew! That was fierce. And not even a hair out of place," he said impulsively running his hand through her short curls. Shocked by his touch, she pulled away.

I'm sorry," he said, though his eyes said otherwise, "but I've been wanting to do that for a long time." She frowned, tight lipped. "Don't take it so seriously, Torry. Besides I want to know how in the world you could have had fly-away hair like Dan said."

The frown disappeared, and she smiled. "I was a fright in some of my pictures as a little girl. When mother didn't take the time to curl my hair on large curlers or braid it, the natural curls went wild. Now you know one of the reasons I keep my hair short. What is that roll of paper?"

"These are the plans I've drawn up for landscaping the yard

around the house," he said, unrolling them and laying them out on the porch.

Torry stared at him in surprise. "Landscaping?"

"Yes, take a look and tell me what you think."

Torry sat down on a step and studied it. "Oh my! This is too elaborate for this little cracker box."

"That's exactly why they are elaborate, to diminish the cracker box look."

"But David, the business can't afford this."

"The business isn't paying for it."

"But David..."

"Don't 'but David' me, Torry. Aren't you the impulsive girl who bought carpet for this house before you should have, because you couldn't stand the brown carpet?"

"Well...yes."

"You couldn't stand the brown carpet, and I can't stand this yard. And didn't you pay for the redecorating with your own funds?"

"Yes..."

"So I'm paying for this with my own funds. And if for any reason, you or we decide that the chicken farm business is not to your or our liking, the resale value will have been improved by your superb decorating and with a yard to match."

"I give up, you win," Torry said. "Let's go over the plans." David sat down, and they both studied them.

"You say you drew these up, David?"

"Yes."

"Why these are professional. Did you study landscape architecture in college?"

"No, I learned it all from ol' Bert."

"And who is he?"

"Our caretaker. He and his wife Belle lived in the caretaker's cottage behind our house. He was a natural landscaper and made our three acres the envy of the neighborhood. He oversaw all the yard care as well as repairs around the house. Bert taught me the names of plants, flowers, and trees. He taught me how to raise them as well as the art of landscape design. He even let me redesign some of it, without my mother's knowledge," he added ruefully.

"How old were you when you learned all this?"

"I began learning when I was in elementary school and continued, as I had time, until I left for college. Soon after that, Bert retired and moved away to make room for the next caretaker."

"You must have liked it to be such an apt pupil."

"I did, but I liked being around Bert even more. Belle even allowed me to eat dinner with them once in a while," he said, smiling as he remembered. "I would liked to have eaten every meal at their table, but Belle was a little tight and didn't want to pay for food to feed me, a rich kid, the son of her husband's rich employer. She was good to me anyway."

"Did you have brother's or sisters?" Torry asked, taking advantage of the moment to learn more about him.

"No, I was an only child." Abruptly he stabbed a finger at the plans, "Are there any changes you'd like to make?"

Knowing it was useless to pursue it further, she said, "What about some fruit trees?"

"Sounds great. However, the grass, bushes and other trees have already been ordered so we'll have to decide what fruit trees you want and I'll order them another time," he said, rolling up the plans.

"Also, could we have a garden plot? We could share it, you could take some home, or do you cook, David?"

"I cook out of desperation when I can't stomach eating in a restaurant."

"You can afford to hire a cook."

"Can I hire you, Torry?" his gaze was intimate.

Flustered more over his gaze than his question, she asked, "Uh...you aren't serious."

"As a matter of fact, I am. And, as I said, I would pay you."

Torry got up and quickly walked around to the back of the house. David caught up with her.

"Hey Torry, I know it's a lot of work to cook for another person. If you'd rather not, just say so, don't walk away from me."

"It isn't that it's too much work, David, it's just not a good idea."

"Why?"

"Owning a chicken farm together is one thing but owning a house and yard together is sometimes uncomfortable for me, so cooking for you and eating together would be even more...uh..."

"Intimate?" he finished.

"Yes, thank you."

"We ate Zelda's meal together in our house," he reminded her.

"I know...once in a while is all right, but...not on a daily basis."

"Well," he grinned, "since I can't hire you as my cook, may I take you up to the Hilltop House tonight, I'm starving."

"I am too, but no thank you."

"Why?" he asked not allowing his disappointment to show.

"David," she said, looking down and nudging a weed with the toe of her shoe, "as I have said before, I would like to keep our relationship as businesslike as possible."

David laughed. "Our businesslike relationship, or I should say my businesslike behavior ceased the day you walked into my office. Our businesslike relationship lasted only one day, Torry. If you remember, it changed that evening in the park."

She glanced up at him, smiling. "I guess it did. I guess we are...are friends."

"I would say that," he said returning her smile, "so why can't friends go out to eat together?"

"I think it's best that we don't socialize."

"Why, for Pete's sake?"

"I...I don't feel comfortable with it."

"Why?"

"Because our relationship has to remain as it is...friends."

This time, David couldn't hide his disappointment, so turning from her, he stared out into the field. The familiar song of a Meadowlark, usually so joyous to his ears, now only saddened him. After a few moments, he turned back. "Do you know what that Meadowlark just said, Torry?"

"No, what?"

"It said, Torry's a stubborn little lady," he said, imitating the lilting song of the bird.

She studied his face, his eyes, and felt heavy hearted.

"Well, Miss Torry Ann, I must be off. Have a good weekend."

Torry watched him walk rapidly away and disappear around the house. She sat down on the back porch, staring at the chicken house, feeling close to tears. Her eyes wandered over to the chicken wire fence that David had helped with, then back to the barbed wire fence and wooden gate, both...repaired by David.

Chapter Sixteen

After a trip to the grocery store Monday morning, Torry returned to find a large truck, a smaller truck and David's car blocking her way. The trucks were labeled Morrison's Landscaping, Salt Lake City. The larger one was filled with plants, flowers, trees, and squares of grass sod. The other one contained lawn equipment. Two men were rototilling the ground and two more were raking up the grass and weeds and bagging them. She sat in the car watching it all, thoroughly amazed at how quickly David got things done. David saw her and came running over.

"Hi partner!" he greeted her, a wide grin on his face. Let me carry those sacks in for you."

"Thank you," she said, following him into the kitchen, marveling at his constant cheerfulness; last Friday night already forgotten, it seemed.

After depositing the sacks in the kitchen, David came over to the window where Torry was standing, watching the landscapers.

"I can't believe they are here already," Torry said.

"I faxed the plans to them ten days ago and then we discussed on the phone the type of plants, flowers and trees that were best for this area. Of course," he said, grinning, "I did all this, knowing I would get your approval."

"Hmmnn...you're a sly one aren't you? But...you are also one efficient man."

"Thank you. Well, Torry, I need to get to the bank. I'll see you later."

~~~~~~~~~~

Wednesday at twelve noon, Zelda drove into Torry's driveway and stared at the yard, her mouth open. She honked the horn and got out. Torry appeared at the front screen door, saw who it was and ran quickly down the steps and over to her obviously stunned friend.

"Quite a change, huh? The landscapers completed it yesterday afternoon."

106

"You could say that again!" Zelda said in awe. "It looks like the back yard's done, too."

"Yes. Come, and I'll show you."

Zelda stared in disbelief at the green lawn, plants, flowers and trees all newly planted. "The minute my back is turned, things always happen," she complained.

"What do you mean?"

"Zak and I have been gone since Monday to a horse show up North. Gilford and Ivan saw what was going on, but did they say a word about it this morning? No."

"Zelda, I was just going to the drugstore to pick up a few things. Can I treat you to a sandwich and a malt?"

"You bet, Torry," she said, grinning. "If I go back home now, those two teenage tapeworms will act helpless and wait for me to make them something for lunch."

"I'll drive for a change, Zelda."

When they were both in the van and Torry had backed out onto the street, she asked, "Did you take both horses to the show?"

"Yes. Zak finally broke down and bought a new horse trailer."

"Good. What happened at the horse show?"

"Both horses won blue ribbons."

"Wonderful, Zelda."

"One of them won two ribbons, one for performance and one for appearance. And I sold it."

"You did? What did Zak think about the ribbons and the sale?"

She grinned. "Zak's quite proud of me."

"He should be." Torry turned the corner at Main. Finding a parking place in front of Allen's Cleaners, they both got out.

In the drugstore, they settled into a booth and ordered. "Did you get the price you wanted for the horse?"

"More than I ever expected. Zak now finally realizes I can make some money with this hobby of mine."

"What about the other horse?"

"It won a blue ribbon on appearance. I have to train her some more. She still has some rough spots, but I expect she'll bring more money than the other one."

"I'm impressed, Zelda."

"Thank you. Now, tell me, Torry, what about that expensive landscape job? You're not even a going business yet."

Torry filled Zelda in on everything, beginning, at Zelda's insistence, where the story had previously left off.

They were almost through with lunch when Zelda's eyes got big. "Don't look now, Torry, but David Mayer is coming into the drugstore and on his arm is one sleek, blonde filly, preening and prancing."

"Really?" Torry asked, her surprise bordering on shock.

David and his companion walked by their booth, unaware of their audience.

Both Torry and Zelda scrutinized the woman who was dressed in an obviously expensive pastel-green linen suit.

"Wow!" Zelda said. "Some classy entry in the David Mayer sweepstakes. And she must be proud of her legs. That skirt's just barely long enough to cover the essentials. Do you know who she is, Torry?"

"No, don't you?" asked Torry surprised, "I thought you knew everyone in town."

"I've never laid eyes on that fake thoroughbred before."

"Fake?"

"Yep. Her hair can't be naturally that blonde...and a couple of other things can't be that uh...natural."

"Zelda, what a cynic you are."

A lovely musical laugh erupted from the booth inhabited by David and company, silencing both Torry and Zelda. The low mellow voice of David was heard followed by another melodious laugh.

"Do you think it's a girlfriend, Torry?"

"How would I know? I'm not his keeper." Remembering this same statement that day on the bleachers, they both started to giggle.

"We're through, Zelda, let's leave."

"I thought you came here to get a few things."

"I did, but I'll get them later."

"Why?" Zelda asked, eyeing her knowingly.

"If you must know, these jeans I'm wearing look a little scuzzy next to that mint green suit."

"Oh really? And why should you care, Torry? David is just your business partner isn't he?"

"Behave, Zelda. Let's go."

They both walked quickly to the cashier. Zelda turned and looked toward David's booth.

"Don't look, Zelda."

"You're talking to the winner of the 'Nosey Josey' contest, remember?

"Don't make me laugh, Zelda," she whispered, as she gave the money to the cashier.

"Hmmn, David is looking quite enamored."

Torry shocked, swiveled around to see for herself just as David gazed in her direction. A surprised expression flitted across his face, then a smile. A gorgeous blonde head peeped out from the booth, curious, then with a condescending smile in their general direction, turned away. David had already turned back to his guest, dismissing them.

Torry and Zelda had just stepped out the door, when they saw Dan Higley and Jesse Jones ambling up.

"Oh good, the rescue team is here," exclaimed Zelda, more to the team than to Torry.

"Hello girls," Jesse said. Both were grinning.

"And who are we to rescue, Zelda?" asked Dan.

"David Mayer. He's pinned in a booth by a blonde heifer."

"Oh-oh!" they exclaimed.

"We'll go unpin him, she's on our time now," said Jesse, and they disappeared into the drugstore, grinning, eager to oust the interloper.

Torry walked quickly to the van, and Zelda followed.

After they were in, Zelda said, "Let's wait and watch." She noted that Torry didn't need coaxing.

Soon, the blonde clipped out of the drugstore and over to a silver colored car parked directly in front. Gracefully easing herself in, she drove off.

"A Mercedes no less!" exclaimed Zelda. "I wonder who she is?"

"Now can we go, Zelda?"

"Yep, unless you want to go back now and get what you needed in the drugstore."

"No, I'll come down later." A moments pause. "Was he really looking enamored?"

Zelda looked over at Torry, "Well yes...and **maybe** no."

"What does that mean?"

"You know that man's eyes are so warm, someone could mistake the meaning if she wanted to."

"Oh?" Torry said, thinking of all the times she had noticed the way he looked at her—wondering if that was the way he looked at every woman.

"But," continued Zelda as if reading her thoughts, "there is no mistaking the way he looks at you, Torry. He certainly doesn't look at me like that."

"Oh?" Relief flooded through her, followed immediately by a feeling of chagrin. Why, she wondered, was she even giving a second thought to David and that...that fake thoroughbred?!

Chapter Seventeen

The equipment had begun to arrive Thursday and the rest arrived Friday. She had not heard from or seen David since the incident in the drugstore, so she called immediately to inform him.

"Great!" exclaimed David. "I'll call the men I've lined up to do the work. I'll have them there Monday."

"Good. I'm enjoying the beautiful yard, David."

"I'm glad. Someone is here to see me so I'll have to go. See you Monday."

Unease settled over Torry as she hung up the phone. Was David different with her or was she imagining it? But what did it matter anyway? If he was different or just indifferent, it would be for the best. The thought came suddenly; she had to solve the mystery of Jack. Even with all the excitement of the building and the landscaping, for some reason the problem was laying heavier on her heart.

When the business got going well, she would train someone to help her, then she could put her mind to it, travel where she needed to, and do whatever she needed to do in order to find the answers. Why hadn't she done it before she got tied down with a business? Of course—the almost forgotten despondency. She had found it difficult to think clearly or accomplish anything more than the bare necessities.

Thinking back, she was amazed that she had accomplished what she had toward the business while under that crippling emotion—but then she had prayed for help.

"I need help now, Dear Father," she prayed aloud. "I need help to find the answers concerning Jack so I can lay it to rest once and for all. I need to be free. It's hindering my progress. I don't feel free and whole." She went into the bedroom and knelt down to finish praying.

~~~~~~~~~

Monday morning early, the workers arrived and so did David, dressed for work in his jeans.

Torry went outside to watch them unpack the equipment, not quite believing that having the chicken farm was so close to a reality.

David looked up and smiled, "Hi Torry."

She smiled back. "Hi."

It took some maneuvering, figuring and studying of the plans before they could get started. But finally, they began installing the equipment.

David turned to Torry. "I need to talk to you, can we go into the kitchen?"

"Of course." She led him in.

"Let's sit at the table so I can see when they need to talk to me. I have a confession, Torry. I have to be up front with you," he said as they both sat down at the table.

A sliver of concern pierced her heart. Her imagination took flight. Was this about that blonde beauty she had seen him with in the drugstore? Did he want to cancel their partnership so that he and the blonde could...

"Torry?"

"What?"

"I've been talking to you."

"I'm sorry. My mind was elsewhere for a moment. What were you saying?"

"I was saying that I didn't know for certain how you would take this...but I have a pretty good idea. I did this, knowing that it would upset you...but I do have a good reason."

Her breath shallow, her heart pounding, she hesitantly asked, "What is it, David?"

"I paid quite a bit extra to get the equipment here this soon, and extra for the experienced men who are here."

This wasn't the confession she had expected.

"What did you say?"

"Torry, where are you this morning?" he asked, smiling, repeating it again.

Torry sat there a moment, letting the words sink in. "You what?" She shot from her chair.

David grinned. "Whew! Back to your old self, Torry. I was beginning to wonder if I'd lost you."

"David, how could you?"

"Easy, I'm rich, remember?"

"How dare you take this so lightly."

"I'm not. I thought it all out very carefully, weighed the odds and took the chance—the chance that I could explain it to you and that you would accept it graciously."

"Well, I'm not accepting it graciously."

"I can see that," he said grinning.

"Take that persistent grin off your face and be serious, David."

"I am serious, very serious." His eyes reinforced the words.

She quickly turned her back to him and stared out the window. He noticed that the back of the pink cotton dress was as becoming as the front.

"You look nice in that pink dress, Torry."

She whirled around, her eyes blazing. "Oooh! You are impossible. You think you can sweet talk me into this like you do other women?"

He looked puzzled. "Other women? Where did that come from, Torry?"

"Well...uh" she felt herself flushing, "you seem to be quite the ladies man, remember that...uh...all those women I rescued you from at the park?" she finished in a rush.

"Oh. I assure you, Torry Anderson, other women are a heck of a lot easier to sweet talk than you are."

Her eyes narrowed. "Is that right? Well you just go use up your sweet talk on...on them because it's not going to get you out of this. How will I know if we can be successful if you help like this? And how can we ever make a profit if you spend extra just...just because you can?"

"The business isn't paying for it, I am."

"Oh? And how often are you personally going to give the business extra perks?"

"I hope this will be the last. I may not live through another one," he grimaced.

"Why did you do it, David?"

"Because I wanted it all in place before your parents came down. It seemed important to you."

Her mouth dropped open, then closed, stunned into silence. Finally, after a few moments, she said, her voice subdued. "How kind of you...but it wasn't necessary."

"Torry, there aren't many ways I can serve...help people...one way, if I'm judicious, is with the money that I've given my life for...which hasn't been a good thing, but that's the way it is. I need blessings. Are you going to deny me the blessings of doing this for you?"

Torry stared at him, not believing her ears. "What...or how did you..."

David smiled. "Dan and Jesse have shared many stories with me. I have learned this from them, for which I'm grateful. It will enable me to help the few who are hesitant when I want to help."

"Like me?"

"No one is like you, Torry, no one reacts like you. But I'm glad you're the way you are...I think," he offered tentatively, chuckling.

Torry took a deep breath and let it out. "You have learned well from Dan and Jesse. I'm...I'm sorry for reacting the way I did. I didn't realize..." Tears appeared in her eyes which she quickly blinked away. "Thank you."

It seemed to David that a hug was perfectly in order at this moment. With great effort, he resisted.

~~~~~~~~~~

By Wednesday afternoon, the equipment had been completely installed. All the chicken feed had arrived, including the special meal she had ordered from Dale's Feed store. Torry and David had spread the litter carefully over the floor. She was excited.

"Now all we need are the chicks, David. Can you believe it?"

"Well," he grinned, "if anyone told me two years ago that I would own a chicken farm and actually oversee the building of the chicken house, I would have laughed in their face."

Torry smiled, "It is all rather strange isn't it?"

"Yes." He heaved a sigh, "I don't want to, but maybe I'd better go shower and go down to the bank, late as it is."

As they came out of the coop, Torry exclaimed, "Look, David, there is the Chelsey Farm truck driving in. Our chicks are here!"

"Now that is what I call timing."

"Do you want to stay and help me put them in the incubators?"

"Do I! Forget the bank today."

Torry smiled, thinking how David sounded like an excited little boy...this man who ran large and complex enterprises. She marveled that it had only been twenty-five days and everything was in place for her parents to see...all because of David's kindness.

The man got out of his truck and walked up to them. "Mrs. Torry Anderson?"

"Yes, I'm Mrs. Anderson."

"I have one hundred and fifty chicks for you if you'll sign here."

After the man had placed the crates in the chicken house and opened them for Torry's inspection, he left, wishing her good luck.

A few minutes later, David and Torry were kneeling down in the chicken house marveling at the mass of peeping yellow puffs.

"They're cute little things. Can I pick one up?" David asked.

"Yes. I know I have to," Torry said, tickled over his reaction. "Besides I don't know how we'll get them into the incubators if we don't."

David picked up one gingerly, feeling its softness with gentle hands, smiling. "Missy would love these." He looked over at Torry. "Could I invite the Baker family over to see them tonight?"

Torry hesitated, not wanting to disappoint David in his eagerness. "The trip to Green Valley was hard on them and at this age they're very fragile—but it would be wonderful to give each of the children an opportunity to pick one up. Oh well, let's chance it, David. Go ahead and invite them."

"Great! I'll see that they're careful—in fact, to cut down on the handling, maybe they can help us place them into the incubators."

"That's a good idea, David."

Carefully putting the chick down and looking at his watch, he said, "I'll go call Tom right now. May I use your phone?"

"Of course."

He was back shortly, smiling. "They're all coming over right now." David could hardly contain his excitement. At last, he was going to get the Baker family and Torry together.

After admiring the chicks for a while, David and Torry walked outside to watch for the Bakers. Soon, their big tan Suburban drove into the driveway. The car doors opened and children spilled out; all running toward David. The three younger girls threw their arms around him, the littlest one wound hers around his legs. The other children gathered around, everyone talking at once.

"We haven't seen you for a long time, David!" a small accusing voice piped up.

David leaned down and picked up the small girl. "I know, Missy, and I've missed you. I want you and your family to meet a very special friend of mine, Torry Anderson."

Everyone turned eager eyes toward Torry. "Torry, this is Josh who is sixteen, Elizabeth who is fifteen, Sam is twelve, Jake here is eleven, Rebecca is ten, Rachael is eight and Missy who is forty."

"Forty? I'm not forty, David, I'm only four!"

"Oh, that's right, I forgot."

"I'm glad to meet all of you," Torry said, smiling at each one.

"You already know Tom," David continued, "but I would like you to meet the mother of this brood, Jenny."

"We're all glad to meet you too, Torry," Jenny said. "We almost thought we were at the wrong place, it looks so different with this beautiful landscaping."

"Yeah, Dave! You're some landscaper—I'm impressed," Tom said, grinning broadly.

"Thank you. Now—we invited you over to help us with our new baby chicks."

"That's what Daddy told us!" exclaimed Missy, her eyes wide with excitement.

"We have one hundred and fifty baby chicks," Torry explained, "who have to be transferred very carefully into the incubator. Do you think you all can help us?"

An exuberant round of affirmative answers came from the seven children, including sixteen-year-old Josh.

"Torry will tell you how to do it, how to pick them up and place them," David added. "All of you follow us into the chicken house. Squeals of delight issued from the girls when they saw the chicks.

"Wow, I've never seen so many baby chicks at one time!" exclaimed Sam and Jake almost at the same time.

David stood back and watched as Torry explained how careful they needed to be and then showed them how by depositing several chicks herself. He noticed Tom grinning from ear to ear as he watched his family. Jenny was in the midst of the children, helping and enjoying it as much as they were. She stood up with a chick in her hand and gave it to Tom.

He chuckled. "Cute little things aren't they?"

The older children, Josh and Elizabeth, seemed to be enjoying the chicks as much as their gleeful little four-year-old sister, Missy.

David wondered, what is it with these Mormons that gives them such a zest for life? He had watched the Baker children interact with each other and with their parents on many occasions and their awareness and vibrant interest in each other, down to the smallest thing, was amazing to him. This interest exhibited itself to others outside of the family as well, to him in particular.

In his circle, the wealthy children he grew up with seemed self-ish compared to the Baker children, more interested in themselves and what they could get out of life.

The wealthy orthodox Jewish families were closer knit than the wealthy gentiles he'd known. Yet, even they came out on the short end of the stick compared to the Bakers, compared to Torry and her sons, and compared to Dan and Jesse. What makes them different? He felt that he knew. The Orthodox Jewish families do not believe in Christ. From what he understood, Mormons do.

A squeal from Missy drew his attention back to the menagerie in front of him.

"Look, David, they are eating and drinking now!"

David was pleased over the children's excitement. Torry stood up and walked over to him smiling.

"I'm glad you invited them," she whispered.

"I would like to take everyone out to eat, Torry. Is that all right with you?"

"I can't leave the chicks right now, I have to check on them often, all night tonight in fact."

"Hey gang, I have an idea!" exclaimed David.

"What? What is it, David?" Missy asked, running to him, the rest following her.

"How about us having a picnic on Torry's back lawn. We can go get hamburgers and root beer from the Old Mill."

"Yippee!" exclaimed Missy, Rachael and Rebecca. The rest grinned and nodded their agreement.

"Is that all right with you?" David asked, looking at Tom and Jenny.

"It's too late now if it weren't, Dave," Tom said, grinning.

"It's more than all right with me, David," Jenny said enthusiastically. "I haven't even had time to think of what I was going to have for dinner tonight."

"Who wants to go with me to get the food?" David asked.

A cacophony of "I do's" greeted his ears.

"Oh-oh," Tom said, "I guess we'll have to take the 'Sub' as he called their Suburban.

After the children had all scrambled in and Tom and David placed themselves in the front seat, they drove off. Jenny smiled at Torry. "Whew! peace and quiet for a little while."

"Come on in the house, Jenny, and let's relax until they get back."

"Sounds good, Torry."

When they were seated in the front room chairs by the window, Jenny looked around, smiling. Torry suspected that this was her demeanor most of the time, suggesting a cheerful disposition. Out on the lawn, Torry had studied this mother of seven: the sun-bleached blonde hair, pulled back into a short pony tail, the high cheek bones, the expressive blue eyes set into her arresting sun-tanned face. Her tall slim, angular body seemed to be made for perpetual motion, her strong-looking hands for hard work.

"I was in this house once, Torry, and I can't believe what you've done to it. It's lovely."

"Thank you. And I can't believe what David has done to the yard."

"David really did the yard?"

"Yes. Apparently landscaping is a hobby with him. He designed it and had it done."

"He's a surprising man and...a much happier one now."

"Now? What do you mean?"

"For about two months before you arrived, David had become

very low in spirits. He wouldn't accept any invitations to dinner, and he didn't invite us out like he usually did. The children were beside themselves as they've become quite attached to him. Tom and I were very worried about him."

"That doesn't sound like the David I know."

"It isn't like him...but the minute you walked into his office..." Her hand flew to her lips. "Oh dear, I don't think I should be telling you this, Torry."

"I don't think I want you to either, Jenny."

"I...I'm sorry, Torry."

The look of concern on Jenny's face compelled Torry to explain. "Please don't be upset, Jenny. I'm the problem, not you. I'm trying to keep everything concerning David as businesslike as possible and as impersonal as possible."

"Oh?" The look of disappointment was plain. "Why?"

"I have a personal problem to work out."

"Can I help in any way?"

"I wish you could, but no one can help right now. However, I do have hopes that I can find some answers before too long."

"I hope so. I know that David is Jewish, Torry, but Tom and I and the children have great hopes that we will be able to do missionary work with him when the time is right."

"I hope you can." Torry became silent, thinking, then a puzzled frown appeared. "Jenny...I don't know why, but I...I'm feeling that it's important for me to hear what you were going to say, after all."

Relief flooded Jenny's face. "Really? Then maybe it wasn't a mistake that I almost blurted it out. Tom said that David's gloom was getting worse. There was even something David said that gave Tom the impression he was planning to leave Green Valley. One day the despondency was there and the next day, after you had come to the bank, it was gone."

Torry stared at Jenny. "You mean...you mean this was a constant state in David for two months straight?"

"Yes, so it seemed to us."

"And then it was gone, all of a sudden it was gone?"

"Yes."

"That is...very strange," Torry murmured almost to herself. As happens so often in the Church, she felt an immediate kinship with

Jenny. She longed to confide the experience of her own despondency that had disappeared so miraculously about the same time. Instead, she expressed one of her concerns.

"Jenny, after watching David with your children, it seems to me he needs children of his own. If he could find some one around thirty-two or thirty-three..."

"I know. After the first time David came to our home for dinner, I arranged, very casually of course, for David to meet a couple of choice friends of mine in that age bracket."

"And?"

"And nothing. He wasn't interested in either one. We thought perhaps he just needed to get to know them better, so we invited one special one to dinner more than once when we invited him."

"How did David react?"

Jenny considered a moment, "I think he was a little amused over it all. He asked her many questions and seemed to enjoy her, just as he had the other one, but then David enjoys people in general."

"Did anything come of it?"

"Not a thing," sighed Jenny.

For some absurd reason Torry felt a rush of relief, then caught herself. What possible difference did it make to her? Anyway, what made Jenny and Tom think she had anything to do with David feeling better? Maybe it was that blonde. The thought brought a prickle of irritation. Well, he can have her!

Suddenly, she thought of a time in high school when her mother reprimanded her. "Torry, you're like a dog-in-the-manger," her mother said, "you don't want Al, but you don't want anyone else to have him." Torry frowned. Now why in the world did that come into my mind?

She was saved from having to answer herself by the slamming of car doors, happy squeals and running feet announcing the arrival of the hamburgers and root beer. Torry and Jenny smiled at each other and headed for the back yard. Torry brought a tablecloth to spread on the lawn. When the happy group were all seated in a circle with the food placed in front of them, Torry asked which one would like to say the blessing. Missy's hand flew up.

David smiled as Missy blessed the chicks, him, the cat, the dog, her family, Torry and finally somehow managed to squeeze in a blessing on the food.

Silence prevailed for a while as the hungry crew ate. Torry just nibbling, studied each child in the family.

"Jenny, I envy you your large family. I wanted a lot of children, but I was only able to have two."

"Oh? I do feel blessed to have this many—most of the time anyway," she added, laughing.

Torry went on, "My grandmother Thomas was only able to have one, and my mother was only able to have two, me and my older brother, Bill. My brother, however, has six children so I'm hoping my boys will also be able to break the cycle and have more than a couple."

"Where is your daddy?" Missy asked Torry.

"You mean my husband, like your daddy is to your mother?"

"Yes."

"Well, Missy he died quite some time ago. He went home to Heavenly Father."

"Oh." She frowned, "I'm sorry you don't have a daddy." Her eyes brightened. "I know, I'll let you marry David, too!"

There was a moment of silence, then laughter erupted around the circle and all eyes were on Torry. David, thoroughly delighted over Missy's remark, noticed Torry's embarrassment. Nevertheless, she smiled.

"Thank you, Missy. That is very nice of you to share David with me. Now if all of you will excuse me a minute, I had better go check on our little brood in the chicken house."

Chapter Eighteen

George and Ruth Conway had driven up and down Farm
Road 6 twice and couldn't find the small frame house with
a weed-filled lawn that Torry had described to them some weeks
ago. They hadn't thought to get the house number from Torry, after
all this was Ruth's home town. Driving slowly back into town on
Farm Road 6, they looked carefully on both sides of the street.

"Drive into this driveway, George. It's the only one it could be.
It has a wide graveled driveway with a detached one-car garage like
Torry described, and it has a new building in the back."

"But look at that yard, Ruth. It isn't the yard Torry described,"
he said, driving in as his wife had requested.

"I know, but I'd like to go in and check. I'll be right back."
Opening the car door, Ruth swung long legs and white sandaled
feet out and stood up, straightening her blue cotton skirt. It felt
good to stretch her legs after the drive down from Salt Lake.
Walking toward the house, a movement caught her eye. She turned
toward it and saw a man coming from the building out back. She
stopped and walked over to him as he came through the gate. He
smiled.

"Hello, may I help you?"

"I'm looking for Torry Anderson's place."

"This is it. I'm David Mayer, her partner."

"I'm Ruth Conway, Torry's mother."

His face lit up. "I'm very glad to meet you." He held out his
hand.

"I'm glad to meet you, too, Mr. Mayer," she said, smiling.

"Please call me David."

"I will if you'll call me Ruth."

"I just got here, Ruth, so I don't know if Torry is home. I've
been so busy, I haven't seen her in almost a week."

"David, come over and meet Torry's father, and then we'll go
see if Torry's home."

George Conway, seeing Ruth and the young man coming

toward the car, got out. Just as they reached him, Torry came running down the front steps.

"Mother, Dad, I've been expecting you for a week!"

David stood back and watched Torry greet her parents: a warm embrace for her mother, a brief and stiff one for her father.

Ruth Conway, a tall elegant lady with dark hair, flanked by gray streaks at the temples, was beautiful still. Torry resembled her in features, except for Ruth's deep blue eyes and height.

Apparently, it was from her father that she had inherited her hazel eyes and shorter stature. George Conway was at least an inch shorter than his wife but his stocky build was still trim and in shape. Sandy gray hair contrasted strikingly with a tan, suggesting many hours on the golf course and an air that went with it; the superior aloofness of the affluent that David had lived with and seen so many times.

"Mother and Dad, I want you to meet my banker and partner, David Mayer."

David reached his hand toward George who hesitated a moment before taking it.

"How do you do, Mr. Mayer."

"I'm glad to meet you, Mr. Conway. But please call me David." George Conway's response was silence.

"I've already met David, Torry," her mother said quickly, covering the awkward moment.

"We couldn't find this place, Torry," her father said tersely. "It isn't at all what you described to us."

"Oh, I forgot to tell you about the new landscaping. I'm sorry."

"A little extravagant isn't it Torry?" questioned her father.

David bristled at the way he talked to his daughter. "The landscaping was my idea," he said firmly, "not Torry's and...my gift. You see, Mr. Conway, landscaping is a hobby of mine."

George Conway gave him a terse nod but Ruth's face lit up. "It's beautifully done, David. You are very talented."

"Well, let's see this so-called chicken farm, Torry," demanded her father in a skeptical tone of voice.

Feeling embarrassed for her father, Torry glanced at David, uneasy over how this was affecting him. "Come on, David, let's show them."

David took over for Torry, explaining the equipment, the type of feed that they were giving the chicks, the uniqueness of this type of concept and the potential of it.

Ruth, allowing her husband a chance to respond first, saw only his cool silence, so expressed her own admiration. "The chicks look so healthy. Did you lose any?"

"We've had them a week and we haven't lost one, Mother. I used several tricks Grandmother taught me."

"We'll be anxious to hear how it progresses and how the restaurants like them. Now, may we see your house, Torry?"

Torry looked up at David, her eyes asking for help. "Will you join us, David?"

"I'd be glad to."

Her parents were silent as they walked into the kitchen and then into the front room. Her father remarked in biting sarcasm. "This isn't the way you described the house to your sons in the beginning, Torry. Another 'gift,' Mr. Mayer? Is redecorating your hobby also?"

David, glad the attack was aimed at him instead of Torry, held his tongue. He glanced at Torry's furious face and Ruth's pale one.

"You see, Mr. Conway, this house and property needed improving for resale value in case we want to change locations or in case we decide chicken farming isn't for us."

"Or in case it fails."

"I assure you, Mr. Conway, it won't fail. I always make profits on my investments because I choose wisely what I invest in." He looked over at Ruth and smiled. "I'll be leaving you now, Ruth, Mr. Conway, so that you can visit with your daughter. It's nice to meet you. Good night, Torry."

"I'll walk you out, David."

It wasn't until they reached David's car that Torry spoke. "Thank you for your help, David."

"Is he always like this?"

"Yes, to me, but rarely in front of my mother and never in the presence of other people. This was unusual, and I'm concerned about my mother."

"I like your mother, Torry," he said getting into his car.

"Thank you, David, I'll see you soon."

Coming in, Torry found her father alone, staring out the window. He'd been watching them.

"He's a Jew isn't he?"

"Yes, how did you know?"

"His name, his face. If that Jew is so successful in his investments, why is he only driving a Ford?"

"Is that what it is?" asked Torry, surprised. Well chalk up another one for David, she said to herself.

"You never could tell one car from another, Torry."

"Well...I and everyone else, I'm sure, can tell that your car is a Mercedes, Dad." She left to find her mother.

Ruth Conway had retreated to Torry's beautiful back yard to collect herself.

"There you are, Mother," Torry said, coming down the back steps, "let me show you something." She led her over to the far side of the yard. "We've planted lilac shoots on both sides of the yard."

"How nice," Ruth said, unable to smile.

"Mother, I'm sorry Dad acted that way in front of you and David, but it's all right, really."

"It's not all right, Torry."

"But, Mother, I'm used to it, he always talks to me like this when you aren't around."

"He does?" Ruth asked, shocked. "How long has he been doing it?"

"Well, as you know, Dad and I are too much alike. We are both confrontive, but he started becoming more openly critical and sarcastic nine or ten years ago when I asked him to do something for me. Remember when he began inviting Jack to go out of town with him to see all the professional football games? Well, I asked him not to invite him anymore since Jack's job as Regional manager of Frasier Sports Equipment already took him away from home two weeks out of the month. Jim and Scott were at such vulnerable ages they needed their father around more."

"What did he say?"

"He said that I was dominating Jack, and I said that he cared more about having a football buddy than for the welfare of his grandsons. Well, Dad kind of hangs on to things, and I haven't apologized."

"It appears that I've been hiding my head in the sand long enough, Torry. We're going back home tonight."

"Oh, Mother, no."

"I don't want him talking to David like he did, let alone you, Torry."

"David handled it well."

"He handled it very well. He's a nice man, I like him. How about you, Torry, are you feeling all right about going into partnership with him?"

Torry was silent as she thought about her mother's question. "Yes I am...but it's uncomfortable at times."

"What do you mean?"

"I'll tell you another time. I would like you to at least stay the night. I need to talk to Dad. He may have some answers for me concerning Jack."

"All right, Torry, but we are leaving tomorrow. Your father and I have some talking to do."

Torry looked at her watch. "It's six o'clock, you and Dad must be starved. I want to take you out to the Old Mill tonight for dinner."

"The Old Mill?"

"Yes, you'll enjoy it. You love barbershop quartets, and that's the entertainment."

"Sounds like something I need tonight, Torry."

Chapter Nineteen

Early the next morning after taking care of the chicks, Torry and her mother prepared breakfast together.

During breakfast, George Conway ate in glum silence. His wife had informed him late last night that they were going home this morning. Ruth just did not give him edicts like this, and he didn't quite know how to deal with it.

Torry and Ruth ignored his silence and talked about the kitchen wallpaper, Zelda, the Baker family and the town park.

When the meal was over and the dishes done, Ruth informed her husband that she needed to go for a walk before the four-hour drive back to Salt Lake. She and Torry had prearranged this so Torry could talk to her father alone.

Torry puttered in the kitchen trying to gather courage. Finally she sat down at the table across from him.

"Dad?"

He showed no recognition that he'd been spoken to, his head still buried in the paper.

"Dad, I need your help."

Slowly her father lowered the paper, his gaze cool.

Feeling great uneasiness, she blurted out, "I desperately need some answers concerning Jack. I believe you got to know him quite well, and I'm sure you noticed the change that came over him. I don't know when it started, it was so gradual at first and then it accelerated as the years went by until he became a totally different person. I tried every way I could to find out why, but Jack denied that there was anything wrong. The question I have for you, Dad, is...do you have any idea, any clue as to what caused this change in him?"

"You really don't know, Torry?" His expression was hard.

"I wouldn't be asking you if I did. You know something don't you?"

"Of course I know something and so should you." The contempt in his voice sounded a warning note to Torry.

"Maybe I should, Dad, but I don't. Please tell me what you think I should know."

"Jack told me that you usurped his role as head of the house."

Torry gasped. "That can't be true."

"You mean I'm lying, Torry?"

"I...I don't mean that, I mean you must have misunderstood him."

"Hardly, he said it many times. You could take a lesson from your mother, but no, you have to always do things your way, no matter how it affects your husband."

"How did it affect him, Dad?"

"If a man doesn't feel like a man in his own home, he goes elsewhere."

"Are you telling me Jack was unfaithful?"

"I didn't say that...figure it out for yourself."

Torry choked with emotion. "When did this happen? Did he tell you anything that gave you the idea he was looking elsewhere or did you notice something that made you suspect?"

"I noticed something."

Torry leaned toward him, "What? Please, I need to know."

"I paid for the trips to the games but he always had to have his own room and was willing to pay the extra."

Torry was stricken. Another lie! Jack had told her they always shared a room to save expenses.

Looking at her father for some sign that he understood her anguish and heartache, she was met only with coldness.

Anger suddenly replaced the hurt. Rising, she went around the table and stood looking down at her father. "And tell me, Dad, what were you doing while Jack was looking elsewhere?"

Shoving his chair back abruptly, he stood up. "Why you impudent little..." His hand reached out and slapped Torry across the mouth. She stared at him numbly. Her hand flew to her face, and the taste of blood made her feel sick.

But not as sick as the expression on her father's face. "Torry...I...didn't mean to do that...I..."

The front screen door slammed. "I'm home," announced Ruth.

George Conway whirled around."Ruth! Why are you back so soon? I thought you were going for a walk?"

"Oh, I felt a little tired today so I decided not to walk very far." A partial truth, since she hadn't slept well the night before, but the real truth of it was that she had a strong feeling she should turn around and come back to the house. Her husband and daughter had not heard her come in. Not meaning to eavesdrop, their shocking conversation stopped her from entering the kitchen. Ruth, heartsick, went over and slammed the screen door to announce her early return.

Pretending not to notice that anything was wrong, or that one side of Torry's lips were red and beginning to swell, she quickly hugged her. "Thank you, darling, for the lovely evening last night. We'll be down again. Come, George, we need to be going." She turned and walked out.

George glanced at his daughter, who was standing at the sink, her back to him. Hesitating a moment, he turned and left.

The moment Torry heard them shut the front door, she gagged, spit out the blood that she'd been holding in, then began sobbing.

Fifteen minutes later, still standing by the sink, the sobbing subsided; now instead, every muscle began shaking. Her legs gave way, and she sank to the floor. Grabbing her knees, she continued to shake. She had no idea how much time had elapsed or when the shaking stopped, but she continued to sit there, unable to focus on anything.

A tapping was coming from somewhere. Wanting to ignore it, she remained huddled up on the floor. More tapping, the back door opened—then she heard a low gentle voice.

"Torry, what...what is it? What is the matter?" David asked as he opened the door wider. No answer came. A stab of fear passed through him and he stepped quickly around, hunkering down to face her.

Her head buried in her arms, she didn't move. The voice was David. Her thoughts reeled. He can't see me like this. Not lifting her head, she said, "Go away, David!"

"Where are your parents, Torry?"

"They've gone home. Please go."

"Look at me, Torry," he commanded gently.

"No."

"Why?"

"I want you to go, David...right now."

"I'm going to pick you up and carry you to your bed, Torry."

"Don't you dare!"

"I will if you don't look at me."

Torry slowly lifted her head. David, shocked and horrified at her swollen lips and red puffy eyes, did not bat an eye.

"Let me help you to a chair, Torry." Taking hold of her upper arms he lifted her gently to a standing position. "Can you walk?"

"Of course," she snapped.

He smiled. "I can see that you're all right." Taking her arm, he led her to a chair. "There you go, Torry my girl."

"I'm not your girl."

David laughed. "Yes, I can definitely see that you're all right."

"Stop saying that. I'm not all right."

"Oh? And what is the matter?"

"I have swollen lips."

"Would you like me to get some ice for your swollen lips?"

"I'll get it," Torry tried to stand up. David pushed her back down.

"No, I'll get it."

"You don't know where anything is."

"Tell me where to find a plastic bag and a dish towel."

Torry pointed to two different drawers and watched him prepare it. Soon she had the ice pack against her lips. She grimaced at the cold and the pain that it produced.

"What are you doing here at this hour, David?" she mumbled under the pack, noticing that it was 10:00 A.M.

"I came by to tell you I'd take care of the chicks so you'd have more free time to spend with your parents."

"Thank you. No need now, so go on to the bank. I'm fine."

David went only as far as the back door, opened it and stood looking out through the screen door, his hands in his pockets jingling coins in concert with his thoughts. He didn't like George Conway, but he certainly didn't expect this of him! Anger swelled up inside him, his fists clenched. He wanted to fire questions at Torry, to find out why. Instead, he remained standing, thinking.

As the cold numbed the pain and soreness, Torry stared at David's back, noticing that he was dressed for the bank in a dark gray suit. Feeling embarrassed that he'd come by and caught her in this condition, she wondered what she could tell him? Why did she have to tell him anything? At least, she thought gratefully, he isn't pressing me with questions.

After twenty minutes had passed, David took the pack from her. "It's time to take it off, Torry. Does it feel any better?"

"Yes, thank you."

"Now," he said smiling, "I'm going to take you to my magic pond."

"You are what?" she asked, sure she hadn't heard correctly.

He repeated it, then added, reaching out his hand, "Come on."

"You're kidding, of course."

"No, I'm not. Let's go," he said, his hand still held out toward her.

"I'm not going anywhere like this."

"No one will see you but me, the water skippers and the pollywogs."

She smiled. "Ouch! it hurts to smile."

"Then you need to smile more often."

"Thanks."

"Come on pard', I want to show you this special place."

"I don't feel like going."

"That's why you need to go."

"Your persistence is wearing me out, David. Let me rinse my face with cold water first."

In the bathroom mirror, Torry examined her lips, deciding that they didn't look so bad. Apparently the ice pack had diminished some of the swelling and at the moment there was no pain. Her concern and embarrassment were over her puffy red eyes. She splashed cold water over her face several times and studied her reflection, finding very little improvement. She sighed, trying not to think about what happened, but as she tried, tears sprang to her eyes. Furious, she blinked them back. Rinsing her face again, she went out to face David.

As they drove out toward the vegetable farms, Torry was silent. After driving some distance past the town proper, David turned off onto a narrower road, passing farm houses now and then on both sides, some large, others small, some neat, some unkempt with junk all around the house and barn. Neat rows of vegetables flourished on the farms, some Torry recognized as corn, and tomatoes.

After a few miles, David turned off on a small dirt road in the middle of an expanse of freshly turned earth. Up ahead she soon saw a small hill that looked like a green oasis of grass and trees, where he pulled off, parking on the grassy area. David got out, removed his suit coat and laid it over the back of the car seat, then came around and opened the door for Torry.

They walked up the knoll together, and Torry noticed the lush stand of green willows and cottonwoods on the top. As they stepped inside the growth, Torry gasped at the small clear pond, surrounded by delicate fern-like plants, wild poppies, and dark green moss. The water sparkled with light where the sun filtered through the leaves of the cottonwoods.

"This is beautiful, David!" she said in subdued tones, "It does look like a magic pond."

"Apparently this is fed by a small spring," he explained.

Torry sat down on the bank feeling peace wash over her.

David loosened his tie, rolled up his shirt sleeves and sat down a couple of feet away from her. He picked up a stone and threw it in the pond watching the ripples, then another and another.

"Why did he strike you, Torry?"

The question disturbed her sense of peace just like David's stones had disrupted the calm surface of the water, bringing back memory of the confrontation with her father. Remembering the things he had revealed about Jack, tears sprang to her eyes. She blinked them away.

"Because I asked for it."

"You didn't deserve that, Torry!"

"I know. I didn't deserve it, but I asked for it."

"That's no excuse for your father's actions."

"I know."

"Has he ever done this before?"

"No, Dad isn't physically abusive...but he's emotionally abusive to me, not to my mother and not to my brother, Bill."

"Why, Torry?" he asked, fighting the urge to reach out to her, to touch her, hold her, comfort her.

Torry was silent, thinking. A few moments passed as David waited for an answer.

"I'm realizing...that I must still have some unresolved anger toward my father. I thought I had worked it out and had gotten over it...but I don't think I have. And I'm sure he's felt it through the years. Besides, we're too much alike. Both of us are too blunt with each other, leading at times to confrontation. And this makes the problem worse."

"That still doesn't give your father reason or a right to strike you."

"I know, but I'm glad it happened..."

David was shocked. "Why?

"Because it has made me realize that I need to repent and work on forgiving my father."

David was silent. He had never heard this from anyone. The Bible taught this, and he believed it even though he wondered many times if he really knew how to put it into practice.

"Have you forgiven your mother, David?"

David was jolted from his thoughts. "How...how did you...what made you ask that?"

"Oh...it just seems there is a sadness in you concerning your mother."

David was astounded. No one had ever guessed this, not even his ex-wife, until circumstances made it necessary for him to tell her. Uneasy that the conversation had turned to him, he stared into the water, feeling even more troubled as he tried to answer the question in his own mind.

Torry watched him, content to wait for an answer. All of a sudden, an overwhelming feeling of gratitude came over her toward him. From the first day she met him until now, David had shown her numerous kindnesses, and he brightened her days with his cheerful constancy. Today, she knew if he hadn't insisted on coming here, she would now be sitting at home wallowing in grief and self pity.

She studied this man, still a stranger in so many ways. Allowing herself for the first time to really notice him, she examined his striking profile. The prominent nose fit nicely with his lips and strong jaw; the dark hair and olive complexion matched his classic Jewish face. His hair, with just enough natural curl to stay in place, accentuated his masculine neck. The breeze, however, tumbled one dark lock upon his handsome forehead, completing, for Torry, a compellingly attractive picture.

Suddenly, his jaw rippled from the abrupt clenching of his teeth. He threw a rock fiercely into the pond.

"David," Torry broke in gently, "I see some water skippers over there." He didn't hear. "You were right, there are water skippers."

"Oh?...Oh yes." David drew in a careful breath, relaxed and smiled.

"Where are the pollywogs?"

"Look carefully, and you'll see them."

Torry bent over and looked. "I see them!" Taking off her shoes and socks she stuck a toe in. "Ooh!" she squealed. "It's cold." Nevertheless, rolling up her jeans, she stepped in and went wading. Putting her hands together, she scooped up a handful of pollywogs, giving David a lopsided smile. "Look! When I was a little girl, pollywogs always intrigued me. They still do."

David was far more intrigued over Torry's childlike enjoyment of them than of the pollywogs themselves. He grinned, as he watched her study them, return them back to the water, wade back to the bank and sit down. She left her feet dangling in the water.

"When did you discover this place, David?"

"About six months ago, but I didn't really take time to enjoy it until you...uh until seven weeks ago," he said, almost divulging that it was at the moment he met her that his appreciation of everything seemed to soar.

"And so whose place are we trespassing upon?"

"Their name is Johnson."

"I take it that it's all right to trespass?"

"Yes, I have their permission."

Torry sighed and swished her feet in the water, wishing this peaceful interlude could last forever. David was wishing the same thing and a comfortable silence settled upon them.

"Hey, David!" A rough male voice came from behind, startling them.

"Oh, hello there, Clive," David said, standing up and shaking his hand.

"I thought that was your car out there," grinned the big ruddy-complexioned farmer, hat in hand, revealing a white forehead and a mop of unruly red hair.

"Clive, I'd like you to meet Mrs. Torry Anderson, my partner in the poultry business. Torry, this is Clive Johnson."

"I'm glad to meet you, ma'am," he said, smiling as he leaned down to shake her hand. "Jesse and Dan have told me about you."

"Glad to meet you too, Mr. Johnson," she mumbled trying to hide her swollen mouth with the other hand. "Thank you for letting us visit your pond."

"My pond? This is David's farm."

"I told her that it was yours, Clive, as it soon will be again if you continue to do as well as you have been."

"Thank you, David. I hope so. I sure do appreciate what you've done for me and my family. Well, I'll be off, just wanted to say hello. Hope to see you again, Mrs. Anderson."

When Torry was sure Clive Johnson was out of ear shot, she squinted her eyes at him. "You said no one would see me but you, the water skippers and the pollywogs."

"Uh-oh, so I did...sorry," he said, sitting beside her.

"And you fibbed again about who owned the farm."

"Not really," David contradicted. "I may own the farm technically, but I consider it Clive's. He inherited the farm from an uncle, but he didn't know much about farming and in addition to that, he and his wife, Madge, didn't know how to manage their money. They borrowed from the bank, but couldn't pay it back. Before the bank could foreclose on him, I bought the farm from them. He has five children and a nice wife. I hated to see him lose his inheritance, so I'm leasing it back to him at a small fee which will be applied to the price of the farm when he's ready to buy it back.

This was on condition that he accept some counseling from Dan and Jesse on how to farm, and some counseling from me on money management. They are learning and doing well on both counts, so I'm sure he's going to get the farm back, so...Miss Torry Ann, I wasn't fibbing."

"Chalk up another one to you, David."

"What do you mean?"

She smiled lopsidedly. "You've earned quite a few 'brownie points.'"

His face brightened. "I have? And how did I earn these points?"

"For one, by helping Clive and Madge Johnson." And, she added to herself, for trying to keep it a secret.

"Oh? Hmmn, it's been plenty hard winning 'brownie points' from you. Now—as much as I hate to, I have to get back to the bank. He pulled out a clean handkerchief. "Hand me a foot, Torry, and I'll dry it for you."

"No thank you, I'll do it," she said, reaching for the hanky.

He pulled it away. "No you don't, it's my handkerchief, hand me your foot."

"My feet are ticklish," she complained.

"I'll be very careful."

"This is not going to rack up another brownie point, David."

He chuckled. "I didn't expect it to. In fact, I suspect you'll dock me a point."

Torry laughed. "Ouch!" her hand flew to her sore mouth, reminding her of the emotional encounter with her father. She had blissfully blotted it out for what seemed to be a suspension of time...a pause that had rejuvenated her soul.

Reluctantly, Torry lifted a foot to David. She felt the tenderness of his touch and watched, with fascination, his attractive, masculine hands as they moved deftly, until both feet were dry.

Chapter Twenty

After David had brought her home, Torry immediately went to work weeding the flower beds, watering them and the lilac plants, the trees and the lawn. All the while, she sang hymns, trying to avoid unhappy thoughts.

However, what she couldn't control, for some reason, were intruding thoughts of David that came now and then, sneaking in at odd moments. But then, why not? she asked herself. The whole yard was David's design, David's gift and David's kindness.

By two o'clock, she felt weak and light headed. Realizing that in her nervousness this morning over the pending talk with her father, she had only eaten a couple of bites of breakfast, and she had forgotten to eat lunch.

After eating a piece of fresh fruit and half a sandwich, she felt better. Restlessness led her to the work room. Sitting on the stool of the drawing table, she began aimlessly sketching, tore off the page and stared at the blank paper.

A peaceful feeling settled over her, and she began sketching the tranquil beauty of David's pond. Before she realized it, she was sketching David. Her hand seemed to have a will of its own, sketching an outline of him sitting on the bank of the pond, shirt sleeves rolled up, tie loosened, arms resting on his knees. Details began to appear: his dark hair, an unruly lock of it falling upon his high forehead, his right hand laying relaxed upon his left arm.

Automatically recording on paper conscious and subconscious memory, his distinctive nose, a slightly thinner upper lip appeared above a full bottom one which she hadn't consciously noticed before. Then came the tenacious jaw and the attractive neck. Her excitement grew as detail after detail came alive; a phenomenon she always experienced when art became true art.

When completed, she stood back and studied it, thrilled at capturing such a true likeness, even down to the half smile that seemed to be ever present, amazed she hadn't consciously noticed that either. Glancing at her watch, she saw that it was late, past time to take care of the chickens.

That night she crawled into bed emotionally and physically exhausted. The minute her eyes closed, she fell into a deep and restless sleep filled with nebulous dreams of working, working, resolving nothing.

She awoke early with a pounding headache, payment for the stress and tension of the last two days. Feeling her lip, she found the swelling down and some of the soreness gone.

She managed to get through the day with the headache, even feeling a perverse gratefulness for it. At least it took her mind off her problems.

Eating an early supper, she showered and put on a cool summer dress. Finally the throbbing pain forced her to take a couple of aspirin and lie down before going out to do the evening chores. At last the headache abated. As she lay there trying to make herself get up and take care of the chickens, she heard the front door open and shut. She jumped up, concerned. Who would be coming in without knocking? To her utter shock, she found her mother standing in the front room—alone, with a small suitcase in her hand.

"Mother! What...what are you doing here? Where's Dad?"

"Your father isn't with me. I drove down from Salt Lake by myself."

Torry shocked, stared at her mother. "You what?!" she exclaimed.

"I know, I can't believe it either. I've never driven this distance alone before."

"How does Dad feel about this?"

"He was very upset, but didn't dare protest too much after what happened."

"Please, Mother, sit down. Can I get you something cold to drink? Even though it's just the first week in June, it's quite warm tonight." Her mother shook her head. Torry sat in the other chair. "Now, tell me, what did you mean when you said... 'after what happened'?"

"When I started on my walk yesterday morning, I felt impressed to come back. You and your father were so intent on your discussion, that you didn't hear me come in. I heard most of it." Ruth Conway choked up. "I saw your mouth where your father struck you..."

"Oh mother! I'm sorry you heard it and saw it. Have you eaten?" Her mother nodded, tears glistening in her eyes. The phone rang, interrupting. "Just a minute, Mother, I'll be right back."

Torry ran into the kitchen. "Hello?"

"Torry, this is David, I'm calling on my car phone because I just drove by and saw your parent's car in the driveway." She heard the concern in his voice.

"It's all right, David, it's just my mother. She drove down by herself because she was concerned about me."

A feeling of relief flooded through David. He didn't know how he would be able to face George Conway and keep his cool. "Look, Torry, why don't you let me take care of the morning and evening chores so that you can relax and visit with your mother?"

"David, you have so much to do at the bank..."

"I want to do it, Torry. Have they been taken care of tonight?"

"No, I've had a headache so I rested until I got over it. I was just going out when Mother came."

"I'll be over and take care of the chickens just as soon as I go home and change my clothes."

"Thank you, David. It would be a great help."

Torry came back and pulled the other chair around closer to her mother and sat down. "That was David. He wants to take care of tonight's chores and tomorrow's so that we can have more time to visit."

"How nice of him." The phone call had given Ruth time to get her emotions under control.

Torry looked into her mother's concerned and sympathetic face. "I'm glad you're here, Mother," she said, feeling like she had many times as a little girl. When hurt, she would hold it in bravely until she saw her mother, then it would all come out in a torrent of tears.

"I'm so sorry for the way your father talked to you, Torry. It's time I take my head out of the sand. I knew there were undercurrents between you and him, but I didn't realize how serious they were. I thought time would take care of the problem, but I see it hasn't. Something has to be done." Tears appeared again in her mother's deep blue eyes. "I can't believe your father hit you."

"I asked for it, Mother. I had no right to insinuate that he had been unfaithful to you. I know he hasn't. He adores you."

"But he sounded so callous and unfeeling when he answered your questions and as he told you of Jack's actions."

"I know. That's what hurt and then I got angry. But...I'm glad he hit me."

"Why?" asked Ruth, horrified.

"Because it knocked some sense into me. I thought that I had taken care of the feelings of resentment, disillusionment and anger that I have felt for Dad...but when I uttered those hateful words to him, I knew I hadn't...not right then, but a little later it came to me."

She gulped back emotion. "Mother, I desperately need to have the Lord's help to find answers concerning Jack, but I feel I have to repent and make amends to Dad first." Unable to hold back any longer, tears rolled down her cheeks. "I need to find answers about Jack. It is such an obstacle to me I can't get past it. I can't get on with my life the way the Lord wants me to. I have even asked the bishop not to give me a calling yet."

Ruth reached over and took her daughter's hand. Relief and gratitude filled her heart, knowing now, at last, the worry she had felt over her daughter, the worry that had become chronic through the years, was over. Torry was going to be all right. In the past, Ruth was unable to get past Torry's fierce independence and private nature, and now...she was opening herself up, ready to accept guidance from the Lord. Now, more humble, Torry could accept help from and through others. It was the way the Lord so often worked, humbling us as we allow it.

"You know," continued Torry, wiping her eyes, "it seems, at the moment anyway, that the two separate problems—Dad and Jack, are entwined with each other."

"What do you mean?"

"You heard what Dad said about Jack feeling that I had usurped his role as head of the house?" Torry's eyes glazed over as her mind went back into the past.

Ruth waited and as she did so, gratitude again filled her heart, gratitude that her daughter was going to confide. This was something Ruth herself needed, but knew that it was now imperative for Torry.

Through the years, she had watched her big, cheerful, happy son-in-law, Jack, change into a glum, dark and moody man. She had tried to talk to Torry about it, but always came up against her daughter's fierce loyalty to her husband. Ruth admired this in her, but because of Torry's cheerful front, to her sons as well as everyone else, she had often wondered with great anxiety if Torry was facing the problem. As a mother, she could do nothing but pray and wait.

Torry interrupted her thoughts, "Mother?"

"Yes, Torry.

"I'll explain. When I was a little girl in Primary, my teachers taught us about family prayer. I remember feeling confused about it because we didn't do it. One day our family started to have family prayer on a daily basis and I was so thrilled that the next week in Primary, I raised my hand and announced proudly to the teacher and class that we were starting to have family prayer now. The teacher seemed surprised and then said how happy she was. A little girl in my class piped up and said, 'we've always had family prayer.' That burst my bubble, but not for long because I was so happy."

Torry noticed tears rolling down her mother's cheeks. She grabbed both of her hands, "Oh mother, I'm so sorry, this is hurting you."

"It doesn't matter, Torry, it has hurt me for years. I'm grateful to talk about it now. We need to talk about it. Please go on."

Torry reflected on this and then agreed. "Yes, we do. I remember...after a while, our family prayers were not regular. I had learned in Primary that we were supposed to have family prayers both night and morning. I was feeling worried about it so I went and talked to Daddy about it early one summer evening."

"I said something like, 'Daddy, we're forgetting to do something very important.'"

"He said, 'What is that my little Torry?' I loved it when he called me that. I remember feeling so proud that I could remind him what I had learned in Primary."

"'We are forgetting to have family prayer every morning and we are supposed to have family prayer every night too.'"

"His smile disappeared and a terrible angry look came over his face. He said, 'Did your mother put you up to this?'"

"'What does 'put-up-to' mean, Daddy?' I think I was starting to cry."

"He said, 'Never mind, Torry Ann, just go out and play.' His voice was cross."

"As I started out the back door, I heard him yell for you. When you came he told you to go into the bedroom with him. I sneaked back to your bedroom door and tried to listen, but all I could hear was Dad's angry voice and you crying."

"Oh Torry," moaned Ruth.

"I ran outside and climbed up into the apple tree and cried. I noticed that we quit having family prayer altogether...and I knew that it was my fault."

"Torry, why didn't you come to me?" cried her mother, this new revelation tearing at her heart. "Why?"

"I didn't want you to know what a terrible thing I had done. And I know you couldn't have dragged it out of me. It is so hard to catch everything that goes on inside a child...and then we find out after they are grown. I just found out something about Jim and Scott that I didn't fully realize. No matter how we try, it happens. Thank you, Mother, for being here, for listening."

"Do go on, Torry. Let's go over everything." Her mind fleetingly reviewed episodes in Torry's life as she was growing up, how she addressed every aspect of a situation and then prayed for understanding. Ruth, inspired by this, learned from her daughter.

"Do you remember when my Primary teacher had to take me out of class and call you because I would start crying for no apparent reason?"

"Yes I do, Torry."

"When anything in the Primary lesson reminded me of family prayer, I would feel so guilty and unhappy that I didn't want to go to Primary anymore...but you always talked me into going back."

"Oh my dear, dear little girl, I should have been more persistent in trying to find out why you were having a problem. The guilt you carried around was terrible." Ruth was now sobbing.

Torry again gripped both her mother's hands in gentle reassurance. "But I got rid of it, Mother. Please don't grieve."

When Ruth got herself under control, she wiped her eyes and asked, "When did you get rid of it?"

"I don't remember exactly, but I do know that you made it possible for me to have a happy childhood. I do remember, however, starting to watch Dad carefully when I was in high school. I knew then that it was Dad's fault we didn't have family prayer.

Dad was never around when we read the scriptures together. Once in a while he happened to be there for family home evening. He wasn't like most of my friend's Dads who all had church callings and did their home teaching. I lost respect for him because the gospel meant so much to me. I know how much the gospel means to you, Mother. How can you respect him?"

"You've asked me this before, Torry, you and Bill both."

"Yes, and you always answered that we need to accept and love Dad as he is. Now, I'm asking you how you've been able to cope with that through the years?"

"The same way you've coped with your grief over Jack."

Torry smiled, "Of course." She studied her mother's beautiful face and saw great weariness there. "There were times when I caught you crying when I was a little girl and when I was a teenager. When I asked you what was the matter, you would quickly wipe away your tears, smile and say, 'Nothing.'"

"Torry, your father still attends church, and I haven't given up hope...but I have made some decisions."

"Can you tell me?"

"Of course," Ruth smiled. "I've gone on the trips around the world as your father wanted me to and I've thoroughly enjoyed our traveling, but I've been telling him for years that I wanted us to go on a mission and work in the temple."

"I know you have...so?"

"I can see, for now, that your father's only interest is golfing and sports...so I've decided to work in the temple on my own. If and when your father has the desire to join me, he can make himself worthy and do so."

Tears filled Torry's eyes. "I'm glad you've decided this, Mother. I know how much it means to you."

Ruth shook her head, "How did we get off on me, Torry, let's get back to you."

Torry looked at her watch. It was 10:00 P.M. David had long ago come and gone and she had not even been aware. "It's late, let's go to bed and finish our discussion tomorrow."

"Yes, let's do that."

They had just finished making up the bed in the work room when Ruth noticed the sketch on Torry's drawing table. She flipped on the light above the table and studied it.

"Torry, this is outstanding work."

"Thank you."

"Did you have him pose for you?"

"No." Torry explained as briefly as she could how it had come about, turned off the table light and kissed her mother good night.

Ruth quickly took off her skirt and blouse, and slipped into an elegant silky nightgown of blue and lavender.

Drawn back to Torry's art work, she turned on the table light and studied it again. Why had she felt relief when Torry told them on the phone about going into business with her banker? She didn't know him or anything about him. Now that she had met him, she felt even greater peace. How strange, she thought, that Torry could sketch him.

Flipping off the table light, she contemplated washing her face, but decided she was too exhausted. Turning off the overhead light, she knelt beside the bed and thanked the Lord for her protection while driving down and then prayed for her daughter.

Chapter Twenty- One

David had just finished the morning chores, and was opening the gate to leave when he saw Ruth sitting on the back steps.

"Ruth! Good morning. It's nice to see you again."

"Thank you. It's nice to see you too. And thank you for doing the chores so Torry could relax.

"It's my pleasure, Ruth," he said, noticing how the blue cotton shirt enhanced her large blue eyes. She wore a white skirt and sandals, silver earrings and a silver chain around her throat. He couldn't remember seeing anyone of her age quite so attractive. Even the lines in her face added to her pleasing appearance. Her dark hair, combed back away from her face, and flipped up in back showing gray streaks at the temple, was very stylish. Everything about her smacked of affluence—but without the air of superiority that emanated from her husband.

"You look very nice this morning," he said, sitting down beside her.

"Thank you again," she replied, smiling.

"And where is my partner?"

"She's still asleep."

David looked at his watch. "It's seven o'clock. What I know of Torry, this is late for her. Is she all right?"

The concern on his face was apparent to Ruth. "I drove down to see how she was, and I can assure you, David, Torry is going to be all right."

David, relieved to hear this, was silent, wanting to ask more, but knew it wouldn't be wise at this time. "How long are you going to be here, Ruth?"

"That depends on how much Torry and I accomplish today. We need to talk some more."

"How fortunate to be able to communicate with each other."

Ruth smiled. "And how rare. I have a very private and independent daughter."

"Do I hear my name being defamed?" came a voice from

behind them. They looked around and saw Torry's head peeking out the door.

"You did," her mother admitted.

"Come on out and join us," David suggested, grinning.

"I can't, I'm still in my pajamas."

"You look mighty good for someone just waking up," he remarked, noticing the hardly rumpled short curls, and it was clear that her lovely sun-tanned face didn't need any makeup.

Torry flushed. "That's why I keep my hair short, so I don't have to comb it when I wake up." She withdrew her head and slammed the door.

"Ouch!" David muttered, glancing over at Ruth, who was smiling.

"How are you two getting along, David?" she asked, still smiling.

"Pretty well, that is, if I walk the tightrope carefully. As you see my foot slipped off just then." Ruth laughed. "And," he continued, "I think that is my cue to leave, and let you two get on with your visit. I'll come again tonight and every night you're here, Ruth."

"Thank you, David."

Torry found her mother starting breakfast as she walked back in the kitchen dressed in white knee length cut-offs and blue knit shirt.

"David left, I see."

"I was tempted to invite him for breakfast," Ruth said, scrutinizing her daughter.

Torry thought about this for a moment. "He gets so tired of restaurant food, and I doubt if he takes time to cook for himself very often...and it's nice of him to do the chores, maybe...No. I'm not going to mother him. I'm glad you didn't invite him."

"Inviting him to breakfast is hardly mothering him, Torry. I would think it would be the gracious thing to do."

"Well, I was never gracious like you, Mother."

"Torry...why are you being testy?"

Torry frowned. "I don't know. I'm sorry."

When breakfast was over, Ruth and Torry sat down in the front room to resume their painful discussion.

"These chairs are comfortable."

"And just big enough for me to curl up in," Torry said, smiling as she did so.

Ruth looked around the room carefully. "I think this is the first time I've had the opportunity to tell you how lovely this room is, Torry. In fact, you've managed to make this little house very homey."

"Thank you, Mother." Torry sighed, "I guess we'd better get on with our talk."

"Start where you want to, Torry."

"I have to continue about Dad because he figured in a decision I made that affected Jack. In my last year in high school, I began to feel that you should have taken over the spiritual leadership of family prayer and let Dad join in or not, as he chose." Torry paused and searched her mother's face for hurt, but saw only concern.

"But, in my college years I began to understand that Dad had an ego to satisfy and that it wouldn't have worked for you to do that. I watched Dad more carefully. He knows the Church is true but that's where it ends. The Church, to him, is a 'social' organization. He has a lot of charm when he chooses, and I watched him turn it on the leadership of the ward, of the stake and on the wealthy or accomplished. I made the decision then not to marry anyone like Dad." Torry stopped, shaking her head, "But that is just what I did."

"In what way do you think they are alike, Torry?"

"In worldliness. Jack's worldliness was different from Dad's. Jack would rather have his boys excel in sports than grow in their testimonies. Of course, this didn't come out for a few years. When I met Jack, as you know, he had just returned from his mission and he served well and he was truly converted, I felt."

"Because of Dad, I made a firm decision when Jack and I decided to get married. I decided to take over the spiritual leadership if my husband would not. Jack and I had this understanding before we were married. He understood how I felt because of the lack in his own home, and he agreed whole-heartedly. He promised me that he wouldn't let male pride be a problem."

"After we were married, because of the traveling his job required, I was forced to take over while he was away. When he returned, I relinquished it while he was home. He did well at first but being gone so much, he got out of the habit and I had to remind him now and then. I could see that sometimes he resented the reminder, so I would discuss it with him and then all was well...so I thought."

"Gradually, however, he began to change. He chose not to take over. I talked with him many times, but each time he became more insistent that I do it all and wouldn't tell me why. I questioned each time how he felt. Did it bother him? What scared me is that it really didn't bother him that I completely took over. He had become totally indifferent. I wanted him to be belligerent, angry, defensive...anything but indifferent."

"Oh Torry! I didn't know. A person is so helpless in the face of indifference."

"That's why I don't believe Jack meant it when he told Dad I had usurped his role as head of the house. He used that to hide the real problem. And yet I worry. Maybe I should have handled it the way you did, Mother. Somehow I failed as a wife, and I need to understand how and why." Tears rolled down her cheeks. "I don't feel guilty because I know I've tried but..."

"And I, Torry, wonder if I should have handled it the way you did. Your brother, Bill, has a strong testimony but because we didn't develop the habit of family prayer in our home, he's had a hard time being consistent with it in his own home. Did we both fail? I don't think so. I prayed about my decision. You did even better, you prayed and talked about it with Jack before you were married. We have both made mistakes, as humans do, but we have tried. Torry, I know you have tried with all your heart and soul to make a success of your marriage."

Torry was sobbing softly. "There's something I haven't told you, Mother. I haven't told the boys. I felt it would be too painful for all of you." Torry continued to sob.

Ruth, alarmed, knelt by her daughter and cradled her. "What, my dear, what is it?"

Some moments went by before Torry could stop. "Jack's death was horrible."

Ruth leaned back and looked into her daughter's face. "What do you mean?"

"After we took him to the hospital and the doctors diagnosed his heart condition as critical, he begged me to take him home. I explained, the doctors explained, the nurses explained that he couldn't be moved. His face twisted out of shape, his eyes filled with terror and he jumped up, yanked the I.V. out of his arm, pulled off the heart monitors and screamed, 'Take me home, Torry. I'll die if I stay here, and I don't want to die!' The nurse and I were help-less. She ran for help. Two male nurses, the doctor and the regular nurse were barely able to push him back down onto the bed. Then he passed out. His heart, of course, took a turn for the worse. The bishop came and stayed with me most of that night. Every time Jack came to, the terror was still there and he'd scream and fight, then pass out. This went on until he died. The bishop said, 'I've never seen a man so afraid to die.'"

Ruth was horrified and distraught over what Torry had gone through alone without any of her family there to support her. She and George had arrived just after Jack died because Torry had informed them too late.

Torry slid off her chair and hugged her mother. "It's a relief to tell someone in the family."

"I'm grateful you told me, Torry."

Mother and Daughter remained huddled on the floor, silent, in each others arms...relief washing over them. Not knowing if any-thing was solved, both experienced the catharsis that comes when loved ones share and carry, for a short while, each other's burdens.

Chapter Twenty-Two

It was eight o'clock Saturday morning when Ruth said good-bye to her daughter. She had called George to tell him approximately when to expect her, feeling grateful for the four hours of driving time, affording her time to think.

Torry stared out the window long after her mother left. It was hot, muggy and oppressive, more like July weather than the end of the first week in June. Not even a hint of breeze came through the open window.

While savoring the aroma of the humid air, she heaved a sigh, feeling the catharsis that two days of merciful unburdening had provided. Like the oppressive air, however, the question still hung heavy. Why had Jack become a stranger?

A sound of thunder far off in the distance compelled Torry to study the skies. A few clouds were starting to gather over the town, bringing with them a feeling of uneasiness rather than the usual euphoria. She hoped that her mother was a jump ahead of the storm. To keep her mind occupied, she sat down to write to the boys and several friends back in Denver.

Two hours later, a clap of thunder startled her. Getting up from the kitchen table, she walked over to the window and watched the rain, feeling sure that her mother had missed it. Sitting back down, she wrote more long procrastinated letters. At noon she ate lunch while waiting for the call from her mother.

~~~~~~~~~~~~~

After a busy morning, David grabbed a sandwich at the drug-store at one o'clock and headed out to the Johnson's farm for another financial counseling session. David felt that this could possibly be the last one because the Johnsons had been teachable and eager for help. As he drove through the rain, he knew Clive and the other farmers were glad for the moisture.

His mind turned to Torry as it had many times today,

wondering how she and her mother were doing. For some reason, he felt a little anxious about her.

~~~~~~~~~~~~~~

Torry continued with the letter writing, looking at her watch every little while. The phone rang.

"Torry, this is Dad. What time did your mother leave?"

"Right at eight o'clock."

"She should have been here an hour ago!"

"Remember, Mother drives slower so five hours isn't too long. She should be driving in any minute."

"Maybe you're right, Torry."

"Call me the minute she arrives, will you?"

Two o'clock came and still no call. At 2:30, Torry wondered if her parents had just forgotten to let her know. She was walking to the phone when it rang again.

"Torry, your mother still hasn't arrived!" She could hear the fear and panic in his voice.

"Maybe she's had some car trouble."

"No. I keep that car in too good a shape. Damnit, Torry, I didn't want her to go, she's not used to driving distances."

"Have you called the Highway Patrol?"

"Yes. They haven't had a report of an accident on the highway from Green Valley."

"That's good news," she said trying to sound cheerful. "You know Mother, Dad; she has a poor sense of direction, she probably made a wrong turn. If she did, she'll soon realize it and call you."

Her father was silent, thinking. "Maybe so. But if we don't hear soon, I'm going to go looking for her."

~~~~~~~~~~~~~~

The session with the Johnson's was not going well. For some reason, David couldn't keep his mind on it. It was usual for Torry to intrude upon his thoughts, but he still felt anxious about her. Glancing at his watch, he noted that it was 2:45. He had a sudden desire to go see Torry right away, even though the session wouldn't be over until 3:00, after which he usually took a few minutes to visit.

"I'm sorry, Madge, Clive, I haven't been able to keep my mind on the matter at hand. There's something that's concerning me. May I postpone this session? I'm afraid I haven't done right by you today."

"You always do right by us, David," Madge said, tears in her eyes.

As David stood up to go, Clive clapped his big hand over David's shoulder and gave it an affectionate squeeze. "You bet you can postpone it. Go take care of your problem, David, and whenever it's convenient with you, we'll meet again."

~~~~~~~~~~~

Torry hung up the phone from her father, fear eating at her insides. Impulsively, she called David at the bank, forgetting it was Saturday.

Torry hung up and dialed his home phone then hung up before it rang. "What am I calling David for?" she asked herself out loud. "What can he do?"

Restlessly, she walked over to the kitchen window and stared out, trying to come up with a logical reason for her mother being so late. What she had told her father could very well be true but... Following her impulse again, she called David at home. She let it ring. No answer. She hung up and again wondered why she was calling him.

The rain was coming down heavier and great claps of thunder sounded, one after the other, the kind of a storm she usually loved. Now it only added to her fear.

"Torry?" a man's voice yelled from the other room.

Startled, Torry ran into the front room and saw David's wet head peeking inside the door.

"David! Come in, you're getting soaked!"

"I rang the bell," he said, stepping in, looking like he had just fallen into his magic pond, "but I guess you didn't hear it because of the thunder."

"Take off your coat and I'll hang it up, maybe it will dry out a little." He took it off and handed it to her. She pulled out a hanger and hung it over the closet door knob.

"What's wrong, Torry," he said, loosening his tie.

Torry stared at him with wide eyes. "How did you know there was something wrong?"

"I was visiting with the Johnsons at their farm, and I had to cut it short because I felt uneasy about you."

Torry was speechless for a moment. "Maybe it's because...because I was trying to reach you."

"What is it, Torry?"

"I don't know."

"Why were you trying to reach me?"

"I don't know."

David laughed, took her arm and led her into the kitchen, "We'll have to sit in here until my pants dry a little. What's wrong, Torry?"

They sat down and Torry told him. He promptly suggested that they call the the Highway Patrol.

Dad's done that. Maybe we could get in the car and go look for her...no we might miss a call...maybe we should call the Sheriff...or..."

"Slow down, Torry."

"But we've got to do something!"

"I feel a little stupid suggesting this, but..."

"Go on, David."

"I'm sure you've done this...never mind."

"What, David? Please tell me."

"You Mormons are quite religious...so I'm sure you've prayed about it."

Torry looked surprised, "Prayed about it?"

"Yeah, you know..." he smiled, pointing upward.

"Yes, I know," she said studying him curiously.

"Well?"

"Uh...I usually do. I don't know why I haven't. Thank you! Uh...shall I...would you like to join me?"

The phone rang. Torry jumped up and grabbed it. "Hello? Mom! Where are you?"

"I'm home, and I'm all right. I took the wrong road."

"Why didn't you call, you scared us to death!"

"I didn't realize that I was going the wrong direction for a long time. When I did, I called your Dad around 11:40 and he wasn't home. I then remembered that he said he would be playing golf all morning, so I didn't try again. I kept thinking that I would be home before you or he would worry. I'm sorry dear, I should have called you, but my mind was full of many things and I..."

"I understand. I'm just grateful you're home safe. But I hope it scared some sense into Dad."

"It scared him, I don't know about the other."

"Thank you, again, Mother, for coming down, it helped."

Torry hung up the phone and sat down smiling with relief. "She took the wrong turn-off."

"I'm glad she's home safe, Torry."

"I got scared, I'm more dependent on her than I realized."

"If I had a mother like her, I would cherish the time I could spend with her."

"What is your mother like?"

"Was. On one of their trips, she and my step father were killed in a small commuter plane in South Africa when I was in my late twenties. I'd already been taking care of our holdings and businesses, so in accordance with my real father's will, I officially took over.

"David," Torry persisted, "I don't want to talk about your businesses, I want you to tell me about your mother."

David stiffened perceptively. "Torry, I don't want to talk about my mother."

"Why?"

"Because...because I want to see my house or...'our' house."

"I don't understand."

"Do we both own this house?"

"Yes."

"Have you ever shown me all the way through?"

"Clever way of getting out of talking about your mother." She gave in, "Come on, and I'll show you."

Torry took him to her bedroom first. His gaze was immediately drawn to the walls, seeing water colors of what appeared to be Jim and Scott as babies, toddlers, children, teenagers and so on.

"This is a regular art gallery. It's beautiful work. Who is the artist?" he asked, scrutinizing the signature. "Why it's you, Torry! I didn't know you could paint." Torry was silent. "Why don't you hang some of these in the front room?"

"I don't want people to know I paint portraits because they sometimes ask me to do portraits for them and I can't. It's very strange, but I literally can't paint or draw people unless I care for them deeply, such as family. It seems that I have a temperamental muse. I have many more paintings, still packed up, of Mother and Father, my grandparents, my brother, Bill, and so on, but there isn't enough room in this house to hang them all.

"I would like to see all of them—but I don't see a picture here of your husband, Torry."

"I have several. I haven't unpacked them."

"That seems a little strange to me," he said, studying her.

She turned away from him. "Come and I'll show you the one and only bathroom, the laundry room and the second bedroom.

"Clever way of getting out of talking about your husband," he mimicked, following her.

Torry smiled but ignored it, pointing to the bathroom, the small laundry room and then stopping at the door of the second bedroom. "This doubles for my work room and a bedroom for the boys when they come home. The couch has a pull-out bed."

"It's nice that you have a place to draw and paint. I see that you have a sketch on the drawing board," he said walking in and looking at it.

Torry gasped, "David, no!" It was too late.

"Why...this...this is a sketch of me!"

Torry flushed with embarrassment. "Oh dear, with all the worry over Mother, I forgot I left that there."

"But...this is a sketch of me," he repeated, trying to understand.

"You've already said that."

"Why...did you sketch me?"

"I don't know."

"But...you said you couldn't paint or draw people unless..."

"I know what I said, David," she interrupted quickly.

"Well?"

"Well what?"

"You know what."

"Let's go into the kitchen, and I'll get us a cup of hot chocolate." She turned to go.

David grabbed her arm, pulled her to him, then with both hands held her shoulders firmly. His eyes searched her face, "Torry, how could you have sketched me if you didn't...uh..."

"I told you, David, I don't know why I sketched you. That was the day you took me to your magic pond. You were so kind when I needed it..." she stopped, her eyes full of dismay.

"You mean you can draw or paint people who are kind to you?"

"No."

"Then?"

"Then nothing...please let me go, David."

"Torry," he said hoarsely, "I care for you deeply."

Torry blinked back tears. "Please, let's go into the front room. I need to tell you something."

David dropped his hands and followed her, a feeling of dread in his heart.

Torry sat down in one of the love seats while David sat in the other one, facing her.

"Okay, out with it, Torry," he said, his voice curt with apprehension.

"There are obstacles, one insurmountable."

"What do you mean?"

"Obstacles that prevent us from getting any closer than mere friendship."

"Name one," he challenged.

Torry was silent—full of conflicting emotions. It was too soon, she wasn't ready for this. Saying a prayer in her heart, she began, "I feel blocked in my emotions, in my relationships until I resolve something in my life."

"Can you tell me about it?"

"I can, but it's best not to, at least not now."

"Best for whom?"

"Best for me."

"Why?"

"Because I don't want to talk about it, like you don't want to talk about any part of your life."

David was silent, contemplating the truth of her statement. "It looks like we're at an impasse—each carrying secrets we don't want to share. When do you think you can resolve things in your life, Torry?"

"I wish I knew. I wish it were today."

"When it's resolved, can we..."

"There are other obstacles."

"Can you tell me about those?" he asked his frustration mounting.

"Yes, but you wouldn't understand."

"Try me!"

"It would be a waste of time until I resolve the first thing."

David's soaring hope at seeing the sketch was now replaced by a feeling close to despair, and his patience was at the breaking point. He got up to walk out, but stopped himself. Instead, he walked to the window and stared out at the downpour of rain. The silence between them became as oppressive as the dark clouds hovering over them.

After a while, Torry said in almost a whisper, "Thank you for coming over again when I needed you, David."

He turned from the window, his eyes burning into hers. "That's just it, Torry, you need me and I need you."

Torry gripped the arm of the small couch, as if trying to keep her equilibrium—because all of a sudden she knew it was true, on her part, at least. Lightning struck nearby, illuminating for a brief moment the room made dim by the cloudy afternoon sky. Window shaking thunder followed, emphasizing the lightning and its illumination—as well as, it seemed, Torry's new awareness of her need for David.

Immediately, she began rationalizing its depth. "Of course I need you, David," she blurted out. "I need your financial backing and I...uh...need your friendship. Everyone needs a friend, especially in time of crisis. What would people do without friends and..." She stopped, realizing she was rambling.

David smiled in spite of the emotions that were gripping him. He walked over to her and took her hands, lifting until she stood up. She tried to extract them, but he held them tightly as he looked into her eyes. "And, how do I need you?"

"You...you told me that you needed a low stress, physical, outdoor business that you could work at how and when you chose."

"I'm not asking why I needed to go into the poultry business. I'm asking how I need you?"

Torry frowned. "Let go, David, I can't think when you're holding my hands."

"That's funny, I can't either."

"How can I answer that question, David Mayer? That is your problem."

David laughed. "It sure is, and is it ever a problem." He let go of her hands, took her face in his hands instead, gazed into her face a moment then kissed her forehead tenderly.

"It's nice to have a friend." He dropped his hands and walked quickly to the small closet, grabbed his still damp suit coat and opened the front door. The rain seemed to escalate while Torry stood staring at him numbly.

"See you later," he said as he stepped out, almost shutting the door on his last words.

"David don't go, it's raining too..." she said to the already shut door.

She walked quickly over to the window nearest the door and watched David run to the car and get in. A jagged bolt of lightning struck, followed by a clap of thunder, punctuating his too-abrupt departure. She stood there long after, her hands tingling from the touch of his hands and remembering the softness of his lips upon her forehead.

Chapter Twenty-Three

The rain lasted for five days, pouring down incessantly. Letting up to sprinkle now and then, the clouds hovered heavy and dark.

David hadn't been over or called during these five bleak and dreary days. An aching loneliness closed in upon Torry, causing a restlessness she had never experienced before. There were many things she needed to do, but found herself unable to stick to one thing long enough to accomplish it.

The rain finally abated for good in the middle of the night. Friday morning dawned, and as Torry stepped outside to go for a morning walk, she was greeted by the glorious smell of rain freshened foliage, marigolds and sweet alyssum.

The bright sunshine was welcome as she went out to do the morning chores. When she opened the chicken coop door, a mass of peeping, healthy looking young chickens surrounded her legs expectantly. She poured in the special feed and checked the water trough, seeing that it needed cleaning out. All of a sudden, the door burst open and there stood her two sons, grinning.

"Jim and Scott! I can't believe my eyes."

"Today is a holiday at school. We got up at four o'clock so we could spend the day with you," Scott said, hugging her.

Jim's arms reached around her next. "Need some help, Mom?"

"Not really, I just have to clean out the water trough a little. It won't take long then we can go in and visit while I fix you a big breakfast."

"Mom, the chickens look big and healthy. Did you lose any?" Jim asked.

"Not one."

"That's unusual isn't it?" asked Scott.

"Yes. Grandmother Thomas' secrets are working. How long can you boys stay?"

"We both have dates tomorrow night, so we have to leave tomorrow early."

Torry led her boys out of the coop toward the house. "I'm glad to hear you both have dates. I want you to tell me about the girls you're taking out while I fix your breakfast."

The boys stopped before going in. "What about this yard, Mom? We thought at first we'd come to the wrong place," Scott said.

Torry explained how it had come about. "Wow!" Jim exclaimed, "It makes this plain little house look attractive. We know you, Mom, and how much happier you are with beauty around you."

As they entered the kitchen, Torry remembered the sketch of David in the bedroom. Not wanting any questions about it she said, "You boys go in and wash up while I take care of something, then I'll begin breakfast."

The day was a wonderful one for Torry. There was time to question her sons about school, girls, their callings in the ward and their possible vocations. They looked at albums, walked to the park and reminisced about their great grandmother and grandfather Thomas, after which she took them to lunch at the drugstore, treating them to a sandwich and malt. The boys were intrigued with the drugstore and asked her to retell stories about grandfather Thomas.

During dinner that evening, they laughed and joked. Torry couldn't remember the last time the three of them felt so relaxed and happy.

They teased their mother as they helped with the dishes, reminding her how they used to get away with things right under her nose. They told humorous stories on each other that their mother didn't know about and retold others she did.

The dishes done, Torry suggested that they finish their visit in the front room, where they settled comfortably on the two small couches.

"How's David?" Jim asked.

"He's very well."

"How's the partnership going?" asked Scott.

"It's doing well, too."

"We both like David," Scott said.

"I'm glad," she said smiling. Her face became serious. "While I have you both here, I would like to tell you something—I'm so sorry about your father."

They glanced at each other. "What do you mean, Mom?" Scott asked.

"I tried to shield you both so that you wouldn't notice or feel it so much, but I've begun to see that I didn't succeed."

"What do you mean?" Jim asked warily.

"That he neglected you both."

They looked at each other, relieved. "Oh." Jim said, "Don't worry about it, we survived it. We're all right. He neglected you too, Mom."

"Yes—I don't know what happened, but your Dad changed through the years and I don't know why. I'm afraid I failed as a wife, and it has affected you." Tears welled up in her eyes. "I'm so sorry."

"You think you failed as a wife because Dad changed?" Scott asked, concerned.

"Yes, and what's hard, is not knowing how I failed. I tried, in every way I could, to find out what was wrong when your father was alive—but he denied that there was anything wrong. Somehow...I failed. I'm sorry," she repeated, still fighting back tears.

"Mom, would you excuse Scott and me a minute. We need to talk about something. We'll be right back."

Torry nodded, puzzled. They went into their bedroom and closed the door. She frowned, wondering.

Her sons returned shortly. They both sat across from her. "Mom," Jim began, "tell us about some good friends you have here in Green Valley."

"What is it, what's wrong?"

"Mom, please answer Jim's question, and we'll tell you," Scott encouraged.

"I have a good friend who lives on the neighboring farm, named Zelda Blackburn. I like Jenny Baker, the wife of David's loan officer, Tom. Why? Why are you asking me this?" Torry asked, feeling more and more apprehensive.

"Because," said Scott, "when we leave we'll feel better knowing you have someone you can talk with if you need to.

"Mom," began Jim, "we didn't know you were blaming yourself for Dad's problem or we would have told you before now."

"We're sorry for not telling you, but we thought we were protecting you," Scott added, his eyes full of regret.

"What? What are you boys talking about?"

"We know what Dad's problem was," Jim said with a heavy voice.

"You what?! You boys know?" Shock was clearly visible on their mother's face.

"Yes," replied Scott. "We hate to tell you, Mom, but we have to now so that you'll have some peace of mind—so you'll quit blaming yourself for something that was not your fault."

"I can't believe you know—but tell me what you think the problem was."

"We don't think, Mom, we know," Jim said firmly.

"Tell me," she whispered, dread growing inside her.

Jim got up and sat down by his mother. Taking hold of her hands he glanced at his brother, took a deep breath and blurted it out.

"Mom, Dad was addicted to pornography."

"No! You're wrong!" she cried, pulling her hands away. "Your dad was very adamant about not going to R-rated movies, and even many PG's. He never attended them and counseled you not to."

"Yes, he did counsel us not to," Jim said. "I suspect that he truly felt almost as strongly about it as you, Mom, but for a different reason."

"A different reason?"

"We need to start at the beginning. Wait until you hear the whole story. Scott is the one who found out first. Tell it, Scott."

"When I was fourteen years old, my English teacher gave our class an assignment to write a fiction story. I decided to write it on an idea from an article I'd seen in one of Dad's sports magazines about a year before. I knew that he kept some old issues in a box down the basement. I found the box. It was taped up securely, which surprised me, but I cut it open and began searching. They weren't in chronological order, so I ended up searching almost to the bottom of the box. I came across two magazines that were different from the rest. They weren't sports magazines." There was a long pause while Scott regained his composure. "They looked like hardcore pornography."

Fear gripped Torry's heart, and she felt the blood drain from her face. The thought of her fourteen-year-old son seeing those magazines sent terror into her heart as two tragedies flashed quickly through her mind.

Scott was twelve and Jim thirteen when she was Young Women president. A teen-age girl finally came to her in tears over being sexually abused by her father. The second instance was now more frightening to Torry. A thirteen-year-old boy had been caught three times sexually abusing three different children before the bishop was informed. The boy had found his father's stash of pornographic magazines and videos and was trying to imitate what he'd seen.

"Scott...did you see..." asked his mother fearfully.

"I saw just barely enough to tell what the magazines were. But even that was terrible. It has taken years to dim the memory of the two pictures. I put the magazines back where they were and went to find Jim."

Jim took over. "I went down to the basement with Scott and when we got there he told me what he'd found. I didn't believe him. He pulled out the magazines and brushed them past my eyes so quickly I really couldn't tell what they were. I tried to grab his arm to really look at them to see if it was true, but he held them behind his back." Jim's eyes filled with tears. "He said that he didn't want my mind polluted. My little brother was protecting me!" All three, mother and sons, wept.

After gaining some control, Jim went on, "If you, Mom, hadn't told us about the boy in the ward and taught us about the danger of pornography, I'm scared to think what could have happened to us."

Scott added, "I'm grateful that you taught us so well. You didn't fail Dad, and you didn't fail us. You set an example for us. The family prayer and scripture study gave us the strength to keep our thoughts in the right place."

He knelt on the floor and hugged his mother, who was now sobbing.

"Why didn't you come to me?" she asked through her tears.

Scott sat back on the couch. "We confronted Dad instead."

Torry was aghast, her tears stopped, "You did? And what did he say?"

"At first he was angry at me for getting into the box, then when

I pulled out the two magazines and showed him, he actually went pale, didn't he Jim?"

"Yes. He grabbed the magazines and said he thought he had gotten rid of all of them. He sat us down and told us that he had indulged in pornography in high school but had repented before he went on his mission. He claimed that he got rid of all the magazines and didn't know how come these were still there. He assured us that he was going to burn those two, and we believed him—because we wanted to."

"He then gave us a lecture," Scott said, "on the dangers of pornography. He made us promise not to tell you, Mom, saying that it wasn't necessary since he had repented. So we promised."

"As the years went by," Jim added, "we saw Dad continue to change. Scott and I began to suspect he was back into pornography. Every now and then we'd go on a searching party, but never found any more."

"Oh good!" their mother exclaimed in relief.

"I'm sorry, Mom, but there's more," Scott said. "Tell her Jim."

"When Scott returned from his mission, before you asked us about moving from Denver, I told him how dark and morose Dad had become before he died. It was hard for him to hear just coming from a mission, but it didn't surprise him. You had given me a key to a small storage unit, Mom, remember?"

"Yes," she whispered as more fear gnawed at her insides.

"You asked me to clear it out for you and decide if there was anything I wanted to keep. Dad had told you that was where he kept some sporting goods that the company had given him. I didn't want to look inside until Scott got home so he could go with me. I was sure of what I would find. I hated to do that to Scott, but I needed him. Well..." he heaved a shuddering sigh, "there were no sporting goods. But—there were boxes and boxes of magazines and videos, all pornography."

"No! NO!" Torry cried, her hands covering her face, "Oh no!"

Scott knelt beside his mother and took hold of one of her hands while Jim continued.

"I'm glad we had the van. We said a prayer for help, and then put all the stuff in the van and headed for the mountains. We found an empty picnic spot where there was a metal incinerator and built a fire in it. We burned and burned and burned. It took most of the day. What hurt the most for some reason, Mom, is that we found those two magazines he said he was going to burn, on top of one of the boxes right out in plain view."

Torry began to sob again, but quickly achieved a measure of control for the sake of her sons. "Go on," she said.

"The eerie thing, Mom," Scott said, "was that we found those two magazines in the back seat when we got home, and we were sure that they were carried to the fire. We had to turn around and go back up to the mountain and burn them. When we got into the car to go home, we used the power of the priesthood to cast out the evil spirits which had attended that stuff."

"Can you see now, Mom," asked Jim, "why we were so eager to move from Denver? And why we didn't want the bedroom furniture that we picked out with Dad?"

"Yes—and how terrible for you both to carry the burden of that promise to your dad, then as you watched him change, to wonder and worry for fear he was indulging again." Torry closed her eyes as the horror of it sunk in. "And—then to carry for over a year the horrible secret—the knowledge of what you discovered...to...to protect me." She covered her face and sobbed.

"It's all right Mom," Scott said, trying to console her.

"Yes, Mom, we're all right," added Jim anxiously.

But their mother wouldn't be consoled—they had to wait—all the while, struggling with their own emotions.

At last Torry's sobs subsided. She looked up and studied both her sons, her heart still breaking and said, "I didn't tell you boys something because I didn't want to upset you, but now I know I need to. Your dad's death was terrible because he was terrified of dying." She told them the whole story.

There was a long silence. Jim finally said, shaking his head, his eyes full of sadness, "That isn't surprising."

"I feel sorry for Dad," Scott said. "I'm so grateful to the Savior for giving His life so that we can repent and not fear death."

For some time, the three of them sat in emotionally charged silence, then Torry ventured, "It's late, we all need to go to bed. But first, let's kneel down and thank Heavenly Father for protecting you from evil, that you were finally able to unburden yourselves tonight and for answering my prayers through you. Could we each offer one?"

Her sons eagerly agreed. The three of them knelt, each taking turns praying, thanking Him for their blessings and for the Savior and His atonement.

Chapter Twenty-Four

Saturday morning, Jim and Scott said good-bye to their mother and left in the car. Out of sight of the house, Jim pulled over to the side of the road.

"What do you think, Scott?"

"Mom seems all right, but you know her, she always hides how she feels."

"Yeah, like she did for years trying to solve the problem of Dad. We never knew."

"I think we'd better ask a friend of hers to look in on her later."

"Me too, but who?"

"You know, it's funny but I keep thinking of David Mayer."

"So do I!" exclaimed Jim. "I guess that settles it. I wonder if he's at the bank this morning." He looked at his watch and saw that it was eight o'clock.

"Let's go look in the bank parking lot and look for his car," suggested Scott.

"Good idea."

David, working at his desk, heard a pounding on the front door of the bank. "Everyone knows the bank doesn't open on Saturday," he muttered, irritated. He tried to ignore it, but the pounding continued. Finally, he jumped up and walked quickly out of his office toward the door. It couldn't be, he thought, as he saw two young men. It was! He opened the door.

"Jim! Scott! I was ready to kick somebody in the rear for pounding on the door on Saturday morning. Come on in!"

"Thanks," they both said, grinning.

David led them into his office and invited them to sit down. When everyone was seated, he smiled at the two boys, not telling them what a lift to his spirits they were.

"It's good to see you two. When did you arrive?"

They told him and explained that they were now on their way back. David felt disappointment. They visited for about twenty minutes and then Jim said, "David, we'd like to ask a favor of you."

"You bet. What can I do for you?"

"Our mother needs a friend right now."

"Your mother?" he asked, thoroughly surprised.

"Yes," replied Jim. "We've just revealed some very shocking and unhappy news to her, and we don't want her to be alone tonight. We were wondering..."

"I'd be glad to go over and be with her. Actually," he said, smiling, "that would be a favor to me."

"She thinks a lot of you," offered Scott.

"How do you know, did she say that?"

"Not exactly, but..."

David laughed. "That's what I thought. But never mind, I'll go over. Can I tell her you asked me to?"

"Sure," Scott said, "but we don't want you to go over before four or five tonight. Mom has to digest the news, think about it and go over it for a while. She hasn't had time to do that yet."

"And," added Jim, "it would be best not to ask her what we told her."

David smiled. "You certainly know your mother. I'll do just as you ask. She's a fortunate woman to have two sons who look after her like you do."

"We're the fortunate ones," Scott said, "to have her as a Mother."

"I agree," David said, emphatically.

After the boys left, David could hardly continue working, wondering what they could have told their mother that was so shocking. The phone rang. His heart leaped, hoping it was Torry.

"David, this is Jenny," the cheery voice said.

David struggled to hide his disappointment. "Jenny, how are you?"

"I'm fine, David. I know this is the last minute, but Tom and I were wondering if you and Torry could come to dinner tonight."

"I would love to Jenny and I know Torry would, but she's kind of under the weather today and I was going over to keep her company. Did you tell Missy you were inviting us?"

"No, I wouldn't dare until we knew. I'm sorry about Torry—I know, I'll drop over a couple of plates of dinner for you and Torry then."

"Oh, does that sound good, Jenny. I know it will lift Torry's spirits, thank you."

"What time do you want it?"

"Whenever it's convenient for you, but I can come and get it."

"No, Missy would have a fit if you just came and went."

David laughed.

~~~~~~~~~~

It all seemed unreal to Torry—as if she had awakened from a nightmare. But—the nightmare was real. This morning when she and the boys ate breakfast together, they visited as if nothing were wrong, each avoiding the subject. All three knew that there was nothing more to accomplish by discussing it any more. With the Lord's help, the healing would come. Now, they needed to put it out of their minds and get on with life.

It was difficult to believe the answer had been under her nose all these years! How could she have not known? Because she did not, her sons had carried a burden that no youth should ever have to carry.

The counsel at conference from the Prophet and many of the Twelve came to mind concerning movies and videos—warning the members against pornography. She recalled the two tragedies in her ward in Denver. Her bishop had called her in to discuss the young girl who came to her about the abuse. After the discussion, he said, "Many wives go with their husbands to movies, totally unaware of how easy it is for a man to become aroused by only one short scene. If they continue to see movie after movie with illicit scenes, the Spirit leaves and sooner than he realizes the man is addicted, or can become so. How foolish these women are!"

During that time, Torry had called a nationally prominent psychologist who, she knew counseled people with this kind of addiction. He said, among many other things, "In the last ten years, child sexual abuse has increased immeasurably because of pornography."

How far had Jack gone? She had learned from the psychologist many of the horrific things that pornography led a man to do. But she couldn't allow herself to dwell on this. There was no way to know and—she didn't want to know.

Instead, she went back over her life with Jack and as she did, so many things fell into place. The first years of their marriage were relatively happy, even though she sensed that his sales job with its long absences each month, were causing him to neglect his family and church duties.

His reaction, when she had urged him to find a job locally, had shocked her. Defensive and angry, he lashed out at her, "I would feel smothered if I had to go to the same place everyday. I couldn't stand it!"

It was then that Torry recognized in Jack a deeply rooted restlessness. When he was home he seemed far from content. When not involved in watching sports on TV or pushing the boys in an athletic direction, he was constantly inventing reasons to get out of the house.

Suddenly, Torry was seized by an intense feeling of anger. Had their whole life together been a lie? she wondered. Had he been into pornography from the beginning? Had he ever truly repented before his mission?

How could she have been so blind! She had ignored and sometimes rationalized the many signs that should have warned her. Interest in his family had declined, replaced by a moody detachment, making him less and less sensitive to her needs, and the needs of his sons.

As their family relationship deteriorated, so too had their personal relationship. There was no longer an expression of love or tenderness in their private times and her refusal to accept this served only to drive them further apart. The changes had occurred so gradually over the years she wasn't able to see them for what they were.

She thought of a story she once heard. The Chinese, she was told, had a unique view of death. It was better to die quickly of a single mortal wound than to suffer the death of a thousand cuts; for no one small cut, or even several small cuts could cause a person to bleed to death. Nevertheless, as each tiny cut added to the scores which had preceded it, life ebbed away more painfully, yet just as surely. That, she could see, was what had occurred in her marriage. A thousand slights, a thousand broken dreams, and it was gone, irretrievably lost.

It was, she thought ruefully, like having a boarder who occasionally took his meals with the family or passed the night under the same roof.

Thinking of the cheerful, happy Jack she had married, she felt a wave of sadness. How difficult it must have been, to be isolated, lonely, estranged from the healing arms of family. How he must have suffered, enslaved by addictions and out of control. But she had given him opportunity after opportunity through the years to open up, to get help. She reflected on how over the last few years she had begged him to go with her to a marriage counselor, then ended up begging him to seek counseling for himself. The bishop had tried to help him, but he angrily refused all help.

"Why, Jack, why? Why did you do this to yourself, to your sons and to me?!" she cried aloud in anguish. But she was through crying. She had cried most of last night and—half their life together.

No wonder the adversary was able to afflict her with a black depression after Jack's death—no wonder evil hovered around her and in their home.

It would take time to feel the relief of knowing, of finding the answer, of solving the unsolvable. All she could feel now was weariness, numbness and loneliness.

She curled up in one of the chairs in the front room and before long, she dozed then fell into the deep forgetfulness of sleep.

Two hours later, a knock on the screen door aroused her. Feeling disorientated, she remained where she was and called out, "Yes?"

David opened the screen door and stepped in. He saw a wan and subdued Torry curled up in a chair. "Hi, how are you?" he asked, softly.

"I'm all right. What are you doing here?"

Squatting down in front of her, he looked into her face. "I came because Jim and Scott asked me to."

"They did?" she asked, trying to focus on what he was telling her.

"May I sit down?" Several moments passed. He wondered if she was going to answer him.

Finally, she managed a small and weary, "Yes."

He sat down. Torry's eyes glazed over, her lids slowly closed and she fell back to sleep. David watched her, feeling concern over this unusual exhaustion. Finally, he got up and went out to do the evening chores.

He had just come in, washed up and walked back into the front room, when he heard Jenny's car drive up. He quietly stepped out and took the plates of food from her, taking them on into the kitchen while Jenny went back for more. Back on the porch Jenny handed him the dessert and salad.

"I can't tell you what this means to me, Jenny, I think Torry needed an angel today."

"I'm glad I could help, David. I'll be checking back with you to see how she is." With that, she ran down the steps to her car.

David arranged the dinner nicely on the table and went in to wake Torry. He knelt down and taking one of her hands he held it. Still she didn't move. Then he pressed her hand to his lips and as he did so, she stirred and slowly awakened.

"David!" she said, pulling her hand away. "What are you doing here?"

"I already told you."

"You did? Oh yes, something about Jim and Scott?"

"Yes, they asked me to come and be with you tonight. They said that they told you something very shocking and distressing and didn't want you to be alone."

She was thoughtful a moment, then murmured, "Bless them."

"But, they said I was not to ask you what it was."

She smiled. "I'm glad they know me."

"However, if you choose to tell me, I'm all ears and I have a very soft shoulder."

"Thank you, but no, and thank you for coming over. I'm fine, you can leave now."

"Oh no. I promised your sons that I would stay all evening," he stated, his eyes twinkling with pleasure.

"What if I want to go to bed?"

"You won't because you're hungry."

"I am? Yes—I think I am."

"Come on, dinner is on the table."

"It is?" Her eyes were wide with surprise.

They walked into the kitchen and Torry saw two plates, each

laden with fried chicken, string beans, mashed potatoes and gravy. In front of each plate was a bowl of fresh fruit salad and a large piece of chocolate cake.

"Oh my! Where did this all come from, David?"

"From Jenny Baker. She invited us to dinner but I told her you weren't feeling well, so she brought it over."

Tears sprang to Torry's eyes. "How could she do all this with her big family? We've got to do something for our friends, David."

"I'm happy to hear the 'we' and 'our' in that statement," he said, smiling as he pulled out the chair for her.

~~~~~~~~~~~

It was 7:00 P.M. Torry and David were sitting, at Torry's request, on the back porch enjoying the summer evening. The warm balmy breeze brought with it the sweet smell of fresh-mown hay from the farm on the north. The whinny of one of Zelda's horses reached their ears and the chirping of crickets surrounded them.

David worried. Torry was more than subdued, the zip seemed to have gone right out of her. He heard her sigh.

"It's been resolved, David."

"What?" asked David, totally taken by surprise.

"You know, that thing in my life..."

"It has...it really has?" She nodded. "How? When?" he asked, incredulous.

"My sons had the answer to it all along, and I didn't know. They told me."

"I see, that's what they meant," he said. "They said it was very shocking and unhappy news."

"It was."

"How are you feeling?"

"You know, like the string on a bow when kept taut too long? I've worked and prayed so long for an answer, and now that I have the answer and it's over, I feel...limp."

"Do you mind a friend propping you up a little?" he asked, putting his arm around her and pulling her shoulder snugly against his chest. To his surprise, she didn't resist.

"Thanks, David," she mumbled, resting her head against his shoulder. "It's all rather heavenly isn't it?"

"What is?" he asked tentatively, hardly daring to hope.

"The smell of the air, the sounds and sights of this summer evening?"

His heart pounding from the thrill of finally holding her, he whispered, "very heavenly." And then he added to himself, especially the company.

Chapter Twenty-Five

All Sunday morning, David worked at the bank catching up. At noon, realizing he was hungry, he locked up and went over to the drugstore for a sandwich. It was closed. He forgot, it was Sunday! In this Mormon community, all the restaurants and stores closed their doors on the Sabbath. He felt irritated to have to go back to his apartment and rummage for something to eat, knowing that his refrigerator was bare.

Back again at the bank after a few crackers, peanut butter and a coke, he proceeded where he left off. At three o'clock he gave up. It had taken much longer than usual to do anything because his mind was elsewhere.

He leaned back in his chair, giving in to the excitement he felt over last night. His relationship with Torry seemed to be progressing, but—was it really? They weren't yet able to confide their past lives to each other and would they ever be able to? Could he? He would be taking a big risk if he revealed his, but—what chance did he and Torry have if he didn't? He had to take that risk! Sweat broke out upon his forehead as he thought about it—as he made the decision to take the chance of laying himself open. He prayed that by exposing himself and some of his past, that it would strengthen their relationship rather than weaken it as he feared.

On Sundays, he always stayed away from Torry's, knowing that she attended church. But feeling a great need to see her today, he decided to break his rule. He locked up and left.

Torry came to the door looking very attractive in a soft red knit shirt, white skirt and white sandals.

"David!" she exclaimed, smiling, "this is a nice surprise."

"It is?" he asked, surprised himself by the greeting.

"Come in."

"Is your church meeting over?" he asked, stepping inside.

"Yes. It starts at 9:00 A.M. and it's over at 12:00."

"Torry?" She gazed up at him. He studied her—stroking her face. "Are you all right today?"

"I'm much better, thank you. I went to bed right after you left at 8:30, just like you suggested. And today after lunch, I had an hour-and-a-half nap. I've never slept so much in my life. Sit down, David," she said, indicating a chair while she curled up in the other one.

"Thank you."

"What brings you over today?"

"You. I was wondering how you were. And I see you're almost yourself. But...there is a second reason I came over, which is equally important."

"And what is that?"

"I'm not in the mood to be careful or diplomatic today, Torry, so I'm going to get right to the point. The first obstacle to us becoming more than friends has been resolved, right?"

Torry silently asked herself if she was anymore ready for this than she was last week. Realizing that though she might not be ready, at least she was now able to think more clearly about her life and future.

"Torry?"

"Oh...yes, you're right."

"Then, since you have indicated that there are several obstacles, can you tell me of another one?"

"Yes. And I too am going to get right to the point."

"Good!"

"Are you Jewish?"

David was somewhat taken back, "Well...that is getting to the point. Yes, I am. I am a full-blooded Jew. Does that matter?"

"Yes, if you don't believe in Christ as the Messiah."

A look of relief came over David's face. "No problem, Torry. He literally saved my life."

Torry was stunned. "Wait—just because you think He may have helped you in some way, doesn't mean you believe that He is..."

"Torry," he interrupted, "I believe that Jesus Christ is the one the Jewish people have been waiting for. He is the promised Messiah—and more than that, He is the Son of God. And I'm glad He's important to you."

Torry was speechless for a moment and then asked, "Did you ever embrace the Jewish faith?"

"No. My parents didn't embrace any of the Jewish traditions that I know of."

"How and when did your faith in Christ come about?" Torry asked, thoroughly intrigued.

"It's a long and involved story, Torry, but here goes. My parents sent me to the Jewish Community Elementary until I was eight then transferred me to a public school. There I met a lot of boys and girls who were Christian, but there was a special one, Paul. We became friends. Remember, I told you that this room looked familiar and realized that it looked like Paul's house?" Torry nodded.

"I remember loving Christmas because I was invited over to his house on Christmas Eve that first year and for the second time, heard the story of the birth of Christ. I was quite taken with it."

"Your parents didn't mind then?"

"They didn't know. They were rarely home."

"Why?"

David hesitated a moment, still feeling reluctant to discuss it. He reminded himself of his decision today and forced himself to go on. "They were very wealthy people and traveled a lot. My real father died when I was two. He had inherited money but, being a brilliant business man, he increased the wealth three fold. My mother remarried a year after his death. She and my step-father spent their lives spending the money entertaining, and traveling around the world."

"Do you have brothers or sisters?"

"No. I soon learned early in life that my mother didn't want any children. I was a total inconvenience to her, so she hired people to take care of me. The help came and went and finally she hired a Swedish woman named Hildi and that was my good fortune. She was a Christian, and she remained with us until I went away to college."

"You...you sound so matter of fact, David. Your parents abandoned you and your tone of voice is as casual as if you were talking about our chicken farm."

"It has taken years to be objective about it, Torry. Sometimes, though, I have this..." his voice trailed off.

"What, David, what do you have?"

"Nothing," he answered abruptly. "Forget it."

Many thoughts were swirling around in Torry's mind—many questions. This man was a total enigma. How can he be the outgoing, warm, concerned man that he is, yet lack so much in his growing up years?

"David—you haven't wanted to talk about your life, so I have many questions."

"I'll answer what I can. Some, I can't right now, like you, Torry. But I hope soon there will to be a time when we both can."

"I would like to know, David, the steps you've taken in your life that have made you the valuable human being you are today."

"A valuable human being?" Embarrassed by the tears that sprang to his eyes, he got up and walked to the window, hands in his pockets, staring out while he regained control.

Still staring out the window he said, "No one has ever called me a valuable human being." Finally he walked back, sat down, leaned over and took Torry's hand in his. "Thank you."

Torry was touched, but managed to say, "Your welcome."

"Have we hurdled this obstacle, Torry."

"Yes." She gently pulled her hand away. "I would like to know more about how you came to believe in Christ and when it happened."

"It's a very long story. How many evenings can you give me? A month, two months?" his eyes were teasing, entreating.

Torry smiled at him, then looked at her watch. "It's after 4:00 and almost time to take care of the chickens. Before we start on that long story, let's get that out of the way. And then may I fix you dinner?"

"You bet! I forgot to prepare for the Green Valley famine that comes every Sunday. All the restaurants and grocery stores are closed."

Two hours later, dinner over and the dishes done, they were again sitting on the back steps, this time at David's request. The meal Torry prepared consisted of garden fresh vegetables and homemade wheat bread, with a dessert of fresh strawberries. David noted how much better he felt after this meal than the one he had for lunch.

"What are you thinking, David?"

"How much healthier I would be if I could entice you to be my cook."

Torry didn't respond.

"And what are you thinking, Torry?"

"That you must eat atrociously at times."

"Like my lunch of peanut butter and crackers and a coke today?" he asked, grinning.

"David! That's terrible and nothing to smile about."

"I smile to keep from crying."

She allowed herself a smile at his rejoinder. "All right, David, the time has come to tell me the long story."

"These steps are too hard to sit on for a long story. Why don't we get more comfortable by putting a blanket on the lawn?"

After they'd settled themselves on the blanket Torry had quickly retrieved from the house, she looked at David, waiting—but all that came forth was a perplexed frown.

"What's the matter, David?"

"I don't know exactly."

"It's probably because you have forgotten how to talk about yourself."

"You're a fine one to be talking."

"I know. But I've had people throughout my life I could talk to when I chose. Did you? Has there been anyone in your life you could talk to about you?"

David became silent, thinking.

"Your wife maybe?"

An expression of sadness came over his face. "Clara was a poor-little-rich-girl. She didn't even know herself. How could she know me or even want to?"

"Was there anyone else?"

"There was Hildi." David smiled remembering. "She was as near like a real mother as I could possibly get. If it hadn't been for her and old Bert, I would have ended up a delinquent. Bert was a little like a father figure. Hildi, a woman in her forties who never had children of her own, took one look at me and claimed me. Why? To this day I don't know."

"By the time she'd come to be the general housekeeper for my mother—and a Nanny of sorts, I was an angry, hardened kid of eight. It was the beginning of my first year in public school. Even though I considered myself 'tough' by then, Hildi managed to intimidate me. She was a formidable, sturdy-built woman with the demeanor of a drill sergeant." David smiled, shaking his head.

"When we were first introduced, we stared at each other, standing in the stance of bull and bull fighter, daring each other. I finally blinked, and she gave me a smile that spread like sunshine clear across her broad face."

"Immediately, she took over the responsibility for me and began interrogating me after school about my friends, my teacher, and my lessons. Somehow, she seemed to find out about everything, including every fight and every visit to the principal. No matter what I told her, she would hug me with such fierceness, I could hardly move. In her Swedish accent she would tell me, 'I love you, Davey boy. One of these days soon, very soon you'll quit getting into fights, you won't have to be sent to the principal, you'll choose good friends to play with and you will do well in school. Ya?' Then she would gaze intently into my eyes and say, 'Do you hear me, Davey boy?' At first I wouldn't answer her, so she'd repeat the whole discourse again and ask, 'Do you hear me, Davey?' I soon learned to say yes very quickly so that I wouldn't have to hear it all over again."

"What an unusual woman," remarked Torry.

"It was Hildi who introduced me to the Bible and first told me about the birth of Christ."

"I had learned to lie before she came to live with us so when she first started questioning me about school, friends and my activities, I lied sometimes. I don't know when she began to suspect that I was lying, but before long she added to the brainwashing discourse, 'soon you will always tell the truth.' One day after school, she read to me out of the Bible about lying. From then on, reading the Bible became a daily routine. I remember squirming, bored to death, but her strong arms held me tightly, lovingly."

"She would say, 'Davey, I wouldn't have to be so fierce if I could have had you since a baby—but now we have to undo some bad habits that you picked up before I got here. Ya? But—that is okay, Davey, we'll undo them won't we?'"

Torry, relieved that David was sharing so much of his life, was deeply touched, "What a dear."

"One day, my mother and stepfather returned from a trip sooner than expected and caught Hildi reading the Bible to me, the New

Testament to be exact." David's face grew pensive. "I'll never forget the expression that came over my mother's face. She grabbed the Bible out of Hildi's hands and threw it clear across the room and screamed, 'If you ever read the New Testament to my son again, you Christian bitch, I'll fire you and you'll never find work again.'"

Torry gasped, horrified, "Oh no!"

David blinked back tears. "Hildi was crushed. The Bible was an old hard-back one that her father had given her when she was a child. It all came apart when Mother threw it." He stopped, lay on his back, his hands under his head. "Actually Mother did me a favor. The Bible all of a sudden became very important to me. When I saw the grief in Hildi's face over the destruction of her precious book, I promised myself that I would earn money and buy her another one." He became silent.

"And did you?"

"Yes. Mother refused to give me an allowance so I asked her if she would pay me to help Bert in the yard or pay me to help clean the house, but she wouldn't. This also turned out to be a favor. When she was gone, I haunted the neighborhood and found odd jobs. I finally earned enough to buy Hildi that Bible."

Torry, wishing that she could hug that little boy of long ago, impulsively leaned down and kissed the grown up boy on the forehead.

David, startled, blurted out, "Wh...what?"

"I...I was just...uh" Torry began, embarrassed over her impulsiveness, "I was just kissing Hildi's little Davey for earning money to buy her another Bible."

David took hold of her arm and pulled her toward him, a gleam in his eyes. "You can't get away with that, Torry."

"David!" she squealed, "No!" Wrenching her arm from his grasp, she jumped up and ran around the corner of the house.

Thoroughly surprised, he sat up, then grinning, got up and started after her. As he rounded the house, he saw Torry about to cross the street. When she saw him running towards her, she squealed and ran across to the sidewalk.

"Torry! Come back here!" he yelled.

He laughed as he crossed the street after her. Loping behind, he allowed some distance to remain between them, curious to see her final destination. When she **slowed** to a walk, he slowed to a walk. When she turned her head to **check** on the distance between them, he **would** walk faster, propelling her to run again.

She turned into the park **and** headed toward some people who were picnicking, stopping a **few** yards away.

When David reached her, he was smiling with amusement. "What **are** you afraid of Torry?" he asked, his chest heaving.

"You know," she said, gasping for breath. "You know very well what I'm afraid of. Just remember you are a respected member of the community, the bank president."

"So?"

"So you must act accordingly in public places."

He laughed. "So that's what this is all about. You feel safe in public because you think I'll keep my distance? Torry Anderson, you are delightful."

"So?"

"So let's go find those lilac bushes."

"Huh?"

"You know, the lilac bushes that flank both sides of your grandmother's lawn."

"What are you up to, David? You know the house, the lawn and the lilacs aren't here anymore."

"Come on, show me," he enticed, ignoring her attempt to be realistic.

Both curious and wary, she allowed herself to be drawn into the game. Glancing around the park to get her bearings, she said, pointing, "They're over there."

"And the lilac bushes on the right are over here?" he asked, moving across the lawn a few yards.

"No, they're further over, Grandmother's lawn is very wide." She walked over to where she guessed they would be. "Here they are," she said, a smirk on her face.

"They've grown quite bushy and tall."

"Yes, it's time Grandfather trimmed them."

"That would be a shame. I think your grandfather should wait a year because there is still some space between them I see," he said, stepping over a few feet.

"I like to play in there. It's one of my favorite things to do," she said grinning.

"Come on into the space with me."

"They're too bushy, David. I'm afraid there's only room for one person."

"I promise there is enough room in here for two. Come on over."

Torry walked over to him. He grabbed her shoulders and kissed her soundly on the lips.

"David!" she gasped, trying to wiggle herself free of his grasp. "What will people think?"

"But they can't see us, we are in between the lilac bushes."

"And I fell into the trap."

"No, I did, Torry...I love you."

She gazed into his eyes a moment, then leaned her forehead upon his chest.

"Oh David."

Putting his hand under her chin, he lifted her face to his, noticing tears at the corners of her eyes. He leaned down and kissed her lips, first with tenderness and the longing of many weeks, then with the hunger of many lonely years, releasing in Torry a torrent of emotions. Before long, her arms reached up around his neck, returning the kiss with an ardor matching his, no longer caring who was in the park. Weren't the lilac bushes hiding them?

Moments later, forcing herself to let go of him, she pulled back, breathless. "But David..."

"There are no more 'buts' between us Torry." Leaning down he kissed her again, and she gave in, holding him tightly, not wanting to ever let him go. Finally the salt from her tears awakened her to the war going on inside. She pulled away.

"I'm sorry, David."

With his finger, he gently wiped the tears from her cheeks. "Sorry my love?" he asked, tears glistening in his own eyes. "Why should you be sorry, you've just given me the most wonderful gift. You have no idea how long I've wanted to kiss you, to hold you, and now to have you return my kiss the way you have—is more than I dared hope..." He choked up, unable to go on. Instead, he kissed her forehead, her eyes and then again her lips.

Emotions enflamed them. Pulling away at the same time, they searched each other's face. Then Torry hugged him tightly, her face against his chest.

"You are truly a special man, David," she murmured.

Abruptly letting go, she turned, walked to the closest park bench and sat down. Following, he sat beside her, reaching for her hand. Giving it to him willingly, she noticed how strong and safe his hand felt.

Birds called to each other as they flew from tree to tree and the warm evening breeze softly rustled the leaves. They sat holding hands, silent for a long time, savoring the magic.

"Finish, David," Torry said, finally.

"What?"

"Finish your story."

"All I can think about is you, Torry, my darling."

She squeezed his hand and looked up at him. "Please."

He heaved a sigh. "I hate to break the spell of this moment, this evening, but here goes. Needless to say, with the help of Hildi, my delinquent ways ended. I quit picking fights, stayed out of the principal's office and got good grades. I remember feeling determined to make Hildi happy, at least until I earned enough for the Bible and then—I realized I was happier."

"Is this when you gained a testimony of Christ?"

"No. The two years in the Jewish Community Elementary, I learned what it meant to be a Jew. I learned of the promised Messiah and the great tribe of Judah. When Hildi came into my life and began reading to me about Christ, explaining in her own way that He was a Jew as well as the promised Messiah, I wanted to believe because I loved her."

"But I didn't really do anything about it all the years she was with us. Right after I left for my first year in college, she took a trip to Sweden and never came back..." David choked back a sudden rush of grief. "She had a heart attack over there and died."

"Oh no!" Torry exclaimed, feeling disappointment and a sense of loss. "I'm sorry David, I wish I could have known her. I wish I could hug her and say, thank you." After a moments pause, she said, "I believe the Lord sent her to you."

"You think so?"

"Yes. I also believe that it was no coincidence that Bert was there too."

"I would like to believe that, Torry."

The sun had set, the stars were out and neither had noticed the change. The lamp lights now gleamed through the darkness, casting shadows of the trees and flowers, transforming the park into another kind of beauty.

David let go of Torry's hand and put his arm around her shoulders, holding her close. Fearing he'd lose her if he told too much about his life before his conversion to Christianity, he passed over his marriage.

"After my divorce from Clara, my life became so unbearable that I pulled out the Bible that Hildi bought me one year for my birthday. I read the Old Testament and found some help and continued reading on through the New Testament, praying all the while for understanding, praying for the first time in years as Hildi taught me. The Bible soon became a lifeline to me. As I read, I came to know Christ. I wanted to believe like Hildi—that He truly was and is the Son of God, and that He is, as Isaiah said, the Redeemer of Israel."

"So, one night I prayed to know. Nothing happened but I kept on praying long into the night, longer than I had ever attempted before. Finally, two scriptures came to mind. The two were Zechariah 9:9 and Matthew 21:5. It became clear to my mind that the King in Zechariah was the same King as in Matthew 21:5! A powerful feeling of peace filled my heart, permeating my whole body—and I knew, without a single doubt, I knew that Jesus was and is the Christ, the promised Messiah. My life turned around after that. From that moment on, I've made it a practice to read the Bible every day."

Torry was silent, filled with amazement—then joy. Not able to express it adequately, she pulled his face down and kissed his lips, conveying to him what she couldn't say in words.

When she drew back, he said, his voice a hoarse whisper, "Thank you."

She smiled and quickly kissed him again. "It's time to go, David."

"I was afraid that time **would** come." He stood, pulled her up and held her close.

"David?"

"What?"

"I can't believe what has **happened** tonight."

Letting her go, he took her hand in his and they began walking slowly through the park. "I can't either. I'm afraid it's all a dream."

"You know when the boys **came** down and a certain issue in my life was taken care of?"

"Yes."

"Well—it not only freed my heart of a heavy burden but at the same time it seemed to have unlocked the floodgates." She paused, shaking her head. "Even though they were unlocked, they apparently weren't yet open...until....until you kissed me, releasing in me emotions that I didn't know were there, emotions that I didn't realize I was holding back. And—I don't quite know what to do about it."

"Torry, you don't need to do anything about it, just accept it, enjoy it and be grateful."

"But...but David, I'm not being fair to you. Nothing can come of this."

He stopped and gripped her shoulders. "Don't say that, Torry! Don't fight me any more. Don't throw any more roadblocks into our path."

She heard the anguish in his voice. The lamplight a few yards away, cast a soft glow upon the pain in his face. His hands dropped from her shoulders. Those wonderful eyes, usually twinkling with humor, kindness and warmth, were now full of anxiety. It tore at her heart. Suddenly—she knew that she loved David! She loved David Mayer, the non-member, the man she could not have. Stung by this knowledge, she could only gaze into his face and mutter, "David, dearest David."

With her heart free of the burden of Jack, she was becoming aware of something else—insights into David. Insights, she realized only subconsciously, now flooded her consciousness. Reaching up, she cupped his face tenderly in her hands and smiled.

"You are the most endearing man I have ever known." Studying his face, she saw the pain begin to disappear.

"Come on." She took hold of his hand and they resumed walking, the moon lighting their path as they left the park. "You endeared yourself to me that first morning in the bank when you tried to keep me from leaving your office."

"I did?"

The inflection in his voice and the total surprise on his face made her laugh. "Yes. And you endeared yourself to me when you appeared on my doorstep with that armful of lilacs." She smiled, remembering, "You endeared yourself when you gave me that ominous look from the top of the bleachers and again after the quartet when you gripped my arm, your expression begging to be rescued." David laughed. "You charmed me when you threatened to put a goat farm next to my chicken farm." They both laughed. "It touched me as you tried to overpay me and when you requested some lilac shoots from Dan and Jesse."

Noticing that David's expression was that of complete incredulity, she smilingly asked, "Shall I go on, David?"

"Yes! I didn't know that I had done so many things right. I had no clue. You didn't give me one, not even the smallest clue, Torry."

"I know. I didn't have a clue either, David. I didn't know you were entwining yourself around my heart, consciously anyway."

"How could you know, Torry, you were too busy fighting me."

She stopped, covering the hand she held with her other one. "David, I'm not fighting you now."

"I hope not, Torry. I'm grateful for what you've told me. It's...an answer to my prayers." He took her in his arms and kissed her. This time the salty tears she tasted were David's.

They walked, both trying to internalize the wonder of what was happening to them. Torry broke the silence.

"You endeared yourself to me, David, as I watched you interact with Zelda, Dan, Jesse and Missy. You totally captivated me when you invited me to go see the water skippers and pollywogs. And I was terribly impressed when you fibbed to me about who owned the pond. Your charming persistence, your patience, your sense of humor and your kindness endeared you to me."

They reached Torry's front lawn, stopped and gazed at each other. David's expression was one of total amazement.

"Have I really heard all this? I can hardly believe my ears."

"Then believe it with **your** heart. Now," she said hesitantly, leading him up the porch steps, "about those obstacles..."

"Torry don't!"

She put her fingers over **his** lips. "Please, David, listen. I didn't put them there. I don't want **them** either, but they are there. Two of them."

"Torry," he said trying to **keep** his voice calm, "we've already hurdled two haven't we?"

"Yes."

"May I remind you that **one** of them didn't really exist. You thought I wasn't a Christian **and** I am—so maybe the other two don't exist."

"I wish that were true, but **they** do."

"Would you mind telling **me** what they are?" he said, his voice sounding cold as he tried to mask the fear.

Ignoring his question, she pleaded, "I need your help, David. I need you to pray along with me that one will be removed, and that together we can surmount the other one. Please David!"

He took hold of her shoulders, fighting the urge to shake her. "How in the deuce can I pray about them if I don't know what they are?" She remained silent as she struggled with her emotions. He dropped his hands and ran down the steps, trying to distance himself from the frustration.

His voice low with apprehension and anger, he asked, "Why can't you tell me what they are?"

"I can tell you," she said, unable to hold back the tears which now streamed down her cheeks, "but...but you wouldn't understand, especially the second one."

He stood there glaring at her in silence. He saw the tears yet made no move to come closer, to comfort her. "I love you, Torry Anderson," he said, then turned and walked quickly toward his car.

When he was almost there, Torry yelled after him, "I love you, David Mayer!" Then ducking into the house, she shut the door quickly and watched him through the window.

He had turned around and was staring at the front door—then she heard a loud, "Yes!"

Torry laughed through her tears.

Chapter Twenty-Six

Henry's wake up call at 4:30 ended at 5:00, then other roosters from every direction took over, their crows wafting in the window with the cool early morning breeze. But it was Torry's own inner clock that awakened her—to a feeling of excitement akin to that of Christmas morning as a child. She lay there marveling. How long had it been since she looked forward to the day?

Sitting up, she took a deep breath of fresh air, stretched, then smiled as she whispered, "David." It really happened. Her feelings for him—her step by step understanding of why she had grown to love him really did unfold last night! It unfolded like a beautiful bud opening its petals to the morning sun.

How long had she loved him? When did it happen? There was no way of knowing, since only three nights ago, she felt emotionally crippled with the thought that she had played a part in her failed marriage, a part she didn't understand. With this gone, insights into David and his endearing ways seemed to flash through her mind in an amazing fashion.

Was David the reason the Lord had directed her to Green Valley? Was he the reason her despondency left so quickly? If so, she marvelled over the wonderful and unique ways Heavenly Father answers prayers. She smiled, savoring the memories of last night and the newness of it all. Then reality set in, bringing with it unsettling thoughts.

"How can it ever work out?" she asked, mumbling an informal prayer. "He's not a member of the Church and even if he did join, would he want to marry me? Could he accept marriage for time only, since I'm sealed to Jack?"

Slipping to her knees, she thanked the Lord for her joy and happiness, pleading with Him to help her understand how it could possibly work out.

Afterward, she got back into bed and opened the scriptures. Soon, she realized she was only reading words, her thoughts kept straying to David. Putting the book back on the nightstand, she got up and dressed quickly for her morning exercise.

While walking, her mind raced, remembering her days at the university when a young man who was a non-member fell for her. She had introduced him to the gospel and after the missionary lessons, he joined the Church. As time passed he could see that she was not returning his love. He promptly left the Church. Heartsick, she promised herself she would never make that same mistake again. Someone else would have to introduce David to the gospel. And she desperately hoped and prayed someone would.

After the morning chores and a light breakfast, she showered. She had just put on clean jeans and shirt and was about to step out the door to pick up a few items from the drugstore, when the phone rang. Running to the kitchen she answered with a breathless "Hello!"

"Hank Chelsey here, from Chelsey Farms."

"Mr. Chelsey, nice to hear from you."

"Just checkin' in, Mrs. Anderson. Two things. How did the chicks do?"

"They did very well. I didn't lose one."

"You didn't?" he asked, surprised. "You must have taken good care of them."

"I'm pleased with the quality of the chicks, I'm sure that had something to do with it also."

"Good! That brings me to the second thing. I need to plan ahead for your next order of chicks, when and how many."

"When is the latest you need to know, I have to talk to my partner."

"A month is all I can wait to reserve chicks for you."

"That will be more than enough time. I'll give you a call."

Torry realized, with excitement, that she had an excuse to drop in at the bank after her errand to the drugstore, and talk to David. "I can't believe this," she muttered to herself, "I'm acting like a love-sick teenager."

Nevertheless, the excitement remained as she walked out the door and headed for the drugstore and bank. In her eagerness, she walked quickly, soon arriving at Main street where she turned the corner. She had almost reached the drugstore when she stopped in mid-stride. There in the middle of the sidewalk, his back to her, stood David and two women, an older woman and the attractive blonde whom she had seen in the drugstore that day.

Quickly stepping close to the building, she ducked into the drugstore. Curiosity compelled her to watch them through the window, focusing particularly on the younger woman. The light, butter-cream silk dress, accentuating her glorious blonde hair would cause any man's head to swivel around and stare. The thought unnerved Torry. She frowned, noticing how close the young woman was standing to David, chattering vivaciously, using her hands, flaunting long delicate fingers with painted and perfectly manicured nails, touching his arm with them now and then in a very intimate manner.

Torry glanced at her own hands—milk-maid hands with short unpainted nails! She couldn't paint with long nails, but at least she could put some polish on them, she thought miserably. Then she looked down at her own attire, groaning as she compared it to the soft silk dress that clung so tantalizingly to the shapely figure of the tall willowy blonde. Here I am, dressed like a farmer again!

She noticed the older woman wasn't talking but smiled as she looked from one to the other, basking, it seemed, in the glow of their conversation. David suddenly threw back his head and laughed, which brought on more animated conversation from the clinging blonde who now had placed her hand possessively inside the crook of his arm. Again he laughed.

Torry turned from the window, thoroughly irritated. He is certainly enjoying himself! Well let him, I don't care. She fumed as she gathered the items she came for, determined not to even glance in the direction of the obnoxious threesome again.

What am I doing? she asked herself. Hadn't David declared his love for her last night? But the niggling doubt continued. Why was she feeling jealous and insecure? Then she realized why. Hadn't she again thrown up obstacles in David's face? And this time he had become angry, something she hadn't seen before. Maybe after he got home last night and thought about it all, he decided he'd had enough—and could she blame him?

When she had paid for her purchases, she walked cautiously to the door and peered out. To her great relief, she saw that the three were no longer there. She stood for a moment, wrestling with herself. Still in a snit, her first impulse was to head home as fast as she could. The second impulse was to go report to her partner the call from Chelsey Farms. The second won out.

She went next door to the bank, and as she stepped inside, her mind was so full of random, disconnected thoughts, she didn't notice the threesome standing a few feet away. Just short of bumping into them, she quickly stepped aside. She was almost past them when a firm hand grabbed her arm.

"Whoa there, Torry, where are you going so fast?" David asked.

Torry's lips tightened as she tried to pull away, but his grip became a vise. Refusing to answer, she just glared at him, thoroughly embarrassed at finding herself in this position.

"I want you to meet some friends of mine, Torry. This is Madge Barber and her daughter, Silvia. Silvia is a new attorney here in town. Silvia and Madge, this is Torry Anderson."

Torry noted with some concern that David omitted the fact that they were partners in the chicken farm business. And she noticed that Silvia's ice blue eyes seemed to be enjoying her obvious discomfort.

"It's nice to meet you," Silvia said in a low smooth voice as cold as the blue eyes. Her mother Madge just stared at Torry in silence.

"It's nice to meet you both," Torry said, forcing a smile, trying to sound sincere for David's sake.

Silvia turned to David and continued the interrupted conversation, conspicuously ignoring Torry's presence. Her sentences ran together, giving David no opening to end it. Torry subtly tried to pull away from David's grasp but with no success.

"David," Silvia went on, "I thoroughly enjoyed our dinner date the other night..." her smile was alluring, intimate. "I had a wonderful time...I'm looking forward to another one soon...this time at my place...did I tell you I specialize in gourmet cooking...I think you said you love Crab Bisque and I've been told my Crab Bisque beats that of the finest restaurants...I remember when I was in New Orleans, the governor invited me along with a small group of his friends to..."

"Silvia," David broke in, "I have an appointment. It has been nice to see you both."

He turned abruptly and propelled Torry toward his office, his hand still holding her fast. Torry glanced back and saw Silvia Barber's mouth open in shock. She didn't have time to look in

Madge's direction, and so was spared her hot resentful gaze.

Inside the office, David closed the door. "Where were you headed in such a hurry, Torry?"

"To transact some business with you."

"Then why were you passing me by?"

Torry stared at her tennis shoes, silent.

"Why, Torry?"

"Because...because every time I run into that blonde and you together, I'm...I'm dressed like this, and she's dressed like she just stepped out of a fashion magazine."

"Every time?"

"Well...both times. Once in the drugstore and today—and it seemed that both times you were thoroughly enjoying her beauty and charms."

David laughed. "Are you serious?"

"Yes, I'm serious. And where did you take her out to dinner, the Hilltop House?"

David scrutinized her, a half smile on his face.

"Well, did you?"

"It was at the Hilltop House but..."

"I have to go, David. My business can wait," she said as she turned to leave.

He grabbed her arm. "You are not leaving, Torry."

"Yes I am, David."

David grinned. "Torry, I believe you're jealous, which gratifies me immensely."

"Jealous?"

"Yes, jealous."

Torry looked down, mortified that it was so obvious.

David crooked his finger under her chin and lifted her face to his. "Torry, my beautiful Torry. Silvia Barber can't hold a candle to you. And she is the one who invited me to the Hilltop House, insisting that it was payment for some business advice I'd given her. She asked me one Saturday night not long ago when I was feeling unbearably lonely for you."

"I feel foolish, David. I was jealous."

David smiled, his eyes melting her. "But—Silvia and her mother were more jealous of you. They were both unforgivably rude."

"Jealous of me?" she asked, in disbelief, looking down at her clothes then up at him. "How in the world could you know that?"

"When a man is single and wealthy, he has a plethora of women throwing themselves at him—and he learns by experience. Come, sit down and tell me what you wanted to see me about."

Torry sat down in one of the chairs in front of the desk and David sat in his chair behind it.

"Chelsey Farms called today and said that we need to let them know within a month how many chicks we'll need for our next order."

"You are the expert, Torry. How many do you want to order this time?"

"The coop can handle more, but maybe we had better not get more than one hundred and fifty again until we get the chicken tasting like it should. We need to look for some property outside of town so we can raise layers if we need to. In either case, we won't make money until we expand."

"You're right, but do you really want to work that hard, Torry?"

"Isn't that what we planned, David? This will be my living and the only way you'll make a profit on your investment."

"Why are you sitting on the other side of the desk, Torry? Remember when you pulled your chair around and faced me straight on?" he asked, grinning.

Torry pulled a little face. "I uh...think I need the protection of the desk between us, Mr. Mayer."

"No fair, Torry." Jumping up, he walked around and pulled her and the chair around the desk, facing his own chair as Torry herself had done two months ago.

"David, no!" she protested.

Ignoring her protests, he sat down taking both her hands in his. "Do you realize that you have on the same red and white shirt and faded jeans that you had when you first walked into this office—even down to the little red belt? I'll never forget that moment, for it was at that moment my life changed. Did last night really happen, Torry?"

His hands feeling so safe, warm and strong enfolding hers, broke down the rest of the flimsy barrier she had put up when she saw him with Silvia Barber. "I'm not sure, David if last night really did happen. It seems like a beautiful dream."

"Speaking of dreams," David said, "Was I dreaming, or did I hear you say that..."

"I love you? Yes, David, you heard right. "I love you.""

"It is real then! I woke up this morning and wondered if I heard you right. My beautiful Torry, I love you! I've loved you from the moment I saw you standing in the doorway of my office. How it could happen so quickly, I don't know. I've never believed in love at first sight—but it happened to me. And as I've come to know you, my love has grown until I am about to burst with it—Torry, my darling, will you marry me?"

"Oh David!" Torry sucked in her breath. Her heart pounding against her chest, she looked down at her hands clenching his. For a moment there was silence. Then her head came up to meet his gaze. She let out an involuntary cry, "David how I want to!"

"Then, let's get married—soon!"

Their eyes locked, each silently pleading with the other.

"Did you do as I requested David?" she asked tentatively.

"Yes I did, I prayed for the imaginary obstacles to disappear— and you know what?" he said, grinning, "they have."

"Be serious, David."

"I am serious, my darling. Our love can conquer all obstacles— with God's help."

The sound of the buzzer on his desk intercom was a jarring intrusion.

While David answered, Torry struggled with her feelings. Oh, how she wanted him to be right. She prayed that he was.

"Darn!" David muttered, taking Torry's hands again. "I have an appointment. Can we talk tonight?"

"Yes, come for dinner—as early as you can, David."

"Thank you, my darling. See you tonight." He reluctantly let go of her hands and she, just as reluctantly, got up and walked out of his office.

Chapter Twenty-Seven

Just as David reached the landing of Torry's porch, a whiff of freshly baked bread came through the screen door. Before he could knock, Torry was there opening the door for him.

Her smile and the expression in her eyes sent David's pulse racing.

"Hi," she said softly.

His breath caught. "You are the loveliest thing I've seen since this morning." Her hot pink blouse matched the rosy flush of her cheeks.

"You mean, this morning when you saw Silvia Barber?" she teased.

"Who's Silvia Barber?" he asked, his eyes twinkling as he took her in his arms and kissed her forehead.

"I forget," she said. Then pulling away, she took his hand and led him into the kitchen.

He immediately noticed the four loaves of bread cooling on a rack. "Mmmm, I smelled those as I stepped up onto the porch. I'm starving." Then he saw the kitchen table covered with a rose colored table cloth, set with white plates and crystal glasses. In the center was a small center piece of freshly cut flowers. "How nice Torry. Are we celebrating something?"

"Yes," she said smiling up at him. "I'm celebrating last night and this morning."

"Oh my darling, thank you," he said taking her hands in his. "I'm celebrating too. I'm celebrating that first meeting in my office—including the moment you lifted that lilac to your nose," he smiled, "and then slammed it down on my desk, leaving it there."

"I'm celebrating everything we've done together since then." He shook his head in wonder. "Even the rough times, the frustration, everything. I'm celebrating meeting your sons, who I wish were my own—and your mother."

"I'm celebrating how you've inspired me to be a better person. I hope I deserve you, Torry."

"David, dear David," tears glistening in her eyes, she pulled his face down to hers and kissed him tenderly.

He put his arms around her and returned her kiss, then lifting his head, he searched her face longingly, expectantly, looking for the answer he had waited for so long. Willing her to say the words, he waited. When Torry's eyes slid away, he felt a stab of disappointment and frustration. He pulled her roughly to him, kissing her, unleashing a tide of pent up passion.

The fire in his lips caused a stirring inside of Torry, a growing warmth, a sudden rush of passion overtaking her. A warning bell sounded inside her. With every ounce of will power, she pulled back and pushed him away.

She said in a rush of breath, "We have to be careful, David."

"Why Torry? he asked hoarsely, his breathing heavy, "We love each other."

She answered almost inaudibly. "You read the Bible, David, you know why."

"But these are different times, Torry."

She gazed up at him, shocked. "You don't really believe that. You're rationalizing, David."

He turned from her, walked to the back door and stared out the window, furiously jingling the coins in his pocket. Torry sat down at the table and waited. After a while, he turned around, the grief plain in his eyes. "You're right, Torry. It's just that...I've really screwed up haven't I? I know your standards. I'm sorry, Torry."

"Come and sit down, David."

After he had seated himself, Torry pulled her chair close to him. Taking his hand in both hers, she said, "David, we're two lonely people who are in love. It was a natural thing to happen. The important thing is that we stopped."

"You stopped. I didn't want to."

"I know...it's because...it's one of the obstacles I was talking about."

David pulled his hand away. "You're talking in riddles again, Torry. I'm tired of you dodging the question whenever I ask you what in the devil these so-called barriers are!"

The phone rang, jarring Torry as much as had David's anger. "You're angry, David." The phone rang insistently.

"Answer the phone, Torry," he said coldly, standing up abruptly and walking back to the window.

She stared at a David she didn't know. She numbly got up and walked to the phone.

"Hello?....Dad?....What....what did you say?....Mom? Oh no Dad, no!" Her face turned pale.

David, still trying to get his emotions under control only felt irritation at the interruption.

"She's got to make it, Dad, we all need her, the boys need her....The boys?....They're coming here to pick me up tonight?....That wasn't necessary Dad....Oh, maybe you're right, I haven't driven distances at night before....We have to have faith that she'll be all right, Dad....Yes, I will....Take care of yourself, see you soon, good-bye."

Ashamed of his feelings of irritation, David forced himself to focus on the unsettling phone call. "What is it, Torry?"

"Mom is in the hospital. She's hemorrhaging. They've taken a biopsy of a tumor in her uterus and found it cancerous. They haven't been able to stop the bleeding. When they get it stopped, they'll operate. They think it will be in the morning."

Seeing the fear and grief on Torry's face, David's heart softened. He stepped over to her, his hands cupping her shoulders. "I'm sorry, Torry."

"Thank you," she said, twisting out of his hands and walking to the pot of vegetable soup on the stove and stirring it.

"What's happening to us, Torry?"

"Maybe we don't really know each other, David."

"Of course we don't. You've avoided my questions, and we have each avoided sharing things about ourselves."

Sounds of running feet came through the screen door. Then they heard a voice. "Mmmm, smell that bread, Scott." The screen door slammed, and the two boys bounded into the kitchen.

"Scott, Jim!" exclaimed Torry hugging each one.

"Did Grandfather call you?" Scott asked. At her nod he continued, "Are you all right, Mom?"

"Yes, I'm all right," she said, blinking back the tears that his solicitude brought to the surface.

"We know you're scared, Mom. We are too," Jim said.

Torry smiled through her tears, "Thank you, Jim."

"David!" Scott exclaimed. "I'm glad you're here. It's good to see you again." He shook his hand heartily.

"I'm sorry about your grandmother."

"Thanks," Jim said. "I'm also glad you're here."

"Thank you, Jim." The sincerity of the boys' affection toward him was a balm to his aching heart.

"If you want to freshen up boys," their mother said, "dinner is ready."

For the first time the boys noticed the table. Scott was the first to speak. "It looks like we've interrupted something special."

"It sure does. Sorry, David and Mom. It looks like you'll have to postpone it until after you get back. Well, come on Scott, let's go wash up."

Torry set two more plates and bowls on the table.

"I'm not staying for dinner, Torry. You three need to be alone."

"We'll be alone four hours back to Salt Lake. I want you to stay, David."

"Are you sure?"

"Yes."

"I'll take care of the chickens while you're away."

"I forgot about the chickens! What if you need to leave town? I know—Ivan and Gilford can help. All you have to do is show them how. Zelda said that Gilford is quite taken with the idea of chicken farming. I think he'd like to learn."

"All right, I'll do that."

The boys walked back into the kitchen. "Boy does that bread look good, Mom!" exclaimed Jim.

"Before we sit down, may we have a prayer for Grandmother?" requested Torry. The boys immediately knelt by their chairs. "David, would you like to join us?"

"Yes, I would, thank you."

"Jim, would you say it?"

"Yes, thank you, Mom."

For a moment it seemed to be deja vu for David. This felt familiar. Jim's prayer was sincere, humble and filled with emotion as he prayed for their grandmother and mother. Suddenly a flash of memory came into his mind. He was a little boy kneeling with...with his friend Paul and Paul's family—remembering the familiar aching as he longed to have a family like this, even wanting to belong to this happy, loving family—wanting it so badly it hurt—the hurt beginning in his chest. His fists clenched as the wrenching pain moved down into his gut.

As the prayer ended, everyone stood up except David who remained kneeling, his head bowed. Torry noticed the clenched fists and beads of perspiration on his brow. Motioning silently for the boys to kneel back down again, Torry knelt beside David, taking one of his fists in her hands. She pried it open and placed her hand in his, holding it tightly while whispering, "I love you, David."

Somewhere far off, someone was taking him by the hand and pulling him back out of a pain filled world. His mind cleared. It was Torry!

Seeing that he was now aware, she let go and stood up. The boys, taking the cue, also stood. David followed.

"Thank you, Jim." Torry said putting on a cheerful face, "All of you be seated, and I'll dish out the soup and cut the bread."

Jim clapped his hands together, "Great, Mom, we're starving."

David, mortified over his attack, looked at each one. It didn't appear that they had noticed—but why was Torry holding his hand? She wasn't before the prayer. Maybe she had just reached over and taken his hand, and he hadn't noticed. He relaxed somewhat, but agonized over why it had happened. Both times it had come on while here with Torry and the boys! Why?

"David," Torry said, "I have a refrigerator full of food and all this bread. Would you do me a favor and eat here so it won't go to waste? I'm sure your refrigerator isn't as full."

"My refrigerator is empty. I'd like to eat here Torry—but I'll miss you not being here," he said cheerfully, trying to mask the deep loneliness that had suddenly descended upon him.

In spite of the concern over their grandmother, the boys enjoyed the meal immensely, and now were exclaiming over the fresh peach cobbler with the rich, thick cream, courtesy of Zelda's Jersey cow.

When he was finished, David excused himself. "Thank you for the delicious meal, Torry. I'm going to leave now so that you can get your packing done, and so the boys will feel free to do the dishes." The boys laughed and said their good-byes.

"I'll walk you to your car, David."

"Thank you, Torry."

Standing by the car, they gazed at each other. It was seven o'clock and still light. A lone Meadowlark's song from the pasture, a symbol of their time together here in Green valley, now seemed to remind them of their forthcoming separation. Neither knew what to say—each burdened by their own private griefs.

Finally David said, "I'll be praying for your mother, Torry."

"Thank you, David."

"How long do you think you'll be gone?"

"I have no way of knowing at this point, I'll call you."

"Good, thank you."

The rift which had been created between them became more apparent, more uncomfortable. It hurt Torry to see David without the twinkle in his eyes and the half smile on his lips that, over any excuse, turned into a heart melting smile. She desperately wanted to tell him that it would all work out, but knew there was no way she could. They stared at each other, motionless, then David took Torry's hand and kissed it.

"I'll be seeing you soon, I hope," he said, letting go of her hand and opening the car door.

Torry watched him get in, start the car and drive off. A devastating feeling of loss engulfed her. "Dear God, help me. Help David. Help us."

Chapter Twenty-Eight

David drove straight to his apartment but couldn't make himself go into the emptiness. He sat in the car thinking about his attack, finally facing the full implication of it. He thought the first one was just an aberration, but now he knew it wasn't.

There was no way he could marry Torry if this was going to become a pattern. He couldn't inflict on Torry what he had put Clara through! Overwhelmed with grief, he sat—staring at the windshield.

Thirty minutes later leaning his head upon hands that gripped the top of the steering wheel, he began to pray. "Dear God, help me...help me..." was all he could utter. He left it to his God—the God of Abraham, Isaac and Jacob—to fill in the blanks.

Still unable to go up to his empty apartment, he backed the car out, and began driving aimlessly.

~~~~~~~~~~

All three were in the wide front seat of George Conway's old Lincoln that he had given his grandsons. Torry was in the middle and Jim was driving. They rode together in silence for several miles, then Jim spoke.

"Mom, you know when David remained on his knees after the prayer, he seemed to be suffering over something. Do you know what it was?"

"No I don't."

"Maybe it was the combination of grandmother's crisis and you leaving," suggested Scott. "Apparently something is going on between you and David."

"Yeah, we heard you whisper that you loved him, Mom."

It all happened so recently, Torry hadn't even had time to wonder how her sons would feel about her and David. "I do love him. He's been so kind to me, so wonderful..." her voice caught with emotion.

Scott squeezed her hand. "We're glad he's been there for you, Mom. It's kind of taken a load off our minds."

"I want you both to know that I didn't realize how I felt about David until last night. Not knowing what was wrong with your father made it impossible to know my own feelings. He's Jewish you know," she stated abruptly.

Jim frowned. "Does that mean he doesn't believe in Christ, Mom?"

"It's kind of a long story, but some time ago, he studied and prayed and gained a strong testimony of Christ."

"Wow! That's unusual. Tell us this long story."

"I would rather he tell you and Scott, if he will." She hesitated a moment then said slowly, "This morning, he asked me to marry him."

The boys glanced at each other and turned silent. Torry waited for their reaction. Finally Jim spoke.

"We knew something was up."

Scott's face was one of concern. "Did...did you accept, Mom?"

"I haven't given him an answer yet, because as you know, he isn't a member of the Church."

Scott let out a breath of relief. "Good. If you marry again, Mom, it should be to a member. You wouldn't be happy otherwise."

"If he believes in Christ, he may accept it," Jim said, thinking aloud. "Has anyone approached him about it?"

"I don't believe so, and of course, I can't." She then reminded them of her experience in college. "But the real question at the moment is—how do you both feel about me marrying David if he does accept the gospel?"

~~~~~~~~~~~~

David found himself in front of Tom Baker's house. Turning off the motor, he listened to the happy shouts and laughter of neighborhood children, still outside playing. He studied Tom's humble home, envying it because it housed a family, a loving close knit family—something he never had but still longed for.

Why was he here? he asked himself. He knew, of course. He desperately needed to talk to someone. But, how could he tell Tom everything? He felt uneasy and a little embarrassed at the thought of inflicting his grief upon this happy family. He started up the car and was about to drive off when he heard Tom's voice.

"Dave, hold up!"

He saw Tom through his side view mirror, running towards him on the sidewalk. He turned off the motor and waited.

Tom stuck his head down and looked at David through the open window. "Why are you driving off without even ringing the doorbell? Jenny's home. I had just gone over to the neighbor's house a minute."

"Well I uh..."

"Where's Torry? I thought you two might be together tonight from the way Torry looked as she left your office this morning."

"We were."

"Oh?"

"She got a call from her father. Her mother is having an emergency surgery in the morning so he sent her sons down to pick her up. They're on their way to Salt Lake right now."

"I'm sorry to hear that, Dave. Why don't you get out of the car, and let's sit here on the lawn and talk a while."

"Thanks, Tom," David said gratefully. "I think I need some company—I miss Torry."

David got out of the car and both men sat down on the lawn.

Tom, sensing that David wanted more than small talk, said, "I have a feeling there's something else bothering you besides missing Torry."

Startled, David looked at Tom. "How did you know? You're right."

"I feel I need to be frank, Dave...are you in love with Torry?"

"I guess I need to be frank too, Tom. The answer is an emphatic yes."

"Have you told her?"

"Yes, yesterday, and I blurted out a proposal this morning."

"And?"

"And all she could do is bring up these damnable barriers she's referred to over and over."

"Does she love you?"

"I can hardly believe it, Tom, but she said she did—last night and again today. You know that first day when you sent her in to see me?"

Tom laughed. "Do I! I can't handle a customer so I send her in to the president of the bank, and what happens?"

Both men laughed, then David became serious. "I owe you one, Tom, for sending her in that day. My life turned around from that moment. But it has been quite a challenge. She's had a pretty high wall built up around herself."

"So what's the matter, Dave?"

"Her obstacles and mine."

"Are you going to discuss them?"

"I'm feeling that when she really knows me, I won't stand a chance."

"I'm wondering if you aren't underestimating Torry."

"I hope you're right...but I don't know..."

"Hey Dave, I have something that will take your mind off your troubles for ten minutes."

"Oh?"

"Yeah, some homemade ice cream and cookies."

David's eyes lit up. "That sounds great. I had dinner at Torry's but my appetite wasn't up to par then. Somehow it has improved," he said grinning.

Upon entering the front door, Tom yelled, "Jenny, I have a surprise for you!"

Jenny came into the front room, wiping her hands on a dish towel. "David! What a nice surprise," she exclaimed, a glowing smile on her face.

David knew he'd come to the right place. His spirits were lifted by Tom and now seeing Jenny's genuine delight over his uninvited presence, they rose even higher. "It's good to see you too, Jenny."

"I invited Dave in for some ice cream. I think there is enough left for three bowls isn't there?"

"Just barely, Tom, just barely," she said, laughing. "The kids dived in pretty heavy. Come on into the kitchen, David, and sit down."

~~~~~~~~~~~

The question remained suspended in the silence that followed, neither boy answering. Torry waited—wondering what she would do if they were against the idea.

At last her oldest spoke. "Mom, the moment I met David, I liked him—but it was more than that—it's hard to describe. I kinda felt a kinship with him, almost like I'd known him before. I felt comfortable with him from the beginning."

"About you marrying him, I don't know. It has already crossed my mind several times, but I'm not quite used to the idea. A part of me wants you to be happy and another part is selfish, not wanting to share you with anyone yet. All three of us have just been relieved of the millstone we've been carrying all these years, and I guess I just want to enjoy our relationship without it for a while—or see what it would be like without it."

Torry choked up with hurt for Jim. Of course he'd want that! When she regained control of herself, she said, "Yes, we three need to have time to enjoy each other without that burden. Now, how about you, Scott, how do you feel?"

"I feel like you and Jim. We need to know what it's going be like without anything hanging over us," Scott began, "but I like David. In fact, I like to be around him so much I find myself wishing I could be around him more. I've missed having a father. Dad never really could relate to me because I didn't enjoy sports to the extent he wanted me to. I feel David relates to both Jim and me. I'm not quite used to the idea of sharing you either, but I feel you've been lonely all your married life, Mom, and I know you wouldn't be lonely with David."

Chapter Twenty-Nine

David and Tom sat down at the large, round oak table. The Lazy Susan in the middle, usually laden with food when David ate there, was now piled high with what looked like Bibles. Jenny cleared off the empty bowls and wiped up the melted droplets of ice cream and cookie crumbs.

"It's mighty quiet around here," remarked David.

"Yes," smiled Tom, "a rare moment in our household."

"Where are all the children?"

"Josh is showing off his driving skills to his older sister, Elizabeth. Sam and Jake coerced Rebecca and Rachael into going to the school yard to play a little baseball. Of course, Missy wanted to play ball, too."

"So why homemade ice cream? Did I miss someone's birthday?"

"No," replied Jenny. "It's just a family home evening dessert. It was Elizabeth's turn to make the dessert, and hers are always elaborate and time consuming."

"Family home evening? It seems I've heard you mention that before. What is it?"

Jenny placed a bowl of strawberry ice cream in front of David and a plate of sugar cookies.

"It's a night the Church designates for families to spend time together," explained Tom, "a night when nothing else takes precedence. Of course, not every family can have it on a Monday night because of their schedules, so some families choose another night."

"What do you do on this family night?"

"We usually have lessons. We and the children take turns giving the lesson, conducting, leading the singing and being in charge of the dessert. Once in a great while we will have an activity instead of a lesson."

Jenny sat down after placing a bowl of ice cream in front of Tom and herself. "We usually eat the dessert with the children and join with them in their activities on a family night, but tonight, Tom and I wanted to eat our ice cream in peace and quiet. We're glad we waited so we could enjoy it with you, David."

"Me too, Jenny. This is delicious ice cream. So are the cookies."

"You can thank Elizabeth," Jenny said, smiling. She made it all. However, she did enlist Josh's help in turning the handle of the ice cream freezer."

"This is all quite amazing and impressive. Every family should do this."

"I agree, David," Jenny said. "Where is Torry this evening?"

David explained.

"I'm so sorry to hear that. Let us know how her mother gets along."

"I will, Jenny."

As they finished their ice cream, David became more curious about the books in the middle. "Most people have food on the Lazy Susan, but you have Bibles?" he teased.

"Yes, along with some modern-day scripture," Tom said, eager to clarify.

"Modern-day scripture?"

"Yes, this book," said Tom, holding it up then laying it on the table in front of David. It was brought forth by the hand of the Lord and published in 1829."

David looked at the title. The Book of Mormon. "Yes, I've heard of this book. This is why you are called Mormons?"

"Yes."

Picking up the book, he looked at it more closely—reading the smaller print under the title. He read it again slowly, out loud.

"Another Testament of Christ." Something inside David came alive. "What does that mean exactly?"

"Dave, you are of Jewish descent and most Jews don't believe in Christ, so before I answer your question, I need to know if this is your belief also?"

"No, Tom, I know he is the promised Messiah in the full sense of that title. The Jews historically do not believe that the Messiah to come will be the Son of God, but will be, as Isaac Lesser said in his History of the Jews and Their Religion, 'a man eminently endowed, like Moses and the prophets in the days of the Bible.' However, I believe that Jesus Christ, the Messiah, is the Son of God."

Tom and Jenny were speechless for a moment, then Tom spoke.

"We're thrilled to hear this, Dave. Have you always believed this?"

"No." David contemplated sharing this very personal and sacred experience. He had never shared it with anyone except Torry, but as he studied the faces of these dear friends, he found himself wanting to tell them. "When I was a young boy," he began, "I learned how to pray from my mother's housekeeper, Hildi, and from my friend Paul's family. Hildi also introduced me to the New Testament."

"Years later as an adult and at a time when my life had become unbearable, I decided to pick up the Bible Hildi had given me as a young boy. It was at this time I read it seriously. I began by reading the Old Testament and continued on into the New Testament. As I came to know Christ, the Bible became a lifeline to me."

"I decided that I wanted to find out if Christ really was the Messiah as promised very obscurely in the Old Testament and as testified in the New Testament, and—as Hildi had told me in her undeviating and positive manner. So—I prayed to know. I had a...a powerful experience. I don't know quite how to describe it, but...but suddenly I knew that He was and is the Messiah. Since then I've read out of the New Testament almost everyday."

"How wonderful!" murmured Jenny, her eyes already full of tears.

"Yes, Dave," said Tom echoing Jenny. "That is really great for us to hear. Now I'm even more excited to answer your question." Tom proceeded to explain, "The Book of Mormon is another witness that Jesus is the Christ. It prophesies of his birth and of His Atonement. It is a record of Christ's visit to the Americas, to this side of the world, after his resurrection."

The air was electric with excitement as David asked where the Book came from, how it had come about. Feeling the Spirit strongly, Tom told him the Joseph Smith story and then bore his testimony. When he finished, he and Jenny watched David stare into space, first with an expression of incredulity, then wonder. They waited, anxiously, hardly daring to breath. The Spirit permeated the silence. David finally spoke.

"It's strange," he said, shaking his head, "but the feeling I have now is like the feeling I had when—I need to have this book, Tom! I have to read it, though my head tells me it's all too good to be true. Where can I get a copy?"

Just a minute, and I'll get you one. Returning shortly, Tom handed David a Book of Mormon with a black cover.

David eagerly accepted it, then looked at the pile of books on the table. "Why does that Book of Mormon have a blue cover and a picture on it?" he asked.

Tom reached for it and handed it to David. "This is Missy's Book of Mormon. It just has a different cover, but the book is the same."

David studied Missy's book with the golden figure holding a trumpet. "Who is that?" he asked, pointing to the figure.

"Moroni, he was the last person to record the history of this special people who lived in the Americas." Tom showed David where to find Moroni 10:3-4 in his own book and instructed him to study it carefully before he began reading the book.

David read the verses immediately, then lifted his eyes to Tom and Jenny, "I certainly will follow the instructions because I can hardly believe this really is more information on Christ—that it's a record of His visit to another part of the world." His dark brows knitted together, his face became troubled. "But what concerns me—is that Torry hasn't told me about this. If she truly believes it—why?"

Tom and Jenny looked at each other knowingly, then Jenny replied, "Trust us, David, Torry has a good reason."

David was silent, contemplating her answer. Soon the concern disappeared from his face. "Thanks, Jenny, I'll accept that for now."

He studied the book in his hands, opening up to the title page and then to the next. He looked up, excitement in his eyes again. "Thanks to both of you, this comes at just the right time. It will help pass the time while Torry's away."

"You're certainly welcome, David," Jenny said, beaming, trying to conceal her rising hopes. "We're thrilled that you want to read it. The children love it. Reading the Book of Mormon separately and together has helped our family become closer, to love one another more and has helped us overcome our personal problems."

"It has?" asked David, hope springing alive in his heart concerning his own personal problems. "Speaking of the children, apologize for me not waiting to see them. I'm anxious to get home and start reading."

"They'll understand, David," replied Jenny, still beaming, her blue eyes dancing.

"Tell Elizabeth how much I enjoyed the ice cream and cookies—and thanks again to both of you."

Tom and Jenny stood on the front porch gripping each other's hand while they watched David almost run to the car—a different David than the one who arrived earlier. As he drove off, Jenny looked up at her husband, tears of hope in her eyes. He squeezed her hand and smiled, tears welling up in his own.

~~~~~~~~~~

Each was deep in thought as they drove toward Salt Lake. Torry's emotions seesawed. One minute she was fighting back fear over her mother's condition; the next, she was feeling hope and excitement over David. Her sons needed someone like him. No. There was no one like David. They needed David.

Somehow, the rift between her and David had dissipated, leaving hardly a memory as to why it happened. But—the haunting question returned. Would David accept the gospel? If so, when? If he didn't, there was no way she could marry him. The gospel was her life. If he did accept it, how would he deal with the fact that they couldn't be sealed, that Jim and Scott were sealed to Jack?

In her heart, she knew that this separation, though hard, would be good for them, giving them time to think—clear the air. However, an overriding thought came to her; they needed time to know each other better. This of course, meant spending more time with each other when she got back, as well as opening up and sharing things each was holding back.

She frowned, feeling great concern as she remembered David's episode during the prayer. What was David holding back? This was twice now that David seemed to be unaware of the present and far away, suffering both physically and emotionally. What could it be?

Chapter Thirty

Davidwoke with a start, fully clothed, still sitting in the chair, the Book of Mormon open in his lap. Glancing at his watch, he saw that it was 8:30 A.M.! He should have taken care of the chickens and been to the bank before now. The last time he looked, it was 5:00. He had read all night, afire with excitement over this startling record containing more information about the Messiah—all the while praying, hoping that what he was reading was as true as it felt.

Jumping up, he went to the phone and called Tom at the bank, "Tom, it's Dave."

"Good morning!" boomed the cheerful voice. "What's goin' on?"

"I read the book all night. Apparently I fell asleep at 5:00, and I just woke up! I have to go take care of the chickens, and then arrange for Gilford Blackburn to take over until...uh I need to ask you a favor, Tom."

"Sure, Dave."

"I think I have an appointment this morning. Will you check with Mrs. Ames? If I do, could you take the appointment for me? I've got to finish this book."

There was silence on the phone.

"Tom?"

"Yes," he managed to say through the lump in his throat.

"Is there something wrong, Tom?"

Tom cleared his throat. "No, just the opposite, Dave. I'm happy to hear how anxious you are to finish it—more than I can say. I'll take care of everything here at the bank. Take off tomorrow, too, if you need to."

"Thanks, Tom. Thanks for everything."

Tom hung up, his heart full of joy as he dialed Jenny.

"Hello?" came Jenny's cheerful, strong voice.

Tom told her the good news and asked her to call the stake missionaries and see if they would be available tonight at seven o'clock and every night the rest of the week for a possible crash course in the missionary lessons and that he would check back with them to confirm it.

"I can hardly believe it, Tom," she said.

David undressed and stepped into the shower, thinking about Torry. She was probably at the hospital. In all the rush, he hadn't even found out which hospital Ruth was in!

His insides ached with loneliness for her. If only she were here to share his excitement. He longed to discuss with her the things he had found that were so satisfying to his hungry soul. Again, he wondered how she could have kept all this to herself? He was certainly going to ask her.

After shaving and dressing, he threw on his jeans, grabbed a bowl of cold cereal, not even feeling a need for his usual morning coffee.

He drove to Zelda's, slipped out from behind the wheel, ran to her front door and rang the bell. Zelda came to the door, an expression of shock on her face.

"David Mayer! What are you doing on my doorstep?"

"I came to see my favorite horse trainer," he said, grinning.

"Come on in this minute," she said, a wide, infectious smile on her face.

"Thank you, Zelda."

~~~~~~~~~~~

At 9:15 A.M. Torry walked into her parents home after exchanging places with her father at the hospital. Before showering and changing, she picked up the phone to call David at the bank and was informed that he wouldn't be in today. No answer at his apartment. She rang her house. No answer. She was disappointed. She was anxious to hear his voice—to learn how he was this morning. Remembering his face as they parted, she ached with pain and loneliness. Reluctantly she decided the call would now have to wait until after the operation, which was scheduled to begin at 10:30.

They had arrived at the hospital after midnight the night before, finding her father in a distraught state and her mother pale and weak. The doctors had stopped the bleeding at one point but about a half hour before they arrived, it had started again.

Ruth greeted her daughter **and** grandsons with a smile. "I'm so glad you're here. Thank you **for** coming. Could I have a blessing now?"

Ruth's grandsons immediately, with their grandfather assisting, gave her a blessing. Within five minutes the hemorrhaging stopped completely. Torry had convinced her harried father to go home with the boys while she remained with her mother the rest of the night.

Seated in Zelda's comfortable living room, David felt right at home. Zelda seated herself across from him.

"Now, my curiosity, like the cud in our old Jersey's throat, is about to choke me. Why are you here, David?"

Amused at her choice of metaphors, David replied, "It's a long story, but the gist of it is, I need Gilford to take care of the chickens for a couple of days if he can."

"I'm sure he can, are you going out of town?"

David thought about how to answer and found himself wanting to tell her but, since he wanted to share it with Torry first, he only said, "I'll be in town but out of pocket so to speak, so I need his help."

"You answer questions about as obliquely as Torry. By the way, where is Torry?"

David related what had happened. Zelda's face clouded up. "I'm sorry to hear this. I haven't met her mother yet, but I know Torry is very close to her."

"I've met her and found her to be a very kind and lovely woman. I'm praying that all will turn out well. Now," he said, scooting to the edge of the chair, "I need to be on my way, could I see Gilford?"

Zelda was confused. She knew how David felt about Torry, saw his sincere concern over her mother, yet sensed, rather than saw, that he was in the grip of some major emotion. The air seemed charged with excitement. Her curiosity peaked, wondering what he was doing that prevented him from taking care of the chickens— and why he was so excited about it.

"All right, David, since you are chomping at the bit, I'll give you some rein." She paused, hoping he'd share a little more information. It wasn't forthcoming so she said, "I'll go get Gilford."

~~~~~~~~~

David sat down and picked up the Book of Mormon, chafing at the time it had taken to arrange everything. It was already 10:30. He held the book in his hands, marveling over the things he read during the night. They validated what he thought he understood in the Old Testament and what he had learned in the New Testament! The Book of Mormon made both more clear. He was immediately fascinated with Lehi and his family and the prophecy of the destruction of Jerusalem. But more important, the book contained prophecies about Jesus Christ.

When he reached 1 Nephi 21, he almost jumped out of his seat as he read the summary of the chapter. After reading the chapter itself, he picked up the Bible and turned to Isaiah 49 and reread it. It was, as he thought, a prophecy of the Messiah's mission! Though difficult to understand, Isaiah had always fascinated him. He was moved when he read King Benjamin's speech and the prophet Abinadi's stirring appeal to King Noah concerning the Atonement. Longing to talk with Torry about all this, he got up, called information for the phone number of George Conway and then called the residence. There was no answer. If they had an answering machine, it wasn't on. Assuming they were still at the hospital, he settled back to read.

At 1:00, he reluctantly gave in to his growling stomach and with the book in hand, headed out the door to Torry's well-stocked refrigerator.

~~~~~~~~~

Torry drove home to her parents house to call David and report the results of the operation. It was one o'clock when she picked up the phone to call his apartment. No answer. She called her house, thinking he might be there to eat lunch. No answer. She frowned, wondering where he could be. Deciding to quiz Mrs. Ames at the bank, she called, only to be informed that she had no idea where he was.

Emotionally and physically exhausted from the events of the last twenty-four hours, tears of frustration and disappointment filled her eyes. Where was David when she needed him?

Almost at once, she felt contrite, and her tears became tears of gratitude to the Lord for the miraculous healing of her mother. How she wanted to share this with David. She wanted to tell him how puzzled the doctors were not to find any cancer or even a trace of the tumor. She got on her knees and thanked the Lord.

After a bowl of Torry's delicious vegetable soup and a piece of homemade bread, he sat down in the front room to read, feeling refreshed and satisfied. He wanted to take time to investigate the cross references at the bottom of each page, but resisted. He was too anxious to get through the book. Later, he decided, he'd ask Tom about those references and study them next time around.

Two hours later, his heart full, he slid to his knees to again plead with the Lord. He had to know if what he was reading was as true as it felt. Before he had uttered a word, a powerful feeling of peace filled his whole being. Overwhelmed with joy and gratitude, he sobbed.

It was true. There was no room for doubt. The Book of Mormon was the word of God! Just as quickly, he was struck by another thought. If the Book of Mormon was true—what did that say about Joseph Smith? Tom had testified to him that Joseph Smith was a prophet.

But a prophet in these modern times? Especially one so young and uneducated? On the other hand, he recalled, Christ had chosen uneducated fisherman to be his disciples. He needed to talk to Tom.

When Tom answered, the words came out with a rush. "Tom, I haven't finished the book, but I know it's true. But I still have some questions. Where do I go from here?"

Even though Tom was hoping and even expecting this possibility, he was speechless.

"Tom?"

"I hope it's okay with you," Tom said slowly, "but I've already made some arrangements. If you'll come over to my home tonight about seven o'clock, there will be two men, missionaries who can teach you the basic principles of the gospel in six discussions."

"You have?" asked David, totally surprised.

I have, Dave. You seem to be a man in a hurry for the truth."

"You're so right, Tom. How long will it take me to get through these discussions?"

"It depends on you, how fast you can understand the principles."

"Thanks, Tom, thanks. I appreciate this more than I can say."

"See you tonight, Dave."

Torry was concerned. She had tried to reach David from the restaurant at 7:30 P.M. and he was still not at his apartment or at her house. She had eaten dinner with her sons before they went back to school and before she returned to the hospital.

She went back to the Hospital, but her stay was fairly short. Since her mother was resting comfortably, she decided to go home and try to reach David.

Looking at her watch as she unlocked the front door of her parent's house, she saw that it was now ten o'clock. She quickly went to the phone and called David. No answer. Again, she tried her house. No answer. Where could he be? He knew that she would be calling, so why would he not be where she could reach him?

Pushing back a discomforting possibility, she got ready for bed. Finally, forced to confront her nagging suspicion—Silvia Barber, the beautiful young attorney may have manipulated him into going out with her and feeling lonely, he may have... No, she thought, David loves me, he wouldn't. Besides where was he during the day?

She needed to tell him that her mother came through the operation beautifully—but more than that, she needed to hear his voice.

Seeking relief from these disturbing thoughts, she offered a silent prayer. Almost at once she realized that her concerns were only in her mind. In her heart she felt that all was well.

David arrived back at his apartment at 11:00 P.M. so exhilarated he wondered if he would ever be able to sleep again. The stake missionaries, as Tom called them, Brother Clark and Brother Wilson, had given him the first two discussions. He was scheduled to have two more discussions tomorrow night and two on Thursday.

He marveled at these two men. They were just ordinary men: husbands, fathers, going about their everyday employment, and yet they seemed so knowledgeable about the scriptures! Questions that he'd had for years were answered tonight.

When he had arrived at the Baker home, he was greeted by seven happy and excited children. They all, including Missy, sat quietly during the first discussion, their faces happy, almost shining. Missy fell asleep soon after the start of the second one but all the rest of the children remained bright-eyed through all of it and had given him hugs as they said good night and went off to bed.

The minute he stepped into his apartment, he went to the phone to call Torry. Then remembering the lateness of the hour, he groaned, "It's too late." He wondered if she had tried to call. If she had, he hoped that she wouldn't be concerned.

David remained seated by the phone, contemplating the first two discussions. Afterward, he'd peppered the missionaries with additional queries. Reluctantly, but with good humor, they answered them, explaining that these were things usually covered in the third discussion.

Nevertheless, it was plain to David that not only was Joseph Smith a prophet, but that through him the Lord had restored all the principles and teachings of Jesus Christ, as well as His true church!

They taught him about faith, repentance and baptism. He felt himself propelled toward a decision, a decision he thought he'd never make. Baptism! Affiliating himself with a church had always seemed foreign, almost repugnant to him. But now it was different. Each thing he learned led so logically to the next. If the Book of Mormon were true—Joseph Smith had to be a prophet of God. This church, the church that Tom belonged to, that Torry belonged to, has to be the Church of Jesus Christ! He had to be part of it.

Suddenly he knew. The obstacle Torry talked about must be that he wasn't a member of the Church! He himself would now consider it a serious problem to marry a woman who didn't believe in Christ and His true church. He jumped up and paced the floor, unable to contain his happiness over the possibility of having both Torry and the Church.

He planned to stay home again tomorrow and finish the Book of Mormon so that he could get started on the other scriptures. When he had asked, at the conclusion of the first two discussions, about the cross references, a smile spread across Tom's face.

"Just wait until you read the Book of Moses and the Book of Abraham. And—the revelations from the Lord, given to Joseph Smith—the Doctrine and Covenants."

He couldn't believe that there were all these added scriptures available today! Then he thought of Gabe, his friend in Dallas. He knew all this and he hadn't said a word. Even when he had contacted his friend now and then, reporting to him as he had promised, Gabe hadn't said a word about the Church. Dan and Jesse hadn't said a word. How could they all keep it quiet? He felt like shouting it to the world!

Quickly undressing, he got into bed and fell into a deep and restful sleep.

~~~~~~~~~~~~~~

The alarm sounded at 4:00 A.M. Wednesday morning and immediately David was fully awake with more energy than he'd had in a long time. He knelt down beside the bed and prayed again for Torry, her mother and her sons but most of all for the Spirit to be with him as he finished the Book of Mormon, just as Josh had prayed for him last night when they ended the meeting.

Turning the lamp on, he picked up the Book of Mormon and read until the cool morning breeze became soft and warm from the golden hues of the early morning sun.

Reluctantly, at 8:30, he put the book down, showered and dressed, begrudging every interruption that took him away from the most compelling book he'd ever read.

When he was ready, he **pick**ed up the priceless volume and headed for Torry's house to **look** at the chickens and make himself a breakfast that would sustain **him** until early afternoon.

~~~~~~~~~~~~~~~~

At 9:05 Torry called the **bank**. Mrs. Ames answered, "Green Valley Bank."

"Mrs. Ames, this is Torry Anderson, is David in?"

"No he isn't, he won't be **in** again today."

"Do you know where he **is**?"

"No I don't, Mrs. **Anderson**, I'm sorry."

"Is Tom Baker in?"

"Yes, but he's with a customer."

Torry hung up, frowning, then rang David's apartment. No answer. She rang her house. **No** answer. Finally, thoroughly frustrated, she called Zelda.

"Hello?" came the familiar voice.

"Zelda, this is Torry."

"Torry! How are you? How is your mother?"

Torry told her the good news and then asked her how she knew about her mother.

"David came by Monday morning to hire Gil to take care of the chickens for him."

"Did David go out of town?"

"I don't know, but I don't **think** so, he just said that he'd be out of pocket for a few days."

"Did he tell you why?"

"You know me, Torry, I tried to find out but he didn't want to tell me."

Torry frowned and bit her lip. "How was he, Zelda?"

Zelda hesitated, not quite sure how she should answer.

"Zelda, please, we kind of separated on a bad note, I need you to be honest with me."

"Well...uh he seemed all right to me."

"Zelda, what is it you're hiding from me?"

"Well, Torry, he seemed to be concerned about your mother...but..."

"Zelda, Tell me!"

"He seemed pretty upbeat about something and very eager for me to go get Gil so he could leave."

~~~~~~~~~~

After checking on the chickens to see how Gil had done, David walked into the kitchen to fix himself a late breakfast noting that it was already 9:15.

As he looked around the attractive little room, his longing for Torry became unbearable, wanting her there now, yearning to tell her the good news. However, he had made a decision, a difficult decision. He wanted Torry to be at his baptism, and he knew she would want to be there. He had explained this to Tom, telling him he wanted to put off the baptism so she could attend.

Tom was silent for a long, pensive moment, then he said, "Dave, when the Spirit testifies as strongly as it has to you, it's best not to put off baptism. Especially since you have no idea how long Torry will have to be with her mother. Why don't you pray about it?"

When he prayed about going ahead with the baptism without Torry, a peaceful assurance came over him that he should take Tom's advice. This also meant that he couldn't tell her about the baptism over the phone. Certain that Torry felt as strongly about the gospel as he did, she might insist on leaving her mother's bedside to be at the baptism. He couldn't do that to Ruth.

After breakfast he cleaned up then drove to his apartment to call Torry. There was no answer, so he called Mrs. Ames at the bank.

"Mrs. Ames, has Torry Anderson tried to reach me?"

"Yes, Mr. Mayer, she has, and she also called this morning."

"If she calls again today, tell her to call me at home. Channel all my other calls to Tom. I believe I'll be in tomorrow."

Settling down in his chair, David eagerly began reading. Several hours had passed when the phone rang. His heart leaped, hoping it was Torry.

"Hello?"

"David, this is Torry."

He exhaled with relief. "At last we've connected! I'm sorry I've missed your calls."

"I called last night also, David, and you weren't home," she said, resisting the urge to quiz him on his whereabouts.

"I know, I'm sorry," he apologized, offering no further explanation. "I got your father's number from information and I've tried to call you several times."

Relief washed over her. "You have?"

"Yes, I miss you, Torry! And I've been anxious to hear about your mother."

Torry told him the good news, saving the special details until she could see him face to face.

"That's wonderful news, Torry."

"I thought you must have gone out of town, David, when I couldn't reach you at the bank."

"No, I've just taken a couple of days off."

Torry waited, wanting him to tell her he'd hired Gil Blackburn to take care of the chickens, and why. He didn't—and she wasn't about to tell him she had called Zelda. "You sound different, David."

"I do?" It was all he could do to keep from blurting out his good news. Instead, he asked her to give him the number of her mother's hospital room, sounding stilted to himself as he did so. He was sure it did to Torry also.

"I don't know it yet since she is still in intensive care. I'll call Mrs. Ames and give it to her since you are so hard to track down."

Something in her voice, disturbed David. "When will you be home, Torry?"

"I don't know yet."

"Please let me know when you have some idea, will you? I miss you."

"I'll try. I miss you too, David."

"You do? That does my heart good to hear. I don't think I could bear it if...if I wasn't busy. Well, my love, I've got to go—I love you."

"All right..." she said hesitantly. "Goodbye David."

The phone clicked, unnerving him. He hadn't wanted it to end so quickly, so abruptly, but what could he talk to her about? He knew that if he'd kept talking he wouldn't have been able to keep the news from her.

David's eagerness to get off the phone puzzled and disappointed Torry—yet he had told her that he loved her and missed her. Questions flooded her mind. Zelda said he was pretty upbeat. Why? She certainly didn't feel that way apart from him! Why had he taken off work? What could he be involved in away from the bank? His farm? His other businesses? And yes, Silvia Barber again flashed into her mind, but she quickly dismissed the thought. The not-knowing was so unsettling, she grabbed her sketch pad. Aimlessly she began to sketch and soon found herself, once again, sketching David.

~~~~~~~~~~~~

David, finally pulling himself away from his reading long enough to glance at his watch, was shocked to see that it was already 6:15 PM. In forty-five minutes he had to be at the Bakers for the second set of discussions. He had forgotten all about lunch and realized he was starving. Finding his cupboard bare, he went over to Torry's to grab a bite to eat, still thinking about what he had read this afternoon.

He had just finished the Book of Helaman and could hardly wait to start 3 Nephi and read of Christ's birth. He felt as though he was coming to the most important part of the Book of Mormon and wondered if he could finish it tonight after the discussions. If not, he knew he'd have to stay home from the bank again tomorrow.

~~~~~~~~~~~~

David returned to his apartment again at 11:00 P.M. Except for Missy, blinking furiously to keep her eyes open, all the Baker children had remained awake and alert through the whole evening. Everyone was as excited as he. The stake missionaries were able to answer all his questions. Everything he learned made so much sense, seemed so logical if God was, as he believed, a just God.

Tomorrow night, Thursday, they would present him with the last two discussions. The baptism date was set for Saturday morning at 10:00 A.M. following his interview with Bishop Price on Friday night.

Thinking about this momentous step, he felt a sudden qualm. Was this all happening too fast? Should he take more time to consider?

The answer came just as quickly. No! His joy and happiness, his testimony were too great. His heart thrilled at the thought of his coming baptism, and more so because this would remove the obstacle between himself and Torry.

He recalled his reaction to the concept of eternal marriage, of the family as an eternal unit. How could it be any other way? When he saw the love that existed in Tom's family, everything in him rebelled at the thought that a just God would terminate it at death.

He got ready for bed, but finding himself still too excited to sleep, sat down and opened the Book of Mormon. Reading 3 Nephi was a feast to David, requiring time out to ponder. The hours passed—and finally at 5:00 A.M. he closed the Book on the last chapter of Moroni. He went into the bedroom and knelt down beside his bed and expressed gratitude to God that he had found the truth.

Chapter Thirty-One

Friday night David walked into a Mormon Church for the first time. Just as he stepped inside, he was greeted by a short, sturdy-built, brown-haired man who had the typical look of a farmer. A farmer like Dan, Jesse, and Clive Johnson, all with suntanned faces and white foreheads, the result of wearing a hat all year long to protect their heads, summer or winter. The man held out his hand and smiled, his hazel eyes friendly and warm.

"I'm Bishop Price. You are David Mayer."

"Yes I am. I'm glad to meet you, Bishop Price," David said, returning the bishop's firm, affectionate hand shake.

Sitting in the bishop's office, David found his nervousness leaving. He relaxed as the bishop visited with him in a casual, down-to-earth manner. David's testimony increased. This man, a humble, common man called by the Lord as were the humble fisherman of long ago. Unlike a couple of ministers he'd met, who seemed to exalt themselves, making a person feel less, Bishop Price renewed David's faith in himself.

"I understand that you are in a business with one of our ward members, Torry Anderson."

"This is Torry's ward?" asked David, surprised and pleased.

"Yes, it will be nice that you already know someone in the ward since the missionaries and Tom Baker attend other wards."

Bishop Price couldn't remember interviewing a potential member who had such an intense testimony and—being Jewish made it more amazing. This interview, he knew, would always remain a highlight in his life.

David returned home relieved and happy that he had passed the interview, even though the bishop had asked some very personal and probing questions.

Wishing with all his heart that he could talk to Torry right this minute, he paced the floor. Even if he hadn't made the decision to not tell Torry about his conversion at this time, it was something too important to tell on the phone. He wanted to see her face, her eyes when he told her; he wanted to see her incredulity, her excitement.

The dilemma—knowing he couldn't keep it to himself if he called her, yet aching to call her—was tearing him apart. All of a sudden, he realized she hadn't tried to call. The last time he talked to her was Wednesday. So preoccupied with the momentous decision he was making, he wasn't aware of this until now. He felt a vague uneasiness.

Not hearing from David was painful to Torry, but she'd made up her mind not to call him again. The last time they talked, he did sound as though he missed her, but his eagerness to get off the phone, was more than unsettling. Her parent's answering machine was now working, and there wasn't even a message from him. And she was home all evening hoping, waiting. Taking the late shift, she was now sitting in her mother's room feeling puzzled and hurt.

"What is it Torry, what's wrong," her mother asked.

Torry was startled. "I thought you were asleep."

"I was. But I awakened a short time ago and I've been watching you—so I know something is not right."

"Mother, you aren't well enough to take on my worries."

"I'm feeling much better, Torry, please confide in me."

Torry, relieved to unburden herself, told her mother everything about the relationship between herself and David, including his proposal.

Ruth smiled. "This isn't a surprise, Torry, I had a feeling this would happen."

Mother and daughter talked about their concerns over David and the Church. Considering the possibility he might someday accept the gospel, they wondered together how would he react when he found that he and Torry could not be sealed in the temple.

Ruth studied her daughter. "But I have a feeling that these things are not your immediate concern, Torry, what is it?"

"Something's wrong. David hasn't called since we talked Wednesday, and he sounded very eager to get off the phone. As I told you, we parted feeling miles apart. Something is going on, he hasn't been at the bank and he hasn't been out of town. I just don't know what to think. What shall I do, mother?"

"Go home tomorrow."

"I can't leave you. You're going home tomorrow, and I am going to cook and care for you."

"Torry, it will be good for your dad to do that for me."

"It may be good for Dad but not for you. What kind of meals will you get?"

Ruth smiled. "Very simple ones. But I assure you the Relief Society will help, and if we need to, your dad can afford to hire help."

"I can't leave you, Mother."

"I want you to go, Torry, your unhappiness and uneasiness over what is going on with David certainly won't help me get well."

"You're right, Mother, I'm sorry. But the boys weren't planning for this Saturday and besides, I wouldn't want to tell them why I was rushing back to Green Valley. Now close your eyes, and get some sleep."

Ruth closed her eyes, not to sleep, but to think. She had to figure a way for Torry to get home tomorrow. Ever since her grandsons revealed the shocking truth about their father to her and George, she grieved over what Torry had lived through in her marriage. If there was a possibility of Torry finding any happiness, she wanted to help it along. There weren't any buses that serviced small towns like Green Valley...so how? An idea came. She smiled at how it would shock everyone. George would be more than shocked; she would have to deal with his anger. For several reasons, he had made up his mind not to like David, one reason, she knew, was that he was Jewish—the others she could only guess at.

"Torry?"

"Mother, why aren't you asleep yet?"

"I've come up with an idea how to get you home tomorrow without asking the boys to drive you down."

"I'm not going to listen. I'm staying here."

"I'm going to hire a helicopter to fly you down."

Torry's mouth dropped open. "Did I hear you correctly?"

"You most certainly did."

Torry laughed. "You aren't serious."

"I'm very serious."

"Dad will have a hissy if you do."

"He won't have anything to do with it. As you know, my parents left me a good sized inheritance. What you don't know, Torry, is—I didn't combine it with any of your father's funds in case I needed to make some independent decisions. I'm making one now."

"This too surprises me, Mother, but I'm glad you've done it that way." She smiled lovingly at her mother, "It will be far too expensive to hire a helicopter, but thank you for wanting to."

Torry, I have friends who I helped at a very crucial time in their lives and the husband, who owns a helicopter service, told me that if I ever needed to get somewhere fast, to call him and he would fly me himself and only charge me the cost of the gas. He's mentioned this more than once."

"Really?" Torry said, finding herself very tempted. "But that doesn't solve the fact that you need help."

"Please, Torry. I promise I'll call you back if I find that I can't manage."

Torry sighed as she thought about it, then gave in, "All right, Mother." She leaned down and kissed her. "Thank you!"

"I'll call my friend first thing in the morning to see if he's available. If he is, I'll let you help me settle in at home in the morning and even let you do a little grocery shopping and prepare dinner for us early. You may be able to be in Green Valley around 5:00 or 6:00 tomorrow evening."

~~~~~~~~~~

David awakened Saturday morning feeling a mixture of excitement, nervousness—and doubt. He was shocked at the doubt. What was the matter with him? He got on his knees and pleaded with the Lord for reassurance that he was doing the right thing. He got up still feeling uneasy. As he showered, he mulled it over and over trying to figure out what was wrong with him. As he dressed, he tried to understand. Tom was picking him up at nine and the rest of his family were coming later.

He needed a cup of coffee. But he had committed himself to give it up. A dark feeling came over him, bringing with it a more intense feeling of uneasiness. He walked into the kitchen and got the coffee can down, reasoning that just one cup wouldn't matter. He desperately needed the mood lift that morning coffee always gave him. He stopped. Picking up the can, he opened the cupboard under the sink and threw it into the garbage.

Still not feeling better, he paced the floor until he heard the honk of Tom's car. Picking up the small suitcase that contained a change of clothing, he ran downstairs.

He'd never been so happy to see Tom's cheerful face. "Glad you're here, Tom," he said as he got into the passenger side.

Tom studied his friend. "What is it, Dave?"

As they drove to the church, David tried to explain how he felt. "I don't know what to do, maybe this means I shouldn't go through with it."

"Actually, Dave, I expected you to feel this way."

David was puzzled, "You...you did? Why? Why would you expect some one to feel so rotten on such a wonderful day?"

"The reason I wanted to pick you up this early is because I wanted to talk to you about this very thing and forewarn you. I woke up this morning feeling apprehensive about you so I knew what was happening."

"How could you know, Tom?" David asked, skepticism in his voice.

Tom told him briefly about his mission in England and explained how the Adversary, Satan, always tried to thwart the baptism before or after and sometimes both. Even months down the road, some were buffeted Tom told him. He reminded David about the Prophet Joseph's experience in the grove. "You are getting a small taste of what he experienced. In England, we lost a lot of potential members because they gave in to these dark and frightening doubts."

"You, Dave, I know, have the strength to withstand Satan, but you need to be very aware of him and his influence and be on guard. Besides," he added, "you know that the Savior is infinitely more powerful than Satan."

They reached the ward building and parked. As they walked into the church, David was still silent, thinking. Tom led him into a small class room.

"Let's sit down and talk **about** this a few minutes before we dress, Dave."

"Thank you, Tom. I know what you've just told me is true. I now remember feeling this influence in my life—particularly around my mother."

Tom was shocked. "Your mother?"

"Yes. I've learned that the opposite of love is not hate, it's indifference, in my case at least. But I now believe that Torry is right. The Lord sent certain people into my life to sustain me, to help me through life—to help me come to this point today." Tears appeared in David's eyes. "You and your family are some of those people, Tom. Thank you for living what you believed, for sharing yourself and your family with me, and for arranging for the missionary lessons..." he couldn't go on.

"Thank you, Dave for the privilege of letting us be a part of it. Now, let's go get dressed for the most important moment of your life."

David was shocked when he walked into the baptistry. The room was full of people! He had expected the Baker family and Bishop Price, but there were Dan and Jesse and their wives grinning from ear to ear, Zelda and Zak Blackburn and their sons Ivan and Gilford, Mrs. Ames, and other employees of the bank, some of the board of directors, Clive and Madge Johnson and many others! He smiled at them as he followed Tom to their designated seats in the front. Though a little nervous, David was overwhelmed. Never had he felt so surrounded by love and support.

After the welcome by Brother Clark, who turned out to be the stake mission leader, a hymn was sung called, "I Need Thee Every Hour" which expressed David's own feelings, moving him deeply. Jenny Baker led the singing and her daughter, Elizabeth accompanied. Josh Baker gave the opening prayer and to David's surprise, Zelda Blackburn gave a short impressive talk on baptism.

Then he found himself walking down into the water with Tom by his side. The moment was here, the moment when he would be washed clean of all his sins, the moment that would signify his willingness to follow in the footsteps of the Lord.

His heart was hammering against his chest until Tom took hold of his wrist and raised his right hand. With a voice of calm and sure authority, Tom pronounced the prayer and put him under the water, then brought him up. Tom smiled at him, and they walked up out of the font together.

When David and Tom had changed and dressed, they returned to find the Baker children singing a medley of songs. As they sat down, the children began singing a song called, "I am a Child of God." The simple beauty of the melody and words brought tears to David's eyes as he looked into Missey's smiling face.

Jesse Jones smiled at David as he began his talk on the Holy Ghost, a moving talk from his crusty old friend. David was amazed that these common, ordinary people had the ability to stand before a group and talk with such knowledge of the gospel that all who heard were inspired.

When Jesse ended his talk and sat down, Brother Clark asked David to come up to the front. Seated on a chair, a large group of his friends gathered around him, placing their hands upon his head. He not only felt their love, he felt the love of God, his Heavenly Father, as he now thought of Him. His old friend Dan Higley confirmed him a member of the Church, saying, "Receive the Holy Ghost." The blessing that Dan gave him along with it, was one which comforted his soul, one he would never forget.

David returned to his seat, realizing that he was now a member of the Church of Jesus Christ. He blinked back tears of gratitude while Bishop Price welcomed him into the ward.

The closing song, "Because I Have Been Given Much" was almost his undoing. He tried to sing but was too full of emotion. All he could do was silently read the words and listen to the music. The beautiful closing prayer, that came out of the mouth of the big clumsy farmer, Clive Johnson, made him again think of the humble fishermen that Jesus called to follow Him and who became His faithful disciples.

The minute Clive said "Amen", David found small arms wrapped around his neck, hugging him fiercely. Then all the Baker children surrounded him hugging him one by one, tears streaming down their cheeks through their wide smiles. Tom hugged him, both of them fighting tears—then Jenny. One by one his friends, including the bishop and the missionaries, came up and shook his hand.

Dan gripped David's hand with his own knarled, calloused one and grinned, "We kinda suspected you might be worth saving!"

Jesse slapped David's back, "Yeah, you can never tell about city boys, but we had an inkling you might have a back bone."

After Gilford, Ivan and their father Zak shook his hand, Zelda held out hers. David thanked her for her part in the baptism, then he grinned, "Imagine a horse trainer like you giving a talk like that."

She grinned back and quipped, "Yeah, the Lord can make anything out of a sow's ear, can't He?"

David chuckled, then he became serious, "I can't wait to tell Torry. I'm going to go to Salt Lake after church tomorrow. I have to stay long enough to attend my first meeting and then I'm off."

"I think that's a good idea, she called me to find out if I knew where you were and seemed a little concerned. I wish I could see her reaction when she learns about this."

"Hey Dave," Tom said, walking up to him, "Come on, everyone who attended your baptism is heading over to our back lawn for a pot-luck dinner in celebration of your baptism."

Chapter Thirty-Two

David drove towards Torry's house, his heart full, thinking of the back yard get-together, the wonderful food and the gift. He touched the black, leather-bound scriptures with his name embossed in gold. A card with everyone's name on it had been included. On the top of the list were Dan's and Jesse's names.

David had cornered Dan and Jesse at the party and threw the question at them. "Why didn't you two story tellers tell me the true story?" He had expected the usual droll come-back but they both sobered up so quickly, David cocked his head in surprise.

"We have a confession to make, David," Dan began, glancing at Jesse who nodded his assent. "Jesse and I here liked you the minute you opened your mouth. You know how a small town is, everyone knows when some one new comes to town and they get curious. Well, we were no different."

"Yep," Jesse chimed in, "we got real curious when we saw those snappy suits you wore. Class, real class."

"Too much class for a couple of ol' farmers like us," Dan added. "So we stayed our distance a while, but the more we got to know you, the more we liked you."

"We decided to invite you over to the drugstore one Wednesday," Jesse said. "It was right after that, Dan and I made the decision."

"What decision?" David asked, thoroughly intrigued as to where all this was leading.

Jesse continued. "We made the decision to actively fellowship you."

David lifted his brows. "That's an odd term to use for our..."

"It's what we at times call the precursor to missionary work," Dan interrupted. "It's a step above friendship. Jesse and I prayed together about it and as we did, we felt for sure—you were just plain gospel material."

"You did?" David's shock made them both chuckle.

"Yep. Believe it or not." Dan's eyes twinkled with humor.

"But...as I asked before, then why didn't you tell me about the Church?" David insisted.

"Well, now that you know about the gift of the Holy Ghost," Jesse explained, "you'll understand. Dan and I had been going around the barn door, planting little things here and there concerning the gospel in our get-togethers with you on Wednesdays, but we were getting impatient."

"Yeah," Dan said, "in our minds, you were as ready to hear the truth as those chicks of yours were to peck through their shells to the light."

"But," Jesse continued, "when we told the Lord in prayers that we were going to get right to it, and would he confirm this, He told us otherwise. For some darn reason we couldn't understand, David, you weren't ready. So Dan and I just kept on fellowshipping, and praying for some sign from the Lord when we could approach you directly about the Church."

David was thoughtful then shook his head. "Well I'll be darned. All this time—for over a year you two have been plotting..." Suddenly he choked up and couldn't go on, noticing Dan and Jesse were also blinking watery eyes. Finally, he managed to grin and blurt out, "Thanks," then hugged his two friends.

A few minutes later, David said, "I know now why Tom and Torry haven't told me before—and Gabe."

"Gabe?" queried Jesse.

"Who is this Gabe?" asked Dan.

David told them.

He drove into Torry's driveway and stopped. His heart was filled with gratitude for all his friends here in Green Valley and right now especially for Gabe. If it hadn't been for him, he wouldn't have come here, he would never have met Torry. And he wouldn't have been ready to accept the gospel. He knew he had to go to Dallas and tell him the good news in person.

He sat in the car feeling unbearably lonely for Torry. Looking at his watch, he saw that it was a little after five o'clock. He had stayed at the Baker's to help clean up and visit with the family, not wanting to go home to his empty apartment.

Even though Gil had been doing a good job, he came to check on the chickens. In reality, he knew he was here because it brought

Torry closer. As he got out of his car, he noticed a helicopter off in the distance, heading north and he wondered if he could hire anyone to fly him to Salt Lake on a Sunday.

The chickens looked bigger and fatter and everything was in order so he knew that Gil had already been there. He stepped out of the chicken coup, walked to the gate, and had just opened it when he saw Torry come out of the house and down the back steps. He stood there, blinking, not believing his eyes.

"Torry?"

"Hello David," she said, not smiling.

"How...when did you get here?! I think you must be a mirage." He turned, locked the gate then eagerly moved towards her, smiling—but stopped. Icy fear stabbed at his heart. She stared at him coldly, apparently unmoved by his happiness. "What is the matter, Torry?"

"What is the matter? Surely, David, if you put your mind to it, you'll come up with it I'm sure." She walked past him toward the gate. A steely grip stopped her.

"Whoa there Torry, I can't come up with it! What is it?" he asked, turning her towards him.

"I haven't heard from you since Wednesday night—and it was I who called you, remember? The least you could have done is do me the same courtesy—but I guess what you were doing was more important."

"It was, Torry! Do you want to hear about it or don't you?"

"I don't."

David dropped his hands—seeing in Torry, it seemed, the same impenetrability of his cold unresponsive mother. A stab of terror struck him. With a sharp intake of breath, he took a step back, then turned abruptly and walked quickly around the house toward his car.

The expression on David's face frightened Torry. "David stop!" she screamed, running after him. He continued walking. As he put his hand on the car door handle, she reached out to restrain him.

"Please, David, stop—don't go! I do want to hear."

He ignored her pleas. Opening the door, he pulled away from her and got in. The feeling of utter helplessness gripped her. As he backed out of the driveway, he saw Torry's stricken face. He stopped, drove back in and slowly got out.

She looked up into his ashen face. "C...can we talk David?"

"I...I guess."

"Let's go into the house," she said. They walked up to the house together. Torry led the way into the front room, offering him a seat on the small couch. She sat in the other one facing him.

Putting his elbows on his knees, he pressed his clasped hands into his forehead, "Torry," the words stuck in his throat, almost choking him. "I wanted to call you every day, all day but..." He looked up, "I wanted to tell you in person—not on the phone. I knew if I called, I'd give it away."

"What, David? What would you give away?"

He studied her face. Trying to rid himself of the grip his mother still had on him, he said, "Give me a moment, Torry."

He got up and walked to the window and stared out, struggling with conflicting emotions. Since his decision to be baptized, he dreamed of the moment he would tell Torry. This wasn't the way it was supposed to happen! After some time, he went back and sat down and looked into her anxious face.

"Would you mind, Torry, if we wait until tomorrow?" A half smile appeared briefly, "I promise you'll find out tomorrow."

"But...but David, you were anxious to tell me. Aren't you anxious to tell me now?"

"It's not that, Torry...it's just that..." he got up again and walked toward the front door, wanting desperately to leave Torry's presence while in this mood. He stopped and turned back to her. "You know, I haven't had much sleep lately, let's get together tomorrow."

Torry jumped up and went over to him. "No, David, you can't leave! My mother hired a helicopter to get me here today."

That got David's attention. "She did? Why?"

"I'll tell you if you'll sit down."

David sat down on one of the chairs flanking the window. Torry sat in the other one. "I needed to stay with her longer, David, but she insisted that I come home. I didn't want the boys to drive me down, so she hired a helicopter to bring me."

"I think I just saw a helicopter heading north. Was that the one?"

"Yes. I had only been here about ten minutes before you arrived."

"That was very nice of your mother, Torry, but we can still talk tomorrow."

Torry had never seen David like this, what had she done? She got up and knelt before him, "Oh David, I think I've ruined something special for you, and I don't know what." She covered her face and sobbed quietly.

"Torry don't," he pleaded.

She looked up at him, tears streaming down her cheeks. "The reason I was so angry with you is because I was so frightened. You seemed so anxious to get off the phone Wednesday night, and you didn't call, I thought...I thought that maybe because I kept bringing up the obstacles between us, you'd given up on me—and I couldn't bear the thought, I love you so much David..."

The icy fingers that had reached out from his mother's grave and gripped his heart, melted away. He stood up and pulled Torry to her feet and held her close. "It's all right, my darling, it's all right now. Thank you for loving me enough to be angry and afraid. Thank you for not letting me leave."

Torry let out a long shuddering sigh. "Oh, David, David," she murmured. They clung together for many moments, each afraid of letting go. Finally, he crooked his finger under her chin and lifted her face to his.

"Come," he entreated, his eyes filled with love, "I've always wanted to sit on one of those loveseats with you."

Relief coursed through her. David was his old self again. She returned his smile and said, "I'd love to sit there with you."

They sat down and David put his arm around her and pulled her close. "I have something wonderful to tell you, Torry."

Torry sighed, "I haven't ruined it for you then?"

"No." He gazed at her a moment, his eyes radiant, then a slow grin spread across his face. "I just got rid of that obstacle you keep talking about, just kicked it right out the door."

Torry's eyes widened with alarm, "David, I don't think you understand, it isn't something that easy to...to kick out the door."

"Oh...is that right? Well, I did it anyway."

"David, be serious."

"I am serious," he paused then said in a rush, "I was baptized this morning."

Torry pulled away, studying his face trying to internalize what he'd said. "David...I...I've only been gone since Monday, it isn't possible that you were..."

He was enjoying this immensely. He smiled broadly, "Oh, it is possible if you picked up the Book of Mormon Monday night and read all night, sluffed work and read all the next day, got Gilford to take care of the chickens, had a crash course in the missionary discussions, finished the Book of Mormon, and passed the interview with Bishop Price Friday night."

She stared at him hardly able to comprehend, trying to mouth words... "Uh—oh, David—this all really happened?"

"It did, my darling."

"But—do you know for sure it's true, that is do...do you have a testimony?"

"I didn't want to joke about that—but wait right here, I want to show you something." He got up and went outside to his car. Torry was standing in the middle of the room when he returned. He showed her a beautiful set of scriptures with his name embossed in gold. She looked at them in awe, speechless, then he handed her the card.

She read the card and all the names and slowly handed it back to David. She squealed, clapped her hands and started to cry, then laughed. "Oh David...Oh David, I can't believe it! I'm so happy for you." She pulled his face down to hers and kissed him joyfully and then leaned against his chest and sobbed.

Chapter Thirty-Three

When Torry and David walked in the door of the ward building Sunday morning fifteen minutes early, the bishop walked over to them, smiling, holding his hand out to David.

"Good morning, David. It's mighty good to see you here this morning."

"I can't tell you how good it is to be here, Bishop Price."

The bishop shook hands with Torry. "I hear you've been out of town, Sister Anderson. How are you this morning?"

She smiled at this intuitive bishop who had been so understanding with her. "I'm much better, bishop, thank you."

The bishop turned back to David, "If you could stay after the block of meetings, we'll ordain you to the priesthood in my office."

David's eyes lit up. "So soon?"

"Oh yes," he smiled. "When a man is worthy to be baptized, he may be given the priesthood immediately. In the meeting, notice the young men who bless the sacrament and those who pass it. They all hold the Aaronic Priesthood. As soon as a boy turns twelve he may be ordained to the office of a deacon—that is, if in my interview he's found worthy. When he reaches the age of fourteen, he may be ordained to the office of a teacher, then at sixteen to the office of a priest. He then has the privilege of preparing and blessing the sacrament."

"Thank you, Bishop Price, I'll be here after the meetings."

When they entered the chapel, the Blackburn family descended upon them, shaking David's hand vigorously.

Zelda, shocked at seeing Torry, said, "When did you get here, Torry?"

"Last night." She smiled, knowing how Zelda would react. "A helicopter let me off right in my weed filled meadow."

Zelda' mouth dropped open and before she could say anything, Ivan blurted out, "I told you, Mom, I saw a helicopter rise up out of Torry's back yard."

Before anymore could be said, several people who attended the baptism interrupted, welcoming him to church and then it was time for the meeting to start.

Immediately David noticed the noise level. He looked around and saw families sitting together, many with babies and toddlers, and realized he was now a part of this. He looked at Torry and she looked up, smiled and slipped her hand into his, and led him to a seat. Never in his life had he felt such peace and contentment.

To David's surprise, the bishop, conducting, mentioned his baptism, requesting those present to accept him as a member by raising their right hand, and publicly welcoming him into the ward. The whole meeting was one of amazement to David as he watched the leadership ability of this lay ministry; as he watched the young priests and deacons reverently prepare, bless and pass the sacrament; and as he listened to talks given by youth and adults. But his testimony increased the most as he watched families seated together row on row in front of them. A teenage boy smiled affectionately at his father a couple of times, another one leaned his head briefly on his mother's shoulder. Other teens were helping their parents by trying to keep their younger siblings quiet. A young girl slipped her arm through her father's, smiled up at him and lay her head lovingly against his arm. A toddler hugged her father tightly around the neck. A baby gave his mother a slobbery kiss on the lips and several fathers got up and carried fussy babies and toddlers out. The love and closeness of these families were, to him, the real fruits of the true gospel.

His heart was full as he partook of the sacrament and renewed his covenants with the Lord, covenants he'd made only yesterday. He thought of the Savior, of his atonement, grateful for the understanding he now had of this—yet wondering if he really would ever be able to fully comprehend it.

The Gospel Doctrine class, as they called it, just reinforced what he already knew—how much he yet had to learn. Then to his dismay, he and Torry had to separate while he attended the priesthood meeting and she attended a woman's meeting called Relief Society.

Afterward, they met in the hall outside the bishop's office where they were ushered in by one of his counselors.

They visited for a few minutes and then the bishop said, "David, in my interview with you for baptism, I found you worthy and knowledgeable enough to be ordained an elder in the Melchizedek Priesthood. However, such ordinations require a stake presidency interview and high council clearance. These ordinations are performed under the direction of the stake president or his representative. Usually we ordain a man to the office of a priest in the Aaronic Priesthood, then later a call may be extended for ordination to the office of an elder. How do you feel about this?"

David was silent—thinking, then he said, "I think I would like be ordained a priest, but I thought you said they were sixteen-year-old boys."

The bishop smiled, "Priests usually are ordained at sixteen years old when they have grown up in the church. Ordination to the Aaronic Priesthood would give you an opportunity to prepare before you take on the responsibility of the Melchizedek Priesthood."

"What things would I be expected to do as a priest?"

"As you observed in our meeting, priests prepare and bless the sacrament each Sunday. You would have an opportunity to participate in the sacrament ordinance with the young priests. Does that bother you?"

"No, I don't think so," David replied tentatively.

"Well then," the bishop said, smiling, "are you ready to be ordained?"

"Yes."

As the bishop and his councilors gathered around David, he was happy to see that they allowed Torry to remain. They placed their hands upon his head, and the bishop began. David's heart swelled with the gravity of what was happening to him. He was actually receiving the power to act in the name of God—by men who had that same authority, the authority of Jesus Christ! He listened to the promises and blessings expressed so well by this ordinary man, and felt humbled and privileged.

Immediately after, the three shook his hand, each expressing happiness and appreciation at having him in the Church and part of their ward. Overcome with gratitude, all David could utter was... "Thank you...thank you."

Both Torry and David were silent as they drove home. David pulled into the driveway, got out and went around to open the door for Torry and together they walked to the porch and into the house. They stood in the foyer looking into each other's eyes, both too full of joy to speak. David pulled her to him, and they held each other tightly for some time.

Finally Torry murmured, "If you'll take your coat and tie off, you can help me get dinner while you tell me every single detail of the impressions of your first day in church and how you felt."

He smiled, "I would be more than happy to do all three."

~~~~~~~~~~

It was a beautiful Sunday afternoon in June. Neither wanted to stay inside after dinner, so Torry had suggested they go find those lilac bushes on Grandmother's lawn. David heartily agreed with the idea.

Sitting on the bench where they first sat on that special night, they enjoyed the shade of the pine tree and listened to the rustling leaves of the others. Torry had never felt such happiness—not even with Jack when they were first engaged. She thought about what David told her about his impressions of his first day at church when they were preparing dinner. And, remembering the joy she felt as she watched him being ordained a priest was almost too much to contain. Tears filled her eyes.

"What is it, my Darling?"

"I'm just so happy that I can't hold it in, David."

"Come on, let's go over to the lilac bushes," he said, pulling her up.

"I'll go if you'll behave yourself."

"Oh I promise. Since I can kiss you any time, I'll wait till I get you home."

"All right then, I'll go with you, that is—if you promise to kiss me when we get home."

David laughed. "Did I hear correctly?"

"You did."

When they arrived at the spot where they had first kissed, they gazed at each other and smiled.

"Torry, I asked you to marry me, and I would like an answer right now, right here."

"I can't think of a better place to say—yes, my dearest David, yes!"

"You did say...yes, didn't you?"

"I did! I love you and I want to be your wife more than I've ever wanted anything in my life."

"YOFI!" He yelled across the park. Then seeing Torry's puzzled look he explained. "That's an old Yiddish expression I learned as a boy. It's sort of the equivalent of 'Hurray!'"

Torry laughed. "You sound like you did the night I yelled 'I love you.'"

He grinned. "You heard that did you? Come on, let's run home so I can collect that kiss."

They ran until they were breathless. Stopping, they both laughed. "I guess we'd better walk the rest of the way," Torry said. Hand in hand they walked. "David?"

"Yes, my love?"

"Will you repeat it to me all over again?"

David reading her mind, said, "We were up until midnight last night. You want to hear everything again? The whole conversion story right from the beginning?"

"I do. It won't be so late this time because we're starting earlier."

"I just remembered a question I have wanted to ask you from the first time I got the Book of Mormon." After what Dan and Jesse told him, he felt he knew the answer, but he wanted to hear it from Torry.

"Oh, what?"

"How could you keep it all to yourself? I'm so thrilled with the gospel, I feel like telling everyone. Why didn't you tell me about it, Torry?"

"It was hard not to tell you, David. Especially when I realized that I loved you. I wanted to tell you—so much it hurt." She then told him of the experience with the young man at college. "I was too frightened. I wanted you to investigate the Church for the right reasons."

"I see. I guess you were right not to talk to me about it for several reasons. Maybe it was for the best that I discovered it on my own—when I was ready."

They walked in silence the rest of the way. As they entered, Torry said, "How about a big glass of ice water?"

"Sounds great."

They put their glasses down on the kitchen counter and went into each others arms, their lips touched tenderly, gently—then in joyous rapture.

When they pulled apart, David said, "Let's get married soon. Let's sit down and set a date right now."

"First, you promised that you would relate everything to me again. And—I'm going to buy you a journal, David Mayer. I want you to record everything as soon as possible so that you won't forget one little thing. One day you'll pick up your journal and be able to relive it all again."

"That's a wonderful idea, Torry."

They sat together in the front room. With David's arm around Torry, he once again told her everything about his conversion and baptism, remembering little things he'd forgotten to tell her before, such as the conversation with Dan and Jesse. He enjoyed the retelling of it as much as she did hearing it. Afterward, they sat there enjoying each other's closeness, feeling such joy they couldn't speak for awhile.

David broke the silence. "There isn't any reason for us to wait is there? Let's get married soon, Torry."

"I also want to get married soon, David." Her heart sunk, the time had come—the moment she'd been dreading, but she knew she had to tell him—now. She said a quick prayer, took a deep breath and began, "Remember, David, when I mentioned that there were two obstacles?"

An expression of dread came over David's face. "Torry, aren't we over that? I thought it all had to do with the fact that I wasn't a member of the Church."

"Yes, it was, but there is one more, and this is one we'll both struggle over, my dearest. Together we can live with it—but only if you choose to live with it. It will be entirely up to you."

He spoke almost inaudibly, "Surely you won't keep this one back from me, saying that I won't understand?"

"No, I'll tell you right now. I don't want to but I have to." The serious expression on her face alarmed David. "In the discussions you heard a little about the Temples and how families are sealed for time and eternity, didn't you?"

"Yes."

Torry didn't know how else to tell him but just straight out. "Jack and I were sealed in the temple for time and eternity."

His brows furrowed, thinking... "I assumed that but..."

"That means, Jack and I are still sealed and will be man and wife in the next life." She said it without conviction because she couldn't see how it could be possible after finding out about Jack, but it had to be said anyway. She knew it was the Lord's judgement, not hers.

David became pensive, silent, then slowly asked, "You accepted my proposal, Torry, so surely this doesn't mean we can't be married." He said it with finality, brooking no argument.

"We can be married, David, but only for time—only for this mortal life—not for eternity."

"You mean—we can be married and love each other with all our hearts but after we die...you...you and Jack and the boys will be a family forever?"

"That's what temple marriage means, David. It means being sealed together for eternity."

Yes, he thought, the missionaries taught him that. Of course! Torry would want to be sealed to the man she was married to for so many years and who fathered her sons! What right had he to step in at this late date and expect Torry to want him instead?

In spite of this realization, he burst out, "But—I want you for eternity, Torry. I can't imagine a life hereafter without you. It isn't fair!" He jumped up and began pacing the floor. "I've been denied a family all my life—and now that I've found the gospel and you— I can only have a family for this life? I can't settle for that."

"You don't have to settle for that, David," she said quietly. "There's a solution for you...and that is to marry a younger woman in the temple who has never been married and who can have children. This way you can have a family for eternity. You deserve this, David."

David scoffed bitterly. "I've dated many younger women, but never found one I wanted to date more than three times. I'll never find another woman like you, Torry. This is not a solution for me."

"But David, you haven't dated anyone who is a member of the Church. You have no way to make a comparison."

"You're right, but none of them are you," he groaned. Pulling her up, he took her in his arms and kissed her possessively, passionately, then put his lips to her ear and spoke in a breathless whisper, "You belong to me, Torry, I can feel it."

Torry's heart ached for him—for herself. Clinging to him, she whispered back, "I feel it too, David. But can you marry me for time only?"

David was silent, holding her close. The minutes stretched out while her heart pounded with anxiety, wanting him to answer but afraid to hear the answer.

Reluctantly he let go of her, his pain filled eyes studied hers, "I don't know Torry—I don't know. I need some time to think about it."

"David, we need to dissolve our partnership and put the house and farm up for sale."

Shock flitted across his face. "That's a little rash, Torry."

"No it isn't, David, I've been giving it a lot of thought. If we get married, I wouldn't want to be tied to a chicken farm, I would want to give all my attention to you, to travel with you when you have to oversee your businesses."

"Torry..." groaned David, pulling her close again. "That sounds wonderful."

"On the other hand, David," she said softly, "if you find that you can't marry me for time only, I couldn't bear to live here anymore. There are too many memories of you in this little place."

They clung together desperately, not wanting to face the decision that could separate them. At long last, David let go. Turning away from her, he walked to the door. Torry followed him out to the car. Before he got in he glanced at her, "I need some time to think, Torry. I love you."

"I love you, too," she said before he closed the door. She watched him drive away until he was out of sight.

Chapter Thirty-Four

Again, David found himself driving aimlessly. All he could feel at the moment was frustration and confusion. What did the Lord expect of him anyway? Was this his reward for accepting the gospel?

Growing up, he was abandoned by his mother and step-father, people who were supposed to love him. And now was he to accept being abandoned in the next life? Was he supposed to hand Torry and her sons over to Jack and say "They're yours now," and then go off and wander around alone?

Why did he have to meet Torry anyway? Convinced now that God had dealt him a dirty blow, old bitterness began to take over. How could God be a just God and allow this kind of disparity? A feeling of darkness came over him. He couldn't help compare this devastating emotion with the way he felt yesterday, and today just a short time ago. Maybe he'd been deceived. How could this be the true church and allow such injustice. These thoughts startled him—remembering the warning Tom had given him.

He suddenly realized that Satan was already working on what he thought he'd long put behind him—the fear of abandonment. He pulled over to the side of the road and pled with the Lord to help him, to keep Satan from pulling him off the course. His hands shook with fear as he gripped the steering wheel. In spite of his prayer, however, a heavy depression descended upon him.

"David?" came a familiar voice through the window.

David looked up and saw Tom looking at him through the open window. "Tom! Where did you come from?"

"I was driving home after visiting a sick member of the ward, when I saw your car parked here. Is something wrong?"

"I've never been so relieved to see anyone in my life, Tom. I need some help...I...I feel like Satan is trying to destroy me."

"Lock up your car, Dave, and let me drive you to my place. I'll take you in the front and tell Jenny not to let any of the children come in."

"Thank you, Tom. I'm shaking so badly, I don't think I could drive."

"I can see that."

David looked at his watch as they drove. It was only 7:30. It was only a half-hour ago that he left Torry's, yet it seemed like hours.

Seated in the peaceful Baker home, David felt a little calmer. Tom sat across from him.

"Tell me about it, Dave."

David told him of learning about Torry being married to Jack in the temple for time and eternity. "I should have known this as I was hearing about it—but I didn't put it together."

Tom let out a heavy sigh, remembering his worry about this very thing. "That must have been a blow, Dave. I don't know what I would do if I were in your situation."

"I had gotten over feeling bitter about my life a long time ago, but when I heard this, it all came back. What shall I do, Tom?"

"What kind of a man was Jack?"

"I don't know. Torry has never talked about him. In fact, she has avoided it."

"Hmnn, I wonder if she's talked about him to Zelda?"

"Why do you ask that?"

"Well," Tom said, "when someone you love dies, it's usual to talk about him or her from time to time."

"No matter how she feels about him, apparently she's sealed to him."

Tom wanted to tell him that Torry and Jack were only sealed if the Holy Spirit of Promise ratified the sealing, but knew it wasn't his place to give him this kind of information. He didn't know Jack, and even if he did, there is a certain amount of repentance possible in the spirit world and it wasn't his place to judge.

"Are you going to marry Torry for time, Dave?"

"I don't know. All I know is that not being able to marry her for time and eternity in the temple has caused me to doubt God, and doubt the truthfulness of the gospel. You warned me about this...a darkness came over me..."

"Would you like a blessing?"

"A blessing?"

Tom explained again what a priesthood blessing was.

"I would like that, Tom, thanks."

Later, David couldn't remember all that Tom said, but he remembered well the immediate lifting of the dark depression. He sat there, astounded at the power of the priesthood—and at the power of Satan, knowing that his frame of mind had given the Adversary a power over him that he never wanted to experience again.

Standing up, he shook Tom's hand and told him what had happened during the blessing.

Tom, greatly relieved, asked, "Now, Dave, how are you going to deal with this problem without letting yourself become bitter again?"

"Pray a lot, read the scriptures." He smiled for the first time since Tom picked him up. "I can hardly wait to dive into those beautiful books you all gave me."

"Good. You have the answer to it. I don't know why I feel this way, Dave, but I feel that if you continue doing what you've been doing, reading the scriptures, praying, attending church and so on, that everything will turn out all right for you—I don't know how—but this is the way I feel."

"You don't know how good that makes me feel. I know I'll still suffer over not being able to have Torry forever, but—I believe what you said. Thanks, Tom."

After Tom had dropped David at his car, David drove toward Torry's. He said a silent prayer, thanking the Lord for Tom's intervention, and as he did so, two strong impressions came to his mind.

He knocked on Torry's screen door. Seeing him, she opened it and sagged against the doorframe in relief. "David! I'm so glad you came back, I've been so worried. Come in."

"You should have worried, it scares me to think what would have happened if Tom hadn't come by and helped me out."

A look of concern crossed her face, "Come and sit down. Tell me about it."

They walked to the couch, but before Torry could seat herself, David put his arms around her. "Torry, I've missed you—I need you."

"I need you too, David," she murmured. "What happened?"

"I went through a little bit of hell, Torry."

They sat down and David proceeded to tell her what happened, carefully skirting the abandonment issue.

"I've been worried," Torry said, "wondering when the Adversary would buffet you. It always happens. You know David, it wasn't just unusual timing that Tom came by."

"You keep telling me about the Lord putting people in my life, and I'm beginning to believe it. I'm amazed at the things that have happened since the baptism. First, Tom coming by and giving me a blessing that literally saved me and while I was driving back here, two impressions came to my mind—quite forcefully."

"Really?" Torry asked, intrigued. "Can you tell me, David?"

He smiled at her, pulling her closer, feeling greatly relieved to be in her presence again after what he'd been through. "I sure can. The first one is: I feel that we need to go see your mother. I've neglected her. I didn't even call or send her a get well card."

Torry clapped her hands. "Wonderful David! I've been feeling a little concerned about her. What is the second one?"

"This one is about us. I can't imagine life without you, Torry. I'm still struggling over the situation. But as I was in the car going over it all in my mind, I had a strong feeling that you and I need more time together—more time to get to know each other on this different plane. After all, my love," he said smiling at her, "it was only one week today that you told me you loved me."

"Can you believe what has happened in one week? And don't forget the miracle that happened to my mother."

"We have been greatly blessed, as I've heard Jessie and Dan say. I feel ashamed for being greedy—wanting you for more than this life."

"Then I'm greedy too, David."

"You...you mean you don't want to be with Jack in the next life?"

"I want to be with you!" she said emphatically, evading a direct answer.

"Tell me about Jack, Torry."

"I will tell you, but not now, let's finish talking about our plans."

"All right," he said hesitantly, "we'll talk about him later. You are right about selling the chicken farm, Torry—not the house yet. This little house is like home to me, I've never been so happy as here with you. The chickens will be ready to sell in two or three weeks won't they?"

"Yes."

"Since we've decided to make changes in our lives, there are several people I would like to help. You know, Torry, being wealthy is often a burden. There are so many people who need help—and I have helped, often to their detriment."

"There is an art to giving so that it helps people rather than harming them. It has taken me a while to learn. Zelda has been a wonderful friend to us. I would like to give the chicken house with all its equipment and most of the acreage to Zelda and Zak since Gilford has shown an interest in it. What do you think, Torry?"

Torry was so surprised, she couldn't answer for a moment. Finally she said, "What a wonderful idea, David."

"But, Torry—what if I can't resolve my feelings about our situation, what will you do?"

Her heart sunk over the 'if.' "I don't know, David, all I know is that I can't stay here."

"I understand. I don't know how Zak and Zelda will want to handle it with Gil but I feel that giving this to them will be all right."

"Yes, they are sensible people, they'll know how to handle it," she said, her heart heavy.

"But I would like to have the chicken house moved further away, wherever they would like it, so we can keep a third of an acre around this house."

"Why keep the house, David?" she asked.

"Because...because it's ours, Torry."

Torry fought back tears, remembering that David's heart was as heavy as hers. "All right, David, who are the others you want to help?"

"No matter what happens, Torry, my time in Green Valley will be up. This was supposed to be for only a couple of years so—I want to give my stock in the chain of banks to Tom Baker."

"Give your stock to him outright?"

"Yes. What do you think?"

"I think it would be wonderful for that family! They deserve it. But..." she smiled wistfully, "I'm kinda sentimental about the bank. After all, that's where we first met and where you proposed to me."

David leaned over and kissed her tenderly. "Me to, I'm more than a little sentimental over the bank." He shook his head, his face clouding up. "I love you, Torry, I..."

"Tell me who else you would like to help?" she quickly asked.

"I'd like to forgive the loans that Dan and Jesse have taken out this year. Those two need to quit working quite so hard."

"How wonderful to have money to help people like this." Suddenly Torry chuckled.

"Why the amusement?" David asked, surprised.

"I would like to see Bishop Price's face when he sees your first tithing check."

David smiled. "I'm going to enjoy that myself. Giving to the church is going to be very satisfying. Then you approve of what I want to do?" Torry nodded vigorously. "Good. Now about you and me. After we visit your mother, then your sons, I'd like to take you to Dallas with me."

"W...why, David?"

"I told you I felt we needed to spend more time together and...I also want to take you meet a friend of mine—and I want him and his wife to meet you. His name is Gabe. He's the one who convinced me I needed to take a leave of absence and spend a couple of years in a small town. If it hadn't been for him, I wouldn't have met you or joined the Church. He wanted me to look for a Mormon town because he said the lifestyle would be more relaxing." David grinned, "You see, he's a Mormon."

Torry's mouth dropped open, "He...is? Well, there's another one the Lord arranged to help point you in the right direction."

"I haven't told him of my baptism yet. I want to tell him and his wife in person."

Torry laughed with excitement, "What a surprise for them."

"Then you'll come with me?" he asked eagerly.

"Yes—but let's talk to the boys about it. Is that all right with you?"

"Of course, they're your family, and Gabe is the nearest thing I have to a family. He and his wife have taken it upon themselves to look after me."

In spite of their present uncertainty, Torry found herself feeling excited about the trips and anxious to meet David's friends. "When shall we leave David?"

"I think I can get things arranged by Tuesday night so Tom can take over while we're out of town. Then we can go see Zelda and Zak. Could we leave Wednesday morning?"

Chapter Thirty-Five

"You're what?" Tom Baker was sure he hadn't heard right.

David repeated it, "I'm going to have a conference call with the Board of Directors. I'll tell them that you will be taking over as the president of the bank in my place because I have to get back to Dallas."

"But, David, you said that you would be here for at least two years."

"My life has changed, Torry's life has changed. Because of this, I have to cut the time short here in Green Valley and we both feel that we must make other arrangements about the chicken farm."

Tom's face didn't reflect the excitement David had expected, "We'll miss you here at the bank, Dave—and Jenny and the children will miss you. We had hoped to enjoy your company more now that you've joined the Church."

"I can't give up the little house yet, Tom. If Torry and I get married, we'll be back every summer for a while to see everyone. This has felt more like home than any place I've ever lived."

"I'm certainly glad to hear that, Dave," he said, a big smile of relief spreading across his face.

"Do you think the new loan officer we hired will be able to take your place, Tom?"

"I do. I'm impressed with his capabilities. But the big question is, will I be able to take your place?"

"I'm sure you will, Tom, but only if you hire another loan officer because you'll have to travel now and then to check on the other banks in the chain."

"Why? You won't be able to?"

"I'm giving you my stock in the chain."

Tom just stared at him blankly.

David smiled and waited him out.

"Uh...Dave what did you say?"

David repeated it and added, "I'm sure you know how difficult it is to help people financially without it hurting them in some way.

You've told me how the church welfare program works and why. But I feel right about doing this."

"I'm grateful to you, Tom, for living the principles of the gospel and for applying them even in your work here at the bank with me, for your dealings with all the employees as well as the customers. If you hadn't, I wouldn't have been in your home that day when I saw the Book of Mormon."

"It's just a way of saying thank you to you and your family for accepting me into your lives, for introducing me to the gospel, for arranging for the discussions and..." David couldn't speak, emotion momentarily overcoming him, "for baptizing me."

Emotion also gripped Tom for a moment, then he spoke quietly, "Dave, our family doesn't need that kind of thanks. The thanks should be on our side for allowing us the privilege of introducing the gospel to you."

"I understand, Tom. I would like to tell everyone I know about it. But as Dan and Jesse taught me, I need the blessings of doing this for you. Will you accept it?"

He answered in almost a whisper, "Yes, but the offer is a little overwhelming—do you think I can handle it?"

"Definitely. I'll be here for three or four more weeks and I'll work with you. Before I do however, Torry and I need to spend some more time together. I felt that strongly as I drove to her house after you gave me that blessing. We need to go see her mother, and then I want to take her to meet Gabe and spend a few days in Dallas."

"When will you leave?"

"Day after tomorrow, Wednesday. I'll catch up so that you won't have so much to do. Well," he said, standing up, "I better get into my office and get started."

Tom got up and went around the desk, holding out his hand to David, "How can I thank you, Dave? I...I'm in a state of shock. Jenny will be too—but she'll be very grateful, it's been tight with seven children..." He blinked back tears of gratitude. Hugging his friend, they clapped each other on the back with great affection.

~~~~~~~~~~

Monday afternoon, her clothes washed and folded, Torry retrieved several suitcases from the small dingy basement in preparation for the trip.

She stepped into the closet and went through her wardrobe again. She was still convinced she had nothing to take to Dallas. David might take her to a nice restaurant, maybe a musical. She pulled out several of her old favorites, a few casual clothes and decided that she would definitely take time to go to a couple of department stores in Salt lake. Hearing the phone ring, she ran to the kitchen.

"Hello?"

David's low, mellow voice came over the wire, "Hello my darling. I'm in my office trying to catch up, but was so lonesome, I had to call."

"I'm so glad. I'm lonesome, too."

"What are you doing?"

"I'm trying to figure out what to take on the trip to Dallas, but I'm a little discouraged with my wardrobe."

"Torry, I would love to take you to some fashion places in Dallas and buy you whatever you want."

"Ah, that sounds wonderful—but no thanks, I'll find something in Salt Lake."

David smiled to himself. The women he'd known would have jumped at the chance. "Torry, I like your taste in clothes and if you didn't buy another thing, I would find you beautiful and right in style wherever we went."

"Love is blind, my dear David. Have you told Tom about the changes?"

"Yes, I've told Tom. His reaction was just what you'd expect."

"You'll have to tell me more about it when we see each other. What are you doing?"

"I'm trying to catch up on everything that I let go last week. I'm not even going to be able to see you until tomorrow night when we go see Zelda and Zak."

"Not even for dinner?"

"No. I'm going to call Zelda and ask if we can even come by as late as nine o'clock."

"All right, David. I guess I'll just have to be content with that.

I can hardly wait for Wednesday morning so I can be with you every day."

David smiled as he hung up the phone, thinking how happy Torry made him. She said just the right thing to lift his spirits. He, too, could hardly wait until Wednesday, which reminded him he had a standing appointment on Wednesdays with Dan and Jessie.

He pulled out his check book and wrote two checks to the bank for their loans, then two more checks to deposit in their accounts. He would tell Tom to inform them when they came in to 'roust him out of his office,' as they put it. He grinned as he visualized their reactions.

~~~~~~~~~~~~

Tuesday night at 8:55, Zelda and Zak were waiting in their living room for Torry and David, feeling very curious. David had requested that Ivan and Gilford not be there.

Zelda had tried to worm it out of Torry earlier in the day when they had lunch together. Finally the door bell rang, and Zelda jumped up and let them in.

"It's about time you two arrived."

"But, Zelda, we're about two minutes early," Torry said.

"You could have been earlier, you know."

David and Torry laughed, then greeted Zak.

"All right, sit down you two and tell us what's up," Zelda demanded.

David grinned, "Oh...we just wanted to know if Gilford and maybe Ivan too could take care of the chickens for about ten days or so."

Zelda looked askance at him. "So why did it take the corporate herd to come and make this request? And...where are you two going and why?"

As they had earlier agreed, David and Torry explained, with frankness, the present situation between the two of them and why they were taking the trips.

For a moment there was only silence, finally broken by Zak. "We'll be praying for you both. I'm sure the Lord will help you work it out."

"Thank you. We appreciate that," David said. He handed Zelda a card with her parent's Salt Lake phone number, as well as his office number in Dallas.

"Have you told anyone else?" asked Zelda.

"Only Tom and Jenny," answered David. Speaking of telling people, that reminds me, I've got to call the bishop tomorrow morning and tell him we're leaving town for a few days."

"We appreciate you two giving the boys this opportunity," Zak said. "Gil is interested in the chicken farm business and Ivan is getting interested now, so this is a good education for them. Neither one is interested in raising Alfalfa like I do, and they aren't interested in raising horses. Maybe they can both work for you when you expand."

Torry and David smiled at each other, then David said, "I don't think that will work out."

Zak's look of disappointment only lasted an instant. "That's fine David, we appreciate them being able to earn a little money when you need them."

"Zak," David began, "I'm afraid the boys will have to find someone to work for them when they expand."

"Huh?" Zelda asked, clearly bewildered. She and Zak looked at each other, then at Torry and David.

"Here's the deed to nine and two-thirds acres and the chicken house with all its equipment," David said, handing it to Zak. "We want to keep the house and a third-of-an-acre. If Torry and I get married, we'll be moving from Green Valley but..."

"You're moving away?" Zelda interrupted, a look of distress on her face. "Why?"

"I'm sure you didn't know, but I was only intending to stay in Green Valley for about two years and then return to Dallas. Now, as we explained, circumstances have changed. But if things work out like we want, Torry and I will be back every summer for a visit."

A look of relief replaced the distress—then what David had said before began to sink in. "Wait a minute here," Zelda said, "did you say something about the deed to the property?"

David smiled and repeated it. "Also, we'll move the chicken house further back so that it will be more convenient, and we'll plumb it for water. You can use the extra acreage for pasture can't you?"

For once Zelda was speechless but Zak managed to mumble, "It sounds like...uh...I don't understand."

"It's all yours," Torry said. "We want you and Zelda to have it. I'll also give you all the research I've done on the poultry business, as well as the secrets of raising delicious chicken meat from my grandmother."

"I will deposit some money in your account," David added, "for expansion when the time comes, that is, if you'll do us the favor of accepting what brought Torry and me together—the chicken farm. We don't know any one who will take better care of it. Gil has proven himself by taking such good care of the chickens. We're impressed how you've taught your boys to work, so we know that if you choose to carry on the chicken farm, it will be in good hands. If you choose not to, the money deposited for it can go toward something else."

Zelda gulped, finally able to speak, "You...you wouldn't josh about a thing like this would you?"

"Why us?" Zak asked, still so astounded, he could hardly assimilate the information.

"Because," Torry said, "we love you. You've been so kind to us since we've been here. Please accept it. If for any reason you change your mind about staying in the poultry business, I'm sure you'll be able to sell the equipment."

"Well if this just doesn't take the blue ribbon," exclaimed Zelda, then she burst into tears.

Torry went over and hugged her. In a few moments, Zelda blubbered through her tears, "I finally get a neighbor who can put up with Henry, and she moves away."

Torry laughed through hers. "I may miss Henry as much as I'll miss you, Zelda."

Zelda sniffled, pulled away and studied Torry's face. Finally she smiled. "Well...I'm sure you'll be coming back each summer. At least a small carrot is better than none."

"We...we don't quite know how to thank you both," Zak said, moved beyond words.

Chapter Thirty-Six

By Wednesday morning, everything was done. The lawn, shrubs and trees were watered, Gil and Ivan had been over to get final instructions, and Torry's bags were packed and set by the front door. She looked at her watch and saw that it was 8:50 A.M. David said he'd pick her up at 9:00.

She was suffering an attack of nerves. The change that came over David when she told him they couldn't be sealed, brought back some of the old insecurities from her days with Jack.

As she had stared into the mirror earlier, she wasn't sure about her appearance. Studying her ensemble, she frowned. At one time she thought she looked good in the light blue cotton pant set with the accessories: a small silver belt, silver earrings and bracelet. The doorbell rang. Taking a deep breath she went to greet David.

Torry opened the screen door, noticing how handsome he looked in his gray cotton pants and navy shirt. "Come in, David, I'm all ready."

He studied her face, "What's the matter, Torry?" he asked, taking her hands in his. "Hmmn, cold hands, cold feet perchance?"

"I guess I'm just a little nervous about everything."

"Why?"

"Things are so unsettled between us."

"I know...and I'm sorry." He dropped her hands and put his arms around her, kissed her tenderly, then pushed her back. "Let me look at you. You look lovely in blue and silver, and might I add you've got the kind of figure that makes everything look great."

As usual, Torry thought, he said the right thing. Her nervousness left, and she smiled up at him. "Thank you, David. Well, here are my bags. Shall we go?"

"Is this all of them?"

"Yes."

"Only one tote bag and one suitcase?"

"Well the suitcase is large, but not very full. I'm going to do a little shopping in Salt lake."

"But still...I guess I'm used to wealthy women who almost have to have an entourage to carry their luggage. It's rather refreshing to see yours." He picked them up and they went out, and Torry locked the door.

After they had driven a while, Torry asked, "Aren't we going in the wrong direction, David?"

"Nope," he said grinning. "We're going to the airstrip outside of town. I've arranged for a small plane to take us to Salt Lake."

"You have?" Torry asked in surprise. "Is this the way you always go out of town?"

"It is. I have to get to places fast and driving to Salt Lake wastes too much time."

"I haven't called my folks so they'll be surprised to see us. You will stay with us won't you, David?"

"Thanks, Torry, but I don't think that would be wise at this time. Your father doesn't like me, and I'm afraid that it will take all I've got to be civil to him after what he did to you. I've made reservations for a tower suite at the Little America Hotel."

~~~~~~~~~~~~~~~

David parked the rented car in the driveway of the Conway residence. The house was a lovely rambler of light brick in an older neighborhood of upper middle class homes.

They walked hand in hand along the sidewalk to the wide front porch. Torry rang the bell to warn them and soon it opened. A very surprised George Conway stood there, momentarily speechless.

"Torry! What are you doing here?"

"David and I are here to see how Mother is."

"How are you, George?" David said, holding out his hand.

George eyed him a moment then gave his hand a cursory shake. "I'm fine thank you," he said, a slight coolness in his voice.

"May we come in, Dad?"

"Oh...uh yes, come in. Your mother is in the family room."

They found Ruth on a recliner reading. "Hello, Mother."

Ruth looked up from her book and her face was one of shock, then joy. "Torry! David! I can't believe it. What a wonderful surprise," she said as she started to get up.

"Stay down, Mother," Torry said bending down and hugging her.

David hunkered down, taking Ruth's hand in both his. "Am I glad to see you well and getting better, Ruth. You gave us a scare."

"Thank you for the beautiful card and huge bouquet of flowers," she said pointing to them.

Torry looked at the flowers, surprised. "They are beautiful, David, thank you from me." She smiled at him, her eyes filled with love.

George was disturbed to see the expression on Torry's face when she looked at David.

"What are you two up here for?" Ruth asked.

"David wanted to see you, Mother. He says he neglected you during your illness."

"He didn't neglect me, it wasn't his worry."

"Oh he did neglect you, Mother...and for a good reason. We can hardly wait to tell you about it."

"Really? I'm anxious to hear, but first have you two had lunch?"

"No we haven't, have you and Dad?"

"Yes," replied her father. "We had pizza and fruit. There's plenty left over, would you like some?"

"We would, Dad, come show me. It sounds like you've been cookin' up a storm for Mother," she said poking fun. "David, you stay here and visit with Mother, while Dad and I put lunch on."

Ruth smiled at David, "Please sit down. George wanted pizza even though we still have plenty of food in the freezer that Church members have brought over."

"Really?" David said, impressed.

"I don't know how long you're here for David, but we'd like to invite you to stay with us."

"Thank you, Ruth, I'd accept in a minute but you are still recuperating."

"That isn't a problem, Torry and George can handle everything."

"That's nice of you, but no...some other time. I've made a reservation at Little America Hotel."

"It's ready," Torry said, bringing in a tray of pizza and fruit. Dad is setting up TV trays so we can visit in here while we eat."

"What are your plans?" Ruth asked, looking at each of them.

David sat down in front of one of the trays and answered, "I know Torry would like to see the boys, so I thought we'd give them a call and see if it would be convenient to take them out to dinner early tomorrow night, that is," he grinned at Torry, "if it's all right with their mother."

"What do you think?" she replied, beaming. "If we go early, I'll show you around the Brigham Young University campus. And David, while we're here you must see Temple Square and the..."

"Don't you think you're pushing it a little, Torry...as usual," her father said.

David bristled. "Torry knows, George, that I'm anxious to see all the Church historical sights and especially Temple Square."

Torry, still flushing with embarrassment over her father's sarcasm, noticed the grim set of David's jaw and knew he wouldn't buckle under to her father as Jack had done.

"All right you two," Ruth said a little too brightly, "let's hear what you have to tell us."

"First, Mother, tell us about your condition. How do the doctors think you're progressing?"

David and Torry ate as Ruth answered the question in more detail than normally in order to ease the situation. She finished with, "The doctors are very pleased over how quickly I'm recovering. It's probably because your father has been taking such good care of me. He's given up a lot to do so..." she winked at him, "he's given up his golf games. Now it's your turn, Torry and David. What do you have to tell us?"

"You tell it, David," Torry said.

"Well...after Torry left with her boys to be with you, Ruth, I went to visit my friend Tom Baker. We were eating ice cream at the kitchen table when I saw a pile of books which looked like Bibles. They were in center of the table on a Lazy Susan. I asked about them. It was then that I was introduced to the Book of Mormon."

"You mean Torry hadn't foisted it upon you yet?" George asked.

Anger seethed inside David but when he saw Ruth's anxiety he let it go. Knowing now that he couldn't tell the details he knew Ruth would want to hear while in George Conway's presence, he just said, "To make a long story short, I was baptized into the Church last Saturday morning."

Ruth gasped, "You...were? I can hardly believe it!" She looked at Torry and their eyes met, then turning her smile on David, she said, "We're so happy for you David."

"Wasn't that a little fast?" George asked.

"It was at that wasn't it," David replied coldly. "I'm sure, George, that now you can see why I want to see all the Church historical sites and Temple Square. Well," he said standing up, leaving his half-eaten pizza, "I think I'll go bring in Torry's bags and go check into the hotel. Thank you for the pizza. I'll see you both later."

"I'll go with you David," Torry said.

They walked to the car in silence. After David got the bags out, Torry said, "I'm sorry about my father."

"So am I, Torry, mostly for you and your mother. It was all I could do to keep my cool when he talked to you the way he did."

"Please don't worry about it, David, I don't think he's going to change. When I was up here for Mother's operation, I found an opportunity to apologize to him for what I said that provoked him to hit me."

"And?"

"He just said, 'I accept your apology, Torry, it's too bad we got angry with each other.'" He can't say 'I'm sorry' which is too bad...for him especially."

David shook his head then mentally dismissed George Conway. "Torry, I'm going to give you the rest of today and part of tomorrow to spend with your mother and to do some shopping. If you don't mind, I would like to go to Temple Square alone. I have a lot of thinking to do. Is that all right with you?" She nodded, thoughtful, and he added, "Call the boys and make a dinner date for late afternoon tomorrow. Let's plan on leaving Salt Lake for Provo about 3:00 in the afternoon."

"All right, David. I'll spend the rest of the day with Mother, then shop tomorrow. Pick me up at the corner of the department store called ZCMI, at Main Street."

"All right." He picked up the bags and they walked up onto the porch. Torry held the door open and he set the bags inside, then she pulled it closed, remaining on the porch with him.

"I think you're wonderful, David," she whispered, "and I love you even more after seeing you interact with my father."

David couldn't have been more surprised. He shook his head, "I'm afraid you won't always be pleased with me, Torry, I may have to tell him off sometime when your mother isn't around."

"Do whatever you have to do."

David took her in his arms and kissed her, then held her for a long time. "I'll miss you. Tomorrow is a long way off, my darling."

"Thank you for saying that, David. I feel—a little insecure about us."

"Why? Is it because I haven't come to grips with the problem?"

"That's part of it but not all. Sometime when the time is right I'll tell you."

"We're still holding things back from each other, aren't we?"

"It appears so, see you tomorrow," she said smiling at him.

"Tomorrow." He turned and ran to the car.

Torry stepped inside and found her father waiting for her in the entry hall. He picked up her bags and carried them into her bedroom. Torry followed.

He turned to her. "Well, can you tell me what is going on between you and that Jew?"

"I want to freshen up, Dad, then I'll be in to talk to both of you."

George Conway grunted, opened his mouth to say something, then turned abruptly and left. Torry closed the door behind him, relieved that she'd side-stepped an argument.

George returned to the family room. "I don't know whether I like Torry getting mixed up with a Jew, Ruth."

Ruth sighed and a sudden tiredness came over her. "Why not, George?"

"I've had dealings with some and they're aggressive, money grabbing, obnoxious people as a rule."

"You know better than to lump all Jewish people together like that. People have done that to the Mormons. What is really eating at you, George? Is it that you can't manipulate him like you could Jack?"

George was shocked. Ruth was never sharp with him, but lately, she had become quite outspoken. He was about to retort when Torry walked in.

"Well now, I feel better. What is it you both want to know?" she asked smiling.

Ruth's tiredness left. "**Tell** us, Torry, what has happened between you and David—**something** has. It's written all over both of you?"

It was unspoken knowledge between Torry and her mother that they would discuss the details **just** between the two of them later. "David loves me, and I love **him**."

"Oh? And does he know **that** you're sealed to Jack?" her father asked sarcastically.

"Please George, stop this! I can't have it anymore. If needs be, Torry and I will go off and **talk** privately."

"All right, all right."

"Yes he does, Dad. So we **may** not get married. He asked me to marry him before he joined **the** Church. Now he's struggling with the idea that I'm sealed to Jack."

"Did you even think to encourage him to marry someone who hasn't been married?"

"George!" Ruth cried.

"Mother don't, let me handle this." With tears stinging her eyes, she said, "Dad, do you ever give me credit for anything? From the beginning, I looked upon David simply as my banker and friend. I knew anything else would not be fair to him. And yes, I've encouraged him to at least meet and get to know some of the younger single women in the Church. At this point, he won't even discuss it. I'm praying about it, and he's praying about it."

"All right, go on," he grudgingly conceded.

"Go on? Is that all you have to say? Dad, can't you ever say I'm sorry?"

"Don't be ridiculous, Torry, I'm just concerned..."

"Forget it, Dad. I've got to go call the boys and then I'll clean up the kitchen." She leaned down and hugged her mother and whispered in her ear. "I'm fine, I'm happy, I love you."

Torry went into her room to call the boys, and Ruth went into hers to lie down, feeling weary. She desperately needed George to go back to his golf, his investments and his ball games.

"George," Ruth said as he entered the room, "why don't you go play a game of golf and relax, you need it. You've been under a lot of stress this last week. I'll be fine with Torry here, and I may take a nap."

George thought about it a minute. "I believe I'll take you up on that Ruth, a round of golf sounds like what I need."

After George left, Ruth heard Torry come out of her room. "Torry, come into the bedroom, I'm lying down."

"Are you all right, Mother?"

"I'm feeling much better. I sent your father off to play a game of golf. Sit down on the bed and tell me everything, Torry. Tell me what happened when the helicopter dropped you off."

Torry sat down on her mother's bed and sighed. "I'd love to tell you everything, Mother. I need to talk to you."

Chapter Thirty-Seven

David checked into one of Little America's tower suites and freshened up. After checking on the distance, he decided to walk to Temple Square rather than drive. It was only a little after 3:00 and the late June sun was bright and hot, nevertheless, he walked rapidly.

When he walked through the wide open gates to Temple Square, he stopped and looked around, trying to take it all in. The flowers, trees and green lawns surrounding the temple with its spires reaching heavenward, were even more awe inspiring than he expected. He wandered around for a while, feeling the same peace he'd felt when studying the gospel. Drawn to the temple, he walked as close to it as possible, looking up at the glorious architecture of it, longing for the time when he could enter. A year was a long time to wait.

He sat down on the lawn. While gazing at the temple, he silently prayed for help with the conflicting emotions he felt over not being able to marry Torry there for eternity. After some time, he realized he wasn't getting answers here anymore than he was getting answers in the privacy of his bedroom.

He got up and sauntered through every section of the beautiful grounds. A tour group drew him in but he soon had to forego it, his mind too preoccupied with his problem.

Through the huge window of the visitors center, he gazed in awe at the magnificent statue of Christ. He made a mental note to return and go inside on his next visit.

He planned to go see what they called, the Joseph Smith Memorial Building so, reluctantly, he left the peaceful surroundings and walked to the corner. The wide streets of downtown Salt Lake were busy. Never had he seen a city's downtown area better utilized or more productive.

He studied the architecture of the Joseph Smith Memorial Building. A magnificent structure, he thought. As he entered, a lovely older woman greeted him and asked him a few questions. Finding out that he was here for the first time, she suggested he go

in and see the movie called Legacy which was starting in ten minutes. He decided to go. After receiving directions to the theatre, he
thanked her.

Moving on to the center of the historic old lobby, a large white
statue of Joseph Smith caught his eye. He stopped a moment, staring at it. A feeling of awe came over him, and once again the Spirit
testified that Joseph Smith was a prophet of God, and that the
President of the Church today is a prophet, just as surely as were
Moses and Abraham. Thrilled with the comfort and security this
knowledge gave him, he followed the directions to the theatre.

After the movie, choked with emotion, David walked out of the
theatre. Realizing that what he had just seen and experienced while
watching the amazing production of *Legacy* made him want to go
back to Temple Square and ponder it all.

Once again inside the temple grounds, he found a secluded spot
and sat down. His heart swelled with emotion; he felt pain over
what the Mormon pioneers went through; he anguished over his
own people, the Jews who also suffered terrible persecution.
Gratitude for the gospel filled his soul. He studied the temple, overwhelmed with amazement that the early settlers of this valley could
have built such a glorious edifice. His testimony had increased
immeasurably during this short visit and, it made him think of
Torry. "How can I live without her, dear Father?" he whispered,
"And how can I live without her on the other side?"

He sat there till long after dark, seeing the temple light up in
luminous splendor. He got up and walked back to the hotel, no
closer to a resolution than before, but filled with the Spirit and—
love for Torry.

Chapter Thirty-Eight

Torry awoke early feeling excitement at the thought of meeting David and visiting with her sons. While showering and dressing, she let her happiness build, unfettered by the uncertainty over David. She entered the empty kitchen humming and began preparing a big breakfast for the three of them.

Twenty minutes later her father walked into the kitchen carrying the morning paper. "This is a treat, honey," he said, smiling.

"Good morning, darling," her mother said, following her husband in and gingerly sitting down at the kitchen table. "It was nice to wake up to such tantalizing aromas."

"I hope you each have a good appetite this morning, because I've made a breakfast big enough for three hired-hands."

During breakfast, George opened the paper and read while Torry and her mother visited.

When her father was through eating, he folded his paper and smiled at Torry. "That breakfast was as good as your dinner last night. And, I might add, it's good to have you here with us...kinda like old times before you got married and moved away from home, huh?"

Something in her father's expression, tugged at her heart. "It is, Dad, isn't it?"

The three of them visited while she and her father cleaned up.

Back in the bedroom, Torry changed into a cotton dress and sat down to read the scriptures, but her thoughts turned to her father. She had suspected something for a long time, and now she was sure of it.

Shortly after turning twelve, she remembered reading a poem that expressed how she felt about her dad. A couple of months later, she hand printed it, framed it, and gave it to him for Father's day. When he read it, he became thoughtful. He read it again and tears came to his eyes, one of the rare times she saw her father cry. She still knew the poem by heart.

FIRST LOVE

Very little girls, come piquant as elves,
Already woman-hearted
Love their mother's as themselves;
But every little girl...every wide-eyed one...
Owns a special world where her daddy shines
like sun.

He is morning wonderful and hero high,
Voice deep-warm as earth in June...
But his smile is sky.
His arms are willow-wise; safe in their holding.
A little girl finds leaf-bright summer and love's
enfolding."

Growing up, she was always her 'daddy's little girl.' Apparently, her father hoped it might be that way again.

She remembered turning fifteen, and noticing the fathers of some of her friends. They were spiritual leaders in the home. They saw to it that the family studied scriptures together and had family prayer on a regular basis along with family home evening. It was then that she became disillusioned.

Torry's attitude toward her father changed, and she knew now that he'd felt it all these years. Not knowing what was wrong or why his daughter didn't make him feel important and special anymore, he became sarcastic and critical. When she got married, he got worse, but always when her mother wasn't around. Now—the problem had intensified. He cut her down in front of Mother and David.

Tears stung her eyes, "Oh Dad...Dad," she whispered to his unhearing ears, "you thought that when Jack died, I would come home and be your little girl again. You thought you could take care of me and that somehow the clock would turn back and we could once again regain that special relationship when you were 'morning wonderful and hero high.'" She cried softly and then whispered to him, "I love you, Dad. It needn't have been like this. You could have been my hero forever."

~~~~~~~~~~

Torry stood on the corner of Main and South Temple, arms full of packages and sacks, watching for David. She caught sight of him standing on the corner of the Joseph Smith Memorial building waiting for the light to change. He looked so handsome walking across the street, her heart skipped a beat. When he saw her, his face lit up and a big smile spread across his face.

"If you aren't a beautiful sight, standing there in the sun glowing like an angel," he said, walking up and taking all the packages from her.

"You certainly know how to lift a girl's spirits, Mr. Mayer." She slipped her hand through his arm. "Mother's car is parked in the ZCMI parking."

After finding the car, they headed for Provo. Torry sat close to David, feeling joy and contentment in his presence, silently savoring it.

David, too, was quiet, thinking how the richness of his experiences the last day and a half had made Torry even more precious to him.

"Tell me, David, what have you been doing since you left yesterday?"

He expelled a big breath, "Oh Torry, the gospel is wonderful. I've just come from the Genealogy Center. Several years ago," he began, grinning, "I heard about it and wondered, if I could find any dead relatives I'd like any better than the living ones."

Torry smiled. "Did you find any?"

"I didn't look, just went on a tour, asked a lot of questions and found it fascinating. Soon I want to do some serious genealogy. I never knew my father, I was so young when he died, but I always felt my life would have been different if he had lived."

"You know, Torry, it was very strange, we never had relatives from either side come to see us, and we never went to see any. I think my mother must have estranged herself from everyone. She would never answer any of my questions about grandparents, uncles, aunts or cousins."

Torry frowned. "How strange." Suddenly consumed with excitement, she exclaimed, "David, it's possible you have some living relatives somewhere. Let's look for them." She flushed. "I'm sorry, I...I don't mean to put pressure on you about us...or expect..."

"Torry, don't. All that did was make me happy you care enough to want to help me find them."

"I'm glad to hear that," she said, her eyes lingering on his profile, his thick dark hair, his brow, his distinctive nose, his lips. He smiled as he felt her gaze.

"What are you doing, Torry?" he asked, not looking at her.

"I'm just checking you out. Remember, my friend who owns Henry says you're handsome."

They both laughed and David said, "Do you realize how happy that remark made me that day? For a moment I felt like a tongue-tied, love-sick teenager."

"You did? And do you realize how embarrassed I was after I repeated it? Here you were, my banker, no less. I almost feel embarrassed when I think about it now.

David chuckled, "Well, you should feel embarrassed, Mrs. Anderson, you were most definitely out of line. By the way, did you agree with your friend who owns Henry?"

Torry sighed, "Well, I feel like a love-sick teenager now. I'll have to say I've never seen such a handsome profile, and the front view really does me in, especially your eyes."

He grinned. "Now you're embarrassing me. But I asked for it didn't I?"

"Yes. Now tell me what you did yesterday."

He recounted everything, reliving again each one of his spiritual experiences. He heard a sniffle. Glancing over, he saw Torry wiping her eyes. "I take it those are happy tears, my love?"

"They are."

By the time they arrived at the restaurant in Provo, it was 3:55. The boys were to meet them at 4:00. David turned off the motor, put his arm around Torry, leaned down and kissed her hair, then ran his fingers through it.

"I love your hair, it's so soft and silky."

"Mmmm..." she purred. "Thank you."

"You know, Torry, I'm looking forward to visiting with the boys." David wanted to add, I wish they were mine, but thought better of it. He had given Jim and Scott a lot of thought. He wanted to help them out a little, not too much, for their sakes, but at least buy them each a nice small car. That big old car they were driving, was a gas guzzler and they had to share it.

If they hadn't as yet decided on their vocations, he'd like to help them by taking them around to all his various business enterprises. If they found an interest in one of them, they both would be assets wherever he put them. If they weren't interested in business, then he could help them in whatever they chose to do.

Torry's thoughts were also on Jim and Scott. She hoped with all her heart that they would have the opportunity to associate more with David.

"Hey!" came a voice through the window on Torry's side, "Scott and I have been waving at you, trying to get your attention."

"Hey yourself, Jim," David said. "How are you?" he asked, getting out of the car.

"Great. How are both of you?" Jim asked, opening the door for his mother.

"We're great too, Jim," his mother said, getting out and giving him a hug.

"Scott went inside to get us a booth in a corner, so we can visit a little better."

The waitress led them to their table where Scott was waiting, grinning. "Hello Scott," Torry said, scooting into the booth, giving him a hug.

"Hi, Mom, you look pretty chipper! And...so do you, David," Scott said, studying him closely. "What's been going on? Something's different."

David smiled at him, "You are an astute young man, Scott."

The waitress placed the menus on the table and David said, "Give us thirty minutes before we order."

The boys looked at each other, feeling apprehensive, certain that David was going to tell them he and their mother were going to get married.

"I wish we had a more conducive atmosphere to talk about this," David began, "but here goes—I was baptized last Saturday."

David could see that the boys were stunned, but they didn't react as he had expected.

"Uh...David," Jim said, "that was fast."

David smiled. "I see. You both are afraid that I've joined the Church only to please your mother."

"That's about the size of it. Sorry, David," Jim said.

"Frankly, I'm glad you're concerned. But I couldn't possibly join for that reason. I've had an aversion to joining any church, and—I'm sorry to say—I'm one of those stubborn, hard-headed Jews the Bible talks about. It's a miracle that I was able to accept the gospel. Let me tell you about it, step by step, beginning with my friend Gabe in Dallas."

"We're all ears, David," Scott said.

As he shared his life-changing experience with these two young men, he found it totally satisfying. They reacted with amazement, incredulity and joy, each emotion apparent on their open and honest faces.

He glanced now and then at Torry and found her totally reliving it with him. When he was through, the boys were silent, their eyes moist.

Scott finally managed to speak first, "Wow! I haven't seen that kind of a conversion. I've only read about it in church history with some of the early day saints."

"It's especially impressive since you are Jewish, David," Jim said, "It is rare for Jews to respond to the gospel, full-blooded ones like you anyway. But, you know, I've heard that there are groups of Jews now claiming to be Christian, which is a step forward, but not as big a step as you've taken. We're really happy for you, David."

The waitress came and took their orders and when the food arrived, the three of them visited while they ate. At the end of the meal, David asked, "Do you boys have a few minutes to visit with me separately?"

They looked at each other, sure that they knew what was coming, that is, until they looked at the surprised face of their mother.

"Sure, David, I have time," Jim said.

"I do too," Scott said, "where should we talk?"

"I know," their mother said, "I've been wanting to show David the BYU campus. Why don't we go up there and find a place to sit down somewhere."

"Sounds good," David said.

In their own car on the way to the campus, Scott asked Jim, "Well, now how do you feel about them getting married?"

"Since we talked in the car when we drove Mom to Salt Lake, Scott, I've been doing a lot of thinking about the pros and cons. In my mind, the pros have it now that he's a member of the Church. In fact I think I'm for it. How about you?"

"I am too. I like him and I think...no, I know he'll make Mom happy. But...I see a problem. Grandfather. Remember how he feels about David because he's Jewish?"

"Yes." Both were silent for some moments, then Jim blurted out, "I've got the answer."

"What?"

"Let's tell them to elope."

"Your kidding!"

"No, I'm not."

Scott thought about it a while and said, "Come to think about it, that makes sense. We don't need to see them married since they won't be sealed in the temple. It sure would forestall a problem."

When both cars were parked, the four of them walked on to the campus. David looked around. "This is a big campus."

"Yeah," Jim said. "It's a challenge getting to classes sometimes."

"The buildings and grounds are impressive."

The early evening sun was still intense and hot, so after looking around a while, David pointed to the shade under a tree. "How about here? I'd like to talk to you first, Jim."

"Okay. See you around," Jim said, grinning at his mother and Scott.

"Stay in shouting distance will you?" suggested David as Torry and Scott started walking away. They both nodded.

"Well, Jim, I need some help—help probably that no one can give me but myself. To get right to the point, I want to marry your mother, but I don't know whether or not I can."

Jim was shocked. "Why not?"

"Because I want to marry her for eternity as well as for time."

"Oh...of course you would."

"To be frank with you, Jim, I wish you and Scott were my sons, that we could be a family forever." He studied Jim's face trying to see how this revelation affected him, but he couldn't tell, so went on, "I'm sorry if this bothers you—I know you must have loved your father very much."

"Has Mom told you anything about Dad?" Jim asked guardedly.

"No. She's been quite closed on the subject. You see, we both need more time with each other since it's only been about a week-and-a-half since your mother realized that she loved me. I don't know about your mother's past life, and she doesn't know mine. Somehow, sometime, we've both got to share our experiences with each other."

"Good. You need to do that. But let me ask you a question, David. What will you do if you don't marry Mom?"

"I can't think of that."

"Why not?"

"Because I can't imagine life without her."

"Do you think if you gave it enough time, you could find some-one else—a younger woman who could be sealed to you in the tem-ple?"

"That's what your mother asked me, and the answer is an unequivocal no."

"Then the answer seems an obvious one—marry her."

Jim's logic and answer took his breath away. It was the answer he wanted to hear. He smiled at Jim, "You give me permission then?"

Jim grinned, "Not that you need it, but yes. However, there's one problem, Grandfather—he'll give you static."

"I know. He doesn't like me."

"He doesn't know you, David. He just thinks he doesn't like Jews. Sometimes I think he would dislike anyone Mom was inter-ested in. If you and Mom decide to get married, Scott and I would like to see you elope."

David's mouth dropped open, "You...you mean that?"

"I do, there's no reason not to. Grandmother would be fine with it, I know, especially if we tell her it was our idea."

"I can't tell you how much I appreciate this, Jim. Thank you!" He waved to Torry and Scott who were sitting under the shade of another tree. They got up and came right over.

Torry studied both their faces and her spirits lifted. "You ready to exchange boys, David?" she asked, smiling at him.

"I am, thank you."

David reviewed, with Scott, the discussion he had with Jim about his desire to marry their mother and what was bothering him. He told Scott what Jim said. "How do you feel about this?"

"Exactly like my brother."

David exhaled in relief and smiled. "That's good to hear. Now, could you tell me a little about your father, Scott?"

He hesitated a moment, then asked, "Has Mom told you anything about him?"

"No."

"I'll tell you a little about him from my perspective. Dad was an athlete and he reveled in Jim's ability at athletics. I disappointed him. I love sports, but only for fun at the park or church. Because of this, I didn't get the attention from him that Jim did. Jim began noticing this and dropped out of sports, so he didn't enjoy either one of us as much as he could have. His job took him away from the family at least two weeks out of every month so he wasn't even around much for us. Mom never let on, but I know she was lonely much of her married life."

"I'm sorry to hear that, Scott. Then...you also give me permission to marry your mother?"

"I do. She deserves to be happy, and I think you'll make her happy. Besides—I wish my dad had been more like you, David."

David swallowed past the tightness in his throat, "Thank you Scott—I can't tell you what that means to me."

Suddenly, David realized, he had his answer. Like Lehi, in the Book of Mormon, he had received revelation. And like Lehi, he had to trust that his journey would be under the direction of the Lord. He would marry Torry now, for time, and trust that the end of their journey together would be the will of a just God.

David stood up and waved Jim and Torry over. When they walked up, David took both of Torry's hands in his, "Well...I've been praying for guidance—and He gave it to me through your sons." He gazed at Jim then Scott, overcome momentarily with gratitude to them and the Lord. Turning back to Torry, he asked, "Are you still willing to marry me, Torry?"

"Are you sure, David?"

"I'm sure, my darling!"

Torry looked questioningly at each of her sons." They smiled at her, and Jim said, "We gave him permission to marry you, Mom."

Chapter Thirty-Nine

Torry, full of questions on the way back to Salt Lake, wanted to know every detail of the conversations David had with her sons. He covered everything except the boy's suggestion that they elope.

Torry snuggled as close to David as the seat belt permitted and sighed, "I've never felt so happy in my life, David."

He glanced at her, "Does that include your life with Jack?"

"Yes."

"What I'm going to say won't be kind to Jack," David began, "but I wish I could usurp his place in the eternities. However, Torry, I promised myself, after talking to the boys, that I wouldn't think about the next life, that I would trust the Lord, enjoy this one and make you as happy as I possibly can. I'm also anxious to associate more with Jim and Scott. I'd like to help them in any way I can. I know I can't replace their father, but I hope that I'll be able to add something to their lives."

Torry covered her face and sobbed quietly. David, alarmed, asked, "What is it, Torry? Have I said something I shouldn't have?"

She shook her head and pulled a tissue from her purse. "No, David, you said all the right things."

When they reached Salt Lake, David asked, "Would you walk around Temple Square with me?"

"I'd love to, my dearest."

They walked together through the beautiful grounds, hand in hand, experiencing blissful emotions not possible until now.

"Heaven couldn't be any better than this, Torry."

"I know," she murmured.

They came to a cement bench and David suggested they rest a minute. "This is Thursday night, Torry, and I have plane reservations for Dallas on Monday morning. Is that all right with you?"

"Yes."

"May I have a date tomorrow night to take you dancing?"

Torry was surprised. "A date?" She smiled wistfully, "That

sounds wonderful, David. They have a place in Salt Lake where an orchestra plays all the 'oldie-goldies' to dance by."

"Great! I'd also like to take you to dinner, but I think we'd better fix dinner for your parents."

"Why, David, how thoughtful."

"Now..." David said, pulling Torry to her feet, "how about an ice cream sundae?"

~~~~~~~~~~~~

Friday morning after fixing breakfast for the three of them, Torry cleaned the house. Afterward, she showered and dressed, changing into jeans and a red T-shirt, all the while reflecting upon the tenderness she had begun to feel for her dad since arriving. This morning, the sudden realization that it had subtly changed his attitude towards her, brought tears of remorse. She knelt beside her bed, painfully aware now that she had been guilty of self righteousness through the years, judging her dad with unkindness and resentment rather than with righteousness.

She pled for forgiveness as deep sobs burst forth from a broken heart. When they finally subsided, she thanked her Father in Heaven for the principle of repentance.

Later, when she left the bedroom, she went in to find her parents, but found only her mother in the reclining chair reading. She was wearing a light blue cotton dress that accentuated her dark silver-streaked hair and blue eyes.

"You look beautiful, Mother," Torry said, sitting down in the chair next to her.

Ruth looked up and smiled. "Why thank you, darling, so do you." She studied Torry's face in concern. "Have you been crying my dear?"

"Yes, Mother."

"Why, what's wrong?"

"Where is Dad?"

"He went golfing."

"Did you notice a difference in the way Dad has treated me, especially this morning?"

"Yes, I did."

Torry, eyes moist, told her mother what had happened over the past two days. Of the insight she had gained into her father's behavior, as well as the part she had played. Ruth held out her arms to her daughter, and Torry went into them.

"My darling girl, how the Lord loves you—thank you."

The doorbell rang. Torry's face lit up. "It must be David," she said running out of the family room, quickly wiping her eyes.

She opened the door, and there stood David holding a long white box. He stepped inside and handed it to her.

Torry squealed in delight when she opened it and saw two dozen red roses. "Deja vu. They aren't lilacs, but just as beautiful! Thank you."

He leaned down and kissed her. "Mmmm, my lovely, you look good enough to eat."

"We're twins," she said, gesturing to her own outfit. "I've never seen you wear a red shirt with jeans before."

"You haven't seen a lot of my shirts—just you wait, I have all colors: pink ones, purple ones..."

"Come, silly, and say hello to Mother while I find a vase for these."

David went into the family room, walked over to Ruth, leaned down and kissed her cheek. "You look as lovely as Torry, Ruth."

"Thank you, David. I consider that a great compliment. Please sit down."

Torry came in carrying the roses in a vase. "Look what David brought me," she said, placing them on a lamp table.

"How lovely, David," Ruth said, smiling at him and then at Torry who curled up on the floor in front of David's chair. "What's up you two? You are both positively glowing."

Torry turned to David and looked at him tenderly. "Do you want to share with Mother your experiences of the last two days?"

"Yes I do, then we'll tell her about the visit with Jim and Scott."

David told most of it, with a few insightful additions by Torry, and ended with his decision to marry Torry for 'time.'

Ruth was silent a moment, then she smiled at him, "I'm grateful for your decision. I know you'll make Torry happy. And I know she'll make you happy."

"Thank you, Ruth. We don't know when we'll get married. I need to court this beautiful lady for a while first."

Torry smiled at him. "You're doing a good job of it already." She looked at her watch and stood up, "It's 12:30, I'll go throw some lunch together."

George Conway entered just as Torry headed for the kitchen. "Oh hello, Dad, did you have a good golf game?"

"I did, thanks."

"Hello, George," David said, "I always wanted to try golf but never quite got around to it. Uh...could I have a word with you in private?"

George looked at him warily. "Well...I was just going to help Torry."

"It won't take long, I promise you."

"All right," he said reluctantly. "Let's go on into the front room."

David turned to Ruth. "Will you excuse us, Ruth?"

"Of course," she said, a look of concern on her face.

David sat across from George. "I appreciate you letting me talk to you. I'll get right to the point. I love Torry." David saw George's face close. "I want to marry her and would very much like to have your approval."

"You don't have it."

David had expected the worst and was prepared to handle it in the nicest way possible for Ruth's sake. "Why, George?"

"Because I don't know you."

"How long do you think it will take before you feel you do?"

"David, let me be frank. I've had dealings with Jews and every experience I've had has not been a good one."

"I've had dealings with Gentiles and many have been very dishonest. Should I judge you as dishonest because you are a Gentile?"

George squirmed uncomfortably. "Well, I guess neither of us should judge each other by others. But...nevertheless, I don't want you to marry my daughter."

"Why? Do you want her to be alone the rest of her life?"

"Of course not! I think she'll eventually come to her senses about that silly chicken farm and move up here by us like we wanted her to in the first place."

"Torry wants to marry me, George," he said quietly.

"I don't think Torry knows what she wants." George stood up and walked out of the room, dismissing David.

David sat there thinking, and for some reason he felt sorry for George Conway. He got up and slowly walked back into the family room. Apparently, George had gone into the kitchen to talk to Torry. Ruth studied him anxiously, and he gave her a smile.

"I guess you know what I wanted to talk to him about?"

"Yes...and?"

"Don't worry, Ruth. He didn't give us his blessing, but it will be all right—he'll be all right."

"Lunch is ready you two," Torry said sticking her head in the door.

~~~~~~~~~~

After a trip up to see the 'This Is The Place Monument,' Torry and David drove up the canyon. A while later, Torry suggested they park the car and go for a hike. After about an hour of hiking straight up the mountain, they laughingly gave in to a rest. David put his arm around his fiancee, drawing her close. Silently their chests heaved, breathing in the fragrant, mountain scented air. They listened to the rustling leaves of the aspen and the whispering of the pine needles, feeling nature's peace...matching their own inner peace and happiness.

"This has been great, Torry. In all my adult life, I haven't taken time for recreation. Let's continue to do this kind of thing after we're married."

"Oh let's do, David." Finally Torry brought up the subject. "Dad said you asked him for his approval of our marriage."

"Did he tell you what he said?"

"Yes."

"And what did you say?"

"I kissed him, and told him he would always be special to me and not to worry about anything."

"You did?" David asked, surprised.

"David, you are so good for me. You've made me a better person. It's because of your influence that I was able to see what I've done wrong all these years with Dad."

David was incredulous. Abruptly, he stood and pulled Torry to her feet. "Torry, my darling, it's just the other way around, it's you who have made me a better person. I'm going to have to spend the rest of my life trying to be worthy of you." He put his arms around her and gave her a long tender kiss, which suddenly turned into a fervent, passionate one, celebrating the joy of their engagement, their commitment to each other.

David pulled away and gazed down at her. "I wish we were married right now."

She lay her face against his chest, and murmured, "Me too."

"We could get married tomorrow, Torry, but—I have to pay attention to the feeling I had that we need a little more time to get acquainted. And...I think it's time to go start dinner, huh?"

"I guess," she sighed, smiling up at him, adoration in her eyes.

~~~~~~~~~~~~

Ruth listened to the laughing exchanges coming from the kitchen as Torry and David prepared dinner. Her heart was full of joy for them both. She glanced over at George who was glowering and reading the Wall Street Journal. The telephone rang next to him. He picked it up.

"Hello? Bill?...Where are you?...You are?...Are Gwen and the children with you?...What time do you want me to pick you up?...We'll be looking forward to it!"

"What did he say, George?" Ruth asked, eagerly.

"Bill flew into New York last night from England and will be at the airport in Salt Lake tomorrow night at 5:00. Gwen and the children aren't with him this time."

Ruth clapped her hands together in joy. "Oh George, how wonderful! He wrote and told us he and the children were flying in for Thanksgiving, so I guess we can wait that long to see the rest of them."

"Torry," her mother called.

Torry and David came in. "Your brother, Bill, will be in tomorrow night at 5:00."

"Oh Mom, how wonderful! It's been over a year and a half since I've seen him. David, now you'll get to meet him, and he'll get to meet you."

"Torry, why don't you call the boys and see if they can come up tomorrow night for dinner so they can see their Uncle Bill."

"Oh yes, I'll go do that right now, Mother. I hope one of them will be there."

"Well, this is good news," David said. "Could I take you all out to eat tomorrow night? Do you feel up to it, Ruth?"

"I believe I do. Thank you, David, that way no one will be stuck in the kitchen preparing dinner. Is that all right with you, George?"

"Whatever you want, Ruth," he said returning to his paper, ignoring David.

~~~~~~~~~~~~~~~

Romantic strains were coming from the orchestra as the hostess led David and Torry to a table. They watched the dancers for a while, then David stood up.

"May I have this dance, beautiful lady?"

"You may," she said, a glow on her face.

His arms encircled her, he leaned his head down slightly to touch his cheek to her forehead and held her close. Torry felt rusty it had been so long since she was on a dance floor. However, David led her effortlessly, making it feel as though they were gliding upon a cloud—or was it her heart that made it feel that way?

Music always made her feel terribly romantic, and tonight in David's arms her heart thrilled with excitement. Never in her life had she felt this way.

The music stopped and he gazed down at her, the magnetism of his wonderful gray eyes drew her in. Her heart pounded, and she whispered, "You're eyes are melting me, David."

He laughed and pulled her close, just as the music started playing another familiar, haunting love song. Moving together in perfect unison, their hearts beat to the rhythm of their love.

Chapter Forty

Jim and Scott arrived early Saturday morning. Not only did they want to see their uncle Bill, but they wanted to spend some more time with their mother and David.

Saturday turned out to be a glorious day for Torry. She and David played several games of badminton with the boys in the back yard while Ruth watched from the porch and George worked on cross word puzzles.

After a lunch on the back porch, they drank lemonade, visited, told jokes, funny stories and laughed heartily. Even George entered in, telling comical stories about himself when he was a boy. The afternoon passed quickly and soon it was time to get ready so they could pick Bill up and go to dinner.

David, having brought a change of clothes with him, changed in the guest room. George, Ruth and the boys went to the airport to pick up Bill. Torry and David agreed to meet them at the Roof Restaurant on top of the Joseph Smith Memorial Building.

Later, seated at a table overlooking the city, David said, "Salt Lake is a beautiful city. Where do you want to live, Torry, besides our annual visits to Green Valley?"

Torry smiled, a far away look in her eyes. "Can you believe that one day we'll actually be living together as man and wife? It doesn't matter where we live, David as long as I'm with you."

"But, you can choose, my love. You see, I can handle my business affairs from wherever we live, though I will have to spend some time in Dallas."

"You really mean I can choose?"

"You can."

"There they are, David!" The group came over to the table and Torry jumped up. Her tall brother picked her up and swung her around, grinning from ear to ear. Setting her down, he looked over at David. Reaching over, he held out his hand.

"I'm Bill, I take it you're David."

"Yes, glad to meet you, Bill. Sit down all of you so we can get acquainted before we head over to the buffet."

"It's nice of you, David, to treat us to dinner here."

"It's my pleasure, Bill. How long are you here for?"

"I'm sorry to say, I have to leave first thing in the morning in order to get back to London on Monday. I had to see Mom and see how she was doing instead of depending on what she told me over the phone. I had business in New York so I made a long detour to Salt Lake."

"How are Gwen and the children, Bill?" asked Torry.

David watched Bill as he interacted with the family. He was a nice looking man with dark hair and blue eyes like his mother. He also had her height. His countenance was that of one who lived the gospel. He liked him immediately. With joy, David realized that he was about to be part of this family, and he found himself looking forward to meeting Bill's wife and six children.

"Bill," Torry said, "before we go get our food, I would like to tell you that David and I are engaged."

Bill looked at Torry then at David. A wide grin spread across his face. "As Grandfather Thomas used to say, 'Well, I'll be a pill peddlin' poke.' Congratulations! When did this happen?"

"Last night," Scott piped up, "right on the BYU campus in front of Jim and me."

"But only after we gave David permission, Uncle Bill," Jim said, grinning.

Bill chuckled. "I'm glad to hear that you did it right, David."

"Thanks, Bill. Now how about us getting something to eat?"

David noticed how glum and withdrawn George had been during all this, but no one seemed to notice, or more likely, pretended not to.

The food was good, and the visit went well. Every once in a while, Torry reached under the table, and patted David's knee or held his hand. Her constant touching comforted him.

After it was over, Bill rode with Torry and David back to the house. The other four followed in George's Mercedes.

After they arrived, they gathered in the family room to continue their visit. Their conversations veered to memories of Torry and Bill, of Jim and Scott, and soon they were completely caught up with it laughing, accusing each other, and teasing.

David, not able to join in, listened with enjoyment for some time, then all of a sudden he felt completely apart from the group. A flash of memory seized him without warning. He was a little boy sitting on the top of the stairs looking through the rungs of the banister at his parents and their friends.

They were laughing hilariously, telling stories, having a wonderful time. He felt left out—so alone—wrenching pain seized his insides. Suddenly he decided he wasn't going to let them leave him out anymore! He'd leave *them*! Running down the stairs, he ran out the front door and down the street.

David, drenched in sweat, found himself outside on the porch. Panic still gripping him, he ran to his car and got in. He sat there; his breathing heavy; his hands clenched. Finally the panic left. The decision was as rapid as a dart hitting its mark. He turned on the motor and sped off.

The family finally decided it was time to quit reminiscing, and go to bed. Torry turned to David, and found him gone.

"Where's David?" her mother asked.

"He probably went in to get his clothes out of the guest room," she said getting up to go find him. The door to the guest room was open, and his clothes were still there. She looked at the bathroom door, it was open and dark inside. She frowned, starting to feel a little concerned.

Wondering if he had gone out to the car for something, she went out the front door, closing it quietly. Running down the steps of the porch she walked quickly to the driveway looking for his car. It was gone! Fear clutched at her heart. Where was he? Where did he go...why did he go? She paced up and down the driveway thinking. Could...could he have had one of those strange attacks? Whatever—she had to cover for David. She went inside.

She found that the boys had gone down to the basement to their room, her folks had gone into theirs. Relief flooded through her. Hopefully, they all thought that she and David wanted to be alone for a while.

Bill, who was staying in the guest room, was now in the bathroom. She breathed a sigh of relief, grabbed David's jeans and shirt, took them to her room, shut the door, and sat down on the bed. Her breath came out short and explosive. "What is it, David? What is it?" She looked at her watch knowing she had to give him time to get to the hotel before she called his room. She hugged his shirt and jeans, smelling his wonderful cologne and waited. A short while later, a rap on the door startled her. "Just a minute," she said. Quickly placing David's clothes inside the closet, she took several deep breaths, and opened the door.

Bill stood in the doorway. "Hi Sis, I didn't get to say goodbye to David."

"I know. I...uh don't know when we'll be married, Bill, but hopefully not too long, and we'll plan on spending Thanksgiving with the family. I'm anxious to see Gwen and the children."

"Great!" He hugged her, then became more serious, "I'm happy for you, Torry. I'll have to confess, I like him. I like him a lot better than I did Jack."

"I'm afraid I do, too."

Bill lifted one eyebrow quizzically, "Oh? I want to hear all the details. I wish it could be tonight, but I think I'm getting jet lag or something. I'm exhausted."

"We'll tell you and Gwen the whole story at Thanksgiving."

"That's a deal. Good night, sis, I love you." He leaned down and gave her a hug.

"I love you to, 'big' brother," she said, tears threatening. "Good night."

Torry closed the bedroom door and sat down again, folding her arms tightly across her midsection. Her breathing fluctuated between short breaths and long heavy sighs. Finally she picked up the phone, rang the hotel and asked for David Mayer's room. It rang and rang. He hadn't arrived yet. Utterly disappointed, she hung up, her anxiety level peaking.

David sat in his car in the parking lot of the hotel, shaking. He felt numb with humiliation and grief. Finally he opened the car door, walked around to the front, went into the lobby and over to the elevator. His feet felt like lead as he stepped out onto the 8th floor. Shuffling toward his room, he heard the phone ringing. He knew it was Torry. He didn't want to talk to her. He unlocked the door, and just as he walked in, the ringing stopped.

He sat down in a chair, and stared into space, vaguely wondering if these episodes of memory came in a similar manner as the flashbacks that come to war veterans. The phone rang again. He let it ring several times, and then forced himself to pick it up.

"Hello," he said thickly.

"David! What happened? You nearly scared me to death!"

"Torry, I can't talk now. I'll talk to you in the morning."

"But David..."

"Good night, Torry."

Torry held the phone in her hand, the dial tone piercing her heart with its dull, cold hum.

Chapter Forty-One

At 5:00 A.M., Torry woke up with a start, fear seizing her again. She had spent a fitful night, every hour or so waking with fear and worry. Slipping out of bed, she knelt and prayed for David, for herself.

By 6:00, she had breakfast on for the family. By 6:45, they had finished eating and were saying their goodbye's. Jim and Scott were going to drop Bill off at the airport, and then go back to Provo for church in their own ward.

Everyone hugged and promised to see each other at Thanksgiving. "Thank you, Bill," his mother said, "your visit has been such a lift to me."

"Me too, Mom," he said gently holding her. "I'm grateful that the Lord let you stay with us a while longer...we need you."

After they waved goodbye on the steps, Torry dashed into the kitchen, and began cleaning up. She had to get down to David's hotel. Her mother walked in.

"What are yours and David's plans today, Torry?"

"I don't know. We have some decisions to make, so do you and Dad mind if I spend the day with David? We'll probably go to a ward close to the hotel, and maybe go for a drive or something."

"Not at all, dear."

"Mother, David wants to take me to Dallas to meet a friend and his wife who have been kind of like family to him. We may leave in the morning, but I'm not sure."

"You and David do what you have to do to get to know each other better. Feel free to continue to use my car."

"Thank you, and thank you for all your support, Mother." Torry hugged her. "I love you."

In her room, Torry looked in the phone book for ward buildings near Little America Hotel. Finally finding one, she called and found out that the sacrament meetings started at 9:00 A.M. and 11:00 A.M.

Borrowing a duffel bag from her mother, she folded David's jeans and shirt and placed them inside. By 7:30, dressed for church, she grabbed her purse and the bag, and went in to say goodbye to her parents.

The trip downtown seemed to take forever. Reaching the hotel at last, she drove into the parking lot and found a space. She got out, grabbed her purse and the bag, and ran. When she reached the front of the hotel, a young doorman smiled and opened the door for her. She gave him a tight smile, a quick thank you and quickly strode to the elevators, grateful that David had mentioned his room number.

Going up, her heart pounded with anxiousness, not knowing how David would react, realizing more than ever she didn't really know him.

She found his door, which had a 'Do Not Disturb' sign hanging from the door knob. She knocked. No answer. She knocked again, louder. "David, it's Torry. Please let me in." The wait seemed endless.

Finally, the door opened a crack, then a little wider. She was shocked at David's appearance. He looked terrible. He was still in the white shirt and suit pants he had on last night! He had a dark growth of beard, his eyes were heavy, and dark.

He didn't say anything so she ventured, "Please, David, may I come in?"

"I...I can't talk now, Torry. I haven't showered..."

"Please..."

He opened the door wide and let her in, then closed it. He turned and stared at her, not knowing what to say. She dropped the purse and bag, taking his hands in hers.

"May we sit down, David?"

He nodded and followed Torry to the sitting area of the suite. She sat down on the small couch, and patted a place beside her. He sat in one of the chairs instead.

"Can you talk about it, David?" He shook his head. "You had another attack, didn't you?"

A look of surprise flickered across his face. "You...you know about them? I mean—you were aware—when..."

"I've been aware of two, David. You seem to go far away, and then perspiration breaks out on your face, and you look like you're in pain."

"I...I knew you noticed the first one, but..." his voice trailed off.

"I want you to know that we were all so engrossed with our reminiscing last night that no one noticed when you left, including me. When we discovered you weren't there, Mother asked where you were. I told her you probably went in to get your clothes. When I couldn't find you, I went outside to look for you. When I came in, everyone had dispersed to their rooms. I'm sure that they thought we just wanted to be alone."

David didn't register any emotion, not even relief. "It doesn't matter, I won't be seeing them again anyway."

Fear almost immobilized Torry for a moment. She took a deep tremulous breath and uttered, "Why, David?"

"Because," he said slowly, "I won't be marrying you. No way will I put you through what I put Clara through."

"What did you put her through?"

"I don't want to talk about it. Go home, Torry, it's over."

Torry jumped up and stood before him, her hands on her hips, glaring down at him. "Oh no you don't, David Mayer! You can't get out of it that easily. You worked hard to win my love...and now that you've succeeded in making me fall head over heels, madly in love with you...you think you can just tell me to go home? Think again, mister."

A flicker of amusement in his eyes came and went. "My fiery, fiesty Torry, you are really something, but you can't change my mind."

"I'm not. You're going to do it all by your self. With just a little help from me," she added softly.

The familiar half-smile came. "Go home, Torry."

"Have you had breakfast?"

"No."

Torry went over to the phone and dialed room service. "Hello, would you send up a large glass of fresh squeezed orange juice....well juice them anyway even if you have to use twenty... a poached egg and whole wheat toast...that's right. Send it up to room 805. Thank you."

"Well, if you aren't a little busybody," he said with irritation. "If I were hungry, I would have ordered it myself."

Torry was relieved to see some emotion—even if it was anger. "Well, Mr. Mayer, you're going to need every ounce of strength you have, because this is soul-bearing day. You are going to tell me everything you haven't told me, and I'm going to tell you everything I haven't told you."

David stood up and glared down at her. "You are a real nuisance, you know that? I've got a headache and I need a shower."

Torry went over to where she had dropped her purse. Picking it up, she came back and fished around in it until she found two aspirin. "Here take these and go shower. By the time you get out, your breakfast will be here."

David refused to take them from her and began to pace up and down. "If I'd known how bossy you were, I would've drowned you in that pond full of polly wogs."

Torry laughed. "I love you, David Mayer, and you aren't ever going to—you hear me—ever get rid of me."

He shook his head and smiled, then reached for the tablets. "You are the cutest thing I've ever seen, but you won't want to marry me when you know me." He ducked into the bathroom and soon she heard the shower.

She felt more hopeful and more desperately in love with him than ever. She looked around the suite and saw that David was neat, his clothes hung carefully in the closet. Nothing was lying around. The bed, which didn't look slept in, was smoothed out. "Another brownie point for you, David."

Twenty-five minutes later, a knock came at the door. She opened it, took the tray from the young man and thanked him. "Just a minute," she said as she went over to the dresser. Setting the tray down, she picked up David's wallet, pulled out a ten dollar bill, went back and handed it to him. His eyes got big, and he grinned. "Hey, thanks!"

She smiled and said, "You're welcome." Closing the door, she picked up the tray and placed it on the table.

"Hey, Torry," David yelled through the bathroom door, it's Sunday!"

She went to the door and yelled back. "I know. What do you want to do about it?"

"We have to go to church."

She smiled, grateful, bursting with love for him. "I know. I've checked on it, there's a sacrament meeting starting at 11:00 not far from here."

"Well, not only are you **bossy**, you're efficient," he yelled. "Now, will you turn your back, I forgot to bring in clean clothes."

"My back is turned."

He came out, rummaged **around**, and went back into the bathroom. Soon, he came out clean, dressed and shaven.

"You were more sexy with a growth of beard and all rumpled," she stated.

He stared at her, opened his mouth, closed it, shaking his head in disbelief.

"Your breakfast is here. And I tipped him ten dollars out of your wallet."

"You what?"

"You heard me. It's fun being rich, David. I've always wanted to be able to give big tips. You know," she said grinning, "I'm really just marrying you for your money."

David grunted out a chuckle of sorts, "Torry, you're in the craziest mood."

"You put me there. Sit down and eat."

He sat down at the table and shook his head, fighting his amusement, but with no luck. He threw back his head and laughed. Torry laughed with him, then sat down on his lap and kissed him thoroughly. Before he could react, she got up and sat across from him.

"There, I feel much better, how about you?"

He flushed. "It depends on your definition," he muttered, quickly picking up the large glass of orange juice and taking a big swallow. "Mmmm that's good."

"It should be, it's made from expensive Australian Navels."

"You're fast and easy with my money, aren't you?"

"Yes," she said, "and I'm enjoying it immensely."

"Where's the Torry that got all miffed when I wanted to overpay her?"

"She's gone. She was kind of a bore—no fun at all." She got up and went to the window and looked out. David's eyes followed her.

"Is that a new dress?"

"No, I found it in the back of my closet."

"Swallowing a bite of egg and toast, he studied her. "You look beautiful, Torry. By the way," he said, "thanks for being a busybody and ordering breakfast for me."

Torry looked out the window, silent, thinking. Turning around just as David took his last bite, she asked, "Do you think you ought to change our plane tickets to Tuesday?"

"Why? You aren't going with me, Torry."

"Do you think we can get it all done in one afternoon and evening?"

"Get what done?" he asked in exasperation.

"Everything. Our talk, baring our souls, whatever needs to be done."

"Let's go to church, Torry."

She looked at her watch and said, "We have an hour before we have to leave." Waiting a moment she asked, "David?"

"Yes?"

"I told Bill that we'd spend Thanksgiving with him and the family when he comes, and he's looking forward to it."

"You aren't making this any easier, Torry," he said getting up and setting the empty tray outside in the hall. He went into the bathroom and brushed his teeth, came out and began packing his clothes. "I'm leaving tonight."

Torry walked over to him and looked up into his pained face. "No, my dearest David, you are not going unless you take me with you." She reached up and put her arms around his neck.

He pulled them off, "Don't touch me Torry, that kiss you gave me was an unfair tactic."

"All's fair in love and war, and this is war, David."

"I'm nothing to fight for, Torry, so don't waste your time." he said, still packing.

"Let's leave for church, David. It will take time to find the ward building."

"It's a little early...but anything to stop the packing, huh?" Picking up his suit coat, he said, "Let's go."

It took a little longer to find the ward building than they expected. David parked and as they walked toward the door, Torry said, "Let's sit at the back, David, so we can leave right after sacrament meeting. We have to talk."

During the meeting, Torry slipped her hand into his, relieved that he left it there, even returning the squeeze. Both of them felt more at peace during the service. After the closing prayer, they exited quickly.

"Where's your car, Torry?" David asked as he drove into the hotel parking lot.

"Why?"

"I'll **drop** you off, and you **can** go now."

"I left my duffel bag in **your** room."

"I'll go get it."

"Are you being fair to me, David?"

"No, I suppose I'm not."

"Why are you making the **decision** for me? Tell me all the terrible details and let me decide whether you're worth fighting for. You owe me that much."

His dark brows hooded his eyes as he thought about it. "All right," he said hesitantly, "I guess I...uh...wanted us to part with you looking up to me instead of being—disappointed in me." He parked the car. "Come on, Torry I can see that I..." he heaved a sigh, "I was being selfish."

When they were up in the room, Torry slipped out of her heels and curled up on the couch. David took off his suit coat and tie and sat down in the chair.

"I guess I'd better get on with it," David began glumly. "There are two things that happen to me when I get the attacks. First, I get a flashback of a memory from my childhood; second, a feeling of panic comes with it. The seed for the panic attacks may have started when I was about six."

"I went to counseling after Clara and I divorced. It was the counselor who told me that these were a type of panic attack and helped me understand why they were happening."

His brows furrowed, "I have to back up Torry. My mother felt something worse than hate toward me, she felt total indifference, which, I'm convinced, is even more devastating to a child than hate—if that's possible. Why she was that way, I don't know. I don't know whether she was an evil woman or emotionally ill."

"The counselor said it was probable that I began panicking and running, thinking that if I ran away from the hurt, it wouldn't hurt so badly. She said that in many cases of child abandonment the results don't show up until a person is older and begins to have relationships. Some, she said, become obsessively possessive of the spouse, literally smothering him or her, draining the partner until she or he can't stay around any longer. She said I chose the better way, if you can call that better."

"Now to Clara. Torry, I was afraid of relationships. Oh, I dated now and then through the years, but since high school I have put all my energies into work. My mother did me a favor by not helping me through college. All she did was buy me a fancy car and clothes for the sake of appearances. It made her look good."

"I asked to work in each one of the businesses they owned. All my mother and her new husband did was spend the earnings from the businesses my father and grandfather had built."

"When I received the inheritance, its worth had dwindled to about two million. It was easy for me to take over because I had learned a great deal about each business we owned while earning my way through Harvard Business school. After I graduated, I became a workaholic. After years of work and just a little social life, I met Clara. She was a pretty, fragile young woman who was kind and had high morals. She needed someone to look after her, and I needed someone."

"It wasn't long after we were married that I realized she wasn't a strong person emotionally. She was a poor-little-rich-girl, so to speak, who also had been neglected. However, in their way, her parents did love her."

"Clara loved me as much as she was capable, but couldn't give anything to me. I began to feel alone around her. It was then that the flashbacks started, which in turn brought on the panic and desire to run. At first, I would leave the house for only short periods of time, but nevertheless it upset her. I would return and apologize. I tried to explain what had happened and asked her to try to understand when I didn't even understand myself. She couldn't empathize or sympathize, she was too needy herself and wanted more than I could give."

"It got worse and worse, my bouts of panic came more often, and I stayed away from home longer and longer. Finally Clara had a nervous breakdown. I felt so guilty, I was determined to help her get well. I did."

"When she came home from the hospital, I tried to be the husband she needed me to be, but she, in turn, wasn't capable of loving in the normal sense. Finally, we mutually agreed that we weren't good for each other, and we divorced."

"I was so broken up over **the** failed marriage, I went to a counselor. As I said, she helped me **understand** what was happening and why, but gave me no solutions."

"That's when I picked up **the** Bible Hildi had given me. That helped me more than a hundred counselors could have, but I still didn't let myself get too involved with women. I'd date one a few times and then I'd go on to the next one. There wasn't one woman who even slightly interested me...until you, Torry."

"I thought I was over those bouts and then it happened at your house when the boys came down that first time. And now it has happened twice more. I'm not over them, Torry." He shook his head, his face full of anguish. "I can't do to you what I did to Clara." He put his head into his hands, waiting for her response. Torry's silence deepened his despair, fearing the worst. Then he heard her voice, soft and gentle.

"David, are these flashbacks memories you have suppressed or are they memories you've always had?"

He looked up and searched her face for deep disappointment, but saw none. "They are suppressed memories coming to light. This is why I can't control them, they just come when they're ready."

"Do you have memories of your childhood, besides the ones that just come?"

"I don't have memories before I was eight. Then Hildi came into my life and I can remember almost all of my life after she came. Wait—strange, but I remember the summer shortly after I turned eight, just before mother hired Hildi.

That summer, my parents had party after party. My mother hired a butler for parties only. He was called McBain. I used to hide behind a big plant and watch, with fascination, the guests and my parents get drunk. They started out acting normal and gradually started acting crazy and stupid."

"It wasn't long before McBain realized that my parents didn't care a hoot about me so he began tormenting me. He twisted my ears, pinched my shoulders, yanked my hair and called me names and so on. I was determined to get him fired, so I concocted a plan."

"Since McBain was a part time bartender, one of his duties was to carefully spike the fruit punch, just enough to relax the guests but not make them drunk. This is what my mother wanted because she was noted for her fabulous meals. She wanted the guests to be properly impressed with them before they lost their senses. Of course, she didn't do the cooking, she had the best cook around. After dinner, when the meal had been properly praised, cocktails were served."

"I knew where all the liquor was and had learned that Vodka could be put in punch without anyone noticing a change in flavor. A couple of days before a party, I sneaked some bottles of Vodka and hid them. When the punch was made in the kitchen, I poured several bottles in a little at a time when no one was looking."

"When McBain came, all dressed in his butler uniform, I watched him carefully measure out the liquor and pour it in the punch, then I went to my hiding place and watched. My mother who didn't even partake of the punch or other liquor until the meal was over, watched her guests gradually get sloshed. After several drinks on empty stomachs, they were out of their minds drunk."

"I saw my mother storm into the kitchen, so I ran in and listened. She tore into McBain as only Mother could, and then promptly fired him."

"You were a precocious eight-year-old, David."

"Oh, I was smart all right, in a devious sort of way. I had to be, to survive. It was that fall that Mother hired Hildi. I had gotten into so many scrapes that summer, it forced Mother to pay some attention to me, which annoyed her. She advertised for a Nanny/Head Housekeeper. She took one look at the formidable Hildi and hired her, certain that she could keep me in line—and out of her way." He smiled. "Mother had a way of unwittingly doing me favors."

"David, what memory came back to you when you had the first attack in our house that night?"

"Remember, Torry, you took the boys to see the house, and I waited in the front room?" She nodded. "I could hear you three laughing, talking and having a good time and all of a sudden a flash of memory came into my mind. I was seven, I think, sitting alone in my bedroom, hearing my mother and stepfather laughing and talking in their room. I felt so alone and lonely that I longed to run in and join them, but they never allowed me to be with them."

Torry was horrified. Dreading to ask the next question, it came out barely audible. "Tell me about the memory that flashed back to you last night."

David hesitated, not wanting to relive the painful memory again. He'd done enough of that all night long, among other things.

"Please, David, I have to know."

"All right." He told her everything he remembered.

Torry was devastated. Quietly, she fought for control. Succeeding at last, she asked in a whisper, "Did...did you think about it last night?" He nodded. She cleared her throat. "Did you remember anymore? I...I want to know what happened to you when you ran down the street."

"When I came back here to the hotel last night, I thought about it a lot because something about the memory was familiar. Then I remembered. When I was going around the neighborhood trying to drum up jobs so I could buy Hildi another Bible, a neighbor three blocks away recognized me and gave me regular jobs for a while. She told me about the incident of me running down the street, because she found me huddled up in her storage shed the next afternoon."

She was still furious with my parents when she told me about it. She said that it was Bert who came looking for me. It was he who discovered I was missing. It was summer time, and he told her that he and I were going to garden together the next day. He sent one of the maids to look for me and soon the whole house was looking for me, except my parents. They were at the Country Club for a day of golf and didn't know I was even gone."

Torry gasped, all control gone, she covered her face and sobbed.

"Torry, please...don't! It's all right...I'm all right." The sobbing continued. David got up, sat beside her and put his arm around her shoulders, "It's okay, Torry...please don't cry." But Torry was inconsolable.

David stood up and ran his hands through his hair in frustration. He paced around the room listening to the sobs, until he couldn't stand it any longer. He stopped pacing. "Torry, look at me—just look at me." She looked up, still crying softly. "Do you realize that if I hadn't had the trials I've had, I'd be just like those stiffnecked

Israelites Moses led out of Egypt? I would have been one of those who, when Moses turned his back immediately broke the commandments."

"I remember a scripture in the Book of Mormon. It says something to the effect that the Jews were a stiff-necked people, quick to do iniquity, and slow to remember the Lord their God." Tears filled his eyes, "Torry, I needed the trials I've had. "

He paced the floor again, then stopped. "I know me, Torry. I...I know that if I hadn't had the trials, I would have been one of those Jews who...who spit on Christ as He carried the cross to be crucified." David fell to his knees, choked with tears. Torry got up, ran over to him and knelt beside him. Putting her arms around him, they both sobbed.

Chapter Forty-Two

The sobs had long subsided, but Torry and David remained in each other's arms, clinging to one another.

"Torry," David whispered into the soft curls of her hair, "I've never known anyone who listened with her heart like you do."

Torry hoped that after this unburdening David's heart had softened. "Does that mean you'll marry me?" she murmured against his shoulder.

He gently pushed her away and stood up, pulling her up with him. He slid his arms around her and held her close, then leaned down and kissed her with all the desperate longing of his heart, and she returned it with all the love in hers."

"He lifted his head and looked into her warm, beautiful eyes, "Oh, Torry, my darling, I'll always love you. You've given me happiness that I didn't think possible. But, I can't marry you." He let go of her and with a grim set to his jaw he said, "Please go home now."

Fire blazed in her hazel eyes. Placing her hands on her hips, she spoke, "All right, David Mayer, if that is your decision. You are right. You are a stiff-necked Jew!"

She slipped on her heels, quickly stepped over to the table, pulled his jeans and shirt out of the duffel bag, and threw them at him. Grabbing the bag and her purse, she walked briskly to the door, then turned abruptly.

"Do you remember that I called you a valuable human being, David? Do you know why?"

His expression was one of pain and wariness, "Yes I remember and," he said quietly. "I don't even know what you meant by that."

"Well, I'll tell you. It is a person who gives more joy than sorrow, who is careful not to inflict his pain on others and who gives more than he takes. Well, Mr. Mayer—I guess you've decided not to give anymore. You've just decided not to give to me, not to give to Jim and Scott, boys who never really had a father. Goodbye, David." She opened the door, stepped out and pulled the door shut.

David stood there a moment, stunned. Quickly coming to, he ran to the door and stepped out into the hall, "Torry!"

She stopped, and turned around, "Yes?" she asked, her eyebrows raised imperiously.

"Please come back."

"Why?"

"You know why."

"No I don't, tell me."

With a look of exasperation, he said, "Because you promised you would 'bare your soul' to me."

"But apparently you weren't interested. You sent me packing before I could. Goodbye, David." She turned and started to walk away, but found herself immediately swept up into David's arms. His jaw set in stubborn determination, he carried her to the room, stepped inside and kicked the door shut.

She looked up at him and smiled. "How nice."

"Why you little imp!" He set her down abruptly, but before he could let go of her, she pulled his face down and kissed him 'a good one.'

He looked at her, shaking his head, trying not to smile. "You were just baiting me."

"Of course," she said, flouncing into the sitting area, "how else could I unbend that stiff neck of yours?"

Following her in, he glared at her. "Doggone it, Torry, you've kept me in a swivet all day. One minute I feel like my heart is being ripped out. Next I feel so irritated at you, I could turn you over my knee. Next I feel like laughing and then I want to smother you with kisses till you call for help."

She put on an alluring smile. "I promise I won't call for help."

David stepped over to one of the chairs and sat down laughing. "I give up...for the moment anyway, you are some determined woman."

"I am, David," she said sitting on the couch. "I'd follow you across the continent until you gave in and married me."

Concern furrowed his brows. "Torry,...what you said about the boys just as you left...was that true?"

"Yes, David," she said, a grave expression on her face, "I've wanted to tell you about Jack, but you had to make up your mind whether you could marry me for time first. What I'm going to tell you might have made your mind up for you, and I didn't want it that way. It wouldn't have been fair to you."

"Tell me...please."

"It is so terrible, I don't let myself think of it anymore, let alone talk about it." She saw alarm on David's face. "Remember when I told you that something in my life had been resolved? Jim and Scott had the answer all along, and I didn't know it." Torry frowned, thinking.

"Go on, Torry, please."

"Let me go back. When I married Jack, he was a big fun loving young man. He had a smile as bright as sunshine. He loved life. I knew before I married him that he was a little immature, but I felt he had great potential."

"He got a job as a salesman for a national sports equipment company and with his personality and ability, he soon became a regional manager. The problem with the job was, he had to be out of town almost half the month."

"Jack began to change. It was so gradual, that I didn't think it was anything but the stress of the job and having to be away from home so much. Immaturity in adults always equates with selfishness. After a few years, I realized that he was giving in to his selfishness."

"As I look back now with more objectivity, Jack basically wasn't a good father. He didn't enjoy the boys when they were small, always looking ahead for the time when they could play sports. He wanted to live vicariously through them since his dream of being a professional football player didn't happen."

"The only time he really paid attention to them was when they were old enough to play ball, and Scott wasn't an athlete so he paid less attention to him. When he was home, he watched sports on television constantly. In fact, that's what he was doing when he had his heart attack."

"The boys were lonely for a father, I was lonely for a husband. He quit being a spiritual leader in the home, and he became dark and morose as the years went by. I felt like I was failing as a wife. I would talk to him and beg him to tell me what was wrong. He denied that there was anything wrong. I prayed constantly that I could find the answer—but he died—leaving me with unanswered questions, leaving me feeling like a failure, not knowing how I had failed."

"A dark depression came over me and finally after the bishop and my home teacher had given me a blessing, the blackness left, but a form of depression stayed. Miraculously—it went away the day I walked into your office."

"It did?" he asked, astounded. "I also had been experiencing a terrible feeling of emptiness and depression for about two months prior to your visit—and it left the minute you walked in."

"That's what Jenny told me. Doesn't that tell you something, David?"

"Go on with your story," he said, his eyes revealing only anxiousness.

"Well, needless to say, the burden of not knowing what was wrong with Jack, kept me from getting on with my life. I couldn't love you, David, until it was resolved. Do you remember the day the boys came to the bank on a Saturday, and asked you to go over and be with me? That they had told me something shocking?"

"Yes, I do."

Torry continued, "The night before, the boys and I were visiting. The subject of their father came up, and I told them I felt I had failed him as a wife. They both looked shocked and excused themselves to talk together. In a short time they came back and said that they had no idea I felt that way or they would have told me sooner. They were very troubled over it. Then they told me."

Torry's face twisted in pain. "They had been carrying this horrible secret for years." She then reluctantly related every detail of the story, leaving nothing out, watching the blood drain from David's face.

His arms resting on his legs, David gripped his hands together so hard, his knuckles turned white. He stared at the floor in silence, not able to speak. When he spoke, his voice cracked with emotion. "And I thought my life was hard. I wish I could make up to you all those lonely unhappy years, Torry...and I wish I could make up to Jim and Scott for what they had to go through and..." he couldn't go on.

Deeply touched by his empathy, Torry waited until he could speak.

He looked up, "Torry, I can't tell you in words how much I want to be part of your lives and make you happy...but..."

"David," she said softly. "I know that the flashbacks of memory you've been getting are very healing...even if they are painful. At least they're coming out into the light where the Savior can heal them. Satan has more power over things that remain hidden in the dark."

His face reflected the dawning of a true principle. "I've never thought about it like that before, Torry."

"You have the gift of the Holy Ghost, and you hold the priesthood of God. You now have more power, with your faith, to overcome and be healed."

Hope flickered across his face then disappeared. Torry didn't wait for his response. "I think the only thing that worries you, David, is that the panic, which comes with the flashbacks, will cause you to run away from me like you ran from Clara. I'm not Clara, David. I won't let you run away from me. Growing up, I had a wonderful mother named Ruth, remember? I will be very watchful in a group of people and stay by your side."

"I don't want you to have to do that, Torry!"

"Do you want to stay by my side and keep me from being lonely like I was with Jack?"

"With all my heart, I do."

"With all my heart I want to be by your side forever. I hope and pray that it will be you I can be with for eternity—not Jack. I feel he's lost his salvation—but then I can't judge him—only the Lord can do that."

David got up and sat on the couch beside her, so deeply affected by her words, he couldn't speak. He just held her tightly in his arms for many moments, then whispered hoarsely, "Let's go to Dallas and meet Gabe—and get married."

Chapter Forty-Three

The previous day had been so fraught with emotion, that sitting together in first class, flying toward Dallas, Texas, seemed unreal to Torry. Last night she was exhausted driving home, but when she awakened this morning, she felt wonderful. The happiness was still there, real and deep, unhampered by uncertainty and fear.

Torry noticed that David wasn't feeling the same peacefulness. When he picked her up this morning, his usually expressive eyes were unreadable. His demeanor was that of a sleep walker, showing no emotion. She knew her mother noticed it too and probably wondered what had gone on between them yesterday. Nevertheless, Ruth saw them to the door and wished them a good time.

Her father, very much against Torry traveling with David, made arrangements with a friend for an early morning golf game in order to avoid seeing them off.

David knew how he must appear to Torry. He knew he was acting like he felt, like someone pretending not to care if his prize possession was soon to be snatched away because of bad behavior. But he couldn't help it, or rather he felt too emotionally exhausted to do anything about it.

When the overhead signal announced that the seat belts could be unfastened, he put his arm around Torry and pulled her close, his happiness still tentative. This was the first time he had even touched her this morning. She looked over at him and smiled.

"Thank you, David, that's much better."

David was amazed. Torry wasn't even questioning his behavior. He pondered this. When he was trying to win her, her unpredictability constantly kept him on a roller coaster. And now, she was steady and calm, giving him room to collect himself, to believe that she would remain by his side.

"David?"

"Yes?"

"What happened to Clara?"

Why was he surprised at this question? "I've tried to keep in touch with her. The last time I heard from her was a year-and-a-half ago. She was getting married for the fourth time."

"Oh...I hope this marriage lasts."

"Torry, how could you have married a man like Jack? Even in his better days, he doesn't sound like your type."

"He wasn't. I didn't even like him at first, but he was persistent. He grew on me. I grew to love him, so when he asked me to marry him for the tenth time, I accepted. I prayed about it, David. I was supposed to marry him."

"Why?"

"I have asked myself that many times during my marriage. I don't know, David. I know we are supposed to have trials so we can grow. Maybe that's why...maybe it was also to give Jack every chance to pull himself up. That's the way the Lord works. Look what he did for the Israelites. He gave them chance after chance to obey the commandments. So when they chose not to, he could say: I've done everything I could to help you. You brought this on yourself, you made the choice. Or...maybe it was so the Lord could give me Jim and Scott."

"I guess those could be answers...but..."

"Besides, David, where were you when I was ready to get married?"

"Well, I guess that puts it into perspective."

They both fell silent, each in their own private world of thought. Then Torry, savoring the new found peace and security with David's arm around her, soon fell asleep.

David, after forty-three years of living lonely and alone, for the most part, found himself unable to completely trust his good fortune, even though she was asleep in his arms.

Two-and-a-half hours later at 12:00 noon, the plane landed at the Dallas/Fort Worth airport.

David and Torry walked hand in hand toward the baggage claim where Gabe was waiting for them. Torry's heart was a flutter, hoping that Gabe would like her. David, on the other hand, now that he was here in Dallas, allowed himself to feel excitement over Gabe meeting Torry.

When they reached the baggage claim, it was already teeming with people. David craned his neck looking for his friend.

"Daveed!" boomed a voice behind him.

David turned around. "Gabe!" The two men hugged, pounding each other's back.

Torry stared at the man who was such an influence on David. Gabe was none other than David's chauffeur! He was wearing a uniform that said, Gabriel's Limo Service.

"Eet's good to see you, Daveed. You said you had a surprise for me?"

"I do, Gabe. Here she is. I want you meet Mrs. Torry Anderson. Torry this is Gabriel Rameriz, the best driver in the whole metroplex, and my best friend."

Gabriel's eyes became big as dollars and his mouth dropped open.

Torry held out her hand. "I'm so glad to finally meet this Gabe whom David has talked so much about," she said, a glowing smile on her face.

"I...I'm glad to meet you, Meesus Anderson," he said, his big hand enveloping hers.

"Please, call me Torry, will you?"

He nodded, studying her while she studied him. The gray at the temples of his dark hair, made his aristocratic face even more distinguished. He was a short well-built man, probably in his fifties. His rich brown eyes snapped with intelligent alertness. Breaking into a wide grin showing a mouthful of even white teeth, he said, "Torry, huh?" He looked over at David. "I like thees beauteeful leetle lady, so what ees going on here?"

David grinned. "Torry is my fiancee, Gabe."

For a moment, Gabe's face registered shock, then lit up with genuine happiness. "Thees lady, she ees worthy of you, I can see eet een her face, her eyes. I can't believe eet, thees ees too good to be true."

"Believe it Gabe, I can't." The words caught in his throat. "Let's get the bags."

After retrieving the bags, David said, "Gabe call Maria and see if it's all right if we...I," he put his finger to his lips, "come by the house for a few minutes."

"Oh thank you, Daveed. Maria has been on peens and needles waiting to hear your surprise."

While Gabe walked a few feet away to call Maria on his cell phone, Torry looked up at David, "You are a man of wonderful surprises, David. I like your friend."

"I'm glad you like him. You certainly passed muster with him, Torry. If we weren't already engaged, I'd ask you to marry me right here and now. Gabe and Maria never liked any of the women I dated."

Gabe came back grinning, still on the phone. "Maria wants you to stay for lunch, she has freshly made tamales for you."

"Great! I'm starving. Tell Maria I accept," David stated emphatically.

Gabe walked away again to give the message, and David asked, "I hope you like tamales, Torry."

"I do."

The two men carried the bags out the door and across the street to the parking area. The limousine was parked close in and soon they were out and on their way.

Torry looked around the country. "Texas is beautiful, who would have ever guessed."

David smiled. "There are so many places in Texas I want to take you to see, Torry. I haven't taken time to see them myself, but all of a sudden I want to."

A deep hearty laugh erupted from the front seat as Gabe looked at Torry through the rear view mirror. "Already you are doing good for Daveed, Torry. Maria and I have been so worried about heem. He worked too hard and deedn't rest. We deedn't want heem to be alone, but all those ladies that came after heem, we were more than worried, my Maria and I."

"Thank you, Gabe. I'm very relieved that you approve of me. I don't think David would marry me without it."

"I'm afraid it's true, Gabe," David chimed in, "but I knew you would like her so I went ahead and asked her to marry me."

Gabe's eyes snapped with eagerness, "Deed you two meet een that small town?"

"Hold your horses, Gabe. We'll tell you and Maria both all about it during lunch."

David gazed at Torry and smiled, giving her a squeeze. Relieved, she noticed the old magnetism was back in his eyes. She sighed with happiness.

They drove into a nice middle class neighborhood and finally into the Rameriz driveway. The home was a well-kept red brick home with magnificent old trees and lots of flowers.

When they stepped inside, a lovely Hispanic woman threw her arms around David. He gave her a squeeze while whispering in her ear, "Maria, I want you to meet my fiancee, Torry Anderson,"

Maria gasped and pulled away. Her brown eyes wide and scrutinizing, focused on Torry.

"Hello, Maria," Torry said, her smile warm. "I want to thank you and Gabe for looking after David for me until I could meet him."

Maria's eyes glistened and her arms opened wide. Torry went into them and returned the warm, motherly embrace. As they pulled apart, Maria laughed.

"I'm so happy for David," then turning to David, she said, "I'm happy for Torry."

"Thank you, Maria," David said, giving her another big hug.

"Now Gabe and I can rest easy. You did well, David. I'm very relieved. I like her."

"Of course, I wouldn't marry anyone you didn't like, Maria."

She smiled, her brown eyes sparkling, "Now come into the kitchen and let's eat lunch while you and Torry tell us all about it, how you met...everything."

David's face became serious. "Before we go into the kitchen, I want to tell you about another surprise."

"Another one?" Maria asked, holding her breath.

"Yes. A week and two days ago, I was baptized into The Church of Jesus Christ of Latter-day Saints."

Maria and Gabe stared at David a moment, speechless, then Maria started to cry.

"Oh David, David, I knew you'd accept the gospel one day!"

Gabe held out his hand to David, tears filling his eyes. "Thees ees what Maria and I have been praying for and hoping for."

Joy over their reaction overcame both David and Torry. David swallowed hard and said, "Gabe, how can I ever thank you for insisting that I take a sabbatical in a small Mormon town? If it hadn't been for you I wouldn't have met Torry."

Gabe smiled and nodded, unable to speak. David continued, "But after giving it some thought, I have to think that even if I hadn't gone to Green Valley, I would have accepted the gospel somewhere, sometime down the road. But, I do know that going to Green Valley hastened it."

Too full for further words, Maria motioned for them to follow her into the kitchen.

Torry was ecstatic over the homemade tamales, the beans and honeydew melon. She was also full of questions over the Rameriz family picture hanging on the kitchen wall. She found out that five of the children were married and that the sixth one was on a mission in Mexico.

Finally she asked, "How did you meet David, Gabe?"

"Ahhh," he smiled, a far away expression in his eyes, "eet was feefteen years ago that thees young man hired me to drive for heem. I had just lost my job, and I was desperate."

He then launched into the whole story; explaining that David had eventually subsidized him in a whole fleet of limousines, refusing any pay except to be at his beck and call as a personal driver whenever he was needed.

To avoid further discussion on the subject, David quickly scooted his chair back and said, "Let's clean up the kitchen, while Torry and I tell you about our courtship and my conversion."

Chapter Forty-Four

Midway between downtown Dallas and North Dallas, Gabe turned west off the highway. After a quarter of a mile, he turned into what appeared to Torry, a private drive, long and winding, canopied by large old trees. The grounds on either side of the road were breathtaking. Beautifully shaped trees, with small dark green leaves, dotted gently rolling hills of green lawn. Soon an architecturally stunning, large five story building appeared. The pastel colors of the weathered brick, trimmed with white stone, gave the structure the soft elegance of a palatial residence. Or was it a residence? Torry was puzzled. Gabe drove under its wide front portico and pulled to a stop. On a brass plate next to the carved fruitwood doors was the name, Live Oak Inn.

"Oh, this is an inn. This is a magnificent place, David."

He smiled, pleased, "You like it?"

"Oh, I do."

Gabe got out and opened the door for them. Torry smiled at him, "Thank you, Gabe."

"Yes, thank you," David added, "I'll call you when I need you."

Gabe nodded formally and then got out their suitcases, set them down, got back in and drove off. A young uniformed doorman came out immediately and carried them inside.

David led Torry into the lobby and up to the desk.

"Mr. Mayer! It's good to see you, sir," the man behind the counter exclaimed.

"Thank you, Roger, it's good to see you, too. I called you for a reservation for my guest, Torry Anderson."

"Oh yes sir, here's the key."

"Thank you, Roger, see that our bags get up." Taking hold of Torry's arm, he led her to the elevator. Glancing at her, he smiled at her expression of awe as she looked around the lobby. They got off at the fourth floor. David led Torry down the wide hall to a door. He unlocked it, swung it open with his arm and stepped back for her to enter.

Torry stepped in and gasped. "David this is a suite! It's...it's so luxurious." She looked up at him in amazement. "You *are* rich if you can afford this."

He threw back his head and laughed. "Torry, weren't you the fiery little chicken farmer-to-be who so indignantly accused me of being a multi-millionaire?"

"Well yes, but...but I had no idea what a multi-millionaire was."

"Come with me, my sweet," he said, grinning. Grabbing her hand, he led her out of the suite to the elevator. They got out on the fifth floor and walked up to a door. Unlocking it, they entered.

Torry sucked in her breath, "Why David, this is even bigger and more luxurious than mine! Is this where you are staying?"

"No. This is where I live."

"You live here?"

"I do."

Stunned and speechless, Torry walked around the big room then walked over to the sliding door and out onto the patio. David followed her out.

"How many suites or condominiums are on this floor?"

"Only this one."

Torry walked along the thirty-foot-wide patio, feeling the heavy heat of Texas, and admiring the pots of flowers, small trees and patio furniture. "Why, David, this patio looks like it goes all the way around." She continued walking, David following, finally arriving back where they started from. "Is this how you exercise each morning?"

David smiled. "No, I exercise on the double wide, walking path that goes all around the grounds."

She leaned out over the brick wall. "I see it, how nice. David! These grounds are a golf course," she stated, as she noticed a couple of golf carts and several men and women with clubs.

"Yes. Do you golf, Torry?"

"No."

"Would you like to learn?"

"No."

"Good, Because I've never golfed and have never wanted to."

"What are those unique trees on the golf course?"

"Live Oak."

"Oh, that's why you named it, Live Oak Inn."

"When I bought the property years ago, there were several old Live Oaks on it, and it gave me the idea."

"You planted more Live Oak then didn't you?" He nodded. "You've made it into a beautiful place, David. Let's go back in and see the rest of your home."

Torry found a large lovely kitchen and a large dinette that led out onto the patio. "Do you cook here for yourself, David?" she asked peeking into the cupboards, finding them mostly bare.

"Rarely, I usually have room service from the five star restaurant down stairs."

"Five star? Ohhh!" she squealed, clapping her hands, "I'm really going to enjoy it here, David."

David, deeply pleased over her child-like excitement, found himself feeling grateful he was rich. "Come on, let me finish showing you the rest of the place."

She followed him to two bedrooms on one side of the suite, each with a private bathroom, and then on the other side they entered the large master bedroom.

Torry walked around the bedroom. "Did you and Clara live here?" she asked tentatively.

"No. We lived in a house. We sold it after the divorce," he said, noting the relief on her face.

Opening the door to the large walk-in closet, she stepped inside. It smelled like David. She looked at his clothes, thinking.

David leaned against the door frame, watching her. "What are you looking for, Torry?"

She turned to him, a hint of a smile on her face. "I just wanted to see if you really lived here in this luxurious place. About the only place I've seen you in is the bank, our little frame house and the chicken coop."

He chuckled. "Don't I fit here?"

She slipped past him out the door and went back into the living room. She slowly walked around, studying everything...the expensive, luxurious looking furniture, frowning.

"What is it, Torry?"

"I don't see you here. I mean, there is nothing that tells me you live here, except your closet."

"I don't live here, Torry, I sleep here. Once in a while I eat here, once in a while I'll entertain here for those who've been kind to me, like the Rameriz family, letting them swim in the pool. I entertain some of my business acquaintances and employees once in a great while."

"Where do you live, David?"

"Mostly at my office."

With a look of distress, she said, "Oh, David, no."

"Work is my life, Torry...or it has been."

"Why?" she asked, still distressed.

"I guess it's a little hard for a woman to understand, but a man has to have...uh, let me put it this way, Torry. It was either hard work or relationships with women. The only way I've been able to remain a moral man is to channel my energy into building my empire."

"Oh." The distress left, replaced by the dawning of understanding. "Oh...of course." She flew into his arms, her arms winding around his chest, hugging him fiercely.

"You are the most wonderful man I have ever known, David."

His heart swelled until it felt like it would burst. Never had he received this kind of admiration and appreciation. Torry made him feel like the valuable person she said he was.

They continued to stay locked in each others arms for many moments, then David leaned down and kissed her long and tenderly. Finally he lifted his head and gazed at her, his eyes captivating her with the love she saw there.

"May I have a date tonight for dinner and dancing?"

"Oh yes. Where?"

"Downstairs."

"You have a ballroom downstairs too?" Torry was finding it difficult to assimilate all of the convenience, luxury and grandeur.

"Yes. It's part of the Live Oak Tree Dining room. I haven't taken time for recreation, but I do love to dance."

She smiled up at him, "I thought so. You dance so well."

"Thank you, so do you. Do you have something dressy to wear?"

"I do. I bought it in Salt Lake."

"Good." He looked at his watch. "May I pick you up at 6:30?"

"You may," Torry said, anticipation dancing in her eyes.

David took Torry back down to her suite and then went back up to his.

Torry just stood there for a moment, tingling with excitement. This dream of an inn, the inn where David only half lived, was turning into a place of happiness for both of them.

She sauntered around in this strange world of David's. She was on his turf now. It was time. He had been on hers. She could get to know David in a way that was not possible in Green Valley.

In the bedroom, she realized suddenly that her suitcases were nowhere to be seen. She stepped quickly to a closet. There were her clothes, already hanging up! She went over to a dresser, opened a drawer and found her underthings neatly placed inside. She bristled. This seemed an intrusion upon her privacy. Soon, however, she relaxed, knowing she could request otherwise.

Getting her robe from the closet, she undressed and went into the bathroom. There were her cosmetics and skin care, neatly placed and ready for use. She had intended to shower but noticing the sunken, marble, jacuzzi, she couldn't resist the luxury of a bath.

She had just put on her hose and slip after her bath when the doorbell rang. "They have doorbells here too?" she muttered. Throwing on her robe, she wondered why David was so early.

She opened the door to a young man holding a vase filled with pink roses.

"Oh!" she gasped.

"Mrs. Torry Anderson?"

"Yes."

"These are for you."

She took them from him. "Thank you."

"Have a good evening." He smiled and walked off.

She smelled the roses, then set them down on the beautifully carved rosewood coffee table in the sofa section. Taking the card from the roses, she read: "To my beautiful Torry. I love you. David."

The thrill of receiving the flowers, staying in this beautiful suite, and the anticipation of spending the evening with David made her feel like Cinderella about to go to the ball and dance in the arms of the handsome prince. She laughed at herself and went into the bedroom to finish getting ready.

When the door bell rang the second time, she was completely ready, but not for the sight before her when she opened the door.

"David!" she uttered breathlessly, "you're in a tuxedo."

He grinned as he stepped inside, "I think that's what they call it."

"You are so handsome in it. It makes your hair look darker and your eyes even grayer. How did I ever resist you for two long months, David?"

"I don't know, how did you?" His eyes turned mischievous. He reached for her, and she backed away.

"No, David, don't touch me, I might faint."

He grabbed her arms and pulled her to him, his eyes full of amusement. "I promise, I won't disturb your makeup." He bent down and ever so lightly, ever so tantalizingly touched her lips with his. She swooned in his arms, and they both laughed.

"Now," he said holding her at arms length, "Let me look at you?"

Torry was dressed in a silky form-fitting dress with a full-swirled skirt in soft muted teal. At the v-neck, she wore a teal crystal necklace with tear drop earrings to match.

David, noting that the dress brought out the green in her hazel eyes, said, "Turn around, Torry." She whirled around. "You are always beautiful, Torry," his eyes shone appreciatively, "but you look especially beautiful tonight."

She walked over to the roses and picked them up, smelled them and put them down. "Maybe it's because I feel like Cinderella. Thank you for the roses," she said softly.

In the dining room, everyone greeted David with a big smile, the hostess, the waiters and the bus boys. He introduced each of them to his fiancee. This brought surprise, smiles and hearty congratulations.

The almost filled dining room was quiet and elegant with smoke blue upholstered chairs surrounding white linen covered tables. In the center of each table candles flickered in crystal bowls surrounded by fresh pink roses. A delicate pattern of pink roses sparsely bordered the soft blue carpet. The tables encircled a rich hardwood maple dance floor above which hung a shimmering chandelier.

David and Torry were seated at a table that edged the dance floor. Across from them on a raised platform behind the tables, the orchestra played soft dinner music.

"I've been in some nice restaurants, David, but nothing like this," she said, wide-eyed.

"I'm glad you like it, my darling."

"Who can afford to eat here, David?" she whispered.

He smiled and whispered, "Only the ultra rich of the city I'm afraid," and only the ultra rich of other cities for that matter. In fact, it attracts the very elite of snobs," he added, grinning.

"If it's that expensive, how can you get enough business?"

"Well, we have a constant waiting list for the suites and the dining room is always filled."

Torry watched the wealthy, beautiful people at the other tables, fascinated by the way they were dressed, the way they talked and ate. And David watched Torry, fascinated.

Never having tasted such wonderful food or been the recipient of such smooth, professional and attentive service from the waiters, Torry was in a state of wonderment.

They had just finished their dessert when Torry noticed the chandelier dim to a soft glow. Couples gravitated to the center and began dancing.

"May I have this dance, my Cinderella?"

"You may, my handsome prince."

They danced together even better than the first time, whirling and dipping, their feet moving together like clockwork. At one point, as the dance ended, they heard clapping. Glancing in that direction they saw four of the waiters standing in a row grinning. Torry noticed that all eyes of the wealthy patrons were upon them, wondering, she was sure, what all the fuss was about. They laughed and bowed, then resumed dancing. The next song was a Strauss waltz, carrying Torry back in time to a romantic world of long ago. When the orchestra played, 'I Could Have Danced All Night,' David held her closer, kissed her forehead then leaned down and whispered in her ear, "How about us eloping day after tomorrow, my love?"

"I would love to," she murmured dreamily.

When the song ended, David took her hand and led her out of

the dining room to the elevator. They got out on the fourth floor and David unlocked her door.

"May I come in?"

"You may."

He closed the door behind them. Torry whirled and danced around the room smiling. "I still feel like Cinderella, David. Thank you for the lovely evening. I had a wonderful time."

"You're welcome, my darling, I had a wonderful time too," he said, sitting down on one of the sofas, "so quit floating around and come and sit down beside me."

"All right." She sat down and snuggled against him.

"Tomorrow we'll go to the courthouse and get the marriage license and..."

"David!" she interrupted. "You were serious about day after tomorrow."

"Of course."

"But...what about the boys, I..."

David put his fingers over her lips and grinned. "I have a secret."

"What? Tell me."

"What will you give me if I tell you?"

"This." She leaned over and kissed him.

"Mmmm, that will do. Here goes, Jim and Scott want us to elope."

"You're teasing."

"I'm not."

"I don't believe you."

"Scouts honor," he held his hand up in the scout sign.

"Were you a Boy Scout?"

"No, but I'm honorable and trustworthy."

Torry laughed. "When did they tell you that?" she asked, still skeptical.

"When I talked to Jim on the BYU campus that day. He said that his grandfather wouldn't be pleased about us getting married and that he and Scott had discussed it and both felt that it would be better if we eloped. He said that he knew his grandmother would approve also."

"Really?" She jumped up and walked around. "I can't believe it, David, that means we really can be married day after tomorrow!"

David, thrilled that she was as excited as he was, said, "Come and sit down by me, please."

"All right. Remember, David," she said, sitting down beside him again, "when our getting married seemed so hopeless? And now...now," she repeated in a voice filled with wonder, "we can be married...day after tomorrow."

"It is unbelievable," he said, putting his arm around her, holding her tightly against him. "Where shall we be married?"

Torry fell silent, thinking. Finally she said, "The next best place to the temple is a home...maybe Maria and Gabe's home?"

"What a remarkable idea, Torry."

"We can have a bishop marry us."

"Of course! I'll call Gabe and ask about one and see if it will be all right to use their home."

"So in the morning we'll go get a license?"

"Yes." He stood up, took her hand and walked to the door. He turned and held her a moment and then gave her a quick kiss. "I'll be glad when you're mine, Torry." He left quickly.

Chapter Forty-Five

Early Tuesday morning, Torry stepped out onto the patio and felt the warmth of the Texas air, realizing it would become a sweltering, hot day. She stepped back in knowing she needed to wear something for both the heat outside and the cool refrigeration inside.

She hummed as she put on her new rich red cotton jersey skirt, the light elastic waist band giving it a subtle flare. Next, she put on the natural-color T-shirt with clamshell embroidery tracing the scooped neckline. The matching red tunic-length cardigan with its gleaming buttons down the front, could be taken off when outside in the heat. Red earrings and white sandals went on next. She smiled at her reflection because she knew David would like it.

And he did. His eyes gleamed with appreciation. He smiled and ran his hand through her curls, then with his fingers, tenderly traced the outline of her face.

~~~~~~~~~~~~

Torry's head was a whirl. So much had taken place already this morning. Having money to make things happen so quickly and orderly, was certainly an advantage, she mused.

While they were eating breakfast in the dining room, David had informed her that Gabe and Maria were thrilled that she and David would even consider getting married in their home. Then Gabe surprised David; he told David he was a branch president, explaining to him that this was the same as a bishop, and that he would consider it a great privilege to marry them. The time was set for 10:00 A.M. Wednesday.

After breakfast, back up in David's suite, he had asked her where she wanted to go on their honeymoon. She had answered, "Why right here."

David, totally surprised at her answer, said, "But, Torry, we can go on a Caribbean cruise, we can go to the beach in Hawaii, you name it."

"But, David, that would be just a waste of money," she had informed him. "Right now I am only interested in you, being with you day and night. Here, we have room service, we can go dancing or swimming if we choose and the rest of the time we can just be together. This is a perfect place for a honeymoon." She was aware how much this pleased David.

At this point, the door bell rang. It was the jeweler. David had arranged for him to make a house call, bringing with him engagement rings and wedding bands!

David was surprised again when she chose not to have a diamond but rather a matching wedding band. The jeweler promised to have them sized and back by 9:00 the next morning.

When they left for the county courthouse, Torry was surprised that David didn't take the usual elevator, instead, he led her to a private one—his. It took them down to his private garage where he picked up his Lincoln Town Car.

And finally the most important thing had been accomplished. They had their marriage license.

Leaving downtown Dallas, Torry asked, "Now what are you going to surprise me with, David?"

He smiled. "That's it for today, my darling. What would you like to do?"

Torry looked at her watch and saw that it was only eleven o'clock. "Go see the house where you grew up."

David exhaled. "That isn't my favorite thing to do, Torry, but I'll take you there."

They drove to Turtle Creek and began driving north along the East side of the lake.

"Slow down, David. This is beautiful!" Her eyes were drawn to the left, to a park-like area separating the street from the lake. Across the lake were gently sloping hills of lush green grass leading up to magnificent homes. On their right were large gracious homes, each unique in their architectural splendor.

"There's a walking path along the creek, David. Will you take me walking there sometime?"

"I will. See across the lake, those bushes up close to the homes and all along the bank?"

"Yes."

"They are Azaleas. Every spring they are covered with big, bright pink blossoms. I'd like to bring you here then."

As they drove out of Turtle Creek into the next area, he explained, his hand making a sweeping gesture, "All this is called Highland Park." Driving a short distance further, he pulled over. "This is where I lived, Torry."

Torry studied the mansion in silence. It was white. The imposing pretentiousness of its modern architecture made her shiver. "It looks like a mausoleum, David." She thought of the little boy who had lived there, so alone and unloved by his parents. Before she realized it, she was crying. She covered her face.

"Torry please don't!" He undid his seat belt and cradled her in his arms. "How can you cry when I am so happy?"

"But little boys are so vulnerable and..."

"Big boys are too, Torry, they also need nurturing."

She wiped her eyes and smiled. "They are, David. And I'm so glad you've given me the job."

David smiled, relieved to see the tears stop. "Now, where do you want to go?"

"I want to see Paul's house."

David's face became thoughtful, his eyes distant. "You know, Torry, I would like to see it, too. I hope it's still there. It's east of the grade school."

They were quiet as he drove out of Highland Park to a neighborhood of smaller homes. He pulled up behind an old Plymouth station wagon parked in front of a tan frame house with light brick wainscoat.

"This is it, Torry!" David exclaimed, excitement in his voice. "Boy, does this bring back memories."

A movement caught their eye. A man got out of the station wagon and lifted the front hood.

"It looks like they're having car trouble," David said, as he got out of the car.

David walked around to the front of the wagon. "Can I help?"

The man pulled his head out, surprised. He shook his head, a grim smile on his face. "Thanks. I wish you could, but we've had car trouble ever since we left Oklahoma City."

"I don't know a thing about cars myself," David said, "but I have a friend who does. He has a limousine service, a tow truck and a garage where he repairs his own cars."

"Uh...do you know how much he charges?"

"He's very reasonable," David quickly assured him. "Excuse me, and I'll call one of his men to tow it in and repair it for you."

"Thank you, I would appreciate that very much."

David went to his car and called Gabe's garage and arranged it, then went back to report that the truck would be there in about twenty minutes.

Torry seeing a woman in the car, got out to visit with her. The woman got out also. Torry smiled at her. "I'm Torry Anderson."

"It's nice to meet you, Torry. My name is Diane Eldredge."

The two men came over. "We really appreciate you helping us out," Diane said, to David, then explained to both of them, "Every time we come to Dallas, we drive by the place where my husband lived when he was a boy."

"Yeah," the husband added, "I always like to see how the old place looks." He indicated the house.

David's head jerked toward the man. "You lived here?"

"Yes, I was born here and lived here until the summer I turned eleven."

"What is your name?" David quickly asked.

"Paul Eldredge."

David stared at him a moment, stunned. "Paul! I'm David...David Mayer!"

Paul Eldredge studied David, frowning, trying to take it in. "You...are David Mayer?"

"Yes."

"David!" Paul reach out his hand and took David's outstretched one. Both men were soon laughing and hugging.

They pulled apart, each grinning from ear to ear.

"I can't believe it, David. What in the world are you doing here?!"

"I've talked about you so often, my fiancée here wanted to see where you lived."

"Really?" Paul asked in amazement.

"Really," confirmed Torry, holding out her hand. "I'm Torry Anderson, Paul. I'm glad to meet you. This is all rather unbelievable."

"It is, Paul," confirmed David. "Is this your wife?"

"Yes. This is Diane. Diane this is the friend I told you about that I missed so much when we moved from here."

Her eyes lit up. "Why this is amazing!"

"Hey, have you two had lunch yet?" asked David.

"No, we haven't," Paul answered.

"May we take you to lunch?"

"Sounds great."

When the tow truck arrived, David drove the four of them back to the inn. Taking them up to his suite, David explained that it would be better to have room service so they could have more privacy.

Paul and Diane looked around the room in awe, and Paul said, "As I've thought about you through the years, David, I felt you would be financially successful, and it looks like I'm right."

"Well, Paul, I started out with an inheritance. My mother and stepfather were killed in a plane crash on one of their many trips around the world."

"Oh. How's Hildi?"

David told him.

"I'm sorry to hear that, I liked her."

"Me too. Now please sit down and I'll get the menus from the kitchen and we'll order."

When they had decided and called it in, David said, "I can't believe we've run into you like this, Paul. For a long time I've wanted to thank you for what you and your family did for me, for what I learned from you."

Paul seemed puzzled. "What did you learn?"

"I learned what a close and loving family was. I felt something in your home that was...uh special. I also learned about family prayer..." All of a sudden it hit David. Of course...they had to be!

Paul noticed the strange expression on David's face. "What? What is it, David?"

"Paul, could you be...I mean, are you...a Mormon?"

"Yes."

"Your family too?"

"Yes."

David jumped up. "I knew it!" He looked over at Torry who

was as excited as he was. "I don't know why I didn't catch it before," he said to Torry then to Paul. "I guess it's because it's all happened so fast."

Paul scooted to the edge of his seat, "What are you trying to tell me, David?"

"That a little over a week ago I was baptized into The Church of Jesus Christ of Latter-day Saints."

Stunned, Paul just stared at him—then shot to his feet and let out a war whoop! He grabbed David's hand and pumped it vigorously. Their wide smiles were mixed with an expression of incredulity.

"I can't believe it, David!"

"It is quite extraordinary since my best friend in grade school happens to be the first Mormon I had contact with."

In a choked up voice, Paul asked, "How did it happen, David? Tell us all about it."

They sat down and as David began, Torry studied Paul and Diane. She liked them immediately. She knew their meeting in front of Paul's house was not just coincidence. Paul was about David's height with sandy hair, blue eyes and a nice looking, intelligent face. Diane had light brown hair and brown eyes. She would have been pretty but her face was too thin and pale and her eyes had a haunted look.

David had just finished his conversion story when lunch arrived. Paul blew his nose, and Diane wiped her eyes.

During lunch, Torry said, "Diane, tell us about you and Paul. Do you have children?"

It was then that Torry learned what was behind the expression in Diane's eyes. Diane informed them that they had six children, but five months ago, their youngest, a little girl, five years old, died of cancer.

"This is what brought us to Dallas this time," explained Paul, "I wanted to take Diane away for a few days. She's still struggling. We both are. Earlier this morning we went to the temple. We needed some special spiritual help. We had only been at the old house a short time when you showed up. I can't tell you what a lift it has been for us to run into you both like this."

"We're sorry to hear about your little girl," David said. "What work do you do, Paul?"

Paul explained that he was a financial officer for a large corporation. "But it has been sold and I'm not impressed with the new management, so I'm going to send out my resume to some other companies. I had hoped to make a few connections while we were here."

"Would you consider moving to Dallas and working with me in my holding company? I would pay you well. I need someone I can trust. Someone who would have my interest at heart. I've made work my life, Paul, and now I want to start living for a change."

Paul looked over at Diane, who smiled and nodded. "I would like that very much, David. Thank you!"

"And," David said, "would you and Diane do Torry and me another big favor?"

Diane spoke up, "We'd be glad to...anything."

"Would you be with us tomorrow morning when Torry and I are married?"

Chapter Forty-Six

Wednesday morning, July second, Gabriel Rameriz, in his Sunday suit and tie, stood before Torry Anderson and David Mayer.

Behind the couple on the right stood Paul and Diane Eldredge, on the left, Maria Rameriz.

Maria, her eyes already glistening with tears, was sure she had never seen such a beautiful and happy couple. Torry, her cheeks flushed with excitement, looked lovely in the simple ivory cotton and linen dress with pearls at her throat. David, in an elegant suit the color of his radiant gray eyes, looked very handsome.

David could hardly believe his good fortune, but here she was by his side smiling up at him, her eyes full of love and happiness, anxiously waiting to be united with him.

To have his friends, Paul, Diane and Maria share in this momentous occasion; to have Gabe, the man responsible for all this, actually marry him and Torry was almost more than his plate of happiness could hold.

In this peaceful, spirit-filled home President Gabriel Rameriz started with simple, clear and inspired words of advice and counsel. Then the ceremony began. Finally came the wonderful words, "I now pronounce you man and wife. You may kiss the bride."

Man and wife—the impossible has happened. Torry thought. She turned to David and their eyes locked for a moment, then he bent down and gently, tenderly kissed his bride.

After the embraces, handshakes and congratulations, Gabe, with Maria by his side, drove everyone in his best limousine to the Live Oak Inn for the wedding luncheon.

A professional photographer, whom David had hired, was waiting for them. He took pictures of the bride and groom in front of a Live Oak tree standing in the courtyard of the inn, next, with each couple separately, then with the three couples together.

In a private dining room of the inn, happiness reigned as the bride and groom and their four friends visited, enjoying each other and the superb meal. The photographer discreetly took pictures at different times, from different angles.

As they finished and were waiting for the dessert David had ordered, the door of the dining room burst open. To David's surprise, as well as Torry's, the cooks, the waiters, the bus boys and the maids all appeared, one of them carrying a beautiful wedding cake.

David laughed with pleasure. "Thank you, all of you...thank you!" He introduced everyone and then insisted that a table be added and that they each sit down and have a piece of the wedding cake with them. The photographer took more pictures.

~~~~~~~~~~~

HONEYMOON DAY ONE: (Wednesday)

David unlocked the door, picked Torry up and carried her over the threshold. She looked at him, and with an impish smile on her face, said, "How nice."

He grinned, kissed her soundly and set her down. Hand in hand they walked into the center of the room. All the fuss and flurry over, they gazed at each other in wonderment.

Torry feeling the unfamiliarity of the wedding band, held up her hand. David did likewise.

"These wedding bands tell us we're married, David...but it doesn't seem real." Their fingers laced together.

David nodded his head. "I know. Of all the times we've had together, Torry, this moment is the most unbelievable."

All of a sudden Torry felt shy. "What...what shall we do now?"

David laughed, picked her up and carried her into the bedroom and set her down. "First of all, I think it would be a very good idea if we both put on something more comfortable. Oh-oh, I forgot to have your things sent over."

A sly smile stole across her face. "You mean you forgot something? The man who is so efficient and thinks of everything...forgot?"

"I did."

"Go look in the closet."

He stepped over to it and peeked in. "Why your clothes are here!"

"And there are my bags by the chair."

"You did it."

"I did. After all, this is my suite now. It's ours. Doesn't that sound good, David? This is ours!"

"Does it ever. My heart nearly leaped out of my chest when I saw your clothes in my closet."

"Do you want to help me find places for the things in my suit-cases?"

"I do."

Torry kicked off her heels. David took off his coat and tie. Then they found drawers and emptied others, laughing...having a good time.

When they were through, they looked at each other, marveling that they really belonged to each other. David took Torry into his arms, his eyes smoldering momentarily with the self-denied desire of years, then they warmed with the deep love and tenderness that he felt for this woman who incredibly had become his wife.

Torry gazed back at him, intoxicated by what she saw in David's eyes, savoring the anticipation—the glorious anticipation that comes only to those who wait until the wedding night.

Allowing passion to inflame them in a way they never allowed before, they kissed. When they pulled apart, breathless, David said, "You are mine Torry, legally and lawfully and in the eyes of God."

"And you are mine, David," she said softly, "The love between a man and a woman...is...is a miracle isn't it?"

He nodded, his heart full.

"And sacred, when approved and sanctioned by the Lord."

"Sacred," he repeated slowly, "I've never thought about it like that, Torry. Sacred. That fits so well how my love for you feels at this very moment."

~~~~~~~~~~~

HONEYMOON DAY TWO: (Thursday)

In the early dawn, David awoke with a start to find Torry lying beside him. It wasn't a dream. He watched her sleep, his eyes tracing her beautiful face, her thick, dark lashes, her cheeks and her full, soft lips. His heart swelled with love and gratitude. How could he be so lucky, so blessed? She turned over, her back to him. Gently slipping his arm around her waist, he pulled her close and promptly fell back to sleep.

The early morning sun seeped through the closed shutters, awakening Torry. Anxiously, she reached for David. He was there. She turned over, leaned up on her elbow and studied David's sleeping face. Her heart skipped a beat, he looked so vulnerable with an unruly lock of hair on his forehead, and so handsome. She leaned down and kissed his wonderful lips. His eyes opened. Smiling, he grabbed her, pulling her close.

~~~~~~~~~~~

Still in their robes, David and Torry enjoyed a leisurely breakfast out on the patio. The air was warm and balmy. Breathing in deeply, Torry exclaimed, "Texas air is so fragrant, David. And listen to those birds. I've never heard so many different kinds."

David listened. "You're right. It took you, Torry, to help me wake up and enjoy the things the Lord put here for us to enjoy."

"I wish we could go on like this forever...almost. I'm so happy, David. How long a honeymoon can we have?"

"I can't leave Tom too long. I have to get back and orient him, and I've really neglected all my other businesses these past two weeks. In fact, if it's okay with you, I do need to make a few phone calls this morning. It won't take long. Back to your question, I thought we could stay until Monday."

Torry clapped her hands with delight. "That's longer than I expected. I'll have you all to myself for four more days."

Happiness filled David's soul. He marveled as he thought of what had happened over the past two-and-a-half months: his fight to win Torry—her persistent rejection—the euphoria over her acceptance and then the utter desolation. And now, here she was, his bride, excited to spend four more days with him!

Quietly he asked, "Shall we call Jim and Scott today and tell them?"

"Oh yes, David! And I'll have them tell my parents. In other words, they can pave the way for us."

"Let's ask them if they can pick us up at the airport late Monday afternoon, and I'll take them and your parents out to dinner to celebrate."

"All right. That would be nice if...if it wasn't for Dad's attitude."

David's brows furrowed, "Torry, your mother and father remind me of something I read in the New Testament. It seems to me they are 'unequally yoked.'"

"I know, but—it may not always be that way. For some reason I have more hope for my dad."

David lifted his brows in surprise, then smiled lovingly at his bride. "I hope you're right."

"When will we leave for Green Valley, David?"

"Tuesday morning. That will give me some time to bring things over from my apartment to our little house. Ahh, that sounds good, Torry."

"Yes, it does, David."

"And how about it if I call Tom today and tell him the good news, and ask him to make a reservation at the Hilltop House Tuesday night and invite our friends for another celebration."

"You mean the Baker family, the Blackburn family, Dan, Jesse and their wives?"

"Exactly."

"Yes! Let's do."

"And now my love, back to you, I would like to take you wherever you would like to go, to a musical, a symphony? Both are on this weekend."

"I'll go if you want to, David, but I would much rather just stay here alone with you."

He sighed, "Ahh just what I was hoping you would say."

Torry got up, went over to him, sat on his lap and kissed him until his toes curled.

HONEYMOON DAY THREE: (Friday)

Before breakfast, Torry stated, "I would love to go for a walk on that inviting walking path right now."

"Your wish is my command, my beautiful bride."

Together, they walked hand in hand in the soothing early morning warmth, breathing in its fragrance, listening to the birds and admiring the beauty of nature.

After the walk, David suggested they take a dip in the pool. After the swim, they sat in the shade of the patio and ordered breakfast. They returned to their suite, relaxed and happy.

That night they took time out to enjoy a bowl of popcorn and watch a couple of videos, a mystery and a romance.

~~~~~~~~~

HONEYMOON DAY FOUR: (Saturday)

Torry curled up on the couch with David's arm around her, and sighed contentedly. "You said I could choose where I wanted to live, David and I've decided."

"You have?" he asked surprised, "Where?"

"Right here."

"You mean Dallas?"

"I mean in Dallas in this very condominium."

"But this isn't a home, Torry."

"Already it's home to me, David. I love it, I love the patio, I love the beautiful grounds surrounding it, the swimming pool and...especially the ballroom." She smiled up at him, "This way we could dance together often."

He smiled back, adoring her, then raised his eyebrows in mock suspicion. "I know how you like that five star restaurant downstairs," he said. "If we live here, will you promise to cook for me most of the time?"

"Are you sure you want me to? The cooks downstairs are much better than I am." ·

"Oh no, Torry, I like your cooking better. I wouldn't trade that for all the five star restaurants in the world."

"Thank you, David." She smiled and said, "I remember when you wanted to hire me to cook for you."

He grinned and stated triumphantly, "I got my way, didn't I?"

"You did, my dearest David. Now...how do you feel about making this our home?"

His face became thoughtful. "With you here, it will become home to me. You can do what you want with it, change the decorating if you wish. At least you must put your own touches on it. I want you to hang all your paintings. How about if I add on a room just for you to paint in?"

"Really?" she asked, excitement in her voice. "I've always wanted a room with just the right lighting."

David leaned over and kissed her forehead and ruffled her curls. "You know what my darling, you're always surprising me. I thought you would choose to live in Salt Lake to be by your sons."

"Our sons."

"Thank you, our sons."

"Isn't your holding company here in Dallas?"

"Yes, because Dallas is more central to my holdings in Texas, Florida, New York, Chicago, Boston and other places."

"I thought it might be, David. I don't want you to have to fly so much in order to take care of business. We can fly to see the boys and my parents once in a while, and we can fly them here."

David, not having had anyone, before or since Hildi, who put his welfare first, was unable to speak. So he just held Torry tightly and thanked the Lord for the privilege of associating with her in this life.

That evening, the bride and groom went down to dinner and dancing and had a memorable and, in Torry's mind, a very romantic evening.

Returning to the room, they stood a moment before entering and smiled at each other, savoring the newness of their relationship.

"Isn't it wonderful," Torry asked, "not to have to say good night at the door?"

David's response proved how right she was.

HONEYMOON DAY 5: (Sunday)

The newlyweds, not knowing which ward was theirs, just picked one and attended church.

In the afternoon, Torry was treated to a Texas thunderstorm. She curled up in David's arms, feeling safe, and watched with great delight the sheets of rain unlike anything she had ever seen before. She loved the rolling claps of thunder that made the walls around them reverberate.

After the storm, Torry began asking questions about David's life. The more he told, the more she asked, then David turned the tables and questioned Torry. They laughed and cried as their lives began to unfold to each other.

Chapter Forty-Seven

The plane dipped down onto the runway of the Salt Lake Airport, gliding to a stop. Torry and David, their eyes full of happiness, smiled at each other.

"Back to real life, Torry," David said, as they prepared to stand in the aisle.

"Heaven must be part of real life then, David."

As they exited the boarding ramp, they saw two eager, smiling young men waiting for them.

"Jim, Scott!" their mother exclaimed. "We thought you would meet us at the baggage claim."

After hugging their mother, they greeted David, "Congratulations!" Scott said.

"Yeah," Jim added, "Congratulations are definitely in order, you both look great!"

"Thank you," David and Torry said together.

"Here's a small wedding gift for you both," Scott said, handing a wrapped package to David.

David smiled at each of them. "This is a surprise." He unwrapped it. It was a book, a biography of the present-day Prophet.

"I have been wanting that book, thank you," Torry said.

"Yes, thank you." David added. "I'm still in awe. Having a prophet today seems almost unreal, let alone being able to read about his life. But do you guys realize how much I have to read and catch up on?"

They grinned and nodded.

Opening up the book, they read the inscription: "July 2. To Mom and Dad. We are happy for you and for us. Love, your sons, Jim and Scott."

David's heart leapt with joy. They had called him Dad! Not able to swallow past the constriction in his throat, he wordlessly embraced each one of his adopted sons.

On the way to the Conway residence, the boys were full of questions but their mother said, "We'll wait and tell you about it when we're all together. Tell us what you two have been doing since we left."

When they reached the house, Torry sent David a nervous glance. He smiled at her reassuringly.

They rang the doorbell and a beaming Ruth answered the door. "Come in, my dear ones."

When they stepped in, everyone embraced. Then Ruth said to David and Torry, "I can't tell you how happy I am for you both."

"Thank you, Mother," Torry said, tears of gratitude in her eyes.

"Yes, thank you, Ruth," David reiterated, "your approval means a lot to us."

"Come in and sit down, all of you."

"Where's Dad?" Torry asked.

"He'll be here in a minute. He stepped outside to check the water sprinklers."

Several minutes later George Conway entered the family room. His head jerked back in surprise. He greeted his grandsons, then coldly stared at David and Torry and sat down.

"Hello, George," David said.

"It's good to see you, Dad," Torry said walking over to him and leaning down and kissing him on the cheek. She whispered in his ear, "I love you, Dad, please be happy for me."

George wanted to respond to his daughter but found himself still hanging on to old hurts.

"Now, tell us everything," Jim said, trying to lighten the atmosphere.

"Yes, do," Ruth encouraged.

"We will," David said, but first, I'd like to make a request of you, George. Actually it's a favor. When we were in Dallas, I made a phone call to my holding company and found out about a problem concerning personnel and sales in one of my companies. It was then that I realized you might be able to counsel me on it. With your particular expertise, I think you just might be the one to help me solve it."

There was a sudden cessation of movement—of sound. The air was charged, electric; it was as though everyone had sucked in a breath of air, and held it expectantly.

George's expression changed to surprise then curiosity.

Hesitating a moment, he spoke cautiously, "Well, I don't know. What is it?"

"Torry and I will be moving from Green Valley to Dallas in about three weeks. When we are moved and settled, I need to travel to all my enterprises and check on them. I want Torry to come with me, and what I'd like, George, is for you and Ruth to accompany us. I will show you the problem then. The expense will be on me. Of course, there will be remuneration for your counsel. Do you think you can help me out?"

Everyone was as surprised as George at David's request and offer. George was silent for a time. It was obvious to those present that he was experiencing an internal conflict. His flattered ego fought with his unremitting pride. Finally he turned to his wife.

"What do you think, Ruth? Do you think you'll feel up to it?"

Ruth held her face carefully neutral as she answered her husband, "I'm feeling so much stronger already, I'm sure I will, George."

"I think Ruth and I can make it. I don't know how I can help you, David, but I'll see what I can do. Just let us know when, so we can plan."

"I will, George, thank you."

There was an inaudible, collective, sigh of relief.

Ruth spoke quickly into the still charged atmosphere. "I have a roast in the oven, David, so we are celebrating here tonight."

"I thought I smelled something good cooking. Thank you, Ruth."

"Now," Scott said, addressing David and his mother, "tell us everything."

Torry and David took turns telling about Gabriel Rameriz, his wife Maria, about running into Paul Eldredge and his wife Diane, and then the marriage itself. Afterward, George begrudgingly admitted to himself that David seemed to have more to him than he first wanted to believe.

Ruth was sure that the Lord had His hand in David and his friend Paul meeting again, just as surely as He had all through David and Torry's courtship.

Jim and Scott found themselves admiring their new stepfather even more.

Everyone helped with the dinner, and during the meal there was an unusually relaxed and happy atmosphere, each privately attributing this to David.

Jim and Scott said their goodbyes as the evening ended, and headed back to school with the promise from their parents, that they'd see them in about three weeks.

In the guest room, preparing for bed, Torry reached up and took David's face in her hands.

"You are an amazing and wonderful man, David and an absolute genius." Then she pulled his face down and covered it with kisses.

"Wow! What did I do to warrant that? And what else can I do to get more?"

"David, Dad is already different because of your request."

"Torry, I did it first for you and your mother, secondly for myself. I'm serious about needing your dad's expertise. I haven't become what I am financially on my own, I have learned how to utilize other peoples talents and learn from them."

"Well, Mr. Mayer, if you ask me, that deserves another reward."

Just then a gentle tap sounded at the door. Torry opened it to find her mother.

"Mother, what a nice surprise. Come in."

Ruth entered, carefully closing the door behind her. "Do you have a few minutes? There is something I would like to talk to you both about."

"Of course, Ruth," answered David. "Sit down," he said, pointing to the chair. "We'll sit here on the bed."

Ruth took a few moments to compose herself, then began. "Now I don't want you two to get your hopes up, but there may be a way to solve your problem about a temple sealing."

David's eyes widened in shock. Torry gasped. "But, Mother, you know I'm sealed to Jack. What do you mean?"

"As I said, don't get your hopes up, but it is possible to get a sealing cancelled, even when one party has died."

"I've never heard of such a thing," Torry protested.

"I've done some checking while you were in Dallas," Ruth continued. "Starting with the bishop, I've gone all the way up to an old friend who is a general authority. To secure a temple cancellation is a very difficult thing. He pointed out that every such application is handled by the First Presidency on a case-by-case basis."

"David, when you have been in the Church for a year, and receive a temple recommend, you, Torry, can apply for a cancellation."

Ruth looked at each of these two who were so dear to her. "You will need a letter from your bishop in Denver, Torry. Also you'll need letters from Jim and Scott since they will be affected by this."

"Again, let me remind you of the difficulties. One thing I do know, absolutely," she said, looking at David. "God is just. If Torry continues to live the commandments, she will have the opportunity to make her choice, whether here or in the hereafter."

Ruth slumped in the chair, exhausted by emotion.

David and Torry, both so stunned by this news that neither were able to do more than just gaze at Ruth incredulously, then at each other.

David was the first to recover. He stood and assisted Ruth to her feet. Putting his arms around her, he said, in a voice choked with emotion, "Thank you, Ruth...Mother, more than I can say."

Chapter Forty-Eight

Tuesday morning, the light plane landed at the small airstrip outside of Green Valley, and David and Torry drove into town.

"So much has happened in the last two weeks, David, it feels like we've been gone two months."

"It does, doesn't it?"

"Driving into this little town, David, it strikes me more than ever what different worlds we've lived in."

David became strangely quiet. It was 10:00 A.M. when he drove into the graveled driveway of the little house on Farm Road 6. Gathering their suit cases together, they walked up onto the porch. Torry unlocked the door and walked in, holding the door open for David. He set the suitcases down and studied the room. All of a sudden, he smiled and picked Torry up in his arms.

"We're home, my darling, we're home!"

"We are?" she asked, touched by his excitement.

"Yes." Do you have any idea how often I wished I lived here with you in this little house? And now I can."

"We can live here always if you wish, my dearest David."

He smiled lovingly at his wife, "Thank you, my darling. I wish it were practical, but it isn't. It will have to be just our place to visit in the summer." He set her down and kissed her.

"Now, I'll check on the chickens, then I'll go get a load of things from the apartment that I'll be needing for the next few weeks."

"And I'll stay here and make some room in my drawers and closet for your things."

On his way out the back door, he said, "We aren't meeting our friends at the Hilltop House until six, so we have plenty of time to get settled."

Torry was glad to see David leave because she had something important to do. She needed to wrap a wedding gift for him. She would do that first. It hadn't started out as a wedding gift, but she couldn't give him anything else that would explain any better what he had done for her, what he meant to her.

An hour-and-a-half later, David returned. He made several trips into the bedroom. On the last trip, he looked around. His heart pounded with excitement as he looked at the bed Torry had been sleeping in during those days he had loved her with such longing. And now he would be sleeping there with her.

Torry walked in. Her heart beat a little faster as she watched him hang his clothes in her closet and put his things in her drawers.

"David," she whispered, "the lonely nights I've slept here alone will all be forgotten with you by my side."

"Come, Torry," he said taking her by the hand, "let's go in and sit down on one of those wonderful loveseats of yours...ours. I have a wedding gift for you."

"You have?" she asked, her eyes wide. "Well...I have one for you, too." She opened a dresser drawer and pulled out a beautifully wrapped package.

He grinned. "Well if you aren't the sly one, come on."

They sat down together. Torry saw her gift, nicely wrapped lying on the magazine table. She set hers down on the table also, and they smiled at each other.

"Who's first?" Torry asked.

"You, of course," David said.

Torry picked it up and opened it carefully. When she saw what it was, she was so astonished she could hardly speak. Beautifully arranged and framed were three dried, pressed lilacs. Underneath it said:

"TORRY MY DARLING, YOU ARE TO ME...WHAT THE FRAGRANCE IS TO THE LILAC...THE VERY ESSENCE OF LIFE. I'LL LOVE YOU FOREVER, DAVID."

"What is it, Torry?" David asked as he watched her, puzzled.

"Open your gift David."

David, a half smile on his face, curiosity in his eyes, picked up his gift and opened it. Astounded, his mouth dropped open. Before him, framed, was a beautiful water color of three lilacs in a small crystal vase. Underneath, it said:

"DAVID DEAREST, WHAT IS THE LILAC WITHOUT FRAGRANCE? WHAT IS LIFE WITHOUT JOY? YOU BROUGHT BOTH BACK TO ME. I'LL LOVE YOU FOREVER, TORRY."

They gazed at each other in awe, clasped hands, laughed a little and cried a little.

"Forever, Torry?"

"Forever, David."